"Rain," by W. Somerset Maugham, needs no introduction here. In the last twenty-odd years it has become a tradition on the stage and on the screen. Gloria Swanson and Lionel Barrymore appeared in the first screen version in 1928. Again, in 1938, it was filmed with Joan Crawford and Walter Huston. Other actresses may in the future attempt to portray the difficult Sadie Thompson.

Another famous Maugham story, "The Vessel of Wrath," was produced in England as "The Beachcomber," a memorable production with Charles Laughton and Elsa Lanchester.

Other authors appearing in this fine anthology are Ben Hecht, Richard Connell, O. Henry, James Street, and Katharine Haviland-Taylor.

Marjorie Barrows and George Eaton, who compiled the book, are to be commended for the excellence of their selections, which are noteworthy both for literary merit and for pure entertainment value.

BOX OFFICE

A Collection of
Famous Short Stories from which
Outstanding Motion Pictures have been made

BOX OFFICE

Compiled by Marjorie Barrows and George Eaton

ZIFF-DAVIS PUBLISHING COMPANY
CHICAGO · NEW·YORK

For
ESTELLA MAE
and
WALTER

FOREWORD

THERE ARE MANY STORIES from which fine motion pictures have been made. The reader may wonder, therefore, on what basis the twelve in this book have been selected. The explanation lies in that difficult-to-define but universally understood phrase, literary merit.

Good plot, characterization and, to some extent, mood, can be transferred from printed page to screen, but fine writing, subtleties and excellencies of style, word cadence and rhythm remain locked in the written text. Moreover, they play no part (except a psychological one) in the choosing of a story for screening.

Here are twelve stories which possess the double virtue of having proved good film material and, at the same time, of having stood the test of literary quality. Preceding each is a brief history of the motion picture which was fashioned from it.

CONTENTS

Samuel Hopkins Adams

*

NIGHT BUS

IT HAPPENED ONE NIGHT, based on Samuel Hopkins Adams' NIGHT BUS, was a movie sensation. It is said to be the picture that made Clark Gable a box office name. The story was adapted by Robert Riskin, directed by Frank Capra, and starred Claudette Colbert, Gable, and Walter Connally. Produced in 1934, the film garnered most of the Academy of Motion Picture Arts and Sciences awards for that year. Both Miss Colbert and Gable were awarded the "Oscars" for the best performances; Capra and Riskin won top honors for directing and adapting, and the film was voted The Best Picture of the Year.

THROUGH THE RESONANT cave of the terminal, a perfunctory voice boomed out something about Jacksonville, points north, and New York. The crowd at the rail seethed. At the rear, Mr. Peter Warne hoisted the battered weight of his carryall, resolutely declining a porter's aid. Too bad he hadn't come earlier; he'd have drawn a better seat. Asperities of travel, however, meant little to his seasoned endurance.

Moreover, he was inwardly fortified by what the advertisement vaunted as "The Best Fifteen-cent Dinner in Miami; Wholesome, Clean and Plentiful." The sign knew. Appetite sated, ticket paid for, a safe if small surplus in a secure pocket; on the whole, he was content with life.

Behind him stood and, if truth must be told, shoved a restive girl. Like him she carried her own luggage, a dressing case, small and costly. Like him she had paid for her ticket to New York. Her surplus, however, was a fat roll of high-caste bills. Her dinner at the ornate Seafoam Club had cost somebody not less than ten dollars. But care sat upon her somber brow, and her expression was a warning to all and sundry to keep their distance. She was far from being content with life.

All chairs had been filled when Peter Warne threaded the

aisle, having previously tossed his burden into an overhead bracket. Only the rear bench, stretching the full width of the car, offered any space. Three passengers had already settled into it; there was accommodation for two more, but the space was piled full of baled newspapers.

"Hi!" said the late arrival cheerfully to the uniformed driver, who stood below on the pavement looking bored. "I'd like one of these seats."

The driver turned a vacant gaze upon him and turned away again.

"Have this stuff moved, won't you?" requested the passenger, with unimpaired good humor.

The official offered a fair and impartial view of a gray-clad back.

Mr. Warne reflected. "If you want a thing well done, do it yourself," he decided. Still amiable, he opened the window and tossed out four bundles in brisk succession.

Upon this, the occupant of the uniform evinced interest. "Hey! What d'you think you're doin'?" He approached, only to stagger back under the impact of another bale which bounded from his shoulder. With a grunt of rage, he ran around to the rear door, yanked it open and pushed his way in, his face red and threatening.

Having, meantime, disposed of the remainder of the papers, Mr. Warne turned, thrust his hand into his rear pocket, and waited. The driver also waited, lowering but uncertain. Out popped the hand, grasping nothing more deadly than a notebook.

"Well, come ahead," said its owner.

"Come ahead with what?"

"You were figuring to bust me in the jaw, weren't you?"

"Yes; and maybe I *am* goin' to bust you in the jor."

"Good!" He made an entry in the book. "I need the money."

The other goggled. "What money?"

"Well, say ten thousand dollars damages. Brutal and unprovoked assault upon helpless passenger. It ought to be worth that. Eh?"

The official wavered, torn between caution and vindictiveness. A supercilious young voice in the aisle behind Peter Warne said: "Do you mind moving aside?"

Peter Warne moved. The girl glided into the corner he had so laboriously cleared for himself. Peter raised his cap.

"Take my seat, madam," he invited, with empressement. She bestowed upon him a faintly speculative glance, indicating that he was of a species unknown to her, and turned to the window. He sat down in the sole remaining place.

The bus started.

Adjustment to the motion of ten tons on wheels is largely a matter of technique and experience. Toughened traveler as he was, Peter Warne sat upright, swaying from the hips as if on well-oiled hinges. Not so the girl at his side. She undertook to relax into her corner with a view to forgetting her troubles in sleep. This was a major error. She was shuttled back and forth between the wall and her neighbor until her exasperation reached the point of protest.

"Tell that man to drive slower," she directed Peter.

"It may surprise you, but I doubt if he'd do it for me."

"Oh, of course! You're afraid of him. I could see that." Leaning wearily away, she said something not so completely under her breath but that Peter caught the purport of it.

"I suspect," he observed unctuously and with intent to annoy, "that you are out of tune with the Infinite."

Unwitherable though his blithe spirit was, it felt the scorch of her glare. Only too obviously he was, at that moment, the focal point for a hatred which included the whole universe. Something must have seriously upset a disposition which, he judged, was hardly inured to accepting gracefully the contrarieties of a maladjusted world.

She looked like that. Her eyes were dark and wide beneath brows that indicated an imperious temper. The long, bold sweep of the cheek was deeply tanned and ended in a chin which obviously expected to have its own way. But the mouth was broad, soft and generous. Peter wondered what it would look like when, as, and if it smiled. He didn't think it likely that he would find out.

Beyond Fort Lauderdale the bus was resuming speed when

the feminine driver of a sports roadster, disdaining the formality of a signal, took a quick turn and ran the heavier vehicle off the road. There was a bump, a light crash, a squealing of brakes, the bus lurched to a stop with a tire ripped loose. After a profane inspection, the driver announced a fifteen-minute wait.

They were opposite that sign manual of Florida's departed boom days, a pair of stone pillars leading into a sidewalked wilderness and flanked by two highly ornamental lamp-posts without glass or wiring. The girl got out for a breath of air, set her dressing case at her feet and leaned against one of the monuments to perishable optimism. As she disembarked, her neighbor, in a spirit of unappreciated helpfulness, had advised her to walk up and down; it would save her from cramps later on.

Just for that she wouldn't do it. He was too officious, that young man. Anyway, the fewer human associations she suffered, the better she would like it. She had a hate on the whole race. Especially men. With a total lack of interest, she observed the parade of her fellow wayfarers up and down the road, before shutting them out from her bored vision.

A shout startled her. The interfering stranger on the opposite side of the road had bounded into the air as if treacherously stabbed from behind, and was now racing toward her like a bull at full charge. At the same time she was aware of a shadow moving away from her elbow and dissolving into the darkness beyond the gates. Close to her, the sprinter swerved, heading down the deserted avenue. Beyond him she heard a crash of brush. His foot caught in a projecting root and he went headlong, rising to limp forward a few yards and give it up with a ruefully shaken head.

"Lost him," he said, coming opposite her.

"I don't know why that should interest me." She hoped that she sounded as disagreeable as she felt. And she did.

"All right," he replied shortly, and made as if to go on, but changed his mind. "He got your bag," he explained.

"Oh!" she ejaculated, realizing that that important equipment was indeed missing. "Who?" she added feebly.

"I don't know his name and address. The thin-faced bird who sat in front of you."

"Why didn't you catch him?" she wailed. "What'll I do now?"

"Did it have much in it?"

"All my things."

"Your money and ticket?"

"Not my ticket; I've got that."

"You can wire for money from Jacksonville, you know."

"Thank you. I can get to New York all right," she returned, with deceptive calm, making a rapid calculation based on the six or eight dollars which she figured (by a considerable over-estimate) were still left her.

"Shall I report your loss at the next stop?"

"Please don't." She was unnecessarily vehement. One might almost suppose the suggestion had alarmed her.

Joining the others, she climbed aboard. The departed robber had left a chair vacant next the window. One bit of luck, anyway; now she could get away from that rear seat and her friendly neighbor. She transferred herself, only to regret the change bitterly before ten miles had been covered. For she now had the chair above the curve of the wheel, which is the least comfortable of bus seats. In that rigorously enforced distortion of the body she found her feet asleep, her legs cramped. Oh, for the lesser torments of the place she had so rashly abandoned!

Twisting her stiffening neck, she looked back. The seat was still vacant. The chatty young man seemed asleep.

Lapsing into the corner, she prepared for a night of heroism. The bus fled fast through the dark and wind. Exigencies of travel she had known before; once she had actually slept in the lower berth of a section, all the drawing-rooms and compartments being sold out. But that was less cramped than her present seat. Just the same, she would have stood worse rather than stay at home after what had happened!

If only she had brought something to read. She surveyed her fellow passengers, draped in widely diverse postures. Then the miracle began to work within her. She grew drowsy.

It was not so much sleep as the reflex anaesthetic of exhaustion. Consciousness passed from her.

Sun rays struck through the window upon her blinking lids. White villas slid by. A milk cart rattled past. Stiff and dazed, she felt as if her legs had been chilled into paralysis, but all the upper part of her was swathed in mysterious warmth. What were those brown, woolly folds?

The tanned, quick-fingered hands explored, lifted a sleeve which flopped loose, discovered a neatly darned spot; another; a third. It had seen hard service, that garment which wrapped her. She thought, with vague pleasure of the senses, that it had taken on a sturdy personality of its own connected with tobacco and wood smoke and strong soap; the brisk, faintly troubling smell of clean masculinity. She liked it, that sweater.

From it, her heavy eyes moved to her neighbor who was still asleep. By no stretch of charity could he be called an ornament to the human species. His physiognomy was blunt, rough and smudgy with bristles; his hair reddish and uncompromisingly straight.

Nevertheless, a guarded approval might be granted to the setting of the eyes under a freckled forehead, and the trend of the mouth suggested strong, even teeth within. Nose and chin betokened a careless good humor. As for the capable hands, there was no blinking the stains upon them.

His clothing was rough and baggy, but neat enough except for a gaping rent along one trouser leg which he had come by in chasing her thief. For the first time in her life, she wished that she knew how to sew. This surprised her when she came to consider it later.

For the moment she only smiled. It was a pity that Peter Warne could not have waked up at the brief, warm interval before her lips drooped back to weariness.

Nearly an hour later, he roused himself at the entrance to Jacksonville where a change of lines was due, and his first look rested upon a wan and haggard face.

"Breakfast!" said he, with energy and anticipation.

The face brightened. "The Windsor is a good place," stated its owner.

"I wouldn't doubt it for a minute. So is Hungry Joe's."

"Do you expect me to eat at some horrid beanery?"

"Beans have their virtue. But oatmeal and coffee give you the most for your money."

"Oh, money! I'd forgotten about money."

"If you want to change your mind and wire for it—"

"I don't. I want to eat."

"With me?"

She speculated as to whether this might be an invitation; decided that it probably wasn't. "If the place is clean."

"It's cleaner than either of us at the present moment of speaking," he grinned.

Thus recalled to considerations of femininity, she said: "I'll bet I look simply *terrible!*"

"Well, I wouldn't go as far as that," was the cautious reply.

"Anyhow, there's one thing I've got to have right away."

"What's that?"

"If you must know, it's a bath."

"Nothing doing. Bus leaves in fifty minutes."

"We can tell the driver to wait."

"Certainly, we can tell him. But there's just a possibility that he might not do it."

This was lost upon her. "Of course he'll do it. People always wait for me," she added with sweet self-confidence. "If they didn't, I'd never get anywhere."

"This is a hard-boiled line," he explained patiently. "The man would lose his job if he held the bus, like as not."

She yawned. "He could get another, couldn't he?"

"Oh, of course! Just like that. You haven't happened to hear of a thing called unemployment, have you?"

"Oh, that's just socialistic talk. There are plenty of jobs for people who really want to work."

"Yes? Where did you get that line of wisdom?"

She was bored and showed it in her intonation. "Why, everybody knows that. Bill was saying the other day that most of these people are idle because they're just waiting for the dole or something."

"Who's Bill?"

"My oldest brother."

"Oh! And I suppose Bill works?"

"We-ell; he plays polo. Almost every day."

Mr. Warne màde a noise like a trained seal.

"What did you say?"

"I said, 'here's the eatery.' Or words to that effect."

The place was speckless. Having a healthy young appetite, the girl disdained to follow the meager example of her escort, and ordered high, wide and handsome. Directing that his fifteen-cent selection be held for five minutes, Peter excused himself with a view to cleaning up. He returned to find his companion gone.

"At the Windsor, having my bath," a scrawl across the bill of fare enlightened him. "Back in half an hour."

That, he figured after consultation of his watch, would leave her just four minutes and twenty seconds to consume an extensive breakfast and get around the corner to the terminal, assuming that she lived up to her note, which struck him as, at the least, doubtful. Well, let the little fool get out of it as best she could. Why bother?

Peter ate slowly, while reading the paper provided free for patrons. At the end of twenty-five minutes, he was craning his neck out of the window. A slight figure turned the corner. Relief was in the voice which bade the waiter rush the order. The figure approached—and passed. Wrong girl. Peter cursed.

Time began to race. Less than five minutes to go now. Half of that was the minimum allowance for getting to the starting place. Peter bore his grip to the door, ready for a flying take-off, in case she appeared. In case she didn't. . . . People always waited for her, did they? Well, he'd be damned if he would! In one short minute he would be leaving. Thirty seconds; twenty; fifteen; five. Sister Ann, do you see anything moving? *Malbrouck s'en va-t'en guerre.* No dust along the road? We're off!

Such was the intention. But something interfered; an intangible something connected with the remembrance of soft contours on a young, sleeping face, of wondering eyes slowly opened. Peter dashed his valise upon the floor, kicked it, cast himself into a chair and sulked. His disposition was distinctly tainted when the truant made triumphal entrance. She was freshened and groomed and radiant, a festal apparition. Up rose then Mr. Warne, uncertain where to begin. She forestalled him.

"Why, how niçe you look!" By virtue of his five minutes, the freedom of the washroom, and a pocket kit, he had contrived to shave, brush up, and make the best of a countenance which, if by strict standards unbeautiful, did not wholly lack points. "How much time have I for breakfast?"

"Plenty," barked Peter.

"Swell! I'm starving. I *did* hurry."

"Did you?" he inquired, between his teeth.

"Of course I did. Didn't you just say I had plenty of time?"

"You certainly have. All day."

She set down her coffee cup. "Why, I thought our bus—"

"Our bus is on its way to New York. The next one leaves at eight tonight."

"I do think you might have telephoned them to wait," she protested. A thought struck her impressionable mind. "Why, you missed it, too!"

"So I did. Isn't that extraordinary!"

"Because you were waiting for me?"

"Something of the sort."

"It was awfully nice of you. But why?"

"Because the poor damfool just didn't have the heart to leave a helpless little hick like you alone," he explained.

"I believe you're sore at me."

"Oh, not in the least! Only at myself for getting involved in such a mix-up."

"Nobody asked you to miss the old bus," she stated warmly. "Why did you?"

"Because you remind me of my long-lost angel mother, of course. Don't you ever go to the movies? Now, do you still want to go to New York?"

"We-ell; I've got my ticket. I suppose that's still good."

"Up to ten days. At this rate, it'll take us all of that to get there. The thing is to figure out what to do now."

"Let's go to the races," said she.

"On what?" he inquired.

"I've got some money left."

"How much?"

She examined her purse. "Why, there's only a little over four dollars," she revealed in disappointed accents.

"How far d'you think that'll take you?"

"I could bet it on the first race. Maybe I'd win."

"Maybe you'd lose, too."

"I thought you had that kind of disposition the minute I set eyes on you," she complained. "Pessimist!"

"Economist," he corrected.

"Just as bad. Anyway, we've got a whole day to kill. What's your dashing idea of the best way to do it?"

"A park bench."

"What do you do on a park bench?"

"Sit."

"It sounds dumb."

"It's cheap."

"I hate cheap things, but just to prove I'm reasonable I'll try it for a while."

He led her a block or so to the area of palms and flowers facing the Windsor where they found a bench vacant and sat down. Peter slouched restfully. His companion fidgeted.

"Maybe the band will play by and by," said he encouragingly.

"Wouldn't that be nah-ice!" murmured the girl, and Peter wondered whether a hard slap would break her beyond repair.

"How old are you, anyway?" he demanded. "Fifteen?"

"I'm twenty-one, if you want to know."

"And I suppose it cost your family a bunch of money to bring you to your present fine flower of accomplished womanhood."

"You shouldn't try to be poetic. It doesn't, somehow, go with your face."

"Never mind my face. If I take you to the station and buy you a ticket to Miami—day coach, of course," he interpolated, "will you go back, like a sensible girl?"

"No, I won't. Think how silly I'd look, sneaking back after having—"

"You'd look sillier trying to get to New York at your present rate of expenditure," he warned, as she failed to complete her objection.

"If you can put up the price of a ticket to Miami," said she, with a luminous thought, "you might better lend me the money. I'll pay you back—twice over."

"Tha-anks."

"Meaning you won't?"

"Your powers of interpretation are positively uncanny."

"I might have known you wouldn't." She turned upon him an offended back.

"My name," he said to the back, "is Peter Warne."

A shrug indicated her total indifference to this bit of information. Then she rose and walked away.

He called after her: "I'll be here at six-thirty. Try not to keep me waiting *more* than half an hour."

Just for that—thought the girl—I'll be an hour late.

But she was not. It annoyed her to find how a day could drag in a town where she knew nobody. She went to a movie. She lunched. She went to another movie. She took a walk. Still, it was not yet six o'clock.

At six-thirty-one she started for the park. At six-thirty-four she was at the spot, or what she had believed to be the spot, but which she decided couldn't be, since no Peter Warne was visible. Several other benches were in sight of the vacant band stand. She made the rounds of all. None was occupied by the object of her search. Returning to the first one, she sat down in some perturbation. Perhaps something had happend to Peter Warne. Nothing short of an accident could explain his absence.

There she sat for what seemed like the better part of an hour, until an ugly suspicion seeped into her humiliated mind that she had been left in the lurch. And by a man. A clock struck seven. She rose uncertainly.

"Oh!" she said, in a long exhalation.

Peter Warne was strolling around the corner of the stand.

"Where have you been?" she demanded, like an outraged empress.

He remained unstricken. "You were late," he observed.

"I wasn't. What if I was? Only a minute."

"Nearer five."

"How do you know? You must have been watching. You were here all the time. And you let me think you'd gone away. Oh! Oh! *Oh!*"

"You're pretty casual about keeping other people waiting, you know."

"That's different." She spoke with a profound conviction of privilege.

"I'm not going to argue that with you. Have you any money left?"

"A dollar and four cents," she announced, after counting and recounting.

Cooly he took her purse, transferred the coins to his pocket, and handed it back. "Confiscated for the common necessity," he stated, and she refrained from protest. "Come along."

She fell into step with him. "Could I please have something to eat?"

"Such is the idea. We'll try Hungry Joe's again."

This time he did the ordering for both of them: soup, hash, thick, pulpy griddle cakes and coffee. Total, sixty-five cents. Fortified by this unfamiliar but filling diet, she decided to give Mr. Peter Warne a more fitting sense of their relative status. Some degree of respect was what her soul demanded to bolster her tottering self-confidence. She had heard that a married woman was in a better position to assert herself than a girl. On that basis she would impress Peter.

"You've been treating me like a child," she complained. "You may as well understand right now that I'm not. I'm a married woman. I'm Mrs. Corcoran Andrews." She had selected this name because Corcoran, who was her third or fourth cousin, had been pestering her to marry him for a year. So he wouldn't mind. The effect was immediate.

"Huh?" jerked out the recipient of the information. "I thought Corker Andrews married a pink chorine."

"They're divorced. Do you *know* Corker?"

"Sure I know Corker."

"You're not a *friend* of his?" The implication of her surprise was unflattering.

"I didn't say that." He grinned. "The fact is, I blacked his boots once for three months."

"What did you do that for?"

"What does a man black boots for? Because I had to. So you're Cor—Mr. Andrews' wife." His regard rested upon her small, strong, deeply browned left hand. She hastily pulled it away.

"My ring's in the bag that was stolen."

"Of course," he remarked. (What did he mean by that?) "Time to be moving."

They emerged into a droning pour of rain. "Can't you get a taxi?" she asked.

"We walk," was the uncompromising reply, as he tucked his hand beneath her arm. They caught the bus with little to spare, and again drew the rear seat.

Outside, someone was saying: "Since Thursday. Yep; a hundred miles up the road. There'll be bridges out."

Feeling sleepy and indifferent, she paid no heed. She lapsed into a doze which, beginning bumpily against the wall, subsided into the unrealized comfort of his shoulder.

Water splashing on the floor boards awakened her; it was followed by the whir of the wheels, spinning in reverse.

"Got out by the skin of our teeth," said Peter Warne's lips close to her ear.

"What is it?"

"Some creek or other on the rampage. We'll not make Charleston this night."

He went forward, returning with dreary news. "We're going to stay in the nearest village. It looks like a night in the bus for us."

"Oh, no! I can't stand this bus any longer. I want to go to bed," she wailed.

He fetched out his small notebook and fell to figuring. "It'll be close reckoning," he said, scowling at the estimate. "But if you feel that way about it—" To the driver he shouted: "Let us off at Dake's place."

"What's that?"

"Tourist camp."

"Aren't they awful places? They look it."

"The Dake's chain are clean and decent enough for any-body," he answered in a tone so decisive that she followed him meekly out into the night.

Leading her to a sort of waiting room, he vanished into an office, where she could hear his voice in colloquy with an unseen man. The latter emerged with a flash light and indicated that they were to follow. Her escort said to her, quick and low: "What's your name?"

"I told you," she returned, astonished. "I'm Mrs. Cor—"

"Your first name."

"Oh. Elspeth. Why? What's the matter?" She regarded him curiously.

"I had to register as Mr. and Mrs.," he explained nervously. "It's usual for a husband to know his wife's first name."

She asked coldly: "What is the idea?"

"Do you mind," he urged, "talking it over after we get inside?"

Their guide opened the door of a snug cabin, lighted a light and gave Elspeth a shock by saying: "Good night, Mrs. Warne. Good night, Mr. Warne. I hope you find everything comfortable."

Elspeth looked around upon the bare but neat night's lodging: two bunks separated by a scant yard of space, a chair, four clothes hooks, a shelf with a mirorr above it. Peter set down his carryall and sat at the head of a bunk.

"Now," said he, "you're free to come or go."

"Go where?" she asked blankly.

"Nowhere, I hope. But it's up to you. You're a lot safer here with me," he added, "than you would be by yourself."

"But why did you have to register that way? To save appearances?"

"To save two dollars," was his grim correction, "which is more to the point. That's the price of a cabin."

"But *you're* not going to stay *here*."

"Now, let me explain this to you in words of one syllable.

We've got darn little money at best. The family purse simply won't stand separate establishments. Get that into your head. And I'm not spending the night outside in this storm!"

"But I—I don't know anything about you."

"All right. Take a look." He held the lamp up in front of what developed into a wholly trustworthy grin.

"I'm looking." Her eyes were wide, exploring, steady, and—there was no doubt about it in his mind—innocent.

"Well; do I look like the villian of the third act?"

"No; you don't." She began to giggle. "You look like a plumber. A nice, honest, intelligent, high-principled plumber."

"The washroom," he stated in the manner of a guidebook, "will be found at the end of this row of shacks."

While she was gone, he extracted a utility kit from his bag, tacked two nails to the end walls, fastened a cord to them and hung a spare blanket, curtain-wise, upon it.

"The walls of Jericho," was his explanation, as she came in. "Solid porphyry and marble. Proof against any assault."

"Grand! What's this?" She recoiled a little from a gaudy splotch ornamenting the foot of her bed.

"Pajamas. My spare set. Hope you can sleep in them."

"'I could sleep," she averred with conviction, "in a strait-jacket." She had an impulse of irrepressible mischief. "About those walls of Jericho, Peter. You haven't got a trumpet in that big valise of yours, have you?"

"Not even a mouth organ."

"I was just going to tell you not to blow it before eight o'clock."

"Oh, shut up and go to sleep."

So they both went to sleep.

Something light and small, falling upon her blanket, woke Elspeth.

"Wha' za'?" she murmured sleepily.

"Little present for you," answered Peter.

"Oh-h-h-h-h-h!" It was a rapturous yawn. "I never slept so hard in my *whole* life. What time is it?"

"Eight o'clock, and all's well before the walls of Jericho."

She ripped the small package open, disclosing a toothbrush.

"What a snappy present! Where did it come from?"

"Village drug store. I'm just back."

"How nice of you! But can we afford it?" she asked austerely.

"Certainly not. It's a wild extravagance. But I'm afraid to cut you off from all luxuries too suddenly. Now, can you get bathed and dressed in twenty minutes?"

"Don't be silly! I'm not even up yet."

"One—two—three—four—"

"What's the count about?"

"On the stroke of ten I'm going to break down the wall, drag you out and dress you myself if neces—"

"Why, you big bum! I believe you wou—"

"—five—six—seven—"

"Wait a *minute!*"

"—eight—ni-i-i-i—"

A blanket-wrapped figure dashed past him and down to the showers. After a record bath she sprinted back to find him squatted above a tiny double grill which he had evidently extracted from that wonder-box of a valise.

"What we waste on luxuries we save on necessities," he pointed out. "Two eggs, one nickel. Two rolls, three cents. Tea from the Warne storehouse. Accelerate yourself, my child."

Odors, wafted from the cookery to her appreciative nostrils, stimulated her to speed. Her reward was a nod of approval from her companion and the best egg that had ever caressed her palate.

"Now you wash up the dishes while I pack. The bus is due in ten minutes."

"But they're greasy," she shuddered.

"That's the point. Get 'em clean. Give 'em a good scraping first."

He vanished within. Well, she would try. Setting her teeth, she scraped and scrubbed and wiped and, at the end, invited his inspection, confident of praise. When, with a pitying glance, he silently did over two plates and a cup before stacking and packing them, she was justifiably hurt. "There's no suiting some people," she reflected aloud and bitterly.

Flood news from the northward, they learned on boarding

the bus, compelled a re-routing far inland. Schedules were abandoned. If they made Charleston by nightfall they'd do pretty well. the driver said. Elspeth, refreshed by her long sleep, didn't much care. Peter would bring them through, she felt . . . .

Yellow against the murk of the night sky shown the lights of Charleston. While Peter was at the terminal office making inquiries, Elspeth, on the platform, heard her name pronounced in astonishment. From a group of company chauffeurs a figure was coming toward her.

"Andy Brinkerhoff! What are you doing in that uniform?"

"Working. Hello, Elspie! How's things?"

"Working? For the bus company?"

"Right," he chirped. "This being the only job in sight and the family having gone bust, I grabbed it. What-ho!"

"How awful!"

"Oh, I dunno. I'd rather be the driver than a passenger. What brought you so low, Elspie?"

"Sh! I've beat it from home."

"Gee! Alone?"

"Yes. That is—yes. Oh, Andy! I never dreamed how awful this kind of travel could be."

"Why don't you quit it, then?"

"No money."

The lad's cherubic face became serious. "I'll raise some dough from the bunch. You could catch the night plane back."

For a moment she wavered. In the distance she sighted Peter Warne scanning the place. There was a kind of expectant brightness on his face. She couldn't quite picture him going on alone in the bus with that look still there. She flattered herself that she had something to do with its presence.

"I'll stick," she decided to herself, but aloud: "Andy, did you ever hear of a man named Peter Warne?"

"Warne? No. What about him?"

"Nothing. What's a telegram to Miami cost?"

"How much of a telegram?"

"Oh, I don't know. Give me a dollar." And then she wrote out a message:

Mr. Corcoran D. Andrews, Bayside Place, Miami Beach, Fla.

Who what and why is Peter Warne Stop Important I should know Stop On my way somewhere and hope to get there some time Stop This is strictly confidential so say nothing to nobody Stop Having a helluvaruff time and liking it Stop Wire Bessie Smith, Western Union, Raleigh, N. C.

El

"Oh, here you are," said Peter, barely giving her time to smuggle the paper into Brinkerhoff's hand. "We're going on. Think you can stand it?"

"I s'pose I've got to," replied Elspeth.

Incertitude had discouraged about half the passengers. Consequently, the pair secured a window chair apiece. At the moment of starting there entered a spindly young male all aglow with self-satisfaction which glossed him over from his cocky green hat to his vivid spats.

By the essential law of his being it was inevitable that, after a survey of the interior, he should drop easily into a seat affording an advantageous view of the snappy-looking girl who seemed to be traveling alone. He exhumed a magazine from his grip and leaned across.

"Pardon *me*. But would you care to look at this?"

Elspeth wouldn't but she looked at Mr. Horace Shapley with attention which he mistook for interest. He transferred himself with suitable preliminaries to the vacant chair at her side and fell into confidential discourse.

His line, so Elspeth learned, was typewriter supplies and he hailed from Paterson, New Jersey. Business was punk but if you knew how to make yourself solid with the girl behind the machine (and that was his specialty, believe *him*), you could make expenses and a little bit on the side.

Elspeth glanced across at Peter to see how he regarded this development. Peter was asleep. All right, then; if he wanted to leave her unprotected against the advances of casual strangers. Unfamilar with this particular species, she was mildly curious about its hopeful antics.

She smiled politely, asked a question or two, and Mr. Shapley proceeded to unfold romantic adventures and tales of life among the typewriters. The incidents exhibited a similarity of climax: "And did *she* fall for me! Hot momma!"

"It must be a fascinating business," commented his listener.

"And how! I'll bet," said Mr. Shapley, with arch insinuation, "you could be a naughty little girl yourself, if nobody was lookin'." He offered her a cigaret. She took it with a nod and tossed it across the aisle, catching the somnolent Peter neatly in the neck. He woke up.

"Hi!"

"Come over here, Peter." He staggered up. "I want you to know" (with a slight emphasis on the word) "Mr. Shapley."

"Pleezetomeetcha," mumbled that gentleman in self-refuting accents.

"He thinks," pursued Elspeth, "that I'm probably a naughty little girl. Am I?"

"You can't prove it by me," said Peter.

"Say, what's the idea?" protested the puzzled Mr. Shapley.

"I don't like him; he nestles," stated Elspeth.

"Aw, now, sister! I was just nicin' you along and—"

"Nicing me along!" Elspeth repeated the phrase with icy disfavor. "Peter; what are you going to do about this?"

Peter ruminated. "Change seats with you," he said brightly.

"Oh!" she choked as she rose. As she stepped across her neighbor to gain the aisle, he gave a yelp and glared savagely, though it was presumably an accident that her sharp, high heel had landed upon the most susceptible angle of his shin. After a moment's consideration, Peter followed her to her new position.

So entered discord into that peaceful community. Mr. Shapley sulked in his chair. Elspeth gloomed in hers. Discomfort invaded Peter's amiable soul. He perceived that he had fallen short in some manner.

"What did you expect me to do about that bird?" he queried.

"Nothing."

"Well, that's what I did."

"I should say you did. If it had been me, I'd have punched his nose."

"And got into a fight. I never could see any sense in fighting unless you have to," he argued. "What happens? You both get arrested. If I got arrested and fined here, how do we eat? If they jug me, what becomes of you? Be sensible."

"Oh, you're sensible enough for both of us." It was plain, however, to the recipient of this encomium, that it was not intended as a compliment. "Never mind. What are we stopping for?"

The halt was occasioned by evil reports of the road ahead, and the chauffeur's unwillingness to risk it in darkness.

"I'll do a look-see," said Peter, and came back, pleased, to announce that there was a cheap camp around the turn. Without formality, the improvised Warne family settled in for the night.

Silence had fallen upon the little community when an appealing voice floated across the wall of their seventy-five-cent Jericho. "Peter. Pe-*ter!*"

"Mmpff."

"You're not a very inquisitive person, Peter. You haven't asked me a single question about myself."

"I did. I asked you your name."

"Because you had to. In self-protection."

"Do you want me to think up some more questions?"

She sniffed. "You might show a *little* human interest. You know, I don't like you much, Peter. But I could talk to you, if you'd let me, as freely as if you were—well, I don't know how to put it."

"Another species of animal."

"No-o-o-o. You musn't belittle yourself," said she kindly.

"I wasn't. And I didn't say an inferior species."

It took her a moment to figure this out, and then she thought she must have got it wrong. For how could his meaning possibly be that her species was the inferior? . . . Better pass that and come to her story. She began with emphasis:

"If there's one thing I can't stand, it's unfairness."

"I thought so."

"You thought *what?*"

"Somebody's been interfering with your having your own sweet way, and so you walked out on the show. What was the

nature of this infringement upon the rights of American womanhood?"

"Who's making this stump speech; you or me?" she retorted.
"It was about King Westley, if you want to know."

"The headline aviator?"

"Yes. He and I have been playing around together."

"How does friend husband like that?"

"Huh? Oh! Why, he's away, you see. Cruising. I'm staying
with Dad."

"Then he's the one to object?"

"Yes. Dad doesn't understand me."

"Likely enough. Go ahead."

"I'll bet you're going to be dumb about this, too. Anyway,
it was all right till King got the idea of finding the lost scientific expedition in South America. Venezuela, or somewhere.
You know."

"Professor Schatze's? South of the Orinoco. I've read about
it."

"King wants to fly down there and locate them."

" 'S all right by me. But where does he figure he'll land?"

"Why, on the prairie or the pampas."

"Pampas, my glass eye! There isn't any pampas within a
thousand miles of the Orinoco."

"What do you know about it?"

"I was there myself, five years ago."

"You were! What doing?"

"Oh, just snooping around."

"Maybe it wasn't the same kind of country we were going
to."

"*We?*" She could hear a rustle and judged that he was sitting
upright. She had him interested at last.

"Of course. I was going with him. Why, if we'd found the
expedition I'd be another Amelia Earhart."

Again the cot opposite creaked. Its occupant had relaxed.
"I guess your family needn't have lost any sleep."

"Why not?" she challenged.

"Because it's all a bluff," he returned. "Westley never took a
chance in his life outside of newspaper headlines."

"I think you're positively septic. The family worried, all right. They tried to keep me from seeing him. So he took to nosing down across our place and dropping notes in the swimming pool, and my father had him arrested and grounded for reckless flying. Did you ever hear anything like that?"

"Not so bad," approved Peter.

"Oh-h-h-h! I might know you'd side against me. I suppose you'd have had me sit there and let Dad get away with it."

"Mmmmm. I can't exactly see you doing it. But why take a bus?"

"All the cars were locked up. I had to sneak out. I knew they'd watch the airports and the railroad stations, but they wouldn't think of the bus. Now you've got the whole story, do you blame me?"

"Yes."

"I do think you're unbearable. You'd probably expect me to go back."

"Certainly."

"Maybe you'd like to send me back."

"You wouldn't go. I did try, you know."

"Not alive, I wouldn't! Of *course* you wouldn't think of doing anything so improper as helping me any more."

"Sure, I will," was the cheerful response. "If you've got your mind set on getting to New York, I'll do my best to deliver you there intact. And may God have mercy on your family's soul! By the way, I suppose you left some word at home so they won't worry too much."

"I did not! I hope they worry themselves into convulsions."

"You don't seem to care much about your family," he remarked.

"Oh, Dad isn't so bad. But he always wants to boss everything. I—I expect I didn't think about his worrying. D'you think he will—much?" The query terminated in a perceptible quaver.

"Hm. I wonder if you're really such a hard-boiled little egg as you make out to be. Could you manage with a bag of pecans for dinner tomorrow?"

"Ouch! Do I have to?"

"To wire your father would come to about the price of two dinners."

"Wire him? And have him waiting in New York for me when we get there? If you do, I'll jump through the bus window and you'll never see me again."

"I see. Westley is meeting you. You don't want any interference. Is that it?"

"I left him a note," she admitted.

"Uh-huh. Now that you've got everything movable off your mind, what about a little sleep?"

"I'm for it."

Silence settled down upon the Warne menage.

Sunup brought Peter out of his bunk. From beyond the gently undulant blanket he could hear the rhythm of soft breathing. Stealthily he dressed. As he opened the door, a gust of wind twitched down the swaying screen. The girl half turned in her sleep. She smiled. Peter stood, bound in enchantment.

In something like panic he bade himself listen to sense and reason. That's a spoiled child, Peter. Bad medicine. Willful, self-centered—and sweet. (How had that slipped in?) Impractical, too. Heaven pity the bird that takes her on! Too big a job for you, Peter, my lad, even if you could get the contract. So don't go fooling with ideas, you poor boob.

Breakfast necessities took him far afield before he acquired at a bargainer's price what he needed. Elspeth had already fished the cooking kit out of the bag and made ready in the shelter of the shack. Not a word did she say about the fallen blanket. This made Peter self-conscious. They breakfasted in some restraint.

A wild sky threatened renewal of the storm. Below the hill a shallow torrent supplanted the road for a space. Nevertheless, the bus was going on. Elspeth washed the dishes—clean, this time.

"You get out and stretch your legs while I pack," advised Peter.

As she stepped from the shack, the facile Mr. Shapley confronted her.

"The cream off the milk to you, sister," said he, with a smile which indicated that he was not one to bear a grudge. I just want to square myself with you. If I'd known you was a married lady—"

"I'm not," returned Elspeth absently.

Mr. Shapley's eyes shifted from her to the shack. Peter's voice was raised within: "Where are your pajamas, Elspeth?"

"Airing out. I forgot 'em." She plucked them from a bush and tossed them in at the door.

"*Oh*-oh!" lilted Mr. Shapley, with the tonality of cynical and amused enlightenment. He went away, cocking his hat.

Warning from the bus horn brought out Peter with his bag. They took their seats and were off.

The bus' busy morning was spent mainly in dodging stray watercourses. They made Cheraw toward the middle of the afternoon. There Peter bought two pounds of pecans; a worthy nut and one which satisfies without cloying. They were to be held in reserve, in case. In case of what? Elspeth wished to be informed. Peter shook his head and said, darkly, that you never could tell.

North of Cheraw, the habits of the bus became definitely amphibian. The main route was flowing in a northeasterly direction, and every side road was a contributory stream. A forested rise of land in the distance held out hope of better things, but when they reached it they found cars parked all over the place, waiting for a road-gang to strengthen a doubtful bridge across the swollen river.

"Let's have a look at this neck of the woods," Peter suggested to Elspeth.

To determine their geographical circumstances was not difficult. Rising waters had cut off from the rest of the world a ridge, thinly oval in shape, of approximately a mile in length, and hardly a quarter of a mile across. On this were herded thirty or forty travelers, including the bus passengers.

There was no settlement of any sort within reach; only a ramshackle farmhouse surrounded by a discouraged garden. Peter, however, negotiated successfully for a small box of potatoes, remarking to his companion that there was likely to be a rise in commodity prices before the show was over.

A sound of hammering and clinking interspersed with rugged profanity, led them to a side path. There they found a well-equipped housekeeping van, the engine of which was undergoing an operation by its owner while his motherly wife sat on the steps watching.

"Cussin' never done you any good with that machine, Abner," said she. "It ain't like a mule."

"It is like a mule. Only meaner." Abner sighted Peter. "Young man, know anything about this kind of critter?"

"Ran one once," answered Peter. He took off his coat, rolled up his sleeves, and set to prodding and poking in a professional manner. Presently the engine lifted up its voice and roared.

Elspeth, perched on a log, reflected that Peter seemed to be a useful sort of person to other people. Why hadn't he done better for himself in life? Maybe that was the reason. This was a new thought and gave her something to mull over while he worked. From the van she borrowed a basin of water, a bar of soap and a towel, and was standing by when he finished the job.

"What do I owe you, young man?" called Abner Braithe, from the van.

"Noth-*uh!*" Elspeth's well-directed elbow had reached its goal in time.

"Don't be an idiot!" she adjured him.

A conference took place.

"You see," said Peter at its close, "my—uh—wife doesn't sleep well outdoors. If you had an extra cot, now—"

"Why, we can fix that," put in Mrs. Braithe. "We haven't got any cot, but if you can sleep in a three-quarter bed—"

"We can't," said both hastily.

"We're used to twin beds," explained Elspeth.

"My wife's quite nervous," put in Peter, "and—and I snore."

"You don't," contradicted Elspeth indignantly, and got a dirty look from him.

It was finally arranged that, as payment for Peter's services, the Braithes were to divide the night into two watches; up to and after one A.M., Elspeth occupying the van bed for the second spell while Peter roosted in the bus. This being settled, the young pair withdrew to cook a three-course dinner over a fire coaxed by Peter from wet brush and a newspaper; first course, thin potato soup; second course, boiled potatoes with salt; dessert, five pecans each.

"We've been Mr. and Mrs. for pretty near three days now, Peter," remarked the girl suddenly, "and I don't know the first darn thing about you."

"What d'you want to know?"

"What have you got in the line of information?"

"Not much that's exciting."

"That's too bad. I hoped you were an escaped con or something, traveling incog."

"Nothing so romantic. Just a poor but virtuous specimen of the half-employed."

"Who employs you?"

"I do. I'm a rotten employer."

"Doing what? Besides blacking boots."

"Oh, I've nothing as steady as that since. If you want to know, I've been making some experiments in the line of vegetable chemistry; pine tar, to be exact. I'm hoping to find some sucker with money to take it up and subsidize me and my process. That's what I'm going to New York to see about. Meantime," he grinned, "I'm traveling light."

"What'll the job be worth if you do get it?"

"Seven or eight thousand a year to start with," said he, with pride.

"Is *that* all?" She was scornful.

"Well, I'll be—Look here, Elspeth, I said per year."

"I heard you. My brother Bill says he can't get along on *ten* thousand. And," she added thoughtfully, "he's single."

"So am I."

"You didn't tell me that before. Not that it matters, of course. Except that your wife might misunderstand if she knew we'd been sl—traveling together."

"I haven't any wife, I tell you."

"All right; all *right!* Don't bark at me about it. It isn't my fault."

"Anything else?" he inquired with careful politeness.

"I think it's going to rain some more."

They transferred themselves to the bus and sat there until one o'clock, when he escorted her to the Braithe van. He returned to join his fellow passengers, leaving her with a sensation of lostness and desertion.

Several small streams, drunk and disorderly on spring's strong liquor, broke out of bounds in the night, came brawling down the hills and carried all before them, including the bridge whereby the marooned cars had hoped to escape.

"I don't care," said Elspeth, when the morning's news was broken to her. She was feeling gayly reckless.

"I do," returned Peter soberly.

"Oh, you're worrying about money again. What's the use of money where there's nothing to buy? We're out of the world, Peter. I like it, for a change. What's that exciting smell?"

"Fish." He pointed with pride to his fire, over which steamed a pot. Dishing up a generous portion he handed it to her on a plate. "Guaranteed fresh this morning. How do you like it?"

She tasted it. "It—it hasn't much personality. What kind of fish is it?"

"They call it mudfish, I believe. It was floping around in a slough and I nailed it with a stick. I thought there'd be enough for dinner, too," said he, crestfallen by her lack of appreciation.

"Plenty," she agreed. "Peter, could I have four potatoes? Raw ones."

"What for?"

"I'm going marketing."

"Barter and exchange, eh? Look out that these tourists don't gyp you."

"Ma feyther's name is Alexander Bruce MacGregor Andrews," she informed him in a rich Scottish accent. "Tak' that to heart, laddie."

"I get it. You'll do."

Quenching his fire, he walked to the van. A semicircle of men and women had grouped about the door. Circulating among them, Abner Braithe was taking up a collection. Yet, it was not Sunday. The explanation was supplied when the shrewd Yankee addressed his audience.

"The morning program will begin right away. Any of you folks whose money I've missed, please raise the right hand. Other news and musical ee-vents will be on the air at five-thirty this P.M. and eight tonight. A nickel admission each, or a dime for the three performances."

Having no nickel to waste on frivolities, Peter moved on. Elspeth, triumphant, rejoined him with her booty.

Item: a small parcel of salt.

Item: a smaller parcel of pepper.

Item: a half pound of lard.

Item: two strips of fat bacon.

Item: six lumps of sugar.

"What d'ye ken about that?" she demanded. "Am I no the canny Scawtswumman?"

"You're a darn bonny one," returned Peter, admiring the flushed cheeks and brilliant eyes.

"Is this the first time you've noticed that?" she inquired impudently.

"It hadn't struck in before," he confessed.

"And now it has? Hold the thought. I can't hurt you." (He felt by no means so sure about that.) "Now Mr. Shapley"—her eyes shifted to the road up which that gentleman was approaching—"got it right away. I wonder what's his trouble."

Gratification, not trouble, signalized his expression as he sighted them. His bow to Elspeth was gravely ceremonious. He then looked at her companion.

"Could I have a minute's conversation apart with you?"

"Don't mind me," said Elspeth, and the two men withdrew a few paces.

"I dont want to butt into your and the lady's private affairs," began Mr. Shapley, "but this is business. I want to know if that lady is your wife."

"She is. Not that it's any concern of yours."

"She said this morning that she wasn't married."

"She hasn't got used to the idea yet," returned Peter, with great presence of mind. "She's only been that way a few days. Honeymoon trip."

"That's as may be," retorted the other. "Even if it's true, it wouldn't put a crimp in the reward."

"What's this?" demanded Peter, eying him in surprise. "Reward? For what?"

"Come off. You heard the raddio this morning, didn'cha?"

"No."

"Well, is that lady the daughter of Mr. A. B. M. Andrews, the yachting millionaire, or ain't she? 'Cause I know she is."

"Oh! You know that, do you! What of it?"

"Ten grand of it. That's what of it," rejoined Mr. Shapley. "For information leadin' to the dis—"

"Keep your voice down."

"Yeah. I'll keep my voice down till the time comes to let it loose. Then I'll collect on that ten thou'. They think she's kidnaped."

"What makes you so sure of your identification?"

"Full description over the air. When the specifications came across on the raddio I spotted the garments. Used to be in ladies' wear," he explained.

"If you so much as mention this to Mi—to Mrs. Warne, I'll—" began Peter.

"Don't get rough, now, brother," deprecated the reward-hunter. "I ain't lookin' for trouble. And I'm not sayin' anything to the little lady, just so long as you and me understand each other."

"What do you want me to understand?"

"That there's no use your tryin' to slip me after we get out of this place. Of course, you can make it hard or easy for me. So, if you want to play in with me and be nice, anyway—I'm ready to talk about a little cut for you . . . No? Well, suit yourself, pal. See you in the mornin'."

He chuckled himself away. Peter, weighing the situation, discovered in himself a violent distaste at the thought of Mr. Horace Shapley collecting Elspeth's family's money for the delivering up of Elspeth. In fact, it afflicted him with mingled nausea and desire for man-slaughter. Out of this unpromising combination emerged an idea. If he, Peter, could reach a wire before the pestilent Shapley, he could get in his information first and block the reward.

Should he tell Elspeth about the radio? Better not, he concluded.

It was characteristic of her and a big credit mark in his estimate of her, that she put no questions as to the interview with Shapley. She did not like that person; therefore, practically speaking, he did not exist. But the mudfish did. With a captivating furrow of doubt between her eyes, she laid the problem before her partner: could it be trusted to remain edible overnight?

"Never mind the fish. Can you swim?"

She looked out across the brown turbulence of the river, more than two hundred yards now to the northern bank. "Not across that."

"But you're used to water?"

"Oh, yes!"

"I've located an old boat in the slough where I killed the fish. I think I can patch her up enough to make it."

"Okay by me; I wouldn't care to settle here permanently. When do we start?"

"Be ready about ten."

"In the dark?"

"We-ell, I don't exactly want the public in on this. They might try to stop us. You know how people are."

"Come clean, Peter. We're running away from something. Is it that Shapley worm?"

"Yes. He thinks he's got something on me." This explanation which he had been at some pains to devise, he hoped would satisfy her. But she followed it to a conclusion which he had not forseeen.

"Is it because he knows we're not married?"

"He doesn't know ex—"

"I told him we weren't. Before I thought how it would look."

"I told him we were."

"Did he believe you?"

"Probably not."

"Then he thinks you're abducting me. Isn't that priceless!"

"Oh, absolutely. What isn't so funny is that there are laws in some states about people—er—traveling as man and wife if they're not married."

She started at him, wide-eyed. "But so long as—Oh, Peter! I'd *hate* it if I got you into any trouble."

"All we have to do is slip Shapley. Nobody else is on." He sincerely hoped that was true.

The intervening time he occupied in patching up the boat as best he might. He had studied the course of various flotsam and thought that he discerned a definite set of the current toward the northern bank which was their goal. With bailing they ought to be able to keep the old tub afloat.

Through the curtain of the rushing clouds the moon was contriving to diffuse a dim light when they set out. The opposite bank was visible only as a faint, occasional blur. Smooth with treachery, the stream at their feet sped from darkness into darkness.

Peter thrust an oar into Elspeth's hand, the only one he had been able to find, to be used as a steering paddle. For himself he had fashioned a pole from a sapling. The carryall he disposed aft of amidships. Bending over Elspeth as she took the stern seat, he put a hand on her shoulder.

"You're not afraid?"

"No." Just the same, she would have liked to be within reach of that firm grasp through what might be coming.

"Stout fella! All set? Shove!"

The river snatched at the boat, took it into its secret keeping—and held it strangely motionless. But the faintly visible shore slipped backward and away and was presently visible no more. Peter, a long way distant from her in the dimness, was active with his pole, fending to this side and that. It was her job to keep them on the course with her oar. She concentrated upon it.

The boat was leaking profusely now. "Shall I bail?" she called.

"Yes. But keep your oar by you."

They came abreast of an island. As they neared the lower end, an uprooted swamp maple was snatched outward in the movement of the river. Busy with her pan, Elspeth did not notice it until a mass of leafy branches heaved upward from the surface, hovered, descended, and she was struggling in the grasp of a hundred tentacles.

"*Peter!*" she shrieked.

They had her, those wet, clogging arms. They were dragging her out into the void, fight them as she would in her terror and desperation. Now another force was aiding her; Peter, his powerful arms tearing, thrusting, fending against this ponderous invasion. The boat careened. The water poured inboard. Then, miraculously, they were released as the tree sideslipped, turning again, freeing their craft. Elspeth fell back, bruised and battered.

"Are you all right?"

"Yes. It t-t-tried to drag me overboard!"

"I know." His voice, too, was unsteadied by that horror.

"Don't go away. Hold me. Just for a minute."

The skiff, slowly revolving like a ceremonious dancer in the performance of a solo waltz, proceeded on its unguided course. The girl sighed.

"Where's my oar?" It was gone.

"It doesn't matter now. There's the shore. We're being carried in."

They scraped and checked as Peter clutched at a small sapling, growing at the edge of a swampy forest. From trunk to trunk he guided the course until there was a solid bump.

"Land ho!" he shouted, and helped his shipmate out upon the bank.

"What do we do now?"

"Walk until we find a road and a roost."

Valise on shoulder, he set out across the miry fields, Elspeth plodding on behind. It was hard going. Her breath labored painfully after the first half-mile, and she was agonizingly sleepy.

Now Peter's arm was around her; he was murmuring some encouraging foolishness to her who was beyond courage, fear, hope, or any other emotion except the brutish lust for rest. . . . Peter's voice, angry and harsh, insisting that she throw more of her weight on him and *keep* moving. How silly! She hadn't any weight. She was a bird on a bough. She was a butterfly, swaying on a blossom. She was nothing. . . .

Broad daylight, spearing through a paneless window, played upon her lids, waking her. Where was the shawl of Jericho? In its place were boards, a raw wall. Beneath her was fragrant hay. She was actually alive and rested. She looked about her.

"Why, it's a barn!" she exclaimed. She got up and went to the door. Outside stood Peter.

"How do you like the quarters?" he greeted her. "Room"— he pointed to the barn—"and bath." He indicated a huge horse trough fed by a trickle of clear water. "I've just had mine."

She regarded him with stupefaction. "And now you're *shaving*. Where's the party?"

"Party?"

"Well, if not, why the elaborate toilet?"

"Did you ever travel on the thumb?"

She looked her incomprehension. He performed a digital gesture which enlightened her.

"The first rule of the thumb," explained Peter, "is to look as neat and decent as you can. It inspires confidence in the passing motorist's breast."

"Is that the way we're going to travel?"

"If we're lucky."

"Without eating?" she said wistfully.

"Tluck-tluck!" interposed a young chicken from a near-by hedge, the most ill-timed observation of its brief life.

A handy stick, flung deftly, checked its retreat. Peter pounced. "Breakfast!" he exulted.

"Where do we go now?" inquired his companion, half an hour later, greatly restored.

"The main highways," set forth Peter, thinking of the radio alarm and the state police, "are not for us. Verdant lanes and bosky glens are more in our line. We'll take what traffic we can."

Hitch-hiking on sandy side roads in the South means slow progress. Peter finally decided that they must risk better-traveled roads, but select their transportation cautiously. It was selected for them. They had not footed it a mile beside Route 1, when a touring car, battered but serviceable, pulled up and a ruddy face emitted welcome words.

"Well, well, well! Boys *and* girls! Bound north?"

"Yes." It was a duet, perfect in accord.

"Meet Thad Banker, the good old fatty. Throw in the old trunk."

"What's the arrangement?" queried Peter, cautious financier that he was.

"Free wheeling," burbled the fat man. "You furnish the gas and I furnish the spark." They climbed in with the valise. "Any special place?" asked the obliging chauffeur.

"Do we go through Raleigh?" asked the girl, and upon receiving an affirmative, added to Peter: "There may be a wire there for me."

Which reminded that gentleman that he had something to attend to. At the next town he got a telegraph blank and a stamped envelope. After some cogitation, he produced this composition, addressed to Mr. A. B. M. Andrews, Miami Beach, Fla.

> Daughter taking trip for health and recreation. Advise abandonment of efforts to trace which can have no good results and may cause delay. Sends love and says not to worry. Undersigned guarantees safe arrival in New York in a few days. Pay no reward to any other claimant as this is positively first authentic information.
>
> Peter Warne

To this he pinned a dollar bill and mailed it for transmission to Western Union, New Orleans, Louisiana, by way of giving the pursuit, in case one was instituted, a pleasant place to start from. Five cents more of his thin fortune went for a newspaper. Reports from the southward were worth the money; there was no let-up in the flood. Competition from Mr. Shapley would be delayed at least another day.

Mr. Thad Banker was a card. He kept himself in roars of laughter with his witty sallies. Peter, in the rear seat, fell peacefully asleep. Elspeth had to act as audience for the conversational driver.

At Raleigh she found the expected telegram from Corcoran, which she read and thrust into her purse for future use. Shortly after, a traffic light held them up and the policeman on the corner exhibited an interest in the girl on the front seat quite disturbing to Peter.

The traffic guardian was sauntering toward them when the green flashed on. "Step on it," urged Peter.

Mr. Banker obliged. A whistle shrilled.

"Keep going!" snapped Peter.

Mr. Banker still obliged, slipping into a maze of side streets. It did not occur to Peter that their driver's distaste for police interference was instinctive. Also successful, it began to appear; when a motor cop swung around unexpectedly and headed them to the curb. The license was inspected and found in order.

"Who's the lady?" the officer began.

"My niece," said Mr. Banker, with instant candor.

"Is that right, ma'am?"

"Yes, of course it is." (Peter breathed again.)

"And this man behind?"

"Search me."

"He thumbed us and Uncle Thad stopped for him." (Peter's admiration became almost more than he could bear.)

"Have you got a traveling bag with you, ma'am?" (So the radio must have laid weight on the traveling bag, now probably in some Florida swamp.)

"No. Just my purse."

The cop consulted a notebook. "The dress looks like it," he muttered. "And the description sort of fits. Got anything on you to prove who you are, ma'am?"

"No; I'm afraid—Yes; of course I have." She drew out the yellow envelope. "Is that enough?"

"Miss Bessie Smith," he read. "I reckon that settles it. Keep to your right for Greensboro at Morrisville."

"Greensboro, my foot! Us for points east," announced the fat man, wiping his brow as the motor cycle chugged away. "Phe-e-ew! What's it all about? Been lootin' a bank, you two?"

"Eloping," said Peter. "Keep it under your shirt."

"Gotcha." He eyed the carryall. "All your stuff in there?"

"Yes."

"How about a breath of pure, country air? I'm not so strong for all this public attention."

They kept to side roads until long after dark, bringing up before a restaurant in Tarboro. There the supposed elopers consulted and announced that they didn't care for dinner. "Oh, on me!" cried Mr. Banker. "Mustn't go hungry on your honeymoon."

He ordered profusely. While the steak was cooking, he remarked, he'd just have a look at the car; there was a rattle in the engine that he didn't like. As soon as he had gone, Elspeth said:

"Wonder what the idea is. I never heard a sweeter-running engine for an old car. What's more, he's got two sets of license cards. I saw the other one when that inquiring cop—"

But Peter was halfway to the door, after slamming some money on the table and snapping out directions for her to wait, no matter how long he took. Outside, she heard a shout and the rush of a speeding engine. A car without lights sped up the street.

With nothing else to do, Elspeth settled down to leisurely eating. . . .

At nine-thirty, the waiter announced the closing hour as ten, sharp. Beginning to be terrified for Peter and miserable for herself, she ordered more coffee. The bill and tip left her a dollar and fifteen cents.

At nine-fifty, the wreckage of Peter entered the door. Elspeth arose and made a rush upon him, but recoiled.

"Peter! You've been fighting."

"Couldn't help it."

"You've got a black eye."

"That isn't all I've got," he told her.

"No; it isn't. What an *awful*-looking ear!"

"*That* isn't all I've got, either." His grin was bloody, but unbowed.

"Then it must be internal injuries."

"Wrong. It's a car."

"Whose car?"

"Ours now, I expect. I had to come home in something."

"Where's the fat man?"

The grin widened. "Don't know exactly. Neither does he, I reckon. That big-hearted Samaritan, my child, is a road-pirate. He picks people up, plants 'em, and beats it with their luggage. Probably does a little holdup business on the side."

"Tell me what happened, Peter. Go on and eat first."

Between relishing mouthfuls, he unfolded his narrative. "You didn't put me wise a bit too quick. He was moving when I got out but I landed aboard with a flying tackle. Didn't dare grab him for fear we'd crash. He was stepping on it and telling me that when he got me far enough away he was going to beat me up and tie me to a tree. That was an idea! So when he pulled up on some forsaken wood road in a swamp, I beat him up and tied him to a tree."

"Why, Peter! He's twice as big as you."

"I can't help that. It wasn't any time for half measures. It took me an hour to find my way. But here we are."

"I'm glad," she said with a new note in her voice.

"Jumping Jehoshaphat! Is *that* all we've got left?" Aghast, he stared at the sum she put in his hands. "And it's too cold to sleep out tonight. It's an open car, anyhow. Oh, well; our transportation's going to be cheap from now on. What price one more good night's rest? Torney's Haven for Tourists is three miles up the highway. Let's get going."

Torney's provided a cabin for only a dollar. Before turning in, Peter returned to the car, parked a few rods away against a fence, to make a thorough inspection. His companion was in bed on his return.

"I've changed the plates to another set that I found under the seat. Indiana, to match the other set of licenses. It'll be safer in case our friend decides to report the loss, after he gets loose from his tree. There's a nice robe, too. We've come into property. And by the way, Elspeth; you're Mrs. Thaddeus Banker till further notice."

Elspeth pouted. "I'd rather be Mrs. Peter Warne. I'm getting used to that."

"We've got to live up to our new responsibilities." Seated on his cot, he had taken off his shoes, when he started hastily to resume them.

"Where are you going?" she asked plaintively. "Looking for more trouble?"

"Walls of Jericho. I forgot. I'll get the robe out of the car."

"Oh, darn the robe! Why bother? It's pouring, too. Let it go. I don't mind if you don't." All in a perfectly matter-of-fact tone. She added: "You can undress outside. I'm going to sleep."

As soon as he withdrew she got out Corcoran's reply to "Miss Bessie Smith," and read it over again before tearing it into fragments. It ran as follows:

> What's all this about P. W.? Watch out for that bird. Dangerous corner, blind road, and all that sorta thing. At any given moment he might be running a pirate fleet or landing on the throne of the Kingdom of Boopadoopia. Ask him about the bet I stuck him on in college, and then keep your guard up. I'm off for a week on the Keys so you can't get me again until then. Better come back home and be a nice little girl or papa spank. And how!
>
> Cork

The scraps she thrust beneath her pillow and was asleep almost at once. But Peter lay, wakeful, crushing down thoughts that made him furious with himself. At last peace came, and dreams.... One of them so poignant, so incredibly dear, that he fought bitterly against its turning to reality.

Yet reality it was; the sense of warmth and softness close upon him; the progress of creeping fingers across his breast, of seeking lips against his throat. His arms drew her down. His mouth found the lips that, for a dizzying moment, clung to his, then trembled aside to whisper:

"No, Peter. I didn't mean— Listen!"

Outside sounded a light clinking.

"Somebody's stealing the car!"

Elspeth's form, in the lurid pajamas, slid away from Peter like a ghost. He followed to the window. Silent as a shadow the dim bulk of the Banker automobile moved deliberately

along under a power not its own. Two other shadows loomed
in its rear, propelling it by hand.

"Shall I scream?" whispered the girl.

He put a hand on her mouth. "Wait."

Another of his luminous ideas had fired the brain of Peter
Warne. In his role of Thad Banker, he would let the robbers
get away, then report the theft to the police and, allowing
for reasonable luck, get back his property (né Mr. Banker's)
with the full blessing of the authorities.

"I'm going to let 'em get away with it," he murmured. "As
soon as they really start, I'll telephone the road patrol."

The dwindling shadow trundled out on the pike, where the
engine struck up its song and the car sped southward. Simultaneously Peter made a rush for the camp office. It was all
right, he reported, on getting back. He'd been able to get the
police at once.

"But suppose they don't catch 'em."

"That'll be just too bad," admitted Peter. He yawned.

"You're sleepy again. You're always sleepy."

"What do you expect at three o'clock in the morning?"

"I'm wide awake," complained Elspeth.

Something had changed within her, made uncertain and
uneasy, since she had aroused Peter and found herself for one
incendiary moment in his arms. She didn't blame him; he was
only half awake at the time. But she had lost confidence in him.
Or could it be herself in whom she had lost confidence? In
any case, the thought of sharing the same room with him the
rest of that night had become too formidable.

"Please go outside again, Peter. I'm going to get dressed.
I'm restless."

"Oh, my gosh!" he sighed. "Can't you count some sheep or
something?"

"No; I can't." A brilliant idea struck her. "How'd you expect
me to sleep when they may be back with the car any minute?"

"And then again, they may not be back till morning."

But Elspeth had a heritage of the immovable Scottish obsti-
nacy. In a voice all prickly little italics she announced that she
was *going to get up*. And she was going to walk off her ner-

vousness. It needn't make any difference to Peter. He could go back to bed.

"And let you wander around alone in this blackness? You might not come back."

"What else could I do?"

The forlorn lack of alternative for her struck into his heart. Absolute dependence upon a man of a strange breed in circumstances wholly new. What a situation for a girl like her! And how gallantly, on the whole, she was taking it! How sensible it would be for him to go back to that telephone; call up her father (reverse charges, of course) and tell him the whole thing. *And* get himself thoroughly hated for it.

No; he couldn't throw Elspeth down. Not even for her own good. Carry on. There was nothing else for it, especially now that luck was favoring them. The car, if they got it back, was their safest obtainable method of travel. Her dress was the weak spot and would be more of a danger point after Horace Shapley contributed his evidence to the hunt. Couldn't something be done about that? . . . The dress appeared in the doorway, and Peter went in to array himself for the vigil.

The two state police found the pair waiting at the gate. Apologetically they explained that the thieves had got away into the swamp. Nothing could have suited Peter better, since there would now be no question of his being held as complaining witness. To satisfy the authorities of his ownership was easy. They took his address (fictitious), wished him and his wife good luck, and were off.

"Now we can go back to bed," said Peter.

"Oh, dear! Can't we start on?"

"At this hour? Why, I suppose we could, but—"

"Let's, then." In the turmoil of her spirit she wanted to be quit forever of Torney's Haven for Tourists and its atmosphere of unexpected emotions and disconcerting impulses. Maybe something of this had trickled into Peter's mind, too, for presently he said:

"Don't you know it's dangerous to wake a sound sleeper too suddenly?"

"So I've heard."

"You can't tell what might happen. I mean, a man isn't quite responsible, you know, before he comes quite awake."

So he was apologizing. Very proper.

"Let's forget it."

"Yes," he agreed quietly. "I'll have quite a little to forget."

"So will I," she thought, startled at the realization.

They packed, and chugged out, one cylinder missing. "I hope the old junk-heap holds together till we reach New York," remarked Peter.

"Are we going all the way in this?"

"Unless you can think of a cheaper way."

"But it isn't ours. It's the fat man's."

"I doubt it. Looks to me as if it had been stolen and gypped up with new paint and fake numbers. However, we'll leave it somewhere in Jersey if we get that far, and write to both license numbers to come and get it. How does that set on an empty conscience?"

"Never mind my conscience. That isn't the worst emptiness I'm suffering from. What's in the house for breakfast? It's nearly sunup."

"Potatoes. Pecans." He investigated their scanty store and looked up. "There are only three spuds left."

"Is that all?"

Something careless in her reply made him scan her face sharply. "There ought to be five. There are two missing. You had charge of the larder. Well?"

"I took 'em. You see—"

"Without saying a word about it to me? You must have pinched them out when we were on the island and cooked them for yourself while I was working on the boat," he figured somberly. Part of this was true, but not all of it. The rest she was saving to confound him with. "Do you, by any chance, still think that this is a picnic?"

Now she *wouldn't* tell him! She was indignant and hurt. He'd be sorry! When he came to her with a potato now, she would haughtily decline it—if her rueful stomach didn't get the better of her wrathful fortitude.

In resentment more convincing than her own, he built the

wayside fire, boiled the water and inserted one lone potato; the smallest at that. He counted out five pecans, added two more, and handed the lot to her. He then got out his pocketknife, opened it, and prodded the bubbling tuber. Judging it soft enough, he neatly speared it out upon a plate. Elspeth pretended a total lack of interest. She hoped she'd have the resolution to decline her half with hauteur. She didn't get the chance.

Peter split the potato, sprinkled on salt, and ate it all.

With difficulty, Elspeth suppressed a roar of rage. That was the kind of man he was, then! Selfish, greedy, mean, tyrannical, unfair, smug, bad-tempered, uncouth—her stock ran thin. How idiotically she had overestimated him! Rough but noble; that had been her formula for his character. And now look at him, pigging down the last delicious fragments while she was to be content with a handful of nuts. Nuts! She rose in regal resentment, flung her seven pecans into the fire, and stalked back to the car.

Somewhere in the vicinity of Emporia, eighty miles north of their breakfast, he spoke. "No good in sulking, you know."

"I'm *not* sulking." Which closed that opening.

Nevertheless, Elspeth was relieved. An oppressive feeling that maybe his anger would prove more lasting than her own had tainted her satisfaction in being the injured party. One solicitude, too, he exhibited. He kept tucking her up in the robe.

This would have been less reassuring had she understood its genesis. He was afraid her costume might be recognized. He even thought of suggesting that she might effect a trade in some secondhand store. In her present state of childish petulance, however, he judged it useless to suggest this. Some other way must be found.

Some money was still left to them. Elspeth saw her companion shaking his head over it when their gas gave out, happily near a filling station. His worried expression weakened her anger, but she couldn't bring herself to admit she was sorry. Not yet.

"There's a cheap camp seventy miles from here," he said.

"But if we sleep there we can't have much of a dinner."

"Potatoes," said the recalcitrant Elspeth. She'd teach him!

They dined at a roadside stand which, in ordinary conditions, she would have considered loathsome. Every odor of it now brought prickly sensations to her palate.

The night presented a problem troubling to her mind. No shared but unpartitioned cabin for her! Last night's experience had been too revelatory. What made things difficult was that she had told him she needed no more walls of Jericho to insure peaceful sleep. Now if she asked him to put up the curtain, what would he think?

Pursuant to his policy of avoiding large cities and the possible interest of traffic cops, Peter had planned their route westward again, giving Richmond a wide berth. They flashed without stop through towns with hospitable restaurants only to pull up at a roadside stand of austere menu, near Sweet Briar.

Never had Elspeth seen the important sum of twenty-five cents laid out so economically as by Peter's method. Baked beans with thick, fat, glorious gollups of pork; a half-loaf of bread, and bitter coffee. To say that her hunger was appeased would be overstatement. But a sense of returned well-being comforted her. She even felt that she could face the morning's potato, if any, with courage. Meantime, there remained the arrangements for the night.

Peter handled that decisively, upon their arrival at the camp. Their cabin was dreary, chill, and stoveless. When he brought in the robe from the car, she hoped for it over her bunk. Not at all; out came his little tool kit; up went the separating cord, and over it was firmly pinned the warm fabric.

With a regrettable though feminine want of logic, Elspeth nursed a grievance; he needn't have been at such pains to raise that wall again without a request from the person most interested. She went to sleep crossly but promptly.

In the morning the robe was tucked snugly about her. How long had that been there? She looked around and made a startling discovery. Her clothes were gone. So was Peter. Also, when she looked out, the car. The wild idea occurred to her that he had stolen her outfit and run away, *à la* Thad Banker. One thing was certain: to rise and wander forth clad in those grotesque pajamas was out of the question. Turning over, she fell asleep again.

Some inner sensation of his nearness awoke her, or perhaps it was, less occultly, his footsteps outside, approaching, pausing. She craned upward to bring her vision level with the window. Peter was standing with his side face toward her, a plump bundle beneath his arm. Her clothes, probably, which he had taken out to clean. How nice of him!

He set down his burden and took off his belt. With a knife he slit the stitches in the leather, carefully prying something from beneath the strips. It was a tight-folded bill.

So he had been holding out on her! Keeping her on a gnat's diet. Letting her go hungry while he gorged himself on boiled potato and salt, and gloated over his reserve fund. Beast! This knowledge, too, she would hold back for his ultimate discomfiture. It was a composed and languid voice which responded to his knock on the door.

"Hello! How are you feeling, Elspeth?"

"Very well, thank you. Where have you been?"

"Act two, scene one of matrimonial crisis," chuckled Peter. "Hubby returns early in the morning. Wife demands explanation. Husband is ready with it: 'You'd be surprised.'" There was a distinct trace of nervousness in his bearing.

"Well, surprise me," returned Elspeth, with hardly concealed hostility. "Where are my clothes?"

"That's the point. They're—uh—I—er—well, the fact is, I pawned 'em. In Charlottesville?"

"You—pawned—my—clothes! Where's the money?" If that was the bill in the belt, she proposed to know it.

"I spent most of it. On other clothes. You said your feet hurt you."

"When we were walking. We don't have to walk any more."

"How do you know? We aren't out of the woods yet. And you don't need such a fancy rig, traveling with me. And we do need the little bit extra I picked up on the trade."

Stern and uncompromising was the glare which she directed upon his bundle. "Let me see."

Her immediate reaction to the dingy, shoddy, nondescript outfit he disclosed was an involuntary yip of distress.

"Don't you like 'em?" he asked.

"They're terrible! They're ghastly!"

"The woman said they were serviceable. Put 'em on. I'll wait outside."

It would have taken a sturdier optimism than Peter's to maintain a sun-kissed countenance in the face of the transformation which he presently witnessed. Hardly could he recognize her in that horrid misfit which she was pinning here, adjusting there.

"Hand me the mirror, please."

"Perhaps you'd better not—"

"Will you be so good as to do as I ask?"

"Oh, all *right!*"

She took one long, comprehensive survey and burst into tears.

"Don't, Elspeth," he protested, appalled. "What's the difference? There's no one to see you."

"There's me," she gulped. "And there's you."

"I don't mind." As if he were bearing up courageously under an affliction.

"I'm a *sight*," she wailed. "I'm hideous! Go and get my things back."

"It can't be done."

"I won't go out in these frightful things. I won't. I won't. I *won't!*"

"Who's going to pay the rent if you stay?"

Obtaining no reply to this pertinent inquiry, he sighed and went out. Down the breeze, there presently drifted to Elspeth's nostrils the tang of wood smoke. Her face appeared in the window.

"About those missing potatoes," said she. (How mean she was going to make him feel in a minute!) "Are you interested in knowing what became of them?"

"It doesn't matter. They're gone."

"They're gone where they'll do the most good," she returned with slow impressiveness. "I gave them away."

"Without consulting me?"

"Do I have to consult you about everything I do?"

"We-ell, some people might figure that I had an interest in those potatoes."

"Well, I gave them to a poor old woman who needed them. She was hungry."

"Umph! Feeling sure, I suppose, that your generosity would cost you nothing, as I'd share the remainder with you. Error Number One."

"Peter, I wouldn't have thought anyone could be so des-des-despicable!"

This left him unmoved. "Who was the starving beneficiary? I'll bet it was that old creature with the black bonnet and gold teeth in the bus."

"How did you know?"

"She's the sort you would help. In case you'd like to know, that old hoarder had her bag half full of almond chocolates. I saw her buy 'em at Charleston."

"Hoarder, yourself!" Enraged at the failure of her bombshell, she fell back on her last ammunition. "What did you take out of your belt this morning?"

"Oh, you saw that, did you? Watchful little angel!"

"I'm not! I just happened to see it. A bill. A big one, I'll bet. You had it all the time. And you've starved me and bullied me and made me walk miles and sleep in barns, while you could just as well have—"

"Hired a special train. On ten dollars."

"Ten dollars is a lot of money." (Ideas change.)

"Now, I'll tell you about that ten dollars," said he with cold precision. "It's my backlog. It's the last resort. It's the untouchable. It's the dead line of absolute necessity."

"You needn't touch it on my account." (Just like a nasty-tempered little brat, she told herself.) "Of course, starvation isn't absolute necessity."

"Can you do simple arithmetic?"

"Yes. I'm not quite an idiot, even if you do think so, Peter."

"Try this one, then. We've got something over five hundred miles to go. Gas will average us seventeen cents. This old mudcart of Banker's won't do better than twelve miles on a gallon. Now, can any bright little girl in this class tell me how much over that leaves us to eat, sleep and live on, not count-ing oil, ferry charge and incidentals?"

"I can't. And I don't want to," retorted Elspeth, very dis-pirited. A long, dull silence enclosed them like a globe. She shattered it. "Peter!"

"What?"

"D'you know why I hate you?"

"I'll bite," said he, wearily. "Why?"

"Because, darn you! you're always right and I'm always wrong. Peter! Peter, dear! A potato, Peter. Please, Peter; one potato. Just one. The littlest. I know I don't deserve it, but—"

"Oh, what's the *use!*" vociferated Peter, throwing up both hands in abject and glad surrender. And that quarrel drifted on the smoke of their fire down to the limbo of things become insignificant, yet never quite to be forgotten.

Two young people, haggard, gaunt, shabby, bluish with the chill of an April storm, drove their battered car aboard the Fort Lee ferry as the boat pulled out. They were sharing a bag of peanuts with the conscientious exactitude of penury: one to you; one to me. Quarter of the way across, both were asleep. At the halfway distance the whistle blared and they woke up.

"We're nearly there," observed the girl without any special enthusiasm.

"Yes," said the man with still less.

A hiatus of some length. "Why didn't you tell me about blacking Corker's boots?"

"What about it?"

"It was on a bet, wasn't it?"

"Yes. In college. I picked the wrong team. If I'd won, the Corker would have typed my theses for the term. What put you on?"

"A telegram from Cork."

"Oh! The one to Bessie Smith that saved our lives in Raleigh?"

She nodded. "Anyway, I knew all the time you weren't a valet," she asserted.

He cocked a mild, derisive eye at her. "You're not building up any rosy picture of me as a perfect gentleman, are you?"

"No-o. I don't know what you are."

"Don't let it worry you. Go back to sleep."

"You're always telling me to go to sleep," she muttered discontentedly. She rubbed her nose on his shoulder. "Peter."

He sighed and kissed her.

"You needn't be so solemn about it."

"I'm not feeling exactly sprightly."

"Because we're almost home? But we'll be seeing each other soon."

"I thought that headliner of the air was waiting to fly you somewhere."

"Who? Oh-h-h-h, King." She began to laugh. "Isn't that funny! I'd absolutely forgotten about King. He doesn't matter. When am I going to see you?" As he made no reply, she became vaguely alarmed. . . . "You're not going right back?"

"No. I've got that possible contract to look after. Down in Jersey."

"But you'll be in town again. And I'll see you then."

"No."

"Peter! Why not?"

"Self-preservation," he proclaimed oracularly, "is the first law of nature."

"You don't want to see me again?"

"Put it any way you like," came the broad-minded permission, "just so the main point gets across."

"But I think that's absolutely lousy!" Another point occurred to her. "There's no reason why you shouldn't if it's because —well, that business about my being married was a good deal exaggerated. If that makes any difference."

"It does. It makes it worse."

"Oh! . . . You don't seem surprised, though."

"Me? I should say not! I've known from the first that was all bunk."

"Have you, Smarty? How?"

"You tried to put it over that you'd been wearing a wedding ring. But there was no band of white on the tan of your finger."

"Deteckative! I haven't had a bit of luck trying to fool you about anything, have I, Peter? Not even putting across the superior-goddess idea. And now you're the one that's being snooty."

"I'm not. I'm being sensible. See here, Elspeth. It may or may not have been called to your attention that you're a not wholly unattractive young person—and that I myself am not yet beyond the age of—"

"Consent," broke in the irrepressible Elspeth.

"—damfoolishness," substituted Peter, with severity. "So," he concluded, with an effect of logic, "we may as well call it a day."

"Not to mention several nights." She turned the brilliance of mirthful eyes upon him. "Wouldn't it be funny if you fell in love with me, Peter?"

"Funny for the spectators. Painful for the bear."

"Then don't mention it, Bear!" Another idea occurred to her. "How much money have you got left?"

"Forty-odd cents."

"Now that you're in New York you can get more, of course."

"Yes? Where?"

"At the bank, I suppose. Where does one get money?"

"That's what I've always wanted to know," he grinned.

"I can get all I want tomorrow. I'll lend you a hundred dollars. Or more if you want it."

"No; thank you."

"But I borrowed yours!" she cried. "At least, you paid for me."

"That's different."

"I don't see how." Of course she did see, and inwardly approved. "But—but I owe you money!" she cried. "I'd forgotten all about that. You'll let me pay that back, of course."

If she expected him to deprecate politely the idea she was swiftly undeceived. "The sooner, the better," said Peter cheerfully.

"I'll bet you've got it all set down in that precious notebook of yours."

"Every cent." He tore out a leaf which he handed to her.

"Where can I send it?"

He gave her an address on a street whose name she had never before heard; Darrow, or Barrow, or some such matter.

In the splendor of the great circular court off Park Avenue, the bedraggled automobile looked impudently out of place. The doorkeeper almost choked with amazement as the luxurious Miss Elspeth Andrews, clad in such garments as had never before affronted those august portals, jumped out, absently responding to his greeting.

"I think your father is expecting you, miss," said he.

"Oh, Lord!" exclaimed Elspeth. "Now, what brought him here?"

Peter could have told her, but didn't. He was looking straight through the windshield. She was looking at him with slightly lifted brows.

"Good-by, Elspeth," said he huskily.

"Good-by, Peter. You've been awfully mean to me. I've loved it."

Why, thought Peter as he went on his way, did she have to use that particular word in that special tone at that unhappy moment?

Between Alexander Bruce MacGregor Andrews and his daughter, Elspeth, there existed a lively and irritable affection of precarious status, based upon a fundamental similarity of character and a prevalent lack of mutual understanding. That she should have willfully run away from home and got herself and him on the front pages of the papers, seemed to him an outrage of the first order.

"But it was your smearing the thing all over the air that got us into the papers," pointed out Elspeth, which didn't help much as a contribution to the *entente cordiale*. Both sulked for forty-eight hours.

Meantime, there arrived by special delivery a decidedly humid shoebox addressed in an uncompromisingly straight-up-and-down hand—just exactly the kind one would expect, thought the girl, knowing whose it was at first sight—full of the freshest, most odorous bunch of arbutus she had ever beheld. Something about it unmistakably defined it as having been picked by the sender.

Elspeth searched minutely for a note; there was none. She carried the box to her room and threw three clusters of orchids and a spray of gardenias into the scrapbasket. After that she went to a five-and-ten-cent store, made a purchase at the toy counter, had it boxed, and herself mailed it to the address given her by Peter Warne. The shipment did not include the money she owed him. That detail had escaped her mind.

"Scotty, dear." She greeted her father in the style of their companionable moods. "Do let's be sensible."

Mr. Andrews grunted suspiciously. "Suppose you begin."

"I'm going to. Drink your cocktail first." She settled down on the arm of his chair.

"Now what devilment are you up to?" demanded the apprehensive parent.

"Not a thing. I've decided to tell you about my trip."

Having her narrative all duly mapped out, she ran through it smoothly enough, hoping that he would not notice a few cleverly glossed passages. Disapproval in the paternal expression presently yielded to amused astonishment.

"Nervy kid!" he chuckled. "I'll bet it did you good."

"It didn't do me any harm. And I certainly found out a few things I'd never known before."

"Broadening effect of travel. Who did you say this young man was that looked after you?"

"I'm coming to that. The question is, what are you going to do for him?"

"What does he want?"

"I don't know that he exactly wants anything. But he's terribly poor, Scotty. Why, just think! He had to reckon up each time how much he could afford to spend on a meal!"

"Yes? I'm told there are quite a few people in this country in the same fix," observed Mr. Andrews dryly. "How much'll I make out the check for?"

"That's the trouble. I don't believe he'd take it. He's one of those inde-be-goshdarn-pendent birds. Wouldn't listen to my lending him some money."

"Humph! That probably means he's fallen for your fair young charms. Be funny if he hadn't."

"I'll tell you what would be funnier."

"What?"

"If I'd fallen for him," was the brazen response.

"Poof! You're always imagining you're in love with the newest hero in sight. Remember that young Danish diplo—"

"Yes; I do. What of it? I always get over it, don't I? And I'll get over this. You'd think he was terrible, Dad. He's sure rough. You ought to have seen Little Daughter being bossed around by him and taking it."

"Is that so?" said her father, spacing his words sardonically. "Bossed you, did he? He and who else?"

"Oh, Peter doesn't need any help."

The grin was wiped off the Andrews face. "Who?"

"Peter. That's his name. Peter Warne."

"*What?*"

"Gracious! Don't yell so. Do you know him?"

"I haven't that pleasure as yet. Just let me make sure about this." He went into the adjoining room, whence he emerged with a sheaf of papers. "Peter Warne. So he's poor, is he?"

"Desperately."

"Well, he won't be, after tomorrow."

"Oh, Scotty! How do you know? Is he going to get some money? I'm so glad!"

"Some money is correct. Ten thousand dollars, to be exact."

"From his tar-pine or something process? How did *you* know about it?"

"From me. I don't know anything about—"

"From you?" Her lips parted; her eyes were wide and alarmed. "What for?"

"Information leading to the discovery and return of Elspeth, daughter of—"

"The reward? For me? Peter? I don't believe it. Peter wouldn't do such a thing. Take money for—"

"He has done it. Put in his claim for the reward. Do you want to see the proof?"

"I wouldn't believe it anyway."

Alexander Andrews studied her defiant face with a concern that became graver. This looked serious. Selecting a letter and a telegram from his dossier, he put them into her reluctant hand. At sight of the writing her heart sank. It was unmistakably that of the address on the box of arbutus. The note cited the writer's telegram of the fourteenth ("That's the day after we got off the island," thought Elspeth. "He was selling me out then.") and asked for an appointment.

"He's coming to my office at ten-thirty Thursday morning."

"Are you going to give him the money?"

"It looks as if I'd have to."

"He certainly worked hard enough for it,' she said bitterly. "And I expect he needs it."

"I might be able to work a compromise," mused the canny Scot. "Though I'm afraid he's got the material for a bothersome lawsuit. If any of the other claimants"—he indicated the sheaf of letters and telegrams—"had a decent case, we could set off one against the other. The most insistent is a person named Shapley."

"Don't let him have it," said the girl hastily. "I'd rather Peter should get it, though I'd never have believed— Sold down the river!" She forced a laugh. "I brought a price, anyway."

"I've a good mind to give him a fight for it. It would mean more publicity, though."

"Oh, no!" breathed Elspeth.

"Enough's enough, eh? Though it couldn't be worse than what we've had."

"It could. Much worse. If you're going to see Pe—Mr. Warne, I'd better tell you something, Father. I've been traveling as Mrs. Peter Warne."

"Elspeth!"

"It isn't what you think. Purely economy—with the accent on the 'pure.' But it wouldn't look pretty in print. Oh, damn!" Her voice broke treacherously. "I thought Peter was so straight."

Her father walked up and down the room several times. He then went over and put his arm around his daughter's shoulders. "It's all right, dawtie. We'll get you out of it. And we'll find a way to keep this fellow's mouth shut. I'm having a detectaphone set up in my office, and if he makes one slip we'll have him by the short hairs for blackmail."

"Peter doesnt make slips," returned his daughter. "It's his specialty not to. Oh, well, let's go in to dinner, Scotty."

Resolutely, she put the arbutus out of her room when she went up to bed that night. But the spicy odor from far spring-time woodlands clung about the place like a plea for the absent.

Stern logic of the morning to which she sorrowfully awoke filled in the case against Peter. Nevertheless and nothwith-standing, "I don't believe it," said Elspeth's sore heart. "And I won't believe it until—until—"

Severe as were the fittings of Mr. Alexander Bruce Mac-Gregor Andrews' spacious office, they were less so than the glare which apprised Peter Warne, upon his entry, that this spare, square man did not like him and probably never would. That was all right with Peter. He was prepared not to like Mr. Andrews, either. On this propitious basis the two con-fronted each other.

After a formidable silence which the younger man bore without visible evidence of discomposure, his host barked:

"Sit down."

"Thank you," said Peter. He sat down.

"You have come about the money, I assume."

"Yes."

"Kindly reduce your claim to writing."

"You'll find it there." He handed over a sheet of paper. "Itemized."

"What's this?" Mr. Andrews' surprised eye ran over it.

"Traveling expenses. Elsp—your daughter's."

The father gave the column of figures his analytical attention. "Boat, twenty dollars," he read. "You didn't take my daughter to Cuba, did you?"

"I had to steal a boat to get through the flood. The owner ought to be reimbursed. If you think that's not a fair charge, I'll assume half of it. Everything else is split."

"Humph! My daughter's share of food, lodging and gasoline, excluding the—er—alleged boat, seems to figure up to eighteen dollars and fifty-six cents. Where did you lodge?"

"Wherever we could."

With the paper before him, Mr. Andrews began to hammer his desk. "You have the temerity, the impudence, the effrontery, the—the—anyway, you come here to hold me up for ten thousand dollars and on top of that you try to spring a doctored expense account on me!"

"Doctored!" echoed Peter. "Maybe you think you could do it for less?"

Taken aback, Mr. Andrews ceased his operations on the desk. "We'll pass that for the main point," he grunted. "Upon what do you base your claim for the ten thousand dollars?"

"Nothing," was the placid reply. "I made no claim."

"Your telegram. Your letter—"

"You couldn't have read them. I simply warned you against paying anybody else's claim. You had others, I suppose."

"Others! A couple of hundred!"

"One signed Horace Shapley?"

"I believe so."

"I don't like him," observed Peter, and explained.

"Then your idea," interposed Mr. Andrews, "was to get in first merely to block off this other person. Is that it?"

"Yes."

"And you aren't claiming any part of the reward?"

"No."

"You're crazy," declared the other. "Or maybe I am. What *do* you want?"

Peter gently indicated the expense account. Mr. Andrews went over it again.

"You mean to tell me that you kept my daughter for five

days and more on a total of eighteen dollars and fifty-six cents?"

"There are the figures."

Mr. Andrews leaned forward. "Did she kick much?"

Peter's grin was a bit rueful. "There were times when—"

"You'd have liked to sock her. I know. Why didn't you present your bill to her?"

"I did. I reckon she just forgot it."

"She would! . . . Have a cigar." As the young fellow lighted up, his entertainer was writing and entering a check.

"As a matter of correct business, I ought to have Elspeth's O.K. on this bill. However, I'll pass it, including the boat. Receipt here, please." The amount was $1,038.56.

Shaking his head, Peter pushed the check across the desk. "Thank you, but I can't take this, Mr. Andrews."

"Bosh! Elspeth told me you were broke."

"I am . . . No; I'm not, either. I forgot. I've just made a deal on a new process of mine. Anyway, I couldn't take that—that bonus."

"That's funny. If you're no longer broke, I should think you'd be above bringing me a trifling expense account for—er —entertaining my daughter."

"It's a matter of principle," returned Peter firmly.

Mr. Andrews rose and smote his caller on the shoulder. "I begin to see how you made that little spitfire of mine toe the mark. More than I've been able to do for the past ten years. Eighteen dollars and fifty-six cents, huh?" He sank back in his chair and laughed. "See here, my boy; I like you. I like your style. Will you take that money as a present from me?"

"Sorry, sir, but I'd rather not."

The older man stared him down. "Because I'm Elspeth's father, eh? You're in love with her, I suppose."

Peter grew painfully red. "God forbid!" he muttered.

"What do you mean, God forbid?" shouted the magnate. "Better men than you have been in love with her."

"All right, Mr. Andrews," said Peter in desperation. "Then I am, too. I have been from the first. Now, you tell me—you're her father—what's the sense of it with a girl like Elspeth? I'm going back to Florida with a contract for eight thousand a year, to complete my process."

"That's more than I was making at your age."

"It's more than I expect to be making at yours," said Peter with candor. "But how far would that go with her? Look me over, sir. Even if I had a chance with Elspeth, would you advise a fellow like me to try to marry her?"

"No, I wouldn't!" roared the father. "You're too darn good for her."

"Don't talk like a fool," snapped Peter.

"Just for that," reflected Mr. Andrews as his caller withdrew, jamming a substituted check into his pocket, "I'll bet you'll have little enough to say about it when the time comes."

He sent for Elspeth and left her alone with the detectaphone. What that unpoetic cylinder spouted forth rang in her heart like the music of the spheres with the morning and evening stars in the solo parts. So *that* was how Peter felt about it.

Memory obligingly supplied the number on Darrow or Farrow or Barrow or whatever strange street it was. The taxi man whom she hailed earned her admiration by knowing all about it.

Peter said: "Come in," in a spiritless manner. With a totally different vocal effect he added: "What are *you* doing *here?*" and tacked onto that "You oughtn't to be here at all."

"Why not?" Elspeth sat down.

He muttered something wherein the word "proper" seemed to carry the emphasis, and in which the term "landlady" occurred.

"Proper!" jeered his visitor. "You talk to me about propriety after we've been traveling together and sharing the same room for nearly a week!"

"But this is New York," he pointed out.

"And you're packing up to leave it. When?"

"Tonight."

"Without the ten thousand dollar reward?"

"How did you know about that? Your fath—"

"I've just come from his office. You might better have taken the check."

"Don't want it."

"That's silly. What," she inquired reasonably, "have you got to get married on?"

"Eight thousand a ye—I'm not going to get married," he interrupted himself with needless force.

"Not after compromising a young and innocent—"

"I haven't compromised anyone." Sulkily and doggedly.

"Peter! I suppose registering me as your wife all over the map isn't compromising. Did you ever hear of the Mann Act?"

"B-b-b-but—"

"Yes; I know all about that 'but.' It's a great big, important 'but,' but there's another bigger 'but' to be considered. We know what happened and didn't happen on our trip, *but* nobody else would ever believe it in this world. I certainly wouldn't."

"Nor I," he agreed. "Unless," he qualified hastily, "the girl was you."

"Or the man was you."

They laughed with dubious heartiness. When they had done laughing, there seemed to be nothing to follow, logically. Elspeth got up slowly.

"Where are you going?" demanded Peter, in a panic.

"If you don't like me any more"—she put the slightest possible stress on the verb, leaving him to amend it if he chose—"I'm sorry I came."

To this rueful observation, Peter offered no response.

"You did like me once, you know. You as much as admitted it."

Peter swore.

"Did you or did you not tell my father that you would never get over it?"

"It?"

"Well—me."

"Your father," said Peter wrathfully, "is a human sieve."

"No; he isn't. There was a detectaphone listening in on everything you said. I got it all from that."

"In that case," said the now desperate and reckless Peter, "I may as well get it off my chest." And he repeated what he had earlier said about his feelings, with a fervor that wiped the mischief from Elspeth's face.

"Oh-h-h-h!" she murmured, a little dazed. "That's the way you feel."

"No, it isn't. It isn't half of it."

"Where do we go from here?" thought the girl. The atmosphere of sprightly combat and adventure had changed. She was not breathing quite so easily. Her uncertain look fell upon an object at the top of the half-packed carryall. "Oh!" she exclaimed. "You got my present."

"Yes; I got it."

"I hope you liked it." Politely.

"Not particularly."

Her eyes widened. "Why not?"

"Well, I may be oversensitive where you're concerned, but I don't care so much about being called a tinhorn sport, because—well, I don't know, but I suppose it's because I let you pay back the money for our trip. What do I know about the way girls look at those things, anyway?" he concluded morosely.

One girl was looking at him with a mixture of contempt, amusement, pity, and something stronger than any of these. "Oh, you boob!" she breathed. "That isn't a tinhorn. That's a trumpet."

"A *trumpet?*"

"The kind What's-his-name blew before the walls of Jericho, if you have to have a diagram. Oh, *Pee*-ter; you're such a dodo!" sighed Elspeth. "What am I ever going to do about you? Would you like to kiss me, Peter?"

"Yes," said Peter. And he did.

"This means," he informed her presently, and dubiously, "our having to live in a Florida swamp—"

"On eighteen dollars and fifty-six cents?"

"On eight thousand a year. That isn't much more, to you. You'll hate it."

"I'll love it. D'you know where I'd like to land on our wedding trip, Peter?"

"Yes. Dake's Two-dollar Cabins; Clean; Comfortable; Reasonable."

"*And* respectable. You're too clever, Peter, darling."

"Because that's exactly what I'd like. Social note: Mr. and Mrs. Peter Warne are stopping in Jaw-jaw on their return trip South."

"Let's go," said Elspeth joyously.

Mrs. Dake, in the wing off the tourist-camp office, yawned herself awake of an early May morning and addressed her husband. "That's a funny couple in Number Seven, Tim. Do you reckon they're respectable?"

"I should worry. They registered all right, didn't they?"

"Uh-huh. Wouldn't take any other cabin but Seven. And wanted an extra blanket. This hot night."

"Well, we could spare it."

"That isn't the only queer thing about 'em. After you was asleep, I looked out and there was the young fellah mopin' around. By and by he went in, and right soon somebody blew a horn. Just as plain as you ever heard. What do you think about that, Tim?"

Mr. Dake yawned. "What they do after they're registered and paid up is their business, not our'n."

Which is the proper and practical attitude for the management of a well-conducted tourist camp.

Richard Connell

*

A FRIEND OF NAPOLEON

*Richard Connell's ingenious tale of the watchman in a Paris
wax-works was produced as a moving picture in 1929 by Fox
Studios. Titled SEVEN FACES, the film introduced Paul Muni
to audiences who wildly acclaimed his sympathetic and competent characterization as Papa Chibou. Directed by Berthold
Viertel the cast also included Margeurite Churchill, Lester
Lonergen and Russell Gleason. Muni as the watchman also
impersonated in the course of a dream sequence, six of the
wax figures under his charge who are supposed to come to life.*

ALL PARIS held no happier man than Papa Chibou. He loved
his work—that was why. Other men might say—did say, in fact
—that for no amount of money would they take his job; no, not
for ten thousand francs for a single night. It would turn their
hair white and give them permanent goose flesh, they averred.
On such men Papa Chibou smiled with pity. What stomach
had such zestless ones for adventure? What did they know of
romance? Every night of his life Papa Chibou walked with
adventure and held the hand of romance.

Every night he conversed intimately with Napoleon; with
Marat and his fellow revolutionists; with Carpentier and
Caesar; with Victor Hugo and Lloyd George; with Foch and
with Bigarre, the Apache murderer whose unfortunate pen-
chant for making ladies into curry led him to the guillotine;
with Louis XVI and with Madame Lablanche, who poisoned
eleven husbands and was working to make it an even dozen
when the police deterred her; with Marie Antoinette and with
sundry early Christian martyrs who lived in sweet resignation
in electric-lighted catacombs under the sidewalk of the Boule-
vard des Capucines in the very heart of Paris. They were all
his friends and he had a word and a joke for each of them, as

61

on his nightly rounds he washed their faces and dusted out
their ears, for Papa Chibou was night watchman at the Musée
Pratoucy—"The World in Wax. Admission, one franc. Children
and soldiers, half price. Nervous ladies enter the Chamber of
Horrors at their own risk. One is prayed not to touch the wax
figures or to permit dogs to circulate in the establishment."

He had been at the Musée Pratoucy so long that he looked
like a wax figure himself. Visitors not infrequently mistook
him for one and poked him with inquisitive fingers or canes.
He did not undeceive them; he did not budge. Spartanlike he
stood stiff under the pokes; he was rather proud of being taken
for a citizen of the world of wax, which was, indeed, a much
more real world to him than the world of flesh and blood. He
had cheeks like the small red wax pippins used in table deco-
rations, round eyes, slightly poppy, and smooth white hair, like
a wig. He was a diminutive man and, with his horseshoe moustache of surprising luxuriance, looked like a gnome going to
a fancy-dress ball as a small walrus. Children who saw him
flitting about the dim passages that led to the catacombs were
sure he was a brownie.

His title "Papa" was a purely honorary one, given him because he had worked some twenty-five years at the museum.
He was unwed, and slept at the museum in a niche of a room
just off the Roman arena where papier-mâché lions and tigers
breakfasted on assorted martyrs. At night, as he dusted off the
lions and tigers, he rebuked them sternly for their lack of
delicacy.

"Ah," he would say, cuffing the ear of the largest lion, which
was earnestly trying to devour a grandfather and an infant
simultaneously, "sort of a pig that you are! I am ashamed of
you, eater of babies. You will go to hell for this, Monsieur Lion,
you may depend upon it. Monsieur Satan will poach you like an
egg, I promise you. Ah, you bad one, you species of a camel,
you Apache, you profiteer—"

Then Papa Chibou would bend over and very tenderly address the elderly martyr who was lying beneath the lion's paws
and exhibiting signs of distress, and say, "Patience, my brave
one. It does not take long to be eaten, and then, consider: The

good Lord will take you up to heaven, and there, if you wish, you yourself can eat a lion every day. You are a man of holiness, Phillibert. You will be Saint Phillibert, beyond doubt, and then won't you laugh at lions!"

Phillibert was the name Papa Chibou had given to the venerable martyr; he had bestowed names on all of them. Having consoled Phillibert, he would softly dust the fat wax infant whom the lion was in the act of bolting.

"Courage, my poor little Jacob," Papa Chibou would say. "It is not every baby that can be eaten by a lion; and in such a good cause, too. Don't cry, little Jacob. And remember: When you get inside Monsieur Lion, kick and kick and kick! That will give him a great sickness of the stomach. Won't that be fun, little Jacob?"

So he went about his work, chatting with them all, for he was fond of them all, even of Bigarre the Apache and the other grisly inmates of the Chamber of Horrors. He did chide the criminals for their regrettable proclivities in the past and warn them that he would tolerate no such conduct in his museum. It was not his museum of course. Its owner was Monsieur Pratoucy, a long-necked, melancholy marabou of a man who sat at the ticket window and took in the francs. But, though the legal title to the place might be vested in Monsieur Pratoucy, at night Papa Chibou was the undisputed monarch of his little wax kingdom. When the last patron had left and the doors were closed Papa Chibou began to pay calls on his subjects; across the silent halls he called greetings to them:

"Ah, Bigarre, you old rascal, how goes the world? And you, Madame Marie Antoinette, did you enjoy a good day? Good evening, Monsieur Caesar; aren't you chilly in that costume of yours? Ah, Monsieur Charlemagne, I trust your health continues to be of the best."

His closest friend of them all was Napoleon. The others he liked; to Napoleon he was devoted. It was a friendship cemented by the years, for Napoleon had been in the museum as long as Papa Chibou. Other figures might come and go at the behest of a fickle public, but Napoleon held his place, albeit he had been relegated to a dim corner.

He was not much of a Napoleon. He was smaller even than the original Napoleon, and one of his ears had come in contact with a steam radiator and as a result it was gnarled into a lump the size of a hickory nut; it was a perfect example of that phenomenon of the prize ring, the cauliflower ear. He was supposed to be at St. Helena and he stood on a papier-mâché rock, gazing out wistfully over a nonexistent sea. One hand was thrust into the bosom of his long-tailed coat, the other hung at his side. Skin-tight breeches, once white but white no longer, fitted snugly over his plump bump of waxen abdomen. A Napoleon hat, frayed by years of conscientious brushing by Papa Chibou, was perched above a pensive waxen brow.

Papa Chibou had been attracted to Napoleon from the first. There was something so forlorn about him. Papa Chibou had been forlorn, too, in his first days at the museum. He had come from Bouloire, in the south of France, to seek his fortune as a grower of asparagus in Paris. He was a simple man of scant schooling and he had fancied that there were asparagus beds along the Paris boulevards. There were none. So necessity and chance brought him to the Museum Pratoucy to earn his bread and wine, and romance and his friendship for Napoleon kept him there.

The first day Papa Chibou worked at the museum Monsieur Pratoucy took him round to tell him about the figures.

"This," said the proprietor, "is Toulon, the strangler. This is Mademoiselle Merle, who shot the Russian duke. This is Charlotte Corday, who stabbed Marat in the bath-tub; that gory gentleman is Marat." Then they had come to Napoleon. Monsieur Pratoucy was passing him by.

"And who is this sad-looking gentlman?" asked Papa Chibou.

"Name of a name! Do you not know?"

"But no, monsieur."

"But that is Napoleon himself."

That night, his first in the museum, Papa Chibou went round and said to Napoleon, "Monsieur, I do not know with what crimes you are charged, but I, for one, refuse to think you are guilty of them."

So began their friendship. Thereafter he dusted Napoleon

with especial care and made him his confidant. One night in his twenty-fifth year at the museum Papa Chibou said to Napoleon, "You observed those two lovers who were in here tonight, did you not, my good Napoleon? They thought it was too dark in this corner for us to see, didn't they? But we saw him take her hand and whisper to her. Did she blush? You were near enough to see. She is pretty, isn't she, with her bright dark eyes? She is not a French girl; she is an American; one can tell that by the way she doesn't roll her *r*'s. The young man, he is French; and a fine young fellow he is, or I'm no judge. He is so slender and erect, and he has courage, for he wears the war cross; you noticed that, didn't you? He is very much in love, that is sure. This is not the first time I have seen them. They have met here before, and they are wise, for is this not a spot most romantic for the meetings of lovers?"

Papa Chibou flicked a speck of dust from Napoleon's good ear.

"Ah," he exclaimed, "it must be a thing most delicious to be young and in love! Were you ever in love, Napoleon? No? Ah, what a pity! I know, for I, too, have had no luck in love. Ladies prefer the big, strong men, don't they? Well, we must help these two young people, Napoleon. We must see that they have the joy we missed. So do not let them know you are watching them if they come here tomorrow night. I will pretend I do not see."

Each night after the museum had closed, Papa Chibou gossiped with Napoleon about the progress of the love affair between the American girl with the bright dark eyes and the slender, erect young Frenchman.

"All is not going well," Papa Chibou reported one night, shaking his head. "There are obstacles to their happiness. He has little money, for he is just beginning his career. I heard him tell her so tonight. And she has an aunt who has other plans for her. What a pity if fate should part them! But you know how unfair fate can be, don't you, Napoleon? If only we had some money we might be able to help him, but I, myself, have no money, and I suppose, you, too, were poor, since you look so sad. But attend; tomorrow is a day most important for

them. He has asked her if she will marry him, and she has said
that she will tell him tomorrow night at nine in this very place.
I heard them arrange it all. If she does not come it will mean
no. I think we shall see two very happy ones here tomorrow
night, eh, Napoleon?"

The next night, when the last patron had gone and Papa
Chibou had locked the outer door, he came to Napoleon, and
tears were in his eyes.

"You saw, my friend?" broke out Papa Chibou. "You observed? You saw his face and how pale it grew? You saw his
eyes and how they held a thousand agonies? He waited until
I had to tell him three times that the museum was closing. I
felt like an executioner, I assure you; and he looked up at me
as only a man condemned can look. He went out with heavy
feet; he was no longer erect. For she did not come, Napoleon;
that girl with the bright dark eyes did not come. Our little
comedy of love has become a tragedy, monsieur. She has refused him, that poor, that unhappy young man."

On the following night at closing time Papa Chibou came
hurrying to Napoleon; he was a-quiver with excitement.

"She was here!" he cried. "Did you see her? She was here and
she kept watching and watching; but, of course, he did not
come. I could tell from his stricken face last night that he had
no hope. At last I dared to speak to her. I said to her, 'Mademoiselle, a thousand pardons for the very great liberty I am
taking, but it is my duty to tell you—he was here last night and
he waited till closing time. He was all of a paleness, mademoiselle, and he chewed his fingers in his despair. He loves you,
mademoiselle; a cow could see that. He is devoted to you; and
he is a fine young fellow, you can take an old man's word for
it. Do not break his heart, mademoiselle.' She grasped my
sleeve. 'You know him, then?' she asked. 'You know where I
can find him?' 'Alas, no,' I said. 'I have only seen him here
with you.' 'Poor boy!' she kept saying. 'Poor boy! Oh, what
shall I do? I am in dire trouble. I love him, monsieur.' 'But you
did not come,' I said. 'I could not,' she replied, and she was
weeping. 'I live with an aunt; a rich tiger she is, monsieur, and
she wants me to marry a count, a fat leering fellow who smells

of attar of roses and garlic. My aunt locked me in my room. And now I have lost the one I love, for he will think I have refused him, and he is so proud he will never ask me again.' 'But surely you could let him know?' I suggested. 'But I do not know where he lives,' she said. 'And in a few days my aunt is taking me off to Rome, where the count is, and oh, dear, oh, dear, oh dear—' And she wept on my shoulder, Napoleon, that poor little American girl with the bright dark eyes."

Papa Chibou began to brush the Napoleonic hat.

"I tried to comfort her," he said. "I told her that the young man would surely find her, that he would come back and haunt the spot where they had been happy, but I was telling her what I did not believe, 'He may come tonight,' I said, 'or to-morrow.' She waited until it was time to close the museum. You saw her face as she left; did it not touch you in the heart?"

Papa Chibou was downcast when he approached Napoleon the next night.

"She waited again till closing time," he said, "but he did not come. It made me suffer to see her as the hours went by and her hope ebbed away. At last she had to leave, and at the door she said to me, 'If you see him here again, please give him this.' She handed me this card, Napoleon. See, it says, 'I am at the Villa Rosina, Rome. I love you. Nina.' Ah, the poor, poor young man. We must keep a sharp watch for him, you and I."

Papa Chibou and Napoleon did watch at the Musée Pratoucy night after night. One, two, three, four, five nights they watched for him. A week, a month, more months passed, and he did not come. There came instead one day news of so terrible a nature that it left Papa Chibou ill and trembling. The Musée Pratoucy was going to have to close its doors.

"It is no use," said Monsieur Pratoucy, when he dealt this blow to Papa Chibou. "I cannot go on. Already I owe much, and my creditors are clamouring. People will no longer pay a franc to see a few old dummies when they can see an army of red Indians, Arabs, brigands and dukes in the moving pictures. Monday the Musée Pratoucy closes its doors for ever."

"But, Monsieur Pratoucy," exclaimed Papa Chibou, aghast, "what about the people here? What will become of Marie

Antoinette, and the martyrs, and Napoleon?"

"Oh," said the proprietor, "I'll be able to realize a little on them, perhaps. On Tuesday they will be sold at auction. Someone may buy them to melt up."

"To melt up, monsieur?" Papa Chibou faltered.

"But certainly. What else are they good for?"

"But surely monsieur will want to keep them; a few of them anyhow?"

"Keep them?" Aunt of the devil, but that is a droll idea! Why should any one want to keep shabby old wax dummies?"

"I thought," murmured Papa Chibou, "that you might keep just one—Napoleon, for example—as a remembrance—"

"Uncle of Satan, but you have odd notions! To keep a souvenir of one's bankruptcy!"

Papa Chibou went away to his little hole in the wall. He sat on his cot and fingered his moustache for an hour; the news had left him dizzy, had made a cold vacuum under his belt buckle. From under his cot, at last, he took a wooden box, unlocked three separate locks, and extracted a sock. From the sock he took his fortune, his hoard of big copper ten-centime pieces, tips he had saved for years. He counted them over five times most carefully; but no matter how he counted them he could not make the total come to more than two hundred and twenty-one francs.

That night he did not tell Napoleon the news. He did not tell any of them. Indeed he acted even more cheerful than usual as he went from one figure to another. He complimented Madame Lablanche, the lady of the poisoned spouses, on how well she was looking. He even had a kindly word to say to the lion that was eating the two martyrs.

"After all, Monsieur Lion," he said, "I suppose it is as proper for you to eat martyrs as it is for me to eat bananas. Probably bananas do not enjoy being eaten any more than martyrs do. In the past I have said harsh things to you, Monsieur Lion; I am sorry I said them, now. After all, it is hardly your fault that you eat people. You were born with an appetite for martyrs, just as I was born poor." And he gently tweaked the lion's papier-mâché ear.

When he came to Napoleon, Papa Chibou brushed him with unusual care and thoroughness. With a moistened cloth he polished the imperial nose, and he took pains to be gentle with the cauliflower ear. He told Napoleon the latest joke he had heard at the cabmen's café where he ate his breakfast of onion soup, and, as the joke was mildly improper, nudged Napoleon in the ribs, and winked at him.

"We are men of the world, eh, old friend?" said Papa Chibou. "We are philosophers, is that not so?" Then he added, "We take what life sends us, and sometimes it sends hardnesses."

He wanted to talk more with Napoleon, but somehow he couldn't; abruptly, in the midst of a joke, Papa Chibou broke off and hurried down into the depths of the Chamber of Horrors and stood there for a very long time staring at an unfortunate native of Siam being trodden on by an elephant.

It was not until the morning of the auction sale that Papa Chibou told Napoleon. Then, while the crowd was gathering, he slipped up to Napoleon in his corner and laid his hand on Napoleon's arm.

"One of the hardnesses of life has come to us, old friend," he said. "They are going to try to take you away. But, courage! Papa Chibou does not desert his friends. Listen!" And Papa Chibou patted his pocket, which gave forth a jingling sound.

The bidding began. Close to the auctioneer's desk stood a man, a wizened, rodent-eyed man with a diamond ring and dirty fingers. Papa Chibou's heart went down like an express elevator when he saw him, for he knew that the rodent-eyed man was Mogen, the junk king of Paris. The auctioneer in a voice slightly encumbered by adenoids, began to sell the various items in a hurried, perfunctory manner.

"Item 3 is Julius Caesar, toga and sandals thrown in. How much am I offered? One hundred and fifty francs? Dirt cheap for a Roman emperor, that is. Who'll make it two hundred? Thank you, Monsieur Mogen. The noblest Roman of them all is going at two hundred francs. Are you all through at two hundred? Going, going, gone! Julius Caesar is sold to Monsieur Mogen."

Papa Chibou patted Caesar's back sympathetically.

"You are worth more, my good Julius," he said in a whisper. "Good-bye."

He was encouraged. If a comparatively new Caesar brought only two hundred, surely an old Napoleon would bring no more.

The sale progressed rapidly. Monsieur Mogen bought the entire Chamber of Horrors. He bought Marie Antoinette, and the martyrs and the lions. Papa Chibou, standing near Napoleon, withstood the strain of waiting by chewing his moustache.

The sale was very nearly over and Monsieur Mogen had bought every item, when, with a yawn, the auctioneer droned: "Now, ladies and gentlemen, we come to Item 573, a collection of odds and ends, mostly damaged goods, to be sold in one lot. The lot includes one stuffed owl that seems to have moulted a bit; one Spanish shawl, torn; the head of an Apache who has been guillotined, body missing; a small wax camel, no humps; and an old wax figure of Napoleon, with one ear damaged. What am I offered for the lot?"

Papa Chibou's heart stood still. He laid a reassuring hand on Napoleon's shoulder.

"The fool," he whispered in Napoleon's good ear, "to put you in the same class as a camel, no humps, and an owl. But never mind. It is lucky for us, perhaps."

"How much for this assortment?" asked the auctioneer.

"One hundred francs," said Mogen, the junk king.

"One hundred and fifty," said Papa Chibou, trying to be calm. He had never spent so vast a sum all at once in his life.

Mogen fingered the material in Napoleon's coat.

"Two hundred," said the junk king.

"Are you all through at two hundred?" queried the auctioneer.

"Two hundred and twenty-one," called Papa Chibou. His voice was a husky squeak.

Mogen from his rodent eyes glared at Papa Chibou with annoyance and contempt. He raised his dirtiest finger—the one with the diamond ring on it—toward the auctioneer.

"Monsieur Mogen bids two hundred and twenty-five," droned the auctioneer. "Do I hear two hundred and fifty?"

Papa Chibou hated the world. The auctioneer cast a look in his direction.

"Two hundred and twenty-five is bid," he repeated. "Are you all through at two hundred and twenty-five? Going, going— sold to Monsieur Mogen for two hundred and twenty-five francs."

Stunned, Papa Chibou heard Mogen say casually, "I'll send around my carts for this stuff in the morning."

This stuff!

Dully and with an aching breast Papa Chibou went to his room down by the Roman arena. He packed his few clothes into a box. Last of all he slowly took from his cap the brass badge he had worn for so many years; it bore the words "Chief Watch-man." He had been proud of that title, even if it was slightly inaccurate; he had been not only the chief but the only watch-man. Now he was nothing. It was hours before he summoned up the energy to take his box round to the room he had rented high up under the roof of a tenement in a near-by alley. He knew he should start to look for another job at once, but he could not force himself to do so that day. Instead, he stole back to the deserted museum and sat down on a bench by the side of Napoleon. Silently he sat there all night; but he did not sleep; he was thinking, and the thought that kept pecking at his brain was to him a shocking one. At last, as day began to edge its pale ways through the dusty windows of the museum, Papa Chibou stood up with the air of a man who has been through a mental struggle and has made up his mind.

"Napoleon," he said, "we have been friends for a quarter of a century and now we are to be separated because a stranger had four francs more than I had. That may be lawful, my old friend, but it is not justice. You and I, we are not going to be parted."

Paris was not yet awake when Papa Chibou stole with infinite caution into the narrow street beside the museum. Along this street toward the tenement where he had taken a room crept Papa Chibou. Sometimes he had to pause for breath, for in his arms he was carrying Napoleon.

Two policemen came to arrest Papa Chibou that very afternoon. Mogen had missed Napoleon, and he was a shrewd man. There was not the slightest doubt of Papa Chibou's guilt. There stood Napoleon in the corner of his room, gazing pensively out over the housetops. The police bundled the overwhelmed and confused Papa Chibou into the police patrol, and with him, as damning evidence, Napoleon.

In his cell in the city prison Papa Chibou sat with his spirit caved in. To him jails and judges and justice were terrible and mysterious affairs. He wondered if he would be guillotined; perhaps not, since his long life had been one of blameless conduct; but the least he could expect, he reasoned, was a long sentence to hard labour on Devil's Island, and guillotining had certain advantages over that. Perhaps it would be better to be guillotined, he told himself, now that Napoleon was sure to be melted up.

The keeper who brought him his meal of stew was a pessimist of jocular tendencies.

"A pretty pickle," said the keeper; "and at your age, too. You must be a very wicked old man to go about stealing dummies. What will be safe now? One may expect to find the Eiffel Tower missing any morning. Dummy stealing! What a career! We have had a man in here who stole a trolley car, and one who made off with the anchor of a steamship, and even one who pilfered a hippopotamus from a zoo, but never one who stole a dummy—and an old one-eared dummy, at that! It is an affair extraordinary!"

"And what did they do to the gentleman who stole the hippopotamus?" inquired Papa Chibou tremulously.

The keeper scratched his head to indicate thought.

"I think," he said, "that they boiled him alive. Either that or they transported him for life to Morocco; I don't recall exactly."

Papa Chibou's brow grew damp.

"It was a trial most comical, I can assure you," went on the keeper. "The judges were Messieurs Bertouf, Goblin, and Perouse—very amusing fellows, all three of them. They had fun with the prisoner; how I laughed. Judge Bertouf said, in sentencing him, 'We must be severe with you, pilferer of hippopotamuses. We must make of you an example. This business of hippopotamus pilfering is getting all too common in Paris.' They are witty fellows, those judges."

Papa Chibou grew a shade paler.

"The Terrible Trio?" he asked.

"The Terrible Trio," replied the keeper cheerfully.

"Will they be my judges?" asked Papa Chibou.

"Most assuredly," promised the keeper, and strolled away humming happily and rattling his big keys.

Papa Chibou knew then that there was no hope for him. Even into the Musée Pratoucy the reputation of those three judges had penetrated, and it was a sinister reputation indeed. They were three ancient, grim men who had fairly earned their title, The Terrible Trio, by the severity of their sentences; evildoers blanched at their names, and this was a matter of pride to them.

Shortly the keeper came back; he was grinning.

"You have the devil's own luck, old-timer," he said to Papa Chibou. "First you have to be tried by The Terrible Trio, and then you get assigned to you as lawyer none other than Monsieur Georges Dufayel."

"And this Monsieur Dufayel, is he then not a good lawyer?" questioned Papa Chibou miserably.

The keeper snickered.

"He has not won a case for months," he answered, as if it were the most amusing thing imaginable. "It is really better than a circus to hear him muddling up his client's affairs in court. His mind is not on the case at all. Heaven knows where it is. When he rises to plead before the judges he has no fire, no passion. He mumbles and stutters. It is a saying about the courts that one is as good as convicted who has the ill luck to draw Monsieur Georges Dufayel as his advocate. Still, if one is too poor to pay for a lawyer, one must take what he can get. That's philosophy, eh, old-timer?"

Papa Chibou groaned.

"Oh, wait till tomorrow," said the keeper gayly. "Then you'll have a real reason to groan."

"But surely I can see this Monsieur Dufayel."

"Oh, what's the use? You stole the dummy, didn't you? It

will be there in court to appear against you. How entertaining! Witness for the prosecution: Monsieur Napoleon. You are plainly as guilty as Cain, old-timer, and the judges will boil your cabbage for you very quickly and neatly, I can promise you that. Well, see you tomorrow. Sleep well."

Papa Chibou did not sleep well. He did not sleep at all, in fact, and when they marched him into the inclosure where sat the other nondescript offenders against the law he was shaken and utterly wretched. He was overawed by the great court room and the thick atmosphere of seriousness that hung over it.

He did pluck up enough courage to ask a guard, "Where is my lawyer, Monsieur Dufayel?"

"Oh, he's late, as usual," replied the guard. And then, for he was a waggish fellow, he added, "If you're lucky he won't come at all."

Papa Chibou sank down on the prisoners' bench and raised his eyes to the tribunal opposite. His very marrow was chilled by the sight of The Terrible Trio. The chief judge, Bertouf, was a vast puff of a man, who swelled out of his judicial chair like a poisonous fungus. His black robe was familiar with spilled brandy, and his dirty judicial bib was askew. His face was bibulous and brutal, and he had the wattles of a turkey gobbler. Judge Goblin, on his right, looked to have mummified; he was at least a hundred years old and had wrinkled parchment skin and red-rimmed eyes that glittered like the eyes of a cobra. Judge Perouse was one vast jungle of tangled grizzled whiskers, from the midst of which projected a cockatoo's beak of a nose; he looked at Papa Chibou and licked his lips with a long pink tongue. Papa Chibou all but fainted; he felt no bigger than a pea, and less important; as for his judges, they seemed enormous monsters.

The first case was called, a young swaggering fellow who had stolen an orange from a pushcart.

"Ah, Monsieur Thief," rumbled Judge Bertouf with a scowl, "you are jaunty now. Will you be so jaunty a year from today when you are released from prison? I rather think not. Next case."

Papa Chibou's heart thumped with difficulty. A year for an

orange—and he had stolen a man! His eyes roved round the room and he saw two guards carrying in something which they stood before the judges. It was Napoleon.

A guard tapped Papa Chibou on the shoulder. "You're next," he said.

"But my lawyer, Monsieur Dufayel—" began Papa Chibou.

"You're in hard luck," said the guard, "for here he comes."

Papa Chibou in a daze found himself in the prisoner's dock. He saw coming toward him a pale young man. Papa Chibou recognized him at once. It was the slender, erect young man of the museum. He was not very erect now; he was listless. He did not recognize Papa Chibou; he barely glanced at him.

"You stole something," said the young lawyer, and his voice was toneless. "The stolen goods were found in your room. I think we might better plead guilty and get it over with."

"Yes, monsieur," said Papa Chibou, for he had let go all his hold on hope. "But attend a moment. I have something—a message for you."

Papa Chibou fumbled through his pockets and at last found the card of the American girl with the bright dark eyes. He handed it to Georges Dufayel.

"She left it with me to give to you," said Papa Chibou. "I was chief watchman at the Musée Pratoucy, you know. She came there night after night, to wait for you."

The young man gripped the sides of the card with both hands; his face, his eyes, everything about him seemed suddenly charged with new life.

"Ten thousand million devils!" he cried. "And I doubted her! I owe you much, monsieur. I owe you everything." He wrung Papa Chibou's hand.

Judge Bertouf gave an impatient judicial grunt.

"We are ready to hear your case, Advocate Dufayel," said the judge, "if you have one."

The court attendants sniggered.

"A little moment, monsieur the judge," said the lawyer. He turned to Papa Chibou. "Quick," he shot out, "tell me about the crime you are charged with. What did you steal?"

"Him," replied Papa Chibou, pointing.

"That dummy of Napoleon?"

Papa Chibou nodded.

"But why?"

Papa Chibou shrugged his shoulders.

"Monsieur could not understand."

"But you must tell me!" said the lawyer urgently. "I must make a plea for you. These savages will be severe enough, in any event; but I may be able to do something. Quick; why did you steal this Napoleon?"

"I was his friend," said Papa Chibou. "The museum failed. They were going to sell Napoleon for junk, Monsieur Dufayel. He was my friend. I could not desert him."

The eyes of the young advocate had caught fire; they were lit with a flash. He brought his fist down on the table.

"Enough!" he cried.

Then he rose in his place and addressed the court. His voice was low, vibrant and passionate; the judges, in spite of themselves, leaned forward to listen to him.

"May it please the honourable judges of this court of France," he began, "my client is guilty. Yes, I repeat in a voice of thunder, for all France to hear, for the enemies of France to hear, for the whole world to hear, he is guilty. He did steal this figure of Napoleon, the lawful property of another. I do not deny it. This old man, Jerome Chibou, is guilty, and I for one am proud of his guilt."

Judge Bertouf grunted.

"If your client is guilty, Advocate Dufayel," he said, "that settles it. Despite your pride in his guilt, which is a peculiar notion, I confess, I am going to sentence him to—"

"But wait, your honour!" Dufayel's voice was compelling. 'You must, you shall hear me! Before you pass sentence on this old man, let me ask you a question."

"Well?"

"Are you a Frenchman, Judge Bertouf?"

"But certainly."

"And you love France?"

"Monsieur has not the effrontery to suggest otherwise?"

"No. I was sure of it. That is why you will listen to me."

"I listen."

"I repeat then: Jerome Chibou is guilty. In the law's eyes he is a criminal. But in the eyes of France and those who love her his guilt is a glorious guilt; his guilt is more honourable than innocence itself."

The three judges looked at one another blankly; Papa Chibou regarded his lawyer with wide eyes; Georges Dufayel spoke on.

"These are times of turmoil and change in our country, messieurs the judges. Proud traditions which were once the birthright of every Frenchman have been allowed to decay. Enemies beset us within and without. Youth grows careless of that honour which is the soul of a nation. Youth forgets the priceless heritages of the ages, the great names that once brought glory to France in the past, when Frenchmen were Frenchmen. There are some in France who may have forgotten the respect due a nation's great"—here Advocate Dufayel looked very hard at the judges—"but there are a few patriots left who have not forgotten. And there sits one of them.

"This poor old man has deep within him a glowing devotion to France. You may say that he is a simple, unlettered peasant. You may say that he is a thief. But I say, and true Frenchmen will say with me, that he is a patriot, messieurs the judges. He loves Napoleon. He loves him for what he did for France. He loves him because in Napoleon burned that spirit which has made France great. There was a time, messieurs the judges, when your fathers and mine dared share that love for a great leader. Need I remind you of the career of Napoleon? I know I need not. Need I tell you of his victories? I know I need not."

Nevertheless, Advocate Dufayel did tell them of the career of Napoleon. With a wealth of detail and many gestures he traced the rise of Napoleon; he lingered over his battles; for an hour and ten minutes he spoke eloquently of Napoleon and his part in the history of France.

"You may have forgotten," he concluded, "and others may have forgotten, but this old man sitting here a prisoner—he did not forget. When mercenary scoundrels wanted to throw on the junk heap this effigy of one of France's greatest sons, who was it that saved him? Was it you, messieurs the judges? Was it I? Alas, no. It was a poor old man who loved Napoleon more than he loved himself. Consider, messieurs the judges; they were going to throw on the junk heap Napoleon—France's Napoleon—our Napoleon. Who would save him? Then up rose this man, this Jerome Chibou, whom you would brand as a thief, and he cried aloud for France and for the whole world to hear, 'Stop! Desecraters of Napoleon, stop! There still lives one Frenchman who loves the memories of his native land; there is still one patriot left. I, I, Jerome Chibou, will save Napoleon!' And he did save him, messieurs the judges."

Advocate Dufayel mopped his brow, and levelling an accusing finger at The Terrible Trio he said, "You may send Jerome Chibou to jail. But when you do, remember this: You are sending to jail the spirit of France. You may find Jerome Chibou guilty. But when you do, remember this: You are condemning a man for love of country, for love of France. Wherever true hearts beat in French bosoms, messieurs the judges, there will the crime of Jerome Chibou be understood, and there will the name of Jerome Chibou be honoured. Put him in prison, messieurs the judges. Load his poor feeble old body with chains. And a nation will tear down the prison walls, break his chains, and pay homage to the man who loved Napoleon and France so much that he was willing to sacrifice himself on the altar of patriotism."

Advocate Dufayel sat down; Papa Chibou raised his eyes to the judges' bench. Judge Perouse was ostentatiously blowing his beak of a nose. Judge Goblin, who wore a Sedan ribbon in his buttonhole, was sniffling into his inkwell. And Chief Judge Bertouf was openly blubbering.

"Jerome Chibou, stand up." It was Chief Judge Bertouf who spoke, and his voice was thick with emotion.

Papa Chibou, quaking, stood up. A hand like a hand of pink bananas was thrust down at him.

"Jerome Chibou," said Chief Judge Bertouf, "I find you guilty. Your crime is patriotism in the first degree. I sentence you to freedom. Let me have the honour of shaking the hand of a true Frenchman."

"And I," said Judge Goblin, thrusting out a hand as dry as autumn leaves.

"And I also," said Judge Perouse, reaching out a hairy hand.

"And, furthermore," said Chief Judge Bertouf, "you shall continue to protect the Napoleon you saved. I subscribe a hundred francs to buy him for you."

"And I," said Judge Goblin.

"And I also," said Judge Perouse.

As they left the court room, Advocate Dufayel, Papa Chibou and Napoleon, Papa Chibou turned to his lawyer.

"I can never repay monsieur," he began.

"Nonsense!" said the lawyer.

"And would Monsieur Dufayel mind telling me again the last name of Napoleon?"

"Why, Bonaparte, of course. Surely you knew—"

"Alas, no, Monsieur Dufayel. I am a man the most ignorant. I did not know that my friend had done such great things."

"You didn't? Then what in the name of heaven did you think Napoleon was?"

"A sort of murderer," said Papa Chibou humbly.

Out beyond the walls of Paris in a garden stands the villa of Georges Dufayel, who has become, everyone says, the most eloquent and successful young lawyer in the Paris courts. He lives there with his wife, who has bright dark eyes. To get to his house one must pass a tiny gatehouse, where lives a small old man with a prodigious walrus moustache. Visitors who peer into the gatehouse as they pass sometimes get a shock, for standing in one corner of its only room they see another small man, in uniform and a big hat. He never moves, but stands there by the window all day, one hand in the bosom of his coat, the other at his side, while his eyes look out over the garden. He is waiting for Papa Chibou to come home after his work among the asparagus beds to tell him the jokes and the news of the day.

Richard Connell

*

THE MOST DANGEROUS GAME

*RKO first released THE MOST DANGEROUS GAME in
1932. The picture adapted by James Ashmore Creelman was
so popular that it was reissued in 1942. Directed by Ernest B.
Schoedsack and Irving Pichel, the film starred Leslie Banks,
"polished and suave" English actor; Fay Wray and Joel McCrea,
supported by Robert Armstrong, Steve Clements and Noble
Johnson. The picture was noteworthy for the imaginative fashion in which it was produced and for its effective staging, which
made of the fantastic theme a highly satisfactory melodrama.*

"OFF THERE to the right—somewhere—is a large island," said
Whitney. "It's rather a mystery—"

"What island is it?" Rainsford asked.

"The old charts call it 'Ship-Trap Island'," Whitney replied.
"A suggestive name, isn't it? Sailors have a curious dread of the
place. I don't know why. Some superstition—"

"Can't see it," remarked Rainsford, trying to peer through the
dank tropical night that was palpable as it pressed its thick
warm blackness in upon the yacht.

"You've good eyes," said Whitney, with a laugh, "and I've
seen you pick off a moose moving in the brown fall bush at
four hundred yards, but even you can't see four miles or so
through a moonless Caribbean night."

"Nor four yards," admitted Rainsford. "Ugh! It's like moist
black velvet."

"It will be light enough in Rio," promised Whitney. "We
should make it in a few days. I hope the jaguar guns have come
from Purdey's. We should have some good hunting up the
Amazon. Great sport, hunting."

"The best sport in the world," agreed Rainsford.

"For the hunter," amended Whitney. "Not for the jaguar."

"Don't talk rot, Whitney," said Rainsford. "You're a big-game hunter, not a philosopher. Who cares how a jaguar feels?"

"Perhaps the jaguar does," observed Whitney.

"Bah! They've no understanding."

"Even so, I rather think they understand one thing—fear. The fear of pain and the fear of death."

"Nonsense," laughed Rainsford. "This hot weather is making you soft, Whitney. Be a realist. The world is made up of two classes—the hunters and the huntees. Luckily, you and I are hunters. Do you think we've passed that island yet?"

"I can't tell in the dark. I hope so."

"Why?" asked Rainsford.

"The place has a reputation—a bad one."

"Cannibals?" suggested Rainsford.

"Hardly. Even cannibals wouldn't live in such a God-forsaken place. But it's gotten into sailor lore, somehow. Didn't you notice that the crew's nerves seemed a bit jumpy today?"

"They were a bit strange, now you mention it. Even Captain Nielsen—"

"Yes, even that tough-minded old Swede, who'd go up to the devil himself and ask him for a light. Those fishy blue eyes held a look I never saw there before. All I could get out of him was: 'This place has an evil name among seafaring men, sir.' Then he said to me, very gravely: 'Don't you feel anything?' —as if the air about us was actually poisonous. Now, you musn't laugh when I tell you this—I did feel something like a sudden chill.

"There was no breeze. The sea was as flat as a plate-glass window. We were drawing near the island then. What I felt was a—a mental chill; a sort of sudden dread."

"Pure imagination," said Rainsford. "One superstitious sailor can taint the whole ship's company with his fear."

"Maybe. But sometimes I think sailors have an extra sense that tells them when they are in danger. Sometimes I think evil is a tangible thing—with wave lengths, just as sound and light have. An evil place can, so to speak, broadcast vibrations of evil. Anyhow, I'm glad we're getting out of this zone. Well, I think I'll turn in now, Rainsford."

"I'm not sleepy," said Rainsford. "I'm going to smoke another pipe up on the after deck."

"Good night, then, Rainsford. See you at breakfast."

"Right. Good night, Whitney."

There was no sound in the night as Rainsford sat there but the muffled throb of the engine that drove the yacht swiftly through the darkness, and the swish and ripple of the wash of the propeller.

Rainsford, reclining in a steamer chair, indolently puffed on his favorite brier. The sensuous drowsiness of the night was upon him. "It's so dark," he thought, "that I could sleep without closing my eyes; the night would be my eyelids—"

An abrupt sound startled him. Off to the right he heard it, and his ears, expert in such matters, could not be mistaken. Again he heard the sound, and again. Somewhere, off in the blackness, someone had fired a gun three times.

Rainsford sprang up and moved quickly to the rail, mystified. He strained his eyes in the direction from which the reports had come, but it was like trying to see through a blanket. He leaped upon the rail and balanced himself there, to get greater elevation; his pipe, striking a rope, was knocked from his mouth. He lunged for it; a short, hoarse cry came from his lips as he realized he had reached too far and had lost his balance. The cry was pinched off short as the blood-warm waters of the Caribbean Sea closed over his head.

He struggled up to the surface and tried to cry out, but the wash from the speeding yacht slapped him in the face and the salt water in his open mouth made him gag and strangle. Desperately he struck out with strong strokes after the receding lights of the yacht, but he stopped before he had swum fifty feet. A certain cool-headedness had come to him; it was not the first time he had been in a tight place. There was a chance that his cries could be heard by someone aboard the yacht, but that chance was slender, and grew more slender as the yacht raced on. He wrestled himself out of his clothes, and shouted with all his power. The lights of the yacht became faint and ever-vanishing fireflies; then they were blotted out entirely by the night.

Rainsford remembered the shots. They had come from the right, and doggedly he swam in that direction, swimming with slow, deliberate strokes, conserving his strength. For a seemingly endless time he fought the sea. He began to count his strokes; he could do possibly a hundred more and then—

Rainsford heard a sound. It came out of the darkness, a high screaming sound, the sound of an animal in an extremity of anguish and terror.

He did not recognize the animal that made the sound; he did not try to; with fresh vitality he swam toward the sound. He heard it again; then it was cut short by another noise, crisp, staccato.

"Pistol shot," muttered Rainsford, swimming on.

Ten minutes of determined effort brought another sound to his ears—the most welcome he had ever heard—the muttering and growling of the sea breaking on a rocky shore. He was almost on the rocks before he saw them; on a night less calm he would have been shattered against them. With his remaining strength he dragged himself from the swirling waters. Jagged crags appeared to jut up into the opaqueness; he forced himself upward, hand over hand. Gasping, his hands raw, he reached a flat place at the top. Dense jungle came down to the very edge of the cliffs. What perils that tangle of trees and underbrush might hold for him did not concern Rainsford just then. All he knew was that he was safe from his enemy, the sea, and that utter weariness was upon him. He flung himself down at the jungle edge and tumbled headlong into the deepest sleep of his life.

When he opened his eyes he knew from the position of the sun that it was late in the afternoon. Sleep had given him new vigor; a sharp hunger was picking at him. He looked about him, almost cheerfully.

"Where there are pistol shots, there are men. Where there are men, there is food," he thought. But what kind of men, he wondered, in so forbidding a place? An unbroken front of snarled and ragged jungle fringed the shore.

He saw no sign of a trail through the closely knit web of weeds and trees; it was easier to go along the shore, and

Rainsford floundered along by the water. Not far from where he had landed, he stopped.

Some wounded thing, by the evidence, a large animal, had thrashed about in the underbrush; the jungle weeds were crushed down and the moss was lacerated; one patch of weeds was stained crimson. A small, glittering object not far away caught Rainsford's eye and he picked it up. It was an empty cartridge.

"A twenty-two," he remarked. "That's odd. It must have been a fairly large animal, too. The hunter had his nerve with him to tackle it with a light gun. It's clear that the brute put up a fight. I suppose the first three shots I heard was when the hunter flushed his quarry and wounded it. The last shot was when he trailed it here and finished it."

He examined the ground closely and found what he had hoped to find—the print of hunting boots. They pointed along the cliff in the direction he had been going. Eagerly he hurried along, now slipping on a rotten log or a loose stone, but making headway; night was beginning to settle down on the island.

Bleak darkness was blacking out the sea and jungle when Rainsford sighted the lights. He came upon them as he turned a crook in the coast line, and his first thought was that he had come upon a village, for there were many lights. But as he forged along he saw to his great astonishment that all the lights were in one enormous building—a lofty structure with pointed towers plunging upward into the gloom. His eyes made out the shadowy outlines of a palatial chateau; it was set on a high bluff, and on three sides of it cliffs dived down to where the sea licked greedy lips in the shadows.

"Mirage," thought Rainsford. But it was no mirage, he found, when he opened the tall spiked iron gate. The stone steps were real enough; the massive door with a leering gargoyle for a knocker was real enough; yet above it all hung an air of unreality.

He lifted the knocker, and it creaked up stiffly, as if it had never before been used. He let it fall, and it startled him with its booming loudness. He thought he heard steps within; the door remained closed. Again Rainsford lifted the heavy knocker, and let it fall. The door opened then, opened as suddenly as if it were on a spring, and Rainsford stood blinking in the river of glaring gold light that poured out. The first thing Rainsford's eyes discerned was the largest man Rainsford had ever seen—a gigantic creature, solidly made and black-bearded to the waist. In his hand the man held a long-barreled revolver, and he was pointing it straight at Rainsford's heart.

Out of the snarl of beard two small eyes regarded Rainsford.

"Don't be alarmed," said Rainsford, with a smile which he hoped was disarming. "I'm no robber. I fell off a yacht. My name is Sanger Rainsford of New York City."

The menacing look in the eyes did not change. The revolver pointed as rigidly as if the giant were a statue. He gave no sign that he understood Rainsford's words, or that he had even heard them. He was dressed in uniform, a black uniform trimmed with gray astrakhan.

"I'm Sanger Rainsford of New York," Rainsford began again. "I fell off a yacht. I am hungry."

The man's only answer was to raise with his thumb the hammer of his revolver. Then Rainsford saw the man's free hand go to his forehead in a military salute, and he saw him click his heels together and stand at attention. Another man was coming down the broad marble steps, an erect, slender man in evening clothes. He advanced to Rainsford and held out his hand.

In a cultivated voice marked by a slight accent that gave it added precision and deliberateness, he said: "It is a very great pleasure and honor to welcome Mr. Sanger Rainsford, the celebrated hunter, to my home."

Automatically Rainsford shook the man's hand.

"I've read your book about hunting snow leopards in Tibet, you see," explained the man. "I am General Zaroff."

Rainsford's first impression was that the man was singularly handsome; his second was that there was an original, almost bizarre quality about the general's face. He was a tall man past middle age, for his hair was a vivid white; but his thick eyebrows and pointed military mustache were as black as the night from which Rainsford had come. His eyes, too, were black and very bright. He had high cheek bones, a sharp-cut nose, a spare, dark face, the face of a man used to giving orders, the face of an aristocrat. Turning to the giant in uniform, the general made a sign. The giant put away his pistol, saluted, withdrew.

"Ivan is an incredibly strong fellow," remarked the general, "but he has the misfortune to be deaf and dumb. A simple fellow, but, I'm afraid, like all his race, a bit of a savage."

"Is he Russian?"

"He is a Cossack," said the general, and his smile showed red lips and pointed teeth. "So am I."

"Come," he said, "we shouldn't be chatting here. We can talk later. Now you want clothes, food, rest. You shall have them. This is a most restful spot."

Ivan had reappeared, and the general spoke to him with lips that moved but gave forth no sound.

"Follow Ivan, if you please, Mr. Rainsford," said the general. "I was about to have my dinner when you came. I'll wait for you. You'll find that my clothes will fit you, I think."

It was to a huge, beam-ceilinged bedroom with a canopied bed big enough for six men that Rainsford followed the silent giant. Ivan laid out an evening suit, and Rainsford, as he put it on, noticed that it came from a London tailor who ordinarily cut and sewed for none below the rank of duke.

The dining room to which Ivan conducted them was in many ways remarkable. There was a medieval magnificence about it; it suggested a baronial hall of feudal times with its oaken panels, its high ceiling, its vast refectory tables where twoscore men could sit down to eat. About the hall were the mounted heads of many animals—lions, tigers, elephants, moose, bears; larger or more perfect specimens Rainsford had never seen. At the great table the general was sitting, alone.

"You'll have a cocktail, Mr. Rainsford," he suggested. The cocktail was surpassingly good; and, Rainsford noticed, the table appointments were of the finest—the linen, the crystal, the silver, the china.

They were eating *borsch*, the rich, red soup with whipped

cream so dear to Russian palates. Half apologetically General Zaroff said: "We do our best to preserve the amenities of civilization here. Please forgive any lapses. We are well off the beaten track, you know. Do you think the champagne has suffered from its long ocean trip?"

"Not in the least," declared Rainsford. He was finding the general a most thoughtful and affable host, a true cosmopolite. But there was one small trait of the general's that made Rainsford uncomfortable. Whenever he looked up from his plate he found the general studying him, appraising him narrowly.

"Perhaps," said General Zaroff, "you were surprised that I recognized your name. You see, I read all books on hunting published in English, French, and Russian. I have but one passion in my life, Mr. Rainsford, and it is the hunt."

"You have some wonderful heads here," said Rainsford as he ate a particularly well cooked *filet mignon*. "That Cape buffalo is the largest I ever saw."

"Oh, that fellow. Yes, he was a monster."

"Did he charge you?"

"Hurled me against a tree," said the general. "Fractured my skull. But I got the brute."

"I've always thought," said Rainsford, "that the Cape buffalo is the most dangerous of all big game."

For a moment the general did not reply; he was smiling his curious red-lipped smile. Then he said slowly: "No. You are wrong, sir. The Cape buffalo is not the most dangerous big game." He sipped his wine. "Here in my preserve on this island," he said in the same slow tone, "I hunt more dangerous game."

Rainsford expressed his surprise. "Is there big game on this island?"

The general nodded. "The biggest."

"Really?"

"Oh, it isn't here naturally, of course. I have to stock the island."

"What have you imported, general?" Rainsford asked. "Tigers?"

The general smiled. "No," he said. "Hunting tigers ceased

to interest me some years ago. I exhausted their possibilities, you see. No thrill left in tigers, no real danger. I live for danger, Mr. Rainsford."

The general took from his pocket a gold cigarette case and offered his guest a long black cigarette with a silver tip; it was perfumed and gave off a smell like incense.

"We will have some capital hunting, you and I," said the general. "I shall be most glad to have your society."

"But what game—" began Rainsford.

"I'll tell you," said the general. "You will be amused, I know. I think I may say, in all modesty, that I have done a rare thing. I have invented a new sensation. May I pour you another glass of port?"

"Thank you, general."

The general filled both glasses, and said: "God makes some men poets. Some He makes kings, some beggars. Me He made a hunter. My hand was made for the trigger, my father said. He was a very rich man with a quarter of a million acres in the Crimea, and he was an ardent sportsman. When I was only five years old he gave me a little gun, specially made in Moscow for me, to shoot sparrows with. When I shot some of his prize turkeys with it, he did not punish me; he complimented me on my marksmanship. I killed my first bear in the Caucasus when I was ten. My whole life has been one prolonged hunt. I went into the army—it was expected of noblemen's sons—and for a time commanded a division of Cossack cavalry, but my real interest was always the hunt. I have hunted every kind of game in every land. It would be impossible for me to tell you how many animals I have killed."

The general puffed at his cigarette.

"After the debacle in Russia I left the country, for it was imprudent for an officer of the Czar to stay there. Many noble Russians lost everything. I, luckily, had invested heavily in American securities, so I shall never have to open a tea room in Monte Carlo or drive a taxi in Paris. Naturally, I continued to hunt—grizzlies in your Rockies, crocodile in the Ganges, rhinoceroses in East Africa. It was in Africa that the Cape buffalo hit me and laid me up for six months. As soon as I recovered I started for the Amazon to hunt jaguars, for I had heard they were unusually cunning. They weren't." The Cossack sighed. "They were no match at all for a hunter with his wits about him, and a high-powered rifle. I was bitterly disappointed. I was lying in my tent with a splitting headache one night when a terrible thought pushed its way into my mind. Hunting was beginning to bore me! And hunting, remember, had been my life. I have heard that in America business men often go to pieces when they give up the business that has been their life."

"Yes, that's so," said Rainsford.

The general smiled. "I had no wish to go to pieces," he said. "I must do something. Now, mine is an analytical mind, Mr. Rainsford. Doubtless that is why I enjoy the problems of the chase."

"No doubt, General Zaroff."

"So," continued the general, "I asked myself why the hunt no longer fascinated me. You are much younger than I am, Mr. Rainsford, and have not hunted as much, but you perhaps can guess the answer."

"What was it?"

"Simply this: hunting had ceased to be what you call 'a sporting proposition.' It had become too easy. I always got my quarry. Always. There is no greater bore than perfection."

The general lit a fresh cigarette.

"No animal had a chance with me any more. That is no boast; it is a mathematical certainty. The animal had nothing but his legs and his instinct. Instinct is no match for reason. When I thought of this it was a tragic moment for me, I can tell you."

Rainsford leaned across the table, absorbed in what his host was saying.

"It came to me as an inspiration what I must do," the general went on.

"And that was?"

The general smiled the quiet smile of one who has faced an obstacle and surmounted it with success. "I had to invent a new animal to hunt," he said.

"A new animal? You're joking."

"Not at all," said the general. "I never joke about hunting. I needed a new animal. I found one. So I bought this island, built this house, and here I do my hunting. The island is perfect for my purposes—there are jungles with a maze of trails in them, hills, swamps—"

"But the animal, General Zaroff?"

"Oh, said the general, "it supplies me with the most exciting hunting in the world. No other hunting compares with it for an instant. Every day I hunt, and I never grow bored now, for I have a quarry with which I can match my wits."

Rainsford's bewilderment showed in his face.

"I wanted the ideal animal to hunt," explained the general. "So I said: 'What are the attributes of an ideal quarry?' And the answer was, of course: 'It must have courage, cunning, and, above all, it must be able to reason'."

"But no animal can reason," objected Rainsford.

"My dear fellow," said the general, "there is one that can."

"But you can't mean—" gasped Rainsford.

"And why not?"

"I can't believe you are serious, General Zaroff. This is a grisly joke."

"Why should I not be serious? I am speaking of hunting."

"Hunting? Good God, General Zaroff, what you speak of is murder."

The general laughed with entire good nature. He regarded Rainsford quizzically. "I refuse to believe that so modern and civilized a young man as you seem to be harbors romantic ideas about the value of human life. Surely your experiences in the war—"

"Did not make me condone cold-blooded murder," finished Rainsford stiffly.

Laughter shook the general. "How extraordinarily droll you are!" he said. "One does not expect nowadays to find a young man of the educated class, even in America, with such a naive, and, if I may say so, mid-Victorian point of view. It's like finding a snuff-box in a limousine. Ah, well, doubtless you had Puritan ancestors. So many Americans appear to have had. I'll wager you'll forget your notions when you go hunting with me. You've a genuine new thrill in store for you, Mr. Rainsford."

"Thank you, I'm a hunter, not a murderer."

"Dear me," said the general, quite unruffled, "again that unpleasant word. But I think I can show you that your scruples are quite ill founded."

"Yes?"

"Life is for the strong, to be lived by the strong, and, if needs be, taken by the strong. The weak of the world were put here to give the strong pleasure. I am strong. Why should I not use my fist? If I wish to hunt, why should I not? I hunt the scum of the earth—sailors from tramp ships—lascars, blacks, Chinese, whites, mongrels—a thoroughbred horse or hound is worth more than a score of them."

"But they are men," said Rainsford hotly.

"Precisely," said the general. "That is why I use them. It gives me pleasure. They can reason, after a fashion. So they are dangerous."

"But where do you get them?"

The general's left eyelid fluttered down in a wink. "This island is called Ship Trap," he answered. "Sometimes an angry god of the high seas sends them to me. Sometimes, when Providence is not so kind, I help Providence a bit. Come to the window with me."

Rainsford went to the window and looked out toward the sea.

"Watch! Out there!" exclaimed the general, pointing into the night. Rainsford's eyes saw only blackness, and then, as the general pressed a button, far out to sea Rainsford saw the flash of lights.

The general chuckled. "They indicate a channel," he said, "where there's none; giant rocks with razor edges crouch like a sea monster with wide-open jaws. They can crush a ship as easily as I crush this nut." He dropped a walnut on the hardwood floor and brought his heel grinding down on it. "Oh, yes," he said, casually, as if in answer to a question, "I have electricity. We try to be civilized here."

"Civilized? And you shoot down men?"

A trace of anger was in the general's black eyes, but it was there for but a second, and he said, in his most pleasant manner: "Dear me, what a righteous young man you are! I assure you I do not do the thing you suggest. That would be barbarous. I treat these visitors with every consideration. They get plenty of good food and exercise. They get into splendid physical condition. You shall see for yourself tomorrow."

"What do you mean?"

"We'll visit my training school," smiled the general. "It's in the cellar. I have about a dozen pupils down there now. They're from the Spanish bark *San Lucar* that had the bad luck to go on the rocks out there. A very inferior lot, I regret to say. Poor specimens and more accustomed to the deck than to the jungle."

He raised his hand, and Ivan, who served as waiter, brought thick Turkish coffee. Rainsford, with an effort, held his tongue in check.

"It's a game, you see," pursued the general blandly. "I suggest to one of them that we go hunting. I give him a supply of food and an excellent hunting knife. I give him three hours' start. I am to follow, armed only with a pistol of the smallest caliber and range. If my quarry eludes me for three whole days, he wins the game. If I find him"—the general smiled—"he loses."

"Suppose he refuses to be hunted?"

"Oh," said the general, "I give him his option, of course. He need not play that game if he doesn't wish to. If he does not wish to hunt, I turn him over to Ivan. Ivan once had the honor of serving as official knouter to the Great White Czar, and he has his own ideas of sport. Invariably, Mr. Rainsford, invariably they choose the hunt."

"And if they win?"

The smile on the general's face widened. "To date I have not lost," he said. Then he added, hastily: "I don't wish you to think me a braggart, Mr. Rainsford. Many of them afford only the most elementary sort of problem. Occasionally I strike a tartar. One almost did win. I eventually had to use the dogs."

"The dogs?"

"This way, please. I'll show you."

The general steered Rainsford to a window. The lights from the windows sent a flickering illumination that made grotesque patterns on the courtyard below, and Rainsford could see moving about there a dozen or so huge black shapes; as they turned toward him, their eyes glittered greenly.

"A rather good lot, I think," observed the general. "They are let out at seven every night. If anyone should try to get into my house—or out of it—something extremely regrettable would occur to him." He hummed a snatch of song from the *Folies Bergère.*

"And now," said the general, "I want to show you my new collection of heads. Will you come with me to the library?"

"I hope," said Rainsford, "that you will excuse me tonight, General Zaroff. I'm really not feeling well."

"Ah, indeed?" the general inquired solicitously. "Well, I suppose that's only natural, after your long swim. You need a good, restful night's sleep. Tomorrow you'll feel like a new man, I'll wager. Then we'll hunt, eh? I've one rather promising prospect—" Rainsford was hurrying from the room.

"Sorry you can't go with me tonight," called the general. "I expect rather fair sport—a big, strong black. He looks resourceful—Well, good night, Mr. Rainsford; I hope you have a good night's rest."

The bed was good, and the pajamas of the softest silk and he was tired in every fiber of his being, but nevertheless Rainsford could not quiet his brain with the opiate of sleep. He lay, eyes wide open. Once he thought he heard stealthy steps in the corridor outside his room. He sought to throw open the door; it would not open. He went to the window and looked out. His room was high up in one of the towers. The lights of the château were out now, and it was dark and silent, but there was a fragment of sallow moon, and by its wan light he could see, dimly, the courtyard; there, weaving in and out in the pattern of shadow, were black, noiseless forms; the hounds heard him at the window and looked up, expectantly, with their green eyes. Rainsford went back to the bed and lay down. By many methods he tried to put himself to sleep. He had achieved a doze when, just as morning began to come, he heard, far off in the jungle, the faint report of a pistol.

General Zaroff did not appear until luncheon. He was dressed faultlessly in the tweeds of a country squire. He was solicitous about the state of Rainsford's health.

"As for me," sighed the general, "I do not feel so well. I am worried, Mr. Rainsford. Last night I detected traces of my old complaint."

To Rainsford's questioning glance the general said: "Ennui. Boredom."

Then, taking a second helping of *Crêpes Suzette*, the general explained: "The hunting was not good last night. The fellow lost his head. He made a straight trail that offered no problems at all. That's the trouble with these sailors; they have dull brains to begin with, and they do not know how to get about in the woods. They do excessively stupid and obvious things. It's most annoying. Will you have another glass of *Chablis*, Mr. Rainsford?"

"General," said Rainsford firmly, "I wish to leave this island at once."

The general raised his thickets of eyebrows; he seemed hurt. "But, my dear fellow," the general protested, "you've only just come. You've had no hunting—"

"I wish to go today," said Rainsford. He saw the dead black eyes of the general on him, studying him. General Zaroff's face suddenly brightened.

He filled Rainsford's glass with venerable *Chablis* from a dusty bottle.

"Tonight," said the general, "we will hunt—you and I."

Rainsford shook his head. "No, general," he said, "I will not hunt."

The general shrugged his shoulders and delicately ate a hothouse grape. "As you wish, my friend," he said. "The choice rests entirely with you. But may I not venture to suggest that you will find my idea of sport more diverting than Ivan's?"

He nodded toward the corner to where the giant stood, scowling, his thick arms crossed on his hogshead of a chest.

"You don't mean—" cried Rainsford.

"My dear fellow," said the general, "have I not told you I always mean what I say about hunting? This is really an inspiration. I drink to a foeman worthy of my steel—at last." The general raised his glass, but Rainsford sat staring at him.

"You'll find this game worth playing," the general said enthusiastically. "Your brain against mine. Your woodcraft against mine. Your strength and stamina against mine. Outdoor chess! And the stake is not without value, eh?"

"And if I win—" began Rainsford huskily.

"I'll cheerfully acknowledge myself defeated if I do not find you by midnight of the third day," said General Zaroff. "My sloop will place you on the mainland near a town." The general read what Rainsford was thinking.

"Oh, you can trust me," said the Cossack. "I will give you my word as a gentleman and a sportsman. Of course you, in turn, must agree to say nothing of your visit here."

"I'll agree to nothing of the kind," said Rainsford.

"Oh," said the general, "in that case— But why discuss that now? Three days hence we can discuss it over a bottle of *Veuve Cliquot*, unless—"

The general sipped his wine.

Then a businesslike air animated him. "Ivan," he said to Rainsford, "will supply you with hunting clothes, food, a knife. I suggest you wear moccasins; they leave a poorer trail. I suggest, too, that you avoid the big swamp in the southeast corner of the island. We call it Death Swamp. There's quicksand there. One foolish fellow tried it. The deplorable part of it was that Lazarus followed him. You can imagine my feelings, Mr. Rainsford. I loved Lazarus; he was the finest hound in my pack. Well, I must beg you to excuse me now. I always take a siesta after lunch. You'll hardly have time for a nap, I fear. You'll want to start, no doubt. I shall not follow till dusk. Hunting at night is so much more exciting than by day, don't you think? *Au revoir*, Mr. Rainsford, *au revoir*." General Zaroff, with a deep, courtly bow, strolled from the room.

Rainsford had fought his way through the bush for two hours. "I must keep my nerve. I must keep my nerve," he said through tight teeth.

He had not been entirely clear-headed when the château

gates snapped shut behind him. His whole idea at first was to put distance between himself and General Zaroff, and, to this end, he had plunged along, spurred on by the sharp rowels of something very like panic. Now he had got a grip on himself, had stopped, and was taking stock of himself and the situation. He saw that straight flight was futile; inevitably it would bring him face to face with the sea. He was in a picture with a frame of water, and his operations, clearly, must take place within that frame.

"I'll give him a trail to follow," muttered Rainsford, and he struck off from the rude path he had been following into the trackless wilderness. He executed a series of intricate loops; he doubled on his trail again and again, recalling all the lore of the fox hunt, and all the dodges of the fox. Night found him leg-weary, with hands and face lashed by the branches, on a thickly wooded ridge. He knew it would be insane to blunder on through the dark, even if he had the strength. His need for rest was imperative and he thought: "I have played the fox, now I must play the cat of the fable." A big tree with a thick trunk and outspread branches was near by, and, taking care to leave not the slightest mark, he climbed up into the crotch, and stretching out on one of the broad limbs, after a fashion, rested. Rest brought him new confidence and almost a feeling of security. Even so zealous a hunter as General Zaroff could not trace him there, he told himself; only the devil himself could follow that complicated trail through the jungle after dark. But, perhaps the general was a devil—

An apprehensive night crawled slowly by like a wounded snake, and sleep did not visit Rainsford, although the silence of a dead world was on the jungle. Toward morning when a dingy gray was varnishing the sky, the cry of some startled bird focused Rainsford's attention in that direction. Something was coming through the bush, coming slowly, carefully, coming by the same winding way Rainsford had come. He flattened himself down on the limb, and through a screen of leaves almost as thick as tapestry, he watched. . . . That which was approaching was a man.

He was General Zaroff. He made his way along with his

eyes fixed in utmost concentration on the ground before him. He paused, almost beneath the tree, dropped to his knees and studied the ground. Rainsford's impulse was to hurl himself down like a panther, but he saw that the general's right hand held something metallic—a small automatic pistol.

The hunter shook his head several times, as if he were puzzled. Then he straightened up and took from his case one of his black cigarettes; its pungent incenselike smoke floated up to Rainsford's nostrils.

Rainsford held his breath. The general's eyes had left the ground and were traveling inch by inch up the tree. Rainsford froze there, every muscle tensed for a spring. But the sharp eyes of the hunter stopped before they reached the limb where Rainsford lay; a smile spread over his brown face. Very deliberately he blew a smoke ring into the air; then he turned his back on the tree and walked carelessly away, back along the trail he had come. The swish of the underbrush against his hunting boots grew fainter and fainter.

The pent-up air burst hotly from Rainsford's lungs. His first thought made him feel sick and numb. The general could follow a trail through the woods at night; he could follow an extremely difficult trail; he must have uncanny powers; only by the merest chance had the Cossack failed to see his quarry.

Rainsford's second thought was even more terrible. It sent a shudder of cold horror through his whole being. Why had the general smiled? Why had he turned back?

Rainsford did not want to believe what his reason told him was true, but the truth was as evident as the sun that had by now pushed through the morning mists. The general was playing with him! The general was saving him for another day's sport! The Cossack was the cat; he was the mouse. Then it was that Rainsford knew the full meaning of terror.

"I will not lose my nerve. I will not."

He slid down from the tree, and struck off again into the woods. His face was set and he forced the machinery of his mind to function. Three hundred yards from his hiding place he stopped where a huge dead tree leaned precariously on a smaller, living one. Throwing off his sack of food, Rainsford took his knife from its sheath and began to work with all his energy.

The job was finished at last, and he threw himself down behind a fallen log a hundred feet away. He did not have to wait long. The cat was coming again to play with the mouse.

Following the trail with the sureness of a bloodhound came General Zaroff. Nothing escaped those searching black eyes, no crushed blade of grass, no bent twig, no mark, no matter how faint, in the moss. So intent was the Cossack on his stalking that he was upon the thing Rainsford had made before he saw it. His foot touched it, the general sensed his danger and leaped back with the agility of an ape. But he was not quick enough; the dead tree, delicately adjusted to rest on the cut living one, crashed down and struck the general a glancing blow on the shoulder as it fell; but for his alertness, he must have been smashed beneath it. He staggered, but he did not fall; nor did he drop his revolver. He stood there, rubbing his injured shoulder, and Rainsford, with fear again gripping his heart, heard the general's mocking laugh ring through the jungle.

"Rainsford," called the general. "if you are within sound of my voice, as I suppose you are, let me congratulate you. Not many men know how to make a Malay man-catcher. Luckily, for me, I, too, have hunted in Malacca. You are proving interesting, Mr. Rainsford. I am going now to have my wound dressed; it's only a slight one. But I shall be back."

When the general, nursing his bruised shoulder, had gone, Rainsford took up his flight again. It was flight now, a desperate, hopeless flight, that carried him on for some hours. Dusk came, then darkness, and still he pressed on. The ground grew softer under his moccasins, the vegetation grew ranker, denser; insects bit him savagely. Then, as he stepped forward, his foot sank into the ooze. He tried to wrench it back, but the muck sucked viciously at his foot as if it were a giant leech. With a violent effort, he tore his feet loose. He knew where he was now. Death Swamp and its quicksand.

His hands were tight closed as if his nerve were something tangible that someone in the darkness was trying to tear from his grip. The softness of the earth had given him an idea. He stepped back from the quicksand a dozen feet or so and, like some huge prehistoric beaver, he began to dig.

Rainsford had dug himself in in France when a second's delay meant death. That had been a placid pastime compared to his digging now. The pit grew deeper; when it was above his shoulders, he climbed out and from some hard saplings cut stakes and sharpened them to a fine point. These stakes he planted in the bottom of the pit with the points sticking up. With flying fingers he wove a rough carpet of weeds and branches and with it he covered the mouth of the pit. Then, wet with sweat and aching with tiredness, he crouched behind the stump of a lightning-charred tree.

He knew that his pursuer was coming; he heard the padding sound of feet on the soft earth, and the night breeze brought him the perfume of the general's cigarette. It seemed to Rainsford that the general was coming with unusual swiftness; he was not feeling his way along, foot by foot. Rainsford, crouching there, could not see the general, nor could he see the pit. He lived a year in a minute. Then he felt an impulse to cry aloud with joy, for he heard the sharp crackle of the breaking branches as the cover of the pit gave way; he heard the sharp scream of pain as the pointed stakes found their mark. He leaped up from his place of concealment. Then he cowered back. Three feet from the pit a man was standing, with an electric torch in his hand.

"You've done well, Rainsford," the voice of the general called. "Your Burmese tiger pit has claimed one of my best dogs. Again you score. I think, Mr. Rainsford, I'll see what you can do against my whole pack. I'm going home for a rest now. Thank you for a most amusing evening."

At daybreak Rainsford, lying near the swamp, was awakened by a sound that made him know that he had new things to learn about fear. It was a distant sound, faint and wavering, but he knew it. It was the baying of a pack of hounds.

Rainsford knew he could do one of two things. He could stay where he was and wait. That was suicide. He could flee. That was postponing the inevitable. For a moment he stood there, thinking. An idea that held a wild chance came to him, and, tightening his belt, he headed away from the swamp.

The baying of the hounds drew nearer, then still nearer, nearer, ever nearer. On a ridge Rainsford climbed a tree. Down a watercourse, not a quarter of a mile away, he could see the bush moving. Straining his eyes, he saw the lean figure of General Zaroff; just ahead of him Rainsford made out another figure whose wide shoulders surged through the tall jungle weeds; it was the giant Ivan, and he seemed pulled forward by some unseen force; Rainsford knew that Ivan must be holding the pack in leash.

They would be on him any minute now. His mind worked frantically. He thought of a native trick he had learned in Uganda. He slid down the tree. He caught hold of a springy young sapling and to it he fastened his hunting knife, with the blade pointing down the trail; with a bit of wild grapevine he tied back the sapling. Then he ran for his life. The hounds raised their voices as they hit the fresh scent. Rainsford knew now how an animal at bay feels.

He had to stop to get his breath. The baying of the hounds stopped abruptly, and Rainsford's heart stopped, too. They must have reached the knife.

He shinned excitedly up a tree and looked back. His pursuers had stopped. But the hope that was in Rainsford's brain when he climbed died, for he saw in the shallow valley that General Zaroff was still on his feet. But Ivan was not. The knife, driven by the recoil of the springing tree, had not wholly failed.

Rainsford had hardly tumbled to the ground when the pack took up the cry again.

"Nerve, nerve, nerve!" he panted, as he dashed along. A blue gap showed between the trees dead ahead. Ever nearer drew the hounds. Rainsford forced himself on toward that gap. He reached it. It was the shore of the sea. Across a cove he could see the gloomy gray stone of the chateau. Twenty feet below him the sea rumbled and hissed. Rainsford hesitated. He heard the hounds. Then he leaped far out into the sea. . . .

When the general and his pack reached the place by the sea,

The Most Dangerous Game 101

the Cossack stopped. For some minutes he stood regarding the blue-green expanse of water. He shrugged his shoulders. Then he sat down, took a drink of brandy from a silver flask, lit a cigarette, and hummed a bit from "Madame Butterfly."

General Zaroff had an exceedingly good dinner in his great paneled dining hall that evening. With it he had a bottle of *Pol Roger* and half a bottle of *Chambertin*. Two slight annoyances kept him from perfect enjoyment. One was the thought that it would be difficult to replace Ivan; the other was that his quarry had escaped him; of course the American hadn't played the game—so thought the general as he tasted his after-dinner liqueur. In his library he read. At ten he went up to his bedroom. He was deliciously tired, he said to himself, as he locked himself in. There was a little moonlight, so, before turning on his light, he went to the window and looked down at the courtyard. He could see the great hounds, and he called: "Better luck another time," to them. Then he switched on the light.

A man, who had been hiding in the curtains of the bed, was standing there.

"Rainsford!" screamed the general. "How in God's name did you get here?"

"Swam," said Rainsford. "I found it quicker than walking through the jungle."

The general sucked in his breath and smiled. "I congratulate you," he said. "You have won the game."

Rainsford did not smile. "I am still a beast at bay," he said in a low, hoarse voice. "Get ready, General Zaroff."

The general made one of his deepest bows. "I see," he said. "Splendid! One of us is to furnish a repast for the hounds. The other will sleep in this very excellent bed. On guard, Rainsford. . . ."

He had never slept in a better bed, Rainsford decided.

Ben Hecht

*

CRIME WITHOUT PASSION

CRIME WITHOUT PASSION was made at Astoria, Long Island, in 1934. It was the first important photoplay to be filmed on the East Coast since THE EMPEROR JONES was made in 1933. Ben Hecht made the adaptation for the screen and produced and directed it in association with Charles Mac-Arthur.

One of the first pictures to use the stream-of-consciousness technique, CRIME WITHOUT PASSION created a sensation both in the movie world and at the box office. The cast included Claude Rains, Whitney Bourne and Margo.

MR. LOU HENDRIX looked at the lady he had been pretending to love for the past six months and, being a lawyer, said nothing. Mr. Hendrix was a gentleman who could listen longer to female hysterics without unbending than was normal. This, he would have said, was due to his aloof and analytical mind. Then, also, the events which were taking place in this boudoir at the moment were of a familiar pattern. Some eight or nine times Mr. Hendrix had been the hero of just such climaxes as this, when new love had entered his life, and necessitated similar farewells.

The young lady who, this time, was doing the screaming was a nymph of the caberets, known as Brownie. Her full name was Carmen Browne. She danced, and very effectively, at the El Bravo Club where, devoid of plumage as an eel, she led the Birds of Paradise number. In this she was ravishing as a Dream of Fair Women.

Why so young and delicious a siren as Brownie should be so disturbed over the amorous defections of Mr. Hendrix would have confused anyone who knew this gentleman or merely took a one minute look at him. He was not Romeo nor was he Adonis, nor was he even such a male as one associates with

CRIME WITHOUT PASSION by Ben Hecht, Copyright, February 7, 1936, by Covici-Friede, Inc.

102

the general practise of seduction. He was a little man with
that objectionable immaculateness which reminds one, instanter, of sheep's clothing. He was one of those popinjays of
the flesh pots with the face of a tired and sarcastic boy. His
sideburns were a wee too long, his smile unduly persistent
(like a ballet dancer's), his voice far too gentle to have de-
ceived anyone, except perhaps a woman, as to his spiritual
composition. But one can always depend on the ladies to misunderstand the combination of gentleness and sideburns.

Brownie, who among her own kind was considered not only
quite a reader of books but a sort of practical authority on
masculine characteristics, had misunderstood Lou Hendrix,
amazingly. Carry on as she would now she was no match for
this *caballero* of the law who, out of a clear sky, was engaged
in giving her what she called "the go-by." As her monologue of
screams, epithets and sobs progressed the lovely and muscular
girl understood it all. She perceived, much too late for any use,
that she had to do with as purring a hypocrite, rogue and
underhanded soul as one might flush in a seven day hunt on
Broadway, which, according to the chroniclers Brownie most
admired, is the world's leading water hole for human beasts
of prey.

Looking around at the pretty apartment in which Mr. Hendrix had installed her and in which she had lorded it over her
friends for the six months and from which she must now exit
—love's dream being ended, Brownie spread herself on the
couch and filled her Sybaritic diggings with a truly romantic
din. From the more coherent utterances of this tearstained
beauty it seemed that she was innocent of all dallyings with a
certain Eddie White, an ex-college hero, and that since leaving this same Mr. White whose love interest she had been before the Birds of Paradise number was staged, she had never
once permitted him to lay a finger on her. She was, wailed
Brownie, being wrongly accused. Then, sitting up, her greenish
eyes popping with rage until they looked like a pair of snake
heads, Brownie laughed, as she would have said, scornfully,
and declared that she could see through Mr. Hendrix and his
so-called jealousy. He was getting rid of her because he

didn't love her any more. He was tiring of her and putting her on the escalator—that was all there was to it.

To this, Mr. Hendrix, thoroughly seen through, made no reply and Brownie, announcing that she was not going to be made a sucker of, fell back on the couch, beat some cushions with her fists and shook with grief. The telephone rang. Brownie straightened on the couch.

"It's probably for you," she said.

"More likely it's Mr. White," said Mr. Hendrix.

The taunt brought Brownie to her feet.

"If it's for me, by any mischance," said Mr. Hendrix, "say I'm not here."

Brownie spoke into the phone.

"Who?" she asked. "No, he's not here. No, I don't know when he'll be here. No, no, I don't expect him." Hanging up she looked bitterly at Mr. Hendrix. "Your office," she said. "Always making me lie for you."

"You might have been a bit more polite," said Mr. Hendrix.

The heartlessness of this suggestion sent Brownie back to the couch and her grief. She resumed her sobs. Mr. Hendrix continued to regard her with creditable, if villainous, detachment. His heart was in the highlands with another lassie. But even discounting that factor Mr. Hendrix felt he was pursuing a wise course in ridding himself of so obstreperous an admirer as lay howling here. He had no use for overemotional types. They were inclined to drive diversion, which was Mr. Hendrix' notion of Cupid, out of the window with their caterwauling.

Mr. Hendrix' soul, in fact, was a sort of china closet and he was firm in his aversion to flying hooves. He belonged to that tribe of Don Juans, rather numerous at the Broadway hole, who never hang themselves for love. Tears he regarded as bad sportsmanship and heartbreak was to him plain blackmail. Beauty—and by beauty Mr. Hendrix meant chiefly those delicious and agile Venuses of the cabaret floor-shows—beauty had been put into Broadway (if not into the world) for man's delight; certainly not for his confusion and despair. And this little barrister lived elegantly, if rather villainously, by this conception.

A number of things, all obvious to the analytical Mr. Hendrix, were now operating in Brownie's mind and making her wail—Eddie's vengeful delight at her getting the go-by from his successor; the tittering of the little group of columnists, hoofers, waiters and good-time Charlies whom she called the World; the lessening of her status as a siren—she might even be demoted from leading the Birds of Paradise Number, and through all these considerations—the Nerve of the Man, throwing her down as if she were some Nobody! As for the more passional side of the business, the pain in her heart at losing someone she had so stupidly loved and misunderstood and at losing the foolish Broadwayish dream of wedlock she had cherished for half a year, Brownie chose not to mention these in her ravings, being too proud.

Mr. Hendrix, still preserving his finest courtroom manner of Reason and Superiority, watched on in silence and fell to wondering what he had even seen in this red-headed, almost illiterate creature with her muscular legs and childish face to have ever considered her charming or desirable. But he was given small time to meditate this problem of idealization. Brownie, with a yell that set the base of his spine tingling, leaped from the couch, stared wildly around and then, emitting a series of shrill sounds, had at the furnishings of the Love Nest. She pulled a portière down, hurled two vases to the floor, swung a chair against the wall and smashed it, beat Mr. Hendrix' framed photograph to bits against the edge of the piano, seized a clock from the mantelpiece and bounced it on the floor and was making for Mr. Hendrix' derby, which he had placed on a chair near the door, when he, with an unexpected shout, headed her off.

The barrister defending his derby received a blow on the side of his face that sent him spinning. A thrown object caught him behind the ear. Brownie's pointed shoes belabored his shins. He retreated. But the hysteria to which he had been cooly and analytically listening seemed suddenly to have been injected, like a virus, into his bloodstream. It had started with the tingling in the base of his spine. Smarting from blows and full of some sort of electric current which gave off oaths in his head, the little lawyer began to out-bellow his now ex-paramour. He came at the lady and in his hand he held, almost unaware of the fact, a large brass candlestick.

What it was that made this popinjay, so renowned for coolness, strategy and cynicism in his twin professions of amour and the law, so completely shed his character, God alone, who was not at Mr. Hendrix' elbow at the moment, could have told; and perhaps a psychiatrist or two might also have made a guess at. But here he was much too far gone for analysis, his own or anyone else's, charging at the lovely Carmen Browne like a bantam cave man, screaming and swinging the heavy piece of brass in the air.

There was no precedent in Mr. Hendrix' life for such a turn of events and no hint in any of his former love doings that passion could so blind his faculties and hate so fill his heart. Yet blind he was and full of a clamorous hate that demanded something of him. From the oaths which escaped Mr. Hendrix during this preliminary skirmish with the brass candlestick, it seemed that what he hated was women; loathed and hated them with a fury out of the Pit. Announcing this he swung the piece of brass and the second swing exhilarated him the more. It had struck squarely against Brownie's head, dropping her to the carpet. Mr. Hendrix, out of breath, stood cursing and grimacing over her like a murderer.

Slowly the little lawyer's rage melted. His heart swelled with terror and the nape of his neck grew warm. Brownie lay as she had fallen. He leaned over. Her skull was cracked. Blood was running. Her eyes were closed. Her legs, exposed in an incongruously graceful sprawl, were inert. He put his ear to her bosom. There was no heart beating. He stood for several minutes holding his breath and listening automatically for sounds outside the door. The choking sensation in his lungs subsided and the cool, analytical mind that was Mr. Hendrix returned like some errant accomplice tiptoeing back to the scene of the crime.

Carmen Browne lay dead on her hearthstone. No more

would she lead the Birds of Paradise number at the El Bravo
Club. But Mr. Hendrix wasted no time considering this senti-
mental phase of the matter. He had committed a murder,
without intent, to be sure, even in self-defense, looked at
factually. But no, self-defense wouldn't hold, Mr. Hendrix was
thinking swiftly. There rushed through his mind all the angles,
holes, difficulties, improbabilities and prejudices of his case
and in less than a minute the little lawyer had put himself on
trial on a plea of self-defense and found himself guilty.

Since a young man, Mr. Hendrix had always been close to
crime. He had had that unmoral and intellectual understanding
of it which helps make one type of excellent lawyer. In action,
defending a criminal, Mr. Hendrix had always been like some
imperturbable surgeon. Guilt was a disease that could be
cured, not by any operation on the soul of its victim, but by
a process of legerdemain which convinced a jury that no guilt
existed. Mr. Hendrix might have said that he served a cause
beyond good and evil, that of extricating the victims of fleet-
ing misadventure from the unjustly permanent results of their
deeds.

Thus, far beyond most men who might have found themselves confronted by the strange and ugly dilemma of having
unexpectedly committed a murder, Mr. Hendrix was prepared
for his new role of criminal. He knew all the ropes, he knew
all the pitfalls of the defense of such a case as this. He knew
the psychology of the prosecution. And with an expert, if
slightly still fevered mind, he knew the perfect details by
which his guilt might be cured, the ideal evidence, persuasive
and circumstantial, by which a jury could be cajoled to the
verdict of not guilty.

In less than a minute, Mr. Hendrix had a full grasp of his
case, seeing far into its convolutions and difficulties. He set
about straightening these out.

But like some dramatic critic who, after observing plays
for years with subtle and intimate understanding of them, is
summoned suddenly on the stage and with the strange foot-
lights glaring in his eyes told to perform the part whose words
he knows, whose ideal gesture and intonation he has always

dreamed about, Mr. Hendrix felt the panic of debut. To know and to act were phenomena surprisingly separate. This was what delayed the cautious barrister for another minute, a minute during which Mr. Hendrix' client, with beating heart and white face, mumbled for speed, chattered even of flight.

But at the end of this second minute Mr. Hendrix had elbowed this ignominious client into a far corner of his mind, seated him as it were at the counsel's table with orders to keep his mouth shut—and taken charge of the case. He leaned over and looked at the clock on the floor. The dial glass was broken. The clock had stopped, its hands at two minutes of four. Mr. Hendrix' thoughts were rapid, almost as if he were not thinking at all but knowing. He could move the hands forward to five o'clock. He could leave the premises undetected, if possible, and attach himself for the next two hours to a group of prospective alibi witnesses, remain with them during the hours between four ten and seven and this would be the proof he had not been in the apartment at the time of the murder. Mr. Hendrix examined the watch on Carmen Browne's wrist. It too had stopped. It registered one minute after four. The two time pieces, evidently synchronized by their owner, told a graphic and substantially correct tale. At 3:58 the struggle had begun. At 4:01 the woman was killed. He would have to set the wrist-watch forward a full hour to preserve this interesting discrepancy in the stopped clocks.

The telephone rang. Mr. Hendrix straightened, not having touched either of the hour hands. He had actually anticipated a telephone ringing, and in this anticipation known the ruse of the forwarded time hands was stupid. At 3:50 Carmen Browne had answered a phone call, a record of which was with the switchboard man in the lobby. Now at 4:03—he consulted his own watch—she failed to answer. Other phone calls might likewise come before five o'clock, all of which Carmen Browne would fail to answer, thus establishing an important series of witnesses against the fact that the murdered woman had been alive between four and five o'clock; thus rendering his alibi of his own whereabouts during that time practically futile. There was also the possibility that the neighbors had heard their quarrel and noted the time of the screaming. And more than all these the chance that someone, a maid or the building agent (Carmen Browne had been consulting him about subletting her place) might enter the room before five o'clock.

It was the hour preceding 4:01 for which Mr. Hendrix needed an alibi. He already knew its vital ground work. At 3:50 Carmen Browne, alive, had told someone on the phone —probably Tom Healey of his own law firm—that he was not in her apartment. Mr. Hendrix' eyes had remained on his own wrist watch as his thought slipped through these pros and cons. It was 4:04. He glanced at the sprawled figure on the floor, shivered, but stood his ground. Another phase of his case had overcome him. He smiled palely, shocked at what had almost been an oversight. He must not only provide an alibi for himself but fortify it with evidence tending to prove someone other than he had done the deed. He must invent a mythical murderer—leave a trail of evidence for the sharp eyes and wits of the prosecution leading to Another—a never to be found another, but yet one always present in the Case.

Carmen Browne's fingerprints were on the broken clock, the smashed chair, the battered photo frame. This was wrong. It would reveal that it was Carmen who had been in the rage, smashing things, demanding something that had resulted in her murder—and this sort of a situation, brought out by the prosecution, might easily point to Lou Hendrix, known to have been her lover. No, said Lawyer Hendrix swiftly, it must have been her assailant, demanding something of Carmen Browne, who had been in the rage and done the smashing and struck the fatal blow. Mr. Hendrix established this fact circumstantially by wiping Carmen Browne's fingerprints from the objects in question with a silk handkerchief. The absence of fingerprints pointed to a certain self-consciousness on the part of the assailant after the deed but that was both legitimate and normal. Men of the deepest passion, and there was precedence for this, remembered to obliterate evidence.

At the door Mr. Hendrix, in his hat, overcoat and gloves, paused. He repeated to himself carefully, Carmen Browne had been attacked by some suitor, jealous of her real sweetheart,

Mr. Hendrix, as witness the destroyed photograph of the latter. But why hadn't she used the gun the police would find in the desk drawer two feet from the spot where her body lay? There were, of course, normal explanations to be put forward. But Mr. Hendrix did not admire them legally. For fifteen seconds Lawyer Hendrix balanced the issue. During this space Mr. Hendrix listened rather than thought. He listened to the prosecution pointing out to the jury that the reason Carmen Browne had not reached for this available weapon with which to defend herself was because she had not expected an attack from her assailant, because the assailant was one familiar to her against whom she had no thought of arming herself; and even further, because the assailant, all too familiar with the premises, knew where this gun was as well as did Carmen Browne, and prevented her from reaching it. All these values pointed shadowly, Mr. Hendrix perceived, at his client. He removed the gun from the drawer and dropped it into his coat pocket. He must be careful in disposing of the weapon and Mr. Hendrix' mind dwelt stubbornly on a dozen cases in which an attempt at post crime evidence disposal had been the connecting link with guilt. But Mr. Hendrix assured his client firmly that he would be more cautious in this regard than any of his previous defendants had been.

With the gun in his coat pocket Mr. Hendrix stepped out of the apartment. Now he was, he knew, purely in the hands of luck. A door opening, a neighbor appearing would ruin his case instantly. But no untoward event happened. He had three floors to descend. He listened at the ornamental elevator doors. Both cages were going up. Mr. Hendrix walked quickly down the three flights and cooly, now, like a gambler rather than a lawyer, rehearsed the possible permutations of Luck.

He had entered the apartment at three o'clock that morning with Carmen Browne. But because it was his habit to preserve a surface air of respectability toward the attendants of the place, though he fancied they knew well enough what was going on, he had walked up to the apartment with Brownie. The switchboard operator concealed in an alcove in the lobby had not seen them come in, nor had the elevator boy on duty, as both were out of sight at the moment. If now he could leave the building with the equal but vitally more important luck of not being seen, his case would be more than launched.

The lobby was empty, but Mr. Hendrix did not make the mistake of slipping out too quickly, and coddling the presumption that no eyes had observed him. He knew too well the possibility of the unexpected witness and he paused to study the premises. The switchboard attendant, half hidden in the alcove, had his back to the lobby and was reading a newspaper. Both elevator cages were out of sight. There was no one else. Mr. Hendrix stepped into the street.

Here again he stopped to look for that unexpected witness. How often, he remembered grimly, had the best of his cases been tumbled by the appearance on the stand of those aimless, incalculable human strays who had "Seen the Defendant." Mr. Hendrix saw two of just that type. Two women were walking, but with their backs to him and away from the apartment. A delivery truck was passing. Mr. Hendrix noticed that the driver was talking to a companion and that neither of these passers looked in his direction. There was no one else. Mr. Hendrix turned his attention to the windows across the street. Only the first three floors mattered. Identification was impossible, or at least could be sufficiently challenged, from any great height. The windows were empty. As for the windows of the building directly over him, if he kept close to the wall none could see him from these.

Satisfied with this rapid but concentrated scrutiny, Mr. Hendrix started walking toward the corner. If the triumph of intellect over nerves, of reason over the impulses of the senses may be called heroism, then this smiling, casually moving little popinjay in the black derby and snug overcoat might well be called a hero. Innocence, even aimlessness, was in his every movement; and in his refusal, despite a driving curiosity to look at the time on his wrist—a tell-tale gesture were it recorded by anyone—there was something approaching the loftiness of purpose which distinguished the ancient Ascetics. As he turned the corner, Mr. Hendrix, still unruffled, still amiably rhythmic in his movements, looked back to make sure no taxicabs had entered the street. None had.

He was now on 6th Avenue and he moved more briskly. He had four blocks to walk and habit sent his eyes looking for a taxicab. But alert to every variety of witness, he shook his head and stayed afoot. He smiled, remembering that his own bed in his own apartment was unmade. He had just turned in the night before when Brownie had telephoned and asked to meet him. Thus his housekeeper, who never arrived before noon, would establish simply the fact that he had slept at home. This was unnecessary, to be sure, unless some passerby had seen Brownie and a man enter the former's apartment at three this morning.

Mr. Hendrix arrived now at a Sixth Avenue cinema palace. He looked carefully over the small crowd, waiting for tickets and then joined the line. In a few minutes he was being ushered into the roped enclosure at the rear of the auditorium. He slipped away quickly, however, and walked in the dark to the other side of the theatre. He approached one of the ushers and demanded to know where he could report the loss of a pair of gloves. After a brief colloquy he was led to the office of the lost and found department and here Mr. Hendrix, very voluble and affable, explained his mishap. He was not, he smiled, usually so careless with his belongings but the picture had been so engrossing that he had forgotten all about his haberdashery. Then Mr. Hendrix gave his name, address, a description of the missing gloves and watched with a glow of deep creative satisfaction the time being written down on the blank form used for cataloguing such matters. "Four-eighteen," the man wrote and Mr. Hendrix, consulting his watch, pretended to be startled. Was it that late, he demanded, good Lord! he had had no idea of the time. It was quite a long picture. And the Lost and Found official, drawn into chumminess by Mr. Hendrix' affability, agreed that the film was a little longer than most, but well worth sitting through—to which Mr. Hendrix heartily assented.

Emerging from the movie palace, Mr. Hendrix rehearsed his case to date. The main body of his alibi was achieved. He had spent the time between two-thirty and four watching a movie. His continued presence at four-eighteen in this theatre was written down in black and white. He had also taken care that it should be a movie he had already seen so as to be able to recite its plot were he questioned in the next few hours. And he had also provided a motive for seeing this particular movie. The film had to do with the character and career of a mythical state's attorney, and a newspaper friend of Mr. Hendrix who conducted a gossip column had asked him to contribute a few paragraphs from a legal point of view carping at the improbabilities of the scenario.

Mr. Hendrix' next port of call was an elegant speakeasy. Here he had a drink, engaged in an exchange of views with the bartender, who knew him, asked the correct time so he might adjust his watch. At 4:50 he stepped into a phone booth in the place and called his office. He inquired whether anybody had been trying to reach him that afternoon. The law clerk on duty for the firm, Tom Healy, answered as Mr. Hendrix had expected. Mr. Healey said he had been trying to find him in relation to a disposition but had been unable to locate him. At this Mr. Hendrix feigned a light anger. Where had the incompetent youth called? He had, said Mr. Healey, tried everywhere, even Miss Carmen Browne's apartment.

At this bit of information Mr. Hendrix, in his mind's eye addressing one of his future star witnesses, changed his voice. He grew angry and very obviously so, for he knew the laziness of people's memory and their slipshod powers of observation. He inquired sourly if Mr. Healey had spoken to Miss Browne. On hearing that he had, Mr. Hendrix said:

"Do you mind telling me how she seemed when you asked if I was there?"

"Well, I don't know," Mr. Healey said.

"Try and think," said Mr. Hendrix, "I'd like to know."

"Well," said Mr. Healey, "come to think of it, she struck me as a little curt or upset about something."

"Ha!" said Mr. Hendrix and, to the surprise of his office underling, called the young lady a villainous name.

"I don't want you to call me up at her place any more," he

raised his voice. The clerk, Mr. Healey, said he would never do it again, but Mr. Hendrix, as though too enraged to notice this promise continued. "I'm all washed up at that telephone number. Understand what I mean? You can just forget about it. Any other calls?"

"No," said Mr. Healey.

"O.K.," said Mr. Hendrix and hung up the phone with an angry bang.

He walked from the speakeasy with the light step which to Mr. Hendrix' office colleagues always characterized a Not Guilty verdict in sight. Now that the tingling at the base of his spine as well as the annoying warmth on the nape of his neck, as if a Prosecuting Staff were actually breathing on him, had gone entirely, Mr. Hendrix was beginning to feel not only relaxed but even amused. He could hear the Prosecution falling into this little trap he had just laid.

Question: So Mr. Hendrix told you that you needn't try to reach him at Miss Browne's apartment any more?

Answer: Yes, sir.

And Lawyer Hendrix looked winningly at the jury that sat in his mind's eye. Gentlemen of the Jury, consider this. As if, having committed a crime the defendant would be so gauche as to give himself away by some such oafish remark to a law-clerk—a type of person trained to remember what he hears. Not a casual stranger, mind you, but a man with sharp and practiced wits.

Mr. Hendrix, skittering happily along the street, cleared his throat, beamed, felt a desire to laugh. He had never quite so enjoyed a case. What subtle and yet vital psychological proof of his innocence was the fact that he had just said to Tom Healey what he had; what perfect proof of the fact that he had been the victim of an obvious coincidence in saying he was washed up with Carmen Browne when she lay dead in her apartment. No guilty man would ever have said that.

From a drug store he was passing, Mr. Hendrix made another telephone call. He called Carmen Browne. Inquiring for her of the apartment switchboard operator a sharp excitement stirred him. Before his eyes the image of her body

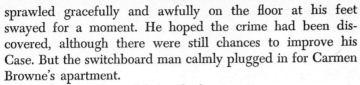

sprawled gracefully and awfully on the floor at his feet
swayed for a moment. He hoped the crime had been discovered, although there were still chances to improve his
Case. But the switchboard man calmly plugged in for Carmen
Browne's apartment.

"She doesn't answer," he said after a pause.

"This is Mr. Hendrix calling," said Mr. Hendrix. "Has she
been in at all? I've been trying to get her all day."

"Hasn't come in while I've been here," said the man.

"How long is that?" said Mr. Hendrix.

"Oh, about three hours," said the man.

"Thank you," said Mr. Hendrix and hung up.

He had told Tom Healey he was washed up with Carmen
Browne and now he was trying to reach her, and Mr. Hendrix
considered this paradox, in behalf of his client, with a smile.
It revealed, Gentlemen of the Jury, a distracted man; a lover
full of confusion as a result of—what? Of the fact, gentlemen, Mr. Hendrix purred to himself, that my client was jealous
of the attentions he had found out someone was paying to
Carmen Browne; that he did not believe the poor girl's pro-
testations of innocence and, driven from her side by suspicions,
was yet lured back to her by his deep love. Jealous, Gentlemen of the Jury, of the attentions being paid to Carmen
Browne by this creature who that very afternoon had entered
her apartment and against whom Carmen Browne had de-
fended herself until struck down and killed.

To augment this phase of the case, Mr. Hendrix returned
now to the apartment building in which Carmen Browne lay
murdered. He approached the switchboard operator, who
greeted him by name. Here Mr. Hendrix controlled a curious
impulse that whitened the skin around his mouth. He felt
impelled to ask this man whether he had noticed Mr. Hendrix
in the building before, whether he had seen him during the
few moments he had walked from the lobby an hour ago.
Astonished at this impulse, Mr. Hendrix held his tongue for
a space, aware that the switchboard man was looking at him
with curiosity.

Question: How did the defendant seem?

Answer: Confused.

Gentlemen of the Jury, and how would a man, consumed with jealousy, seem while inquiring, against all his pride, if the woman he thought was wronging him, was home?

"Has Miss Browne come in since I called?" asked Mr. Hendrix.

"I haven't seen her," said the man. "I'll try her apartment again."

There was no response.

"Give her this note when she comes back," said Mr. Hendrix. He wrote on the lower part of a business letter from his pocket.

"Darling, if you are innocent, don't torture me any more. Give me a chance to believe you. I'm willing to forget what I heard or thought I heard over the phone. As ever Lou."

He placed this in a used envelope, scribbled her name on it, and sealed it.

Gentlemen of the Jury, can you imagine any man who had killed a woman he loved or had loved, so lost to all human reaction, so fiendishly wanton as to have written that little plea when he knew she was lying dead at his hands?

That was merely a rhetorical overtone, the human rather than evidential side of the note, but Mr. Hendrix filed it away in his memory as a bit of decoration. His alibi, Lawyer Hendrix murmured to himself, was now complete. But the secondary phase of the case needed further effort. The beauty of a case lay always in the elaborateness of diverse but corroborating detail—as if the world were crying the defendant's innocence from every nook and cranny. And happily at work, Mr. Hendrix had lawyer-like so far forgotten the human existence of his client as to whistle cheerily the while he turned over and returned over the major psychological problem in his mind.

Defense—Carmen Browne had been murdered by a man to whom she refused, after perhaps leading him on, to surrender herself. Also it might be that the killing had been one of those passional accidents which the sex instinct, run amok, precipitates. It might be that Carmen Browne had led a double life and was discovered in this double life by her slayer.

Ergo—Lou Hendrix, sharp-witted, observant, a veritable connoisseur of women, must suspect the existence of this other man. And Defendant Hendrix must also be jealous of him.

Witness to this—his talk to Tom Healey; his note to Carmen Browne now in the hands of the switchboard operator.

And Lawyer Hendrix, with the thrill of a gambler rolling a third lucky seven, remembered at this point a third witness—a veritable star witness, beautifully, if unwittingly, prepared for her role a few days ago. This was Peggy Moore.

Miss Moore danced at the El Bravo Club as a member of the ensemble. She had been Brownie's confidant for a year. Mr. Hendrix smiled blissfully recalling his conversation with Miss Moore less than a week ago and recalling also her general character, one made to order for the part he was to assign her.

This young lady was a tall, dark-haired Irish lassie with slightly bulging eyes and an expression of adenoidal and not unpleasing vacuity about her face. She was, as Brownie had frequently confided to him, a veritable love slave, a dithering creature incapable of thinking or talking on any subject other than the emotions stirred in her bosom by love or jealousy.

Some days ago Mr. Hendrix had selected this almost congenital idiot as the opening pawn in his decision to rid himself of Brownie. He had confided to Miss Moore's ears, so perfectly attuned to all tales of amorous agony, that he suspected Brownie of being still in love with his predecessor, Eddie White. Miss Moore's eyes had bulged, her mouth opened as if to disgorge a fish hook and simultaneously a shrewd, if transparent emotion, had overcome her. Miss Moore, the victim of so much perfidy, had been convinced instanter of her chum's guilt and had launched at once into a series of lies, all defending Brownie's integrity and offering idiotic details of her devotion to her lawyer lover. Mr. Hendrix, intent on laying some foolish groundwork for his subsequent defection, had persisted, however, and, for no other reason than that he delighted in playing the human fraud whenever he could, had feigned sorrow and talked of woe.

Now Mr. Hendrix summoned Miss Moore on the telephone to meet him at the speakeasy he had recently quitted. He spoke guardedly, hinting at a lovers' quarrel, and pretending he needed her to verify some evidences of Brownie's guilt, just unearthed. Miss Moore, full of a laudable and loyal ambition to lie her head off in Brownie's behalf, as Mr. Hendrix had foreseen, arrived in a rush. And the two sat down at a table in a corner, Miss Moore to invent innocent explanations and alibis for her chum, at which like all over-tearful addicts of passion she was amazingly expert; and Mr. Hendrix to weave her artfully into his case.

But first Mr. Hendrix, aware of the lady's sensitivity toward all matters pertaining to love, proceeded to get himself drunk. He must be the lover stricken with jealousy and seeking to drown his pains in liquor, a characterization which this simple child and student of amour would remember only too vividly on the witness stand. Three drinks were consumed and then, honestly befuddled from such an unaccustomed dose, Mr. Hendrix launched into cross examination. And despite his thickened tongue and touch of genuine physical paralysis, Lawyer Hendrix remained as cool and analytical as if he were in a courtroom. He was not one to betray a client by any human weaknesses.

He put himself at Miss Moore's mercy. He must know the truth and she alone could tell him. Otherwise with too much brooding and uncertainty he would be sure to go out of his mind. His law practice was already suffering. He would lose all his money. Miss Moore nodded tenderly and understandingly at this saga of love woes. In reply she could assure Mr. Hendrix that he was being very foolish to be jealous of Eddie White because Mr. White wasn't even in town and besides Mr. White was engaged to marry a society girl in Newport. Mr. Hendrix sighed appreciatively at this walloping lie.

"It's not Eddie," said Mr. Hendrix, "it's somebody else. You know that as well as I. You're in her confidence. Don't try to lie to me, dearie. I caught her red handed, talking over the phone. She hung up when I came into the room. She was making a date—and not with Eddie White."

Miss Moore paled at the thought of this dreadful contretemps, but kept her wits. Her chum's guilt frightened her but at the same time she saw through Mr. Hendrix' effort to lead her astray. Of course it was Eddie White of whom he was jealous. Miss Moore was certain of this and Mr. Hendrix, listening to her somewhat hysterical defense of Brownie, sufficient to have convicted that young lady of a hundred infidelities had he been interested, realized exactly what was in his companion's mind. He considered for a moment the plan of involving Eddie White in his case. He had thought of it before—Brownie's previous lover, a known hot headed young gentleman given to nocturnal fisticuffs in public places. But for the second time he dismissed this phase. Eddie would have an alibi and the establishing of Eddie's physical innocence, however psychologically promising his guilt might have looked, would embarrass his client's case.

For the next hour Mr. Hendrix drank and discussed his jealousy, pleading with Miss Moore to be kind to him and reveal what she knew; and hinting at gifts in return for such service. But Miss Moore only increased the scope of her lies.

"Have you seen Brownie today?" Miss Moore finally broke off, winded.

Mr. Hendrix weaved in his seat and looked at her with bleary, drunken eyes.

"No," he said. "I don't trust myself to see her. God knows what I would do—feeling this way."

"You're just worked up about absolutely nothing," said Miss Moore and rose. She had to toddle off to the El Bravo where she performed during the dinner hour. Mr. Hendrix accompanied her to the door.

"Tell Brownie," he whispered, "I'll be over to the club tonight. And . . . and give her a last chance to prove her innocence."

"I'll give her the message," said Miss Moore and sighed.

Alone, Mr. Hendrix returned to the phone booth. He sat down heavily and put in a call for Carmen Browne. His case was ready. He desired to hear the news of the finding of the body. An annoying tingle touched the base of his spine as he waited for the apartment switchboard to answer. He wondered how drunk he was. Drunk, to be sure, but sober enough to know exactly every phase and weigh every nuance. The moment he heard of the crime he would rush over, be detained by the police and with the aid of his intoxicated condition act thoroughly irrational and grief stricken. He would hint at no alibis, reveal not a shred of his case until the coroner's inquest.

The switchboard operator finally answered. Mr. Hendrix inquired thickly for Miss Browne. He was told Miss Browne was not in. He hung up. Rising and swaying for a moment, Mr. Hendrix, thoroughly at peace with the world, except for this intermittent tingle, decided on the best course. He would go to the El Bravo Club, order his dinner and wait there till Brownie's absence was noticed and a search started.

The El Bravo orchestra was rendering a dance number. The dance floor was crowded. Mr. Hendrix looked dizzily at the circling figures. He had selected a table far to the side, one of those at which the performers and their friends grouped themselves during the evening. The stuffiness of the air made Mr. Hendrix feel drowsy. Looking up, he beheld a familiar figure approaching. It was Eddie White, whom he had pleased to style the ignorant drop kicker. Mr. Hendrix smiled. He noticed tiredly that Mr. White seemed a little drunk.

The ex-college hero, still a sturdy, tanned and muscular product of the Higher Education, greeted Mr. Hendrix calmly. He dropped into a chair at the table and inquired, with an eye roving over the place, how tricks were. Mr. Hendrix said they were fine.

There was a pause during which the music filled the cafe with glamorous and exciting sounds.

"Didn't know you were such a movie fan," said Mr. White apropos of nothing and Mr. Hendrix felt himself sobering up as if in a cold shower.

"Just what do you mean?" Mr. Hendrix managed to inquire and very casually.

His companion was busy looking them over on the dance floor and offering a roguish eye to a few of the tastier numbers. Mr. Hendrix stared at him in silence and felt the tingle return to his spine.

"Saw you going into the Roxy this afternoon," Mr. White resumed.

"You did," said Mr. Hendrix, and then added, as if he were looping the loop, "what time was that?"

"What time?" Mr. White repeated, looking at the little lawyer with a dull, athlete's stare. "Oh, a little after four, I should say."

"You're crazy," said Mr. Hendrix, "if you think you saw me going into the Roxy after four. Why I came out about twenty after four, after seeing the whole show."

"I don't care what you saw," said Mr. White, "I saw you going in at about a quarter after. I was gonna say hello but I thought the hell with it. How'd you like the picture? Ought to be in your line—all about one of those crooked legal sharks."

In the brief space during which Mr. Hendrix was now silent his thoughts were very rapid. Mr. White, God help Mr. Hendrix, was that most objectionable of all humans known to a legal case—the aimless stray that the Prosecution was wont to drag, rabbit fashion, out of its hat with which to confound the guilty. And Mr. Hendrix knew without thinking the full significance of this witness, Eddie White. If the defendant had been seen entering the movie theater after four, he had been seen entering after the murder had been committed. But that was the least damaging phase. The defendant had left the movie theater at 4:20, having lied to the attendants and told them he had spent an hour and a half in the place. With the fact of this lie established, the prosecution could take apart piece by piece the obvious mechanism of his alibi. There was no alibi. There was no case. In fact, to the contrary, Eddie White's simple statement of the time of day —after four—revealed all of the defendant's subsequent actions as those of a thoroughly guilty man, and Mr. Hendrix leaned across the table and put a hand on the athlete's arm.

"It must have been somebody else you saw," he purred.

"Listen, don't tell me," said Mr. White. "I saw you looking around, buying your ticket and ducking in."

Mr. Hendrix winced at the damning phraseology.

"I know it was about a quarter after four," pursued Mr.

White, "because I had a date outside. And don't get so excited. It wasn't with Brownie."

The tingle at the base of the Hendrix spine was almost lifting him out of his seat.

"That's a lie," said Mr. Hendrix thickly.

"What's that?" Mr. White demanded.

"I said you're lying," Mr. Hendrix repeated slowly. "You didn't see me."

"Oh, that's what you said, is it?" Mr. White was unexpectedly grim. "Listen, I never liked you and I don't take talk off a guy I got no use for. Get that."

And for the second time that day an unprecedented mood overcame the little lawyer. He made an effort to stop the words which suddenly filled his head but he heard himself saying them and wondering confusedly who it was who was drunk—he who was listening or he who was speaking. He was telling Mr. White what a liar, numbskull and oaf he was and Mr. White stood up. Words continued, Mr. Hendrix aware that he and Mr. White were both talking at once. But the music made a blur in his ears and the El Bravo Club swayed in front of his eyes. Then Mr. Hendrix realized, and darkly, that the towering Mr. White's hand was on his collar and that he was being lifted out of his seat. The El Bravo orchestra was rolling out a jazz finale and nobody seemed to have noticed as yet the fracas taking place at this side table. As Mr. Hendrix felt himself being hoisted to his feet, a sense of nausea and helplessness overcame him. He thrust his hand into his coat pocket.

"Calling me a liar, eh?" Mr. White was growling in the Hendrix ear. He added a number of epithets.

The little lawyer saw for an instant a fist pull back that never landed. Mr. Hendrix had removed a gun from his coat pocket, a gun of whose existence in his hand he was as unaware as he had been of the brass candlestick. The gun exploded and Mr. White, with a look of suddenly sober astonishment, fell back into a chair. The music at this moment finished with a nanny goat blare of trumpets. No heads turned. No waiters came rushing. Shaking as if his bones had turned into castanets, Mr. Hendrix stood looking at the crumpled .

athlete and watched his head sink over the table. The mouth was open. The athlete's fingers hanging near the floor were rigid.

Music started again and Mr. Hendrix turned his eyes automatically toward the dance floor. Blue and pink flood lights were shining on it and out from behind the orchestra shell came a line of almost naked girls. White legs kicked, smiles filled the air. Leading this chorus line Mr. Hendrix saw Carmen Browne. She was dancing.

The little lawyer grew sick. He shut his eyes. Then he opened them. They were full of pain and bewilderment. It was no hallucination. It was Brownie. Extending under her ear at the back of her head he saw strips of court plaster. She was alive and restored.

Mr. Hendrix knew exactly what had happened. The last time he had called her apartment, the switchboard man, failing to recognize his liquor thickened voice, had withheld the information he might have offered Mr. Hendrix—that Carmen Browne was alive, that she had summoned a doctor, that she had left the apartment.

And even as he was thinking of this tiny detail, a hundred other details crowded into the Hendrix mind. He remembered his accusations to Brownie that she still loved Eddie White; his statement to Peggy Moore last week and this afternoon that he was too jealous to trust himself; his attack on Carmen Browne, his subsequent drunkenness, his idiotic antics in the movie theater—as if he were shadowing Eddie White—what else could his rushing in and rushing out mean? Everything Mr. Hendrix had accomplished since 4:02 this afternoon pointed only at one conclusion—that he hated Eddie White, that he had almost killed his sweetheart out of jealousy over White, that, still burning with this emotion he had tracked White down and murdered him in cold blood.

Mr. Hendrix, during these brief moments staring at the crumpled athlete, wanted to scream, so macabre did all these events strike him, but his voice trailed off into a moan. What was this insane thing he had done for his client! Exonerated him! Mr. Hendrix, still shaking, slipped down into his chair. He, Lou Hendrix, the shining legal intelligence, had like some

Nemesis convicted himself—and not of manslaughter, which might have been the verdict otherwise—but of premeditated murder in the first degree. There was no case. No defense was possible. There was nothing left to do but to flee like some thug.

Mr. Hendrix looked at his wrist. He had twenty minutes to make the ten o'clock train for Chicago. From Chicago he would travel to New Orleans and thence into Mexico. He had a wallet full of bills. The side exit of the El Bravo was ten feet away. But Mr. Hendrix, struggling to get to his feet, swayed and fell forward. The dozen drinks he had so shrewdly tossed down his gullet to help him act his part, joined the hideous plot he had hatched against himself. He was too drunk, too dizzy to stand up and move quickly.

They found the little barrister hunched in his seat staring at the murdered athlete. The gun was still in his hand. Mr. Hendrix was mumbling passionlessly.

"Guilty. Guilty. Guilty."

O. Henry

*

A DOUBLE-DYED DECEIVER

Released in 1939 by Paramount as THE LLANO KID, with the screenplay written by Wanda Tuchock, O. Henry's A DOUBLE-DYED DECEIVER was popular with movie audiences. The picture was produced by Harry Sherman and was directed by E. D. Venturini. Tito Guizar, Latin Singer, and Gale Sondergaard headed the cast that included Alan Mowbray, Jane Clayton, Emma Dunn, Minor Watson and Cris Pin Martin.

THE TROUBLE began in Laredo. It was the Llano Kid's fault, for he should have confined his habit of manslaughter to Mexicans. But the Kid was past twenty; and to have only Mexicans to one's credit at twenty is to blush unseen on the Rio Grande border.

It happened in old Justo Valdo's gambling house. There was a poker game at which sat players who were not all friends, as happens often where men ride in from afar to shoot Folly as she gallops. There was a row over so small a matter as a pair of queens; and when the smoke had cleared away it was found that the Kid had committed an indiscretion, and his adversary had been guilty of a blunder. For, the unfortunate combatant, instead of being a Greaser, was a high-blooded youth from the cow ranches, of about the Kid's own age and possessed of friends and champions. His blunder in missing the Kid's right ear only a sixteenth of an inch when he pulled his gun did not lessen the indiscretion of the better marksman.

The Kid, not being equipped with a retinue, nor bountifully supplied with personal admirers and supporters—on account of a rather umbrageous reputation, even for the border—considered it not incompatible with his indisputable gameness to perform the judicious tractional act known as "pulling his freight."

Quickly the avengers gathered and sought him. Three of

them overtook him within a rod of the station. The Kid turned and showed his teeth in that brilliant but mirthless smile that usually preceded his deeds of insolence and violence, and his pursuers fell back without making it necessary for him even to reach for his weapon.

But in this affair the Kid had not felt the grim thirst for encounter that usually urged him on to battle. It had been a purely chance row, born of the cards and certain epithets impossible for a gentleman to brook that had passed between the two. The Kid had rather liked the slim, haughty, brown-faced young chap whom his bullet had cut off in the first pride of manhood. And now he wanted no more blood. He wanted to get away and have a good long sleep somewhere in the sun on the mesquite grass with his handkerchief over his face. Even a Mexican might have crossed his path in safety while he was in this mood.

The Kid openly boarded the north-bound passenger train that departed five minutes later. But at Webb, a few miles out, where it was flagged to take on a traveller, he abandoned that manner of escape. There were telegraph stations ahead; and the Kid looked askance at electricity and steam. Saddle and spur were his rocks of safety.

The man whom he had shot was a stranger to him. But the Kid knew that he was of the Coralitos outfit from Hidalgo; and that the punchers from that ranch were more relentless and vengeful than Kentucky feudists when wrong or harm was done to one of them. So, with the wisdom that has character-ized many great fighters, the Kid decided to pile up as many leagues as possible of chaparral and pear between himself and the retaliation of the Coralitos bunch.

Near the station was a store; and near the store, scattered among the mesquites and elms, stood the saddled horses of the customers. Most of them waited, half asleep, with sagging limbs and drooping heads. But one, a long-legged roan with a curved neck, snorted and pawed the turf. Him the Kid mounted, gripped with his knees, and slapped gently with the owner's own quirt.

If the slaying of the temerarious card-player had cast a

cloud over the Kid's standing as a good and true citizen, this last act of his veiled his figure in the darkest shadows of disrepute. On the Rio Grande border if you take a man's life you sometimes take trash; but if you take his horse, you take a thing the loss of which renders him poor, indeed, and which enriches you not—if you are caught. For the Kid there was no turning back now.

With the springing roan under him he felt little care or uneasiness. After a five-mile gallop he drew in to the plainsman's jogging trot, and rode northeastward toward the Nueces River bottoms. He knew the country well—its most tortuous and obscure trails through the great wilderness of brush and pear, and its camps and lonesome ranches where one might find safe entertainment. Always he bore to the east; for the Kid had never seen the ocean, and he had a fancy to lay his hand upon the mane of the great Gulf, the gamesome colt of the greater waters.

So after three days he stood on the shore at Corpus Christi, and looked out across the gentle ripple of a quiet sea.

Captain Boone, of the schooner *Flyaway*, stood near his skiff, which one of his crew was guarding in the surf. When ready to sail he had discovered that one of the necessaries of life, in the parallelogrammatic shape of plug tobacco, had been forgotten. A sailor had been dispatched for the missing cargo. Meanwhile the captain paced the sands, chewing profanely at his pocket store.

A slim, wiry youth in high-heeled boots came down to the water's edge. His face was boyish, but with a premature severity that hinted at a man's experience. His complexion was naturally dark; and the sun and wind of an outdoor life had burned it to a coffee brown. His hair was as black and straight as an Indian's; his face had not yet been upturned to the humiliation of a razor; his eyes were a cold and steady blue. He carried his left arm somewhat away from his body, for pearl-handled .45s are frowned upon by town marshals, and are a little bulky when packed in the left armhole of one's vest. He looked beyond Captain Boone at the gulf with the impersonal and expressionless dignity of a Chinese emperor.

"Thinkin' of buyin' that'ar gulf, buddy?" asked the captain, made sarcastic by his narrow escape from the tobaccoless voyage.

"Why, no," said the Kid gently, "I reckon not. I never saw it before. I was just looking at it. Not thinking of selling it, are you?"

"Not this trip," said the captain. "I'll send it to you C.O.D. when I get back to Buenas Tierras. Here comes that capstan-footed lubber with the chewin'. I ought to've weighed anchor an hour ago."

"Is that your ship out there?" asked the Kid.

"Why, yes," answered the captain, "if you want to call a schooner a ship, and I don't mind lyin'. But you better say Miller and Gonzales, owners, and ordinary plain, Billy-be-damned old Samuel K. Boone, skipper."

"Where are you going to?" asked the refugee.

"Buenas Tierras, coast of South America—I forgot what they called the country the last time I was there. Cargo—lumber, corrugated iron, and machetes."

"What kind of a country is it?" asked the Kid—"hot or cold?"

"Warmish, buddy," said the captain. "But a regular Paradise Lost for elegance of scenery and be-yooty of geography. Ye're wakened every morning by the sweet singin' of red birds with seven purple tails, and the sighin' of breezes in the posies and roses. And the inhabitants never work, for they can reach out and pick steamer baskets of the choicest hothouse fruit without gettin' out of bed. And there's no Sunday and no ice and no rent and no troubles and no use and no nothin'. It's a great country for a man to go to sleep with, and wait for somethin' to turn up. The bananys and oranges and hurricanes and pineapples that ye eat comes from there."

"That sounds to me!" said the Kid, at last betraying interest. "What'll the expressage be to take me out there with you?"

"Twenty-four dollars," said Captain Boone; "grub and transportation. Second cabin. I haven't got a first cabin."

"You've got my company," said the Kid, pulling out a buckskin bag.

With three hundred dollars he had gone to Laredo for his

regular "blowout." The duel in Valdo's had cut short his season of hilarity, but it had left him with nearly $200 for aid in the flight that it had made necessary.

"All right, buddy," said the captain. "I hope your ma won't blame me for this little childish escapade of yours." He beckoned to one of the boat's crew. "Let Sanchez lift you out to the skiff so you won't get your feet wet."

Thacker, the United States consul at Buenas Tierras, was not yet drunk. It was only eleven o'clock; and he never arrived at his desired state of beatitude—a state where he sang ancient, maudlin vaudeville songs and pelted his screaming parrot with banana peels—until the middle of the afternoon. So, when he looked up from his hammock at the sound of a slight cough, and saw the Kid standing in the door of the consulate, he was still in a condition to extend the hospitality and courtesy due from the representative of a great nation. "Don't disturb yourself," said the Kid easily. "I just dropped in. They told me it was customary to light at your camp before starting in to round up the town. I just came in on a ship from Texas."

"Glad to see you, Mr.—," said the consul.

The Kid laughed.

"Sprague Dalton," he said. "It sounds funny to me to hear it. I'm called the Llano Kid in the Rio Grande country."

"I'm Thacker," said the consul. "Take that cane-bottom chair. Now if you've come to invest, you want somebody to advise you. These dingies will cheat you out of the gold in your teeth if you don't understand their ways. Try a cigar?"

"Much obliged," said the Kid, "but if it wasn't for my corn shucks and a little bag in my back pocket I couldn't live a minute." He took out his "makings," and rolled a cigarette.

"They speak Spanish here," said the consul. "You'll need an interpreter. If there's anything I can do, why, I'd be delighted. If you're buying fruit lands or looking for a concession of any sort, you'll want somebody who knows the ropes to look out for you."

"I speak Spanish," said the Kid, "about nine times better than

I do English. Everybody speaks it on the range where I come from. And I'm not in the market for anything."

"You speak Spanish?" said Thacker thoughfully. He regarded the Kid absorbedly.

"You look like a Spaniard, too," he continued. "And you're from Texas. And you can't be more than twenty or twenty-one. I wonder if you've got any nerve."

"You got a deal of some kind to put through?" asked the Texan, with unexpected shrewdness.

"Are you quite open to a proposition?" said Thacker.

"What's the use to deny it?" said the Kid. "I got into a little gun frolic down in Laredo and plugged a white man. There wasn't any Mexican handy. And I come down to your parrot-and-monkey range just for to smell the morning-glories and marigolds. Now, do you *sabe*?"

Thacker got up and closed the door.

"Let me see your hand," he said.

He took the Kid's left hand, and examined the back of it closely.

"I can do it," he said excitedly. "Your flesh is as hard as wood and as healthy as a baby's. It will heal in a week."

"If it's a fist fight you want to back me for," said the Kid, "don't put your money up yet. Make it gun work, and I'll keep you company. But no barehanded scrapping, like ladies at a tea-party, for me."

"It's easier than that," said Thacker. "Just step here, will you?"

Through the window he pointed to a two-story white-stuccoed house with wide galleries rising amid the deep-green tropical foliage on a wooded hill that sloped gently from the sea.

"In that house," said Thacker, "a fine old Castilian gentleman and his wife are yearning to gather you into their arms and fill your pockets with money. Old Santos Urique lives there. He owns half the gold-mines in the country."

"You haven't been eating loco weed, have you?" asked the Kid.

"Sit down again," said Thacker, "and I'll tell you. Twelve

years ago they lost a kid. No, he didn't die—although most of 'em here do from drinking the surface water. He was a wild little devil, even if he wasn't but eight years old. Everybody knows about it. Some Americans who were through here prospecting for gold had letters to Señor Urique, and the boy was a favourite with them. They filled his head with big stories about the States; and about a month after they left, the kid disappeared, too. He was supposed to have stowed himself away among the banana bunches on a fruit steamer, and gone to New Orleans. He was seen once afterward in Texas, it was thought, but they never heard anything more of him. Old Urique has spent thousands of dollars having him looked for. The madam was broken up worst of all. The kid was her life. She wears mourning yet. But they say she believes he'll come back to her some day, and never gives up hope. On the back of the boy's left hand was tattooed a flying eagle carrying a spear in his claws. That's old Urique's coat of arms or something that he inherited in Spain."

The Kid raised his left hand slowly and gazed at it curiously.

"That's it," said Thacker, reaching behind the official desk for his bottle of smuggled brandy. "You're not so slow. I can do it. What was I consul at Sandskan for? I never knew till now. In a week I'll have the eagle bird with the frog-sticker blended in so you'd think you were born with it. I brought a set of the needles and ink just because I was sure you'd drop in some day, Mr. Dalton."

"Oh, hell," said the Kid. "I thought I told you my name!"

"All right, 'Kid,' then. It won't be that long. How does Señorito Urique sound, for a change?"

"I never played son any that I remember of," said the Kid. "If I had any parents to mention they went over the divide about the time I gave my first bleat. What is the plan of your round-up?"

Thacker leaned back against the wall and held his glass up to the light.

"We've come now," said he, "to the question of how far you're willing to go in a little matter of the sort."

"I told you why I came down here," said the Kid simply. "A good answer," said the consul. "But you won't have to go that far. Here's the scheme. After I get the trade-mark tattooed on your hand I'll notify old Urique. In the meantime, I'll furnish you with all of the family history I can find out, so you can be studying up points to talk about. You've got the looks, you speak the Spanish, you know the facts, you can tell about Texas, you've got the tattoo mark. When I notify them that the rightful heir has returned and is waiting to know whether he will be received and pardoned, what will happen? They'll simply rush down here and fall on your neck, and the curtain goes down for refreshments and a stroll in the lobby."

"I'm waiting," said the Kid. "I haven't had my saddle off in your camp long, pardner, and I never met you before; but if you intend to let it go at a parental blessing, why, I'm mistaken in my man, that's all."

"Thanks," said the consul. "I haven't met anybody in a long time that keeps up with an argument as well as you do. The rest of it is simple. If they take you in only for a while it's long enough. Don't give 'em time to hunt up the strawberry mark on your left shoulder. Old Urique keeps anywhere from $50,000 to $100,000 in his house all the time in a little safe that you could open with a shoe buttoner. Get it. My skill as a tattooer is worth half the boodle. We go halves and catch a tramp steamer for Rio Janeiro. Let the United States go to pieces if it can't get along without my services. *Que dice, señor?*"

"It sounds to me!" said the Kid, nodding his head. "I'm out for the dust."

"All right, then," said Thacker. "You'll have to keep close until we get the bird on you. You can live in the back room here. I do my own cooking, and I'll make you as comfortable as a parsimonious Government will allow me."

Thacker had set the time at a week, but it was two weeks before the design that he patiently tatooed upon the Kid's hand was to his notion. And then Thacker called a *muchacho*, and dispatched this note to the intended victim:

El Señor Don Santos Urique,
    La Casa Blanca,
My Dear Sir:

   I beg permission to inform you that there is in my house as a temporary guest a young man who arrived in Buenas Tierras from the United States some days ago. Without wishing to excite any hopes that may not be realized, I think there is a possibility of his being your long-absent son. It might be well for you to call and see him. If he is, it is my opinion that his intention was to return to his home, but upon arriving here, his courage failed him from doubts as to how he would be received.

Your true servant,
Thompson Thacker.

Half an hour afterward—quick time for Buenas Tierras—Señor Urique's ancient landau drove to the consul's door, with the barefooted coachman beating and shouting at the team of fat, awkward horses.

A tall man with a white moustache alighted, and assisted to the ground a lady who was dressed and veiled in unrelieved black.

The two hastened inside, and were met by Thacker with his best diplomatic bow. By his desk stood a slender young man with clear-cut, sunbrowned features and smoothly brushed black hair.

Señora Urique threw back her heavy veil with a quick gesture. She was past middle age, and her hair was beginning to silver, but her full, proud figure and clear olive skin retained traces of the beauty peculiar to the Basque province. But, once you had seen her eyes, and comprehended the great sadness that was revealed in their deep shadows and hopeless expression, you saw that the woman lived only in some memory.

She bent upon the young man a long look of the most agonized questioning. Then her great black eyes turned, and her gaze rested upon his left hand. And then with a sob, not loud, but seeming to shake the room, she cried, "*Hijo mio!*" and caught the Llano Kid to her heart.

A month afterward the Kid came to the consulate in response to a message sent by Thacker.

He looked the young Spanish *caballero*. His clothes were imported, and the wiles of the jewellers had not been spent upon him in vain. A more than respectable diamond shone on his finger as he rolled a shuck cigarette.

"What's doing?" said Thacker.

"Nothing much," said the Kid calmly. "I eat my first iguana steak today. They're them big lizards, you *sabe*? I reckon, though, that frijoles and side bacon would do me about as well. Do you care for iguanas, Thacker?"

"No, nor for some other kinds of reptiles," said Thacker.

It was three in the afternoon, and in another hour he would be in his state of beatitude.

"It's time you were making good, sonny," he went on, with an ugly look on his reddened face. "You're not playing up to me square. You've been the prodigal son for four weeks now, and you could have had veal for every meal on a gold dish if you'd wanted it. Now, Mr. Kid, do you think it's right to leave me out so long on a husk diet? What's the trouble? Don't you get your filial eyes on anything that looks like cash in the Casa Blanca? Don't tell me you don't. Everybody knows where old Urique keeps his stuff. It's U. S. currency, too; he don't accept anything else. What's doing? Don't say 'nothing' this time."

"Why, sure," said the Kid, admiring his diamond, "there's plenty of money up there. I'm no judge of collateral in bunches, but I will undertake for to say that I've seen the rise of $50,000 at a time in that tin grub box that my adopted father calls his safe. And he lets me carry the key sometimes just to show me that he knows I'm the real little Francisco that strayed from the herd a long time ago."

"Well, what are you waiting for?" asked Thacker angrily. "Don't you forget that I can upset your apple-cart any day I want to. If old Urique knew you were an imposter, what sort of things would happen to you! Oh, you don't know this country, Mr. Texas Kid. The laws here have got mustard spread between 'em. These people here'd stretch you out like a frog that had been stepped on, and give you about fifty sticks at every corner of the plaza. And they'd wear every stick out, too. What was left of you they'd feed to alligators."

"I might as well tell you now, pardner," said the Kid, sliding down low on his steamer chair, "that things are going to stay just as they are. They're about right, now."

"What do you mean?" asked Thacker, rattling the bottom of his glass on his desk.

"The scheme's off," said the Kid. "And whenever you have the pleasure of speaking to me address me as Don Francisco Urique. I'll guarantee I'll answer to it. We'll let Colonel Urique keep his money. His little tin safe is as good as the time-locker in the First National Bank of Laredo as far as you and me are concerned."

"You're going to throw me down, then, are you?" said the consul.

"Sure," said the Kid cheerfully. "Throw you down. That's it. And now I'll tell you why. The first night I was up at the colonel's house they introduced me to a bedroom. No blankets on the floor—a real room, with a bed and things in it. And before I was asleep, in comes this artificial mother of mine and tucks in the covers. 'Panchito,' she says, 'my little lost one, God has brought you back to me. I bless His name forever.' It was that, or some truck like that, she said. And down comes a drop or two of rain and hits me on the nose. And all that stuck by me, Mr. Thacker. And it's been that way ever since. And it's got to stay that way. Don't you think that it's for what's in it for me, either, that I say so. If you have any such ideas, keep 'em to yourself. I haven't had much truck with women in my life, and no mothers to speak of, but here's a lady that we've got to keep fooled. Once she stood it; twice she won't. I'm a low-down wolf, and the devil may have sent me on this trail instead of God, but I'll travel it to the end. And now, don't forget that I'm Don Francisco Urique whenever you happen to mention my name."

"I'll expose you today, you—you double-dyed traitor," stammered Thacker.

The Kid arose and, without violence, took Thacker by the throat with a hand of steel, and shoved him slowly into a corner. Then he drew from under his left arm his pearl-handled .45 and poked the cold muzzle of it against the consul's mouth.

"I told you why I come here," he said, with his old freezing smile. "If I leave here, you'll be the reason. Never forget it, pardner. Now, what is my name?"

"Er—Don Francisco Urique," gasped Thacker.

From outside came a sound of wheels, and the shouting of someone, and the sharp thwacks of a wooden whipstock upon the backs of fat horses.

The Kid put up his gun, and walked toward the door. But he turned again and came back to the trembling Thacker, and held up his left hand with its back toward the consul.

"There's one more reason," he said slowly, "why things have got to stand as they are. The fellow I killed in Laredo had one of them same pictures on his left hand."

Outside, the ancient landau of Don Santos Urique rattled to the door. The coachman ceased his bellowing. Señora Urique, in a voluminous gay gown of white lace and flying ribbons, leaned forward with a happy look in her great soft eyes.

"Are you within, dear son?" she called, in the rippling Castilian.

"*Madre mia, yo vengo* [mother, I come]," answered the young Don Francisco Urique.

O. Henry

*

A RETRIEVED REFORMATION

*O. Henry's famous story has become even more famous under
the title ALIAS JIMMY VALENTINE, through its success on
both stage and screen. In 1909 Paul Armstrong adapted it for
the stage. In 1920 Metro Products filmed the story as a six reel
silent picture. Finis Fox wrote the scenario that was directed
by Maxwell Karger and starred Bert Lytell, Viola Vale and
Eugene Pallette. In 1928 MGM produced a new ALIAS JIMMY
VALENTINE with dialogue. This version written by A. T.
Younger and Sara Y. Mason and directed by Jack Conway, starred
Lionel Barrymore and William Haines.*

A GUARD CAME to the prison shoeshop, where Jimmy Valentine was assiduously stitching uppers, and escorted him to the front office. There the warden handed Jimmy his pardon, which had been signed that morning by the governor. Jimmy took it in a tired kind of way. He had served nearly ten months of a four-year sentence. He had expected to stay only about three months, at the longest. When a man with as many friends on the outside as Jimmy Valentine had is received in the "stir" it is hardly worth while to cut his hair.

"Now, Valentine," said the warden, "you'll go out in the morning. Brace up, and make a man of yourself. You're not a bad fellow at heart. Stop cracking safes, and live straight."

"Me?" said Jimmy, in surprise. "Why, I never cracked a safe in my life."

"Oh, no," laughed the warden. "Of course not. Let's see, now. How was it you happened to get sent up on that Springfield job? Was it because you wouldn't prove an alibi for fear of compromising somebody in extremely high-toned society? Or was it simply a case of a mean old jury that had it in for you? It's always one or the other with you innocent victims."

"Me?" said Jimmy, still blankly virtuous. "Why, warden, I never was in Springfield in my life!"

"Take him back, Cronin," smiled the warden, "and fix him up with outgoing clothes. Unlock him at seven in the morning, and let him come to the bullpen. Better think over my advice, Valentine."

At a quarter past seven on the next morning Jimmy stood in the warden's outer office. He had on a suit of the villainously fitting, ready-made clothes and a pair of the stiff, squeaky shoes that the state furnishes to its discharged compulsory guests.

The clerk handed him a railroad ticket and a five-dollar bill with which the law expected him to rehabilitate himself into good citizenship and prosperity. The warden gave him a cigar, and shook hands. Valentine, 9762, was chronicled on the books "Pardoned by Governor," and Mr. James Valentine walked out into the sunshine.

Disregarding the song of the birds, the waving green trees, and the smell of the flowers, Jimmy headed straight for a restaurant. There he tasted the first sweet joys of liberty in the shape of a broiled chicken and a bottle of white wine— followed by a cigar a grade better than the one the warden had given him. From there he proceeded leisurely to the depot. He tossed a quarter into the hat of a blind man sitting by the door, and boarded his train. Three hours set him down in a little town near the state line. He went to the café of one Mike Dolan and shook hands with Mike, who was alone behind the bar.

"Sorry we couldn't make it sooner, Jimmy, me boy," said Mike, "But we had that protest from Springfield to buck against, and the governor nearly balked. Feeling all right?"

"Fine," said Jimmy. "Got my key?"

He got his key and went upstairs, unlocking the door of a room at the rear. Everything was just as he had left it. There on the floor was still Ben Price's collar button that had been torn from that eminent detective's shirtband when they had overpowered Jimmy to arrest him.

Pulling out from the wall a folding-bed, Jimmy slid back a panel in the wall and dragged out a dust covered suitcase. He opened this and gazed fondly at the finest set of burglar's tools in the East. It was a complete set, made of specially tempered steel, the latest designs in drills, punches, braces and bits, jimmies, clamps, and augers, with two or three novelties, invented by Jimmy himself, in which he took pride. Over nine hundred dollars they had cost him to have made at ———, a place where they made such things for the profession.

In half an hour Jimmy went down stairs and through the café. He was now dressed in tasteful and well-fitting clothes, and carried his dusted and cleaned suitcase in his hand.

"Got anything on?" asked Mike Dolan, genially.

"Me?" said Jimmy, in a puzzled tone. "I don't understand. I'm representing the New York Amalgamated Short Snap Biscuit Cracker and Frazzled Wheat Company."

This statement delighted Mike to such an extent that Jimmy had to take a seltzer-and-milk on the spot. He never touched "hard" drinks.

A week after the release of Valentine, 9762, there was a neat job of safe-burglary done in Richmond, Indiana, with no clue to the author. A scant eight hundred dollars was all that was secured. Two weeks after that a patented, improved, burglar-proof safe in Logansport was opened like a cheese to the tune of fifteen hundred dollars, currency; securities and silver untouched. That began to interest the rogue-catchers. Then an old-fashioned bank-safe in Jefferson City became active and threw out of its crater an eruption of bank-notes amounting to five thousand dollars. The losses were now high enough to bring the matter up into Ben Price's class of work. By comparing notes, a remarkable similarity in the methods of the burglaries was noticed. Ben Price investigated the scenes of the robberies, and was heard to remark:

"That's Dandy Jim Valentine's autograph. He's resumed business. Look at that combination knob—jerked out as easy as pulling up a radish in wet weather. He's got the only clamps that can do it. And look how clean those tumblers were punched out! Jimmy never has to drill but one hole. Yes, I guess I want Mr. Valentine. He'll do his bit next time without any short-time or clemency foolishness."

Ben Price knew Jimmy's habits. He had learned them while working up the Springfield case. Long jumps, quick get-aways, no confederates, and a taste for good society—these ways had helped Mr. Valentine to become noted as a successful dodger of retribution. It was given out that Ben Price had taken up the trail of the elusive cracksman, and other people with burglarproof safes felt more at ease.

One afternoon Jimmy Valentine and his suitcase climbed out of the mail-hack in Elmore, a little town five miles off the railroad down in the black-jack country of Arkansas. Jimmy, looking like an athletic young senior just home from college, went down the board side-walk toward the hotel.

A young lady crossed the street, passed him at the corner and entered a door over which was the sign "The Elmore Bank." Jimmy Valentine looked into her eyes, forgot what he was, and became another man. She lowered her eyes and coloured slightly. Young men of Jimmy's style and looks were scarce in Elmore.

Jimmy collared a boy that was loafing on the steps of the bank as if he were one of the stockholders, and began to ask him questions about the town, feeding him dimes at intervals. By and by the young lady came out, looking royally unconscious of the young man with the suitcase, and went her way.

"Isn't that young lady Miss Polly Simpson?" asked Jimmy, with specious guile.

"Naw," said the boy. "She's Annabel Adams. Her pa owns this bank. What'd you come to Elmore for? Is that a gold watch chain? I'm going to get a bulldog. Got any more dimes?"

Jimmy went to the Planters' Hotel, registered as Ralph D. Spencer, and engaged a room. He leaned on the desk and declared his platform to the clerk. He said he had come to Elmore to look for a location to go into business. How was the shoe business, now, in the town? He had thought of the shoe business. Was there an opening?

The clerk was impressed by the clothes and manner of Jimmy. He, himself, was something of a pattern of fashion to the thinly gilded youth of Elmore, but he now perceived his shortcomings. While trying to figure out Jimmy's manner of tying his four-in-hand he cordially gave information.

Yes, there ought to be a good opening in the shoe line. There wasn't an exclusive shoe store in the place. The dry-goods and general stores handled them. Business in all lines was fairly good. Hoped Mr. Spencer would decide to locate in Elmore. He would find it a pleasant town to live in, and the people very sociable.

Mr. Spencer thought he would stop over in the town a few days and look over the situation. No, the clerk needn't call the boy. He would carry up his suitcase himself; it was rather heavy.

Mr. Ralph Spencer, the phoenix that arose from Jimmy Valentine's ashes—ashes left by the flame of a sudden and alterative attack of love—remained in Elmore, and prospered. He opened a shoe store and secured a good run of trade.

Socially he was also a success, and made many friends. And he accomplished the wish of his heart. He met Miss Annabel Adams, and became more and more captivated by her charms.

At the end of a year the situation of Mr. Ralph Spencer was this: he had won the respect of the community, his shoe store was flourishing, and he and Annabel were engaged to be married in two weeks. Mr. Adams, the typical, plodding, country banker, approved of Spencer. Annabel's pride in him almost equalled her affection. He was as much at home in the family of Mr. Adams and that of Annabel's married sister as if he were already a member.

One day Jimmy sat down in his room and wrote this letter which he mailed to the safe address of one of his old friends in St. Louis:

Dear Old Pal:

I want you to be at Sullivan's place, in Little Rock, next Wednesday night, at nine o'clock. I want you to wind up some little matters for me. And, also, I want to make you a present of my kit of tools. I know you'll be glad to get them—you couldn't duplicate the lot for a thousand dollars. Say, Billy, I've quit the old business—a year ago. I've got a nice store. I'm making an honest living, and I'm going to marry the finest girl on earth two weeks from now. It's the only life, Billy—the straight one. I wouldn't touch a dollar of another man's money now for a million. After I get married I'm going to sell out and go West, where there won't be so much danger of having old scores brought up against me. I tell you, Billy, she's an angel. She believes in me; and I wouldn't do another crooked thing for the whole world. Be sure to be at Sully's, for I must see you. I'll bring the tools with me.

Your old friend, Jimmy.

On the Monday night after Jimmy wrote this letter, Ben Price jogged unobtrusively into Elmore in a livery buggy. He lounged about town in his quiet way until he found out what he wanted to know. From the drugstore across the street from Spencer's shoe store he got a good look at Ralph D. Spencer.

"Going to marry the banker's daughter are you, Jimmy?" said Ben to himself, softly. "Well, I don't know!"

The next morning Jimmy took breakfast at the Adamses. He was going to Little Rock that day to order his wedding-suit and buy something nice for Annabel. That would be the first time he had left town since he came to Elmore. It had been more than a year now since those last professional "jobs," and he thought he could safely venture out.

After breakfast quite a family party went downtown to-gether—Mr. Adams, Annabel, Jimmy and Annabel's married sister with her two little girls, aged five and nine. They came by the hotel where Jimmy still boarded, and he ran up to his room and brought along his suitcase. Then they went on to the bank. There stood Jimmy's horse and buggy and Dolph Gibson, who was going to drive him over to the railroad station.

All went inside the high, carved oak railings into the bank-ing-room—Jimmy included, for Mr. Adams's future son-in-law was welcome anywhere. The clerks were pleased to be greeted by the good-looking, agreeable young man who was going to marry Miss Annabel. Jimmy set his suitcase down. Annabel, whose heart was bubbling with happiness and lively youth, put on Jimmy's hat, and picked up the suitcase. "Wouldn't I make a nice drummer?" said Annabel. "My! Ralph, how heavy it is! Feels like it was full of gold bricks."

"Lot of nickel-plated shoehorns in there," said Jimmy coolly, "that I'm going to return. Thought I'd save express charges by taking them up. I'm getting awfully economical."

The Elmore Bank had just put in a new safe and vault. Mr. Adams was very proud of it, and insisted on an inspection by every one. The vault was a small one, but it had a new, patented door. It fastened with three solid steel bolts thrown simultaneously with a single handle, and had a time-lock. Mr. Adams beamingly explained its workings to Mr. Spencer, who showed a courteous but not too intelligent interest. The two children, May and Agatha, were delighted by the shining metal and funny clock and knobs.

While they were thus engaged Ben Price sauntered in and leaned on his elbow, looking casually inside between the railings. He told the teller that he didn't want anything; he was just waiting for a man he knew.

Suddenly there was a scream or two from the women, and a commotion. Unperceived by the elders, May, the nine-year-old girl, in a spirit of play, had shut Agatha in the vault. She had then shot the bolts and turned the knob of the combination as she had seen Mr. Adams do.

The old banker sprang to the handle and tugged at it for a moment. "The door can't be opened," he groaned. "The clock hasn't been wound nor the combination set."

Agatha's mother screamed again, hysterically.

"Hush!" said Mr. Adams, raising his trembling hand. "All be quiet for a moment. Agatha!" he called as loudly as he could. "Listen to me." During the following silence they could just hear the faint sound of the child wildly shrieking in the dark vault in a panic of terror.

"My precious darling!" wailed the mother. "She will die of fright! Open the door! Oh, break it open! Can't you men do something?"

"There isn't a man nearer than Little Rock who can open that door," said Mr. Adams, in a shaky voice. "My God! Spencer, what shall we do? That child—she can't stand it long in there. There isn't enough air, and, besides, she'll go into convulsions from fright."

Agatha's mother, frantic now, beat the door of the vault with her hands. Somebody wildly suggested dynamite. Annabel turned to Jimmy, her large eyes full of anguish, but not yet despairing. To a woman nothing seems quite impossible to the powers of the man she worships.

"Can't you do something, Ralph—*try*, won't you?"

He looked at her with a queer, soft smile on his lips and in his keen eyes.

"Annabel," he said, "give me that rose you are wearing, will you?"

Hardly believing that she heard him aright, she unpinned the bud from the bosom of her dress, and placed it in his hand. Jimmy stuffed it into his vest-pocket, threw off his coat and pulled up his shirt-sleeves. With that act Ralph D. Spencer passed away and Jimmy Valentine took his place.

"Get away from the door, all of you," he commanded shortly.

He set his suitcase on the table, and opened it out flat. From that time on he seemed to be unconscious of the presence of any one else. He laid out the shining, queer implements swiftly and orderly, whistling softly to himself as he always did when at work. In a deep silence and immovable, the others watched him as if under a spell.

In a minute Jimmy's pet drill was biting smoothly into the steel door. In ten minutes—breaking his own burglarious record—he threw back the bolts and opened the door.

Agatha, almost collapsed, but safe, was gathered into her mother's arms.

Jimmy Valentine put on his coat, and walked outside the railings toward the front door. As he went he thought he heard a far-away voice that he once knew call "Ralph!" But he never hesitated.

At the door a big man stood somewhat in his way.

"Hello, Ben!" said Jimmy, still with his strange smile. "Got around at last, have you? Well, let's go. I don't know that it makes any difference, now."

And then Ben Price acted rather strangely.

"Guess you're mistaken, Mr. Spencer," he said. "Don't believe I recognize you. Your buggy's waiting for you, ain't it?"

And Ben Price turned and strolled down the street.

W. Somerset Maugham

*

RAIN

Just as Maugham's story has become a classic, the Hollywood versions have become legendary. First produced in 1928 by United Artists as a silent movie starring Gloria Swanson and Lionel Barrymore, and directed by Raoul Walsh, the picture was later remade as a talkie by United Artists in 1932, with Joan Crawford as Sadie Thompson, and Walter Hutson as the missionary. It was one of the biggest successes of the year.

IT WAS NEARLY bed-time and when they awoke next morning land would be in sight. Dr. Macphail lit his pipe and, leaning over the rail, searched the heavens for the Southern Cross. After two years at the front and a wound that had taken longer to heal than it should, he was glad to settle down quietly at Apia for twelve months at least, and he felt already better for the journey. Since some of the passengers were leaving the ship next day at Pago-Pago they had had a little dance that evening and in his ears hammered still the harsh notes of the mechanical piano. But the deck was quiet at last. A little way off he saw his wife in a long chair talking with the Davidsons, and he strolled over to her. When he sat down under the light and took off his hat you saw that he had very red hair, with a bald patch on the crown, and the red, freckled skin which accompanies red hair; he was a man of forty, thin, with a pinched face, precise and rather pedantic; and he spoke with a Scots accent in a very low, quiet voice.

Between the Macphails and the Davidsons, who were missionaries, there had arisen the intimacy of shipboard, which is due to propinquity rather than to any community of taste. Their chief tie was the disapproval they shared of the men who spent their days and nights in the smoking-room playing poker or bridge or drinking. Mrs. Macphail was not a little flattered to think that she and her husband were the only people on board with whom the Davidsons were willing to associate, and even the doctor, shy but no fool, half unconsciously acknowledged the compliment. It was only because he was of an argumentative mind that in their cabin at night he permitted himself to carp.

"Mrs. Davidson was saying she didn't know how they'd have got through the journey if it hadn't been for us," said Mrs. Macphail, as she neatly brushed out her transformation. "She said we were really the only people on the ship they cared to know."

"I shouldn't have thought a missionary was such a big bug that he could afford to put on frills."

"It's not frills. I quite understand what she means. It wouldn't have been very nice for the Davidsons to have to mix with all that rough lot in the smoking-room."

"The founder of their religion wasn't so exclusive," said Dr. Macphail with a chuckle.

"I've asked you over and over again not to joke about religion," answered his wife. "I shouldn't like to have a nature like yours, Alec. You never look for the best in people."

He gave her a sidelong glance with his pale, blue eyes, but did not reply. After many years of married life he had learned that it was more conducive to peace to leave his wife with the last word. He was undressed before she was, and climbing into the upper bunk he settled down to read himself to sleep.

When he came on deck next morning they were close to land. He looked at it with greedy eyes. There was a thin strip of silver beach rising quickly to hills covered to the top with luxuriant vegetation. The coconut trees, thick and green, came nearly to the water's edge, and among them you saw the grass houses of the Samoans; and here and there, gleaming white, a little church. Mrs. Davidson came and stood beside him. She was dressed in black and wore round her neck a gold chain, from which dangled a small cross. She was a little woman, with brown, dull hair very elaborately arranged, and she had prominent blue eyes behind invisible *pince-nez*. Her face was long, like a sheep's, but she gave no impression of foolishness, rather of extreme alertness; she had the quick movements of a bird. The most remarkable thing about her was her voice, high, metallic, and without inflection; it fell on the ear with a hard monotony, irritating to the nerves like the pitiless clamour of the pneumatic drill.

"This must seem like home to you," said Dr. Macphail, with his thin, difficult smile.

"Ours are low islands, you know, not like these. Coral. These are volcanic. We've got another ten days' journey to reach them."

"In these parts that's almost like being in the next street at home," said Dr. Macphail facetiously.

"Well, that's rather an exaggerated way of putting it, but one does look at distances differently in the South Seas. So far you're right."

Dr. Macphail sighed faintly.

"I'm glad we're not stationed here," she went on. "They say this is a terribly difficult place to work in. The steamers' touching makes the people unsettled; and then there's the naval station; that's bad for the natives. In our district we don't have difficulties like that to contend with. There are one or two traders, of course, but we take care to make them behave, and if they don't we make the place so hot for them they're glad to go."

Fixing the glasses on her nose she looked at the green island with a ruthless stare.

"It's almost a hopeless task for the missionaries here. I can never be sufficiently thankful to God that we are at least spared that."

Davidson's district consisted of a group of islands to the North of Samoa; they were widely separated and he had frequently to go long distances by canoe. At these times his wife remained at their headquarters and managed the mission. Dr. Macphail felt his heart sink when he considered the efficiency with which she certainly managed it. She spoke of the depravity of the natives in a voice which nothing could hush, but with a vehemently unctuous horror. Her sense of delicacy was singular. Early in their acquaintance she had said to him:

"You know, their marriage customs when we first settled in the islands were so shocking that I couldn't possibly describe them to you. But I'll tell Mrs. Macphail and she'll tell you."

Then he had seen his wife and Mrs. Davidson, their deck-chairs close together, in earnest conversation for about two hours. As he walked past them backwards and forwards for the sake of exercise, he had heard Mrs. Davidson's agitated whisper, like the distant flow of a mountain torrent, and he saw by his wife's open mouth and pale face that she was enjoying an alarming experience. At night in their cabin she repeated to him with bated breath all she had heard.

"Well, what did I say to you?" cried Mrs. Davidson, exultant, next morning. "Did you ever hear anything more dreadful? You don't wonder that I couldn't tell you myself, do you? Even though you are a doctor."

Mrs. Davidson scanned his face. She had a dramatic eagerness to see that she had achieved the desired effect.

"Can you wonder that when we first went there our hearts sank? You'll hardly believe me when I tell you it was impossible to find a single good girl in any of the villages."

She used the word *good* in a severely technical manner.

"Mr. Davidson and I talked it over, and we made up our minds the first thing to do was to put down the dancing. The natives were crazy about dancing."

"I was not averse to it myself when I was a young man," said Dr. Macphail.

"I guessed so much when I heard you ask Mrs. Macphail to have a turn with you last night. I don't think there's any real harm if a man dances with his wife, but I was relieved that she wouldn't. Under the circumstances I thought it better that we should keep ourselves to ourselves."

"Under what circumstances?"

Mrs. Davidson gave him a quick look through her *pince-nez*, but did not answer his question.

"But among white people it's not quite the same," she went

on, "though I must say I agree with Mr. Davidson, who says he can't understand how a husband can stand by and see his wife in another man's arms, and as far as I'm concerned I've never danced a step since I married. But the native dancing is quite another matter. It's not only immoral in itself, but it distinctly leads to immorality. However, I'm thankful to God that we stamped it out, and I don't think I'm wrong in saying that no one has danced in our district for eight years."

But now they came to the mouth of the harbour and Mrs. Macphail joined them. The ship turned sharply and steamed slowly in. It was a great landlocked harbour big enough to hold a fleet of battleships; and all around it rose, high and steep, the green hills. Near the entrance, getting such breeze as blew from the sea, stood the governor's house in a garden. The Stars and Stripes dangled languidly from a flagstaff. They passed two or three trim bungalows, and a tennis court, and then came to the quay with its warehouses. Mrs. Davidson pointed out the schooner, moored two or three hundred yards from the side, which was to take them to Apia. There was a crowd of eager, noisy, and good-humoured natives come from all parts of the island, some from curiosity, others to barter with the travellers on their way to Sydney; and they brought pineapples and huge bunches of bananas, *tapa* cloths, necklaces of shells or shark's teeth, *kava*-bowls, and models of war canoes. American sailors, neat and trim, clean-shaven and frank of face, sauntered among them, and there was a little group of officials. While their luggage was being landed the Macphails and Mrs. Davidson watched the crowd. Dr. Macphail looked at the yaws from which most of the children and the young boys seemed to suffer, disfiguring sores like torpid ulcers, and his professional eyes glistened when he saw for the first time in his experience cases of elephantiasis, men going about with a huge, heavy arm or dragging along a grossly disfigured leg. Men and women wore the *lava-lava*.

"It's a very indecent costume," said Mrs. Davidson. "Mr. Davidson thinks it should be prohibited by law. How can you expect people to be moral when they wear nothing but a strip of red cotton round their loins?"

"It's suitable enough to the climate," said the doctor, wiping the sweat off his head.

Now that they were on land the heat, though it was so early in the morning, was already oppressive. Closed in by its hills, not a breath of air came in to Pago-Pago.

"In our islands," Mrs. Davidson went on in her high-pitched tones, "we've practically eradicated the *lava-lava*. A few old men still continue to wear it, but that's all. The women have all taken to the Mother Hubbard, and the men wear trousers and singlets. At the very beginning of our stay Mr. Davidson said in one of his reports: the inhabitants of these islands will never be thoroughly Christianised till every boy of more than ten years is made to wear a pair of trousers."

But Mrs. Davidson had given two or three of her bird-like glances at heavy grey clouds that came floating over the mouth of the harbour. A few drops began to fall.

"We'd better take shelter," she said.

They made their way with all the crowd to a great shed of corrugated iron, and the rain began to fall in torrents. They stood there for some time and then were joined by Mr. Davidson. He had been polite enough to the Macphails during the journey, but he had not his wife's sociability, and had spent much of his time reading. He was a silent, rather sullen man, and you felt that his affability was a duty that he imposed upon himself Christianly; he was by nature reserved and even morose. His appearance was singular. He was very tall and thin, with long limbs loosely jointed; hollow cheeks and curiously high cheek-bones; he had so cadaverous an air that it surprised you to notice how full and sensual were his lips. He wore his hair very long. His dark eyes, set deep in their sockets, were large and tragic; and his hands with their big, long fingers, were finely shaped; they gave him a look of great strength. But the most striking thing about him was the feeling he gave you of suppressed fire. It was impressive and vaguely troubling. He was not a man with whom any intimacy was possible.

He brought now unwelcome news. There was an epidemic of measles, a serious and often fatal disease among the Kanakas, on the island, and a case had developed among the crew of the schooner which was to take them on their journey. The sick man had been brought ashore and put in hospital on the quarantine station, but telegraphic instructions had been sent from Apia to say that the schooner would not be allowed to enter the harbour till it was certain no other member of the crew was affected.

"It means we shall have to stay here for ten days at least."

"But I'm urgently needed at Apia," said Dr. Macphail.

"That can't be helped. If no more cases develop on board, the schooner will be allowed to sail with white passengers, but all native traffic is prohibited for three months."

"Is there a hotel here?" asked Mrs. Macphail.

Davidson gave a low chuckle.

"There's not."

"What shall we do then?"

"I've been talking to the governor. There's a trader along the front who has rooms that he rents, and my proposition is that as soon as the rain lets up we should go along there and see what we can do. Don't expect comfort. You've just got to be thankful if we get a bed to sleep on and a roof over our heads."

But the rain showed no sign of stopping, and at length with umbrellas and waterproofs they set out. There was no town, but merely a group of official buildings, a store or two, and at the back, among the coconut trees and plantains, a few native dwellings. The house they sought was about five minutes' walk from the wharf. It was a frame house of two storeys, with broad verandahs on both floors and a roof of corrugated iron. The owner was a half-caste named Horn, with a native wife surrounded by little brown children, and on the ground-floor he had a store where he sold canned goods and cottons. The rooms he showed them were almost bare of furniture. In the Macphails' there was nothing but a poor, worn bed with a ragged mosquito net, a rickety chair, and a washstand. They looked round with dismay. The rain poured down without ceasing.

"I'm not going to unpack more than we actually need," said Mrs. Macphail.

Mrs. Davidson came into the room as she was unlocking a portmanteau. She was very brisk and alert. The cheerless surroundings had no effect on her.

"If you'll take my advice you'll get a needle and cotton and start right in to mend the mosquito net," she said, "or you'll not be able to get a wink of sleep to-night."

"Will they be very bad?" asked Dr. Macphail.

"This is the season for them. When you're asked to a party at Government House at Apia you'll notice that all the ladies are given a pillowslip to put their—their lower extremities in."

"I wish the rain would stop for a moment," said Mrs. Macphail. "I could try to make the place comfortable with more heart if the sun were shining."

"Oh, if you wait for that, you'll wait a long time. Pago-Pago is about the rainiest place in the Pacific. You see, the hills, and that bay, they attract the water, and one expects rain at this time of year anyway."

She looked from Macphail to his wife, standing helplessly in different parts of the room, like lost souls, and she pursed her lips. She saw that she must take them in hand. Feckless people like that made her impatient, but her hands itched to put everything in the order which came so naturally to her.

"Here, you give me a needle and cotton and I'll mend that net of yours, while you go on with your unpacking. Dinner's at one. Dr. Macphail, you'd better go down to the wharf and see that your heavy luggage has been put in a dry place. You know what these natives are, they're quite capable of storing it where the rain will beat in on it all the time."

The doctor put on his waterproof again and went downstairs. At the door Mr. Horn was standing in conversation with the quartermaster of the ship they had just arrived in and a second-class passenger whom Dr. Macphail had seen several times on board. The quartermaster, a little, shrivelled man, extremely dirty, nodded to him as he passed.

"This is a bad job about the measles, doc," he said. "I see you've fixed yourself up already."

Dr. Macphail thought he was rather familiar, but he was a timid man and he did not take offence easily.

"Yes, we've got a room upstairs."

"Miss Thompson was sailing with you to Apia, so I've brought her along here."

The quartermaster pointed with his thumb to the woman standing by his side. She was twenty-seven perhaps, plump, and in a coarse fashion pretty. She wore a white dress and a large white hat. Her fat calves in white cotton stockings bulged over the tops of long white boots in glacé kid. She gave Macphail an ingratiating smile.

"The feller's tryin' to soak me a dollar and a half a day for the meanest sized room," she said in a hoarse voice.

"I tell you she's a friend of mine, Jo," said the quartermaster. "She can't pay more than a dollar, and you've sure got to take her for that."

The trader was fat and smooth and quietly smiling.

"Well, if you put it like that, Mr. Swan, I'll see what I can do about it. I'll talk to Mrs. Horn and if we think we can make a reduction we will."

"Don't try to pull that stuff with me," said Miss Thompson. "We'll settle this right now. You get a dollar a day for the room and not one bean more."

Dr. Macphail smiled. He admired the effrontery with which she bargained. He was the sort of man who always paid what he was asked. He preferred to be over-charged than to haggle. The trader sighed.

"Well, to oblige Mr. Swan I'll take it."

"That's the goods," said Miss Thompson. "Come right in and have a shot of hooch. I've got some real good rye in that grip if you'll bring it along, Mr. Swan. You come along too, doctor."

"Oh, I don't think I will, thank you," he answered. "I'm just going down to see that our luggage is all right."

He stepped out into the rain. It swept in from the opening of the harbour in sheets and the opposite shore was all blurred. He passed two or three natives clad in nothing but the *lava-lava*, with huge umbrellas over them. They walked finely, with leisurely movements, very upright; and they smiled and greeted him in a strange tongue as they went by.

It was nearly dinner-time when he got back, and their meal

was laid in the trader's parlour. It was a room designed not to live in but for purposes of prestige, and it had a musty, melancholy air. A suite of stamped plush was arranged neatly round the walls, and from the middle of the ceiling, protected from the flies by yellow tissue paper, hung a gilt chandelier. Davidson did not come.

"I know he went to call on the governor," said Mrs. Davidson, "and I guess he's kept him to dinner."

A little native girl brought them a dish of Hamburger steak, and after a while the trader came up to see that they had everything they wanted.

"I see we have a fellow lodger, Mr. Horn," said Dr. Macphail.

"She's taken a room, that's all," answered the trader. "She's getting her own board."

He looked at the two ladies with an obsequious air.

"I put her downstairs so she shouldn't be in the way. She won't be any trouble to you."

"Is it someone who was on the boat?" asked Mrs. Macphail.

"Yes, ma'am, she was in the second cabin. She was going to Apia. She has a position as cashier waiting for her."

"Oh!"

When the trader was gone Macphail said:

"I shouldn't think she'd find it exactly cheerful having her meals in her room."

"If she was in the second cabin I guess she'd rather," answered Mrs. Davidson. "I don't exactly know who it can be."

"I happened to be there when the quartermaster brought her along. Her name's Thompson."

"It's not the woman who was dancing with the quartermaster last night?" asked Mrs. Davidson.

"That's who it must be," said Mrs. Macphail. "I wondered at the time what she was. She looked rather fast to me."

"Not good style at all," said Mrs. Davidson.

They began to talk of other things, and after dinner, tired with their early rise, they separated and slept. When they awoke, though the sky was still grey and the clouds hung low, it was not raining and they went for a walk on the high road which the Americans had built along the bay.

On their return they found that Davidson had just come in.

"We may be here for a fortnight," he said irritably. "I've argued it out with the governor, but he says there is nothing to be done."

"Mr. Davidson's just longing to get back to his work," said his wife, with an anxious glance at him.

"We've been away for a year," he said, walking up and down the verandah. "The mission has been in charge of native missionaries and I'm terribly nervous that they've let things slide. They're good men, I'm not saying a word against them, God-fearing, devout, and truly Christian men—their Christianity would put many so-called Christians at home to the blush—but they're pitfully lacking in energy. They can make a stand once, they can make a stand twice, but they can't make a stand all the time. If you leave a mission in charge of a native missionary, no matter how trustworthy he seems, in course of time you'll find he's let abuses creep in."

Mr. Davidson stood still. With his tall, spare form, and his great eyes flashing out of his pale face, he was an impressive figure. His sincerity was obvious in the fire of his gestures and in his deep, ringing voice.

"I expect to have my work cut out for me. I shall act and I shall act promptly. If the tree is rotten it shall be cut down and cast into the flames."

And in the evening after the high tea which was their last meal, while they sat in the stiff parlour, the ladies working and Dr. Macphail smoking his pipe, the missionary told them of his work in the islands.

"When we went there they had no sense of sin at all," he said. "They broke the commandments one after the other and never knew they were doing wrong. And I think that was the most difficult part of my work, to instil into the natives the sense of sin."

The Macphails knew already that Davidson had worked in the Solomons for five years before he met his wife. She had been a missionary in China, and they had become acquainted in Boston, where they were both spending part of their leave to attend a missionary congress. On their marriage they had been appointed to the islands in which they had laboured ever since.

In the course of all the conversations they had had with Mr. Davidson one thing had shone out clearly and that was the man's unflinching courage. He was a medical missionary, and he was liable to be called at any time to one or other of the islands in the group. Even the whaleboat is not so very safe a conveyance in the stormy Pacific of the wet season, but often he would be sent for in a canoe, and then the danger was great. In cases of illness or accident he never hesitated. A dozen times he had spent the whole night bailing for his life, and more than once Mrs. Davidson had given him up for lost.

"I'd beg him not to go sometimes," she said, "or at least to wait till the weather was more settled, but he'd never listen. He's obstinate, and when he's once made up his mind, nothing can move him."

"How can I ask the natives to put their trust in the Lord if I am afraid to do so myself?" cried Davidson. "And I'm not, I'm not. They know that if they send for me in their trouble I'll come if it's humanly possible. And do you think the Lord is going to abandon me when I am on his business? The wind blows at his bidding and the waves toss and rage at his word."

Dr. Macphail was a timid man. He had never been able to get used to the hurtling of the shells over the trenches, and when he was operating in an advanced dressing-station the sweat poured from his brow and dimmed his spectacles in the effort he made to control his unsteady hand. He shuddered a little as he looked at the missionary.

"I wish I could say that I've never been afraid." he said.

"I wish you could say that you believed in God," retorted the other.

But for some reason, that evening the missionary's thoughts travelled back to the early days he and his wife had spent on the islands.

"Sometimes Mrs. Davidson and I would look at one another and the tears would stream down our cheeks. We worked without ceasing, day and night, and we seemed to make no progress. I don't know what I should have done without her then. When

I felt my heart sink, when I was very near despair, she gave me courage and hope."

Mrs. Davidson looked down at her work, and a slight colour rose to her thin cheeks. Her hands trembled a little. She did not trust herself to speak.

"We had no one to help us. We were alone, thousands of miles from any of our own people, surrounded by darkness. When I was broken and weary she would put her work aside and take the Bible and read to me till peace came and settled upon me like sleep upon the eyelids of a child, and when at last she closed the book she'd say: 'We'll save them in spite of themselves.' And I felt strong again in the Lord, and I answered: 'Yes, with God's help I'll save them. I must save them'."

He came over to the table and stood in front of it as though it were a lectern.

"You see, they were so naturally depraved that they couldn't be brought to see their wickedness. We had to make sins out of what they thought were natural actions. We had to make it a sin, not only to commit adultery and to lie and thieve, but to expose their bodies, and to dance and not to come to church. I made it a sin for a girl to show her bosom and a sin for a man not to wear trousers."

"How?" asked Dr. Macphail, not without surprise.

"I instituted fines. Obviously the only way to make people realise that an action is sinful is to punish them if they commit it. I fined them if they didn't come to church, and I fined them if they danced. I fined them if they were improperly dressed. I had a tariff, and every sin had to be paid for either in money or work. And at last I made them understand."

"But did they never refuse to pay?"

"How could they?" asked the missionary.

"It would be a brave man who tried to stand up against Mr. Davidson," said his wife, tightening her lips.

Dr. Macphail looked at Davidson with troubled eyes. What he heard shocked him, but he hesitated to express his disapproval.

"You must remember that in the last resort I could expel them from their church membership."

"Did they mind that?"

Davidson smiled a little and gently rubbed his hands.

"They couldn't sell their copra. When the men fished they got no share of the catch. It meant something very like starvation. Yes, they minded quite a lot."

"Tell him about Fred Ohlson," said Mrs. Davidson.

The missionary fixed his fiery eyes on Dr. Macphail.

"Fred Ohlson was a Danish trader who had been in the islands a good many years. He was a pretty rich man as traders go and he wasn't very pleased when we came. You see, he'd had things very much his own way. He paid the natives what he liked for their copra, and he paid in goods and whiskey. He had a native wife, but he was flagrantly unfaithful to her. He was a drunkard. I gave him a chance to mend his ways, but he wouldn't take it. He laughed at me."

Davidson's voice fell to a deep bass as he said the last words, and he was silent for a minute or two. The silence was heavy with menace.

"In two years he was a ruined man. He'd lost everything he'd saved in a quarter of a century. I broke him, and at last he was forced to come to me like a beggar and beseech me to give him a passage back to Sydney."

"I wish you could have seen him when he came to see Mr. Davidson," said the missionary's wife. "He had been a fine, powerful man, with a lot of fat on him, and he had a great big voice, but now he was half the size, and he was shaking all over. He'd suddenly become an old man."

With abstracted gaze Davidson looked out into the night. The rain was falling again.

Suddenly from below came a sound, and Davidson turned and looked questioningly at his wife. It was the sound of a gramophone, harsh and loud, wheezing out a syncopated tune.

"What's that?" he asked.

Mrs. Davidson fixed her *pince-nez* more firmly on her nose.

"One of the second-class passengers has a room in the house. I guess it comes from there."

They listened in silence, and presently they heard the sound of dancing. Then the music stopped, and they heard the popping of corks and voices raised in animated conversation.

"I daresay she's giving a farewell party to her friends on board," said Dr. Macphail. "The ship sails at twelve, doesn't it?"

Davidson made no remark, but he looked at his watch.

"Are you ready?" he asked his wife.

She got up and folded her work.

"Yes, I guess I am," she answered.

"It's early to go to bed yet, isn't it?" said the doctor.

"We have a good deal of reading to do," explained Mrs. Davidson. "Wherever we are, we read a chapter of the Bible before retiring for the night and we study it with the commentaries, you know, and discuss it thoroughly. It's a wonderful training for the mind."

The two couples bade one another good night. Dr. and Mrs. Macphail were left alone. For two or three minutes they did not speak.

"I think I'll go and fetch the cards," the doctor said at last.

Mrs. Macphail looked at him doubtfully. Her conversation with the Davidsons had left her a little uneasy, but she did not like to say that she thought they had better not play cards when the Davidsons might come in at any moment. Dr. Macphail brought them and she watched him, though with a vague sense of guilt, while he laid out his patience. Below, the sound of revelry continued.

It was fine enough next day, and the Macphails, condemned to spend a fortnight of idleness at Pago-Pago, set about making the best of things. They went down to the quay and got out of their boxes a number of books. The doctor called on the chief surgeon of the naval hospital and went round the beds with him. They left cards on the governor. They passed Miss Thompson on the road. The doctor took off his hat, and she gave him a "Good morning, doc," in a loud, cheerful voice. She was dressed as on the day before, in a white frock, and her shiny white boots with their high heels, her fat legs bulging over the tops of them, were strange things on that exotic scene.

"I don't think she's very suitably dressed, I must say," said Mrs. Macphail. "She looks extremely common to me."

When they got back to their house, she was on the verandah playing with one of the trader's dark children.

"Say a word to her," Dr. Macphail whispered to his wife. "She's all alone here, and it seems rather unkind to ignore her."

Mrs. Macphail was shy, but she was in the habit of doing what her husband bade her.

"I think we're fellow lodgers here," she said, rather foolishly.

"Terrible, ain't it, bein' cooped up in a one-horse burg like this?" answered Miss Thompson. "And they tell me I'm lucky to have gotten a room. I don't see myself livin' in a native house, and that's what some have to do. I don't know why they don't have a hotel."

They exchanged a few more words. Miss Thompson, loud-voiced and garrulous, was evidently quite willing to gossip, but Mrs. Macphail had a poor stock of small talk and presently she said:

"Well, I think we must go upstairs."

In the evening when they sat down to their high-tea Davidson on coming in said:

"I see that woman downstairs has a couple of sailors sitting there. I wonder how she's gotten acquainted with them."

"She can't be very particular," said Mrs. Davidson.

They were all rather tired after the idle, aimless day.

"If there's going to be a fortnight of this I don't know what we shall feel like at the end of it," said Dr. Macphail.

"The only thing to do is to portion out the day to different activities," answered the missionary. "I shall set aside a certain number of hours to study and a certain number to exercise, rain or fine—in the wet season you can't afford to pay any attention to the rain—and a certain number to recreation."

Dr. Macphail looked at his companion with misgiving. Davidson's programme oppressed him. They were eating Hamburger steak again. It seemed the only dish the cook knew how to make. Then below the gramophone began. Davidson started nervously when he heard it, but said nothing. Men's voices floated up. Miss Thompson's guests were joining in a well-known song and presently they heard her voice too, hoarse and loud. There was a good deal of shouting and laughing.

The four people upstairs, trying to make conversation, listened despite themselves to the clink of glasses and the scrape of chairs. More people had evidently come. Miss Thompson was giving a party.

"I wonder how she gets them all in," said Mrs. Macphail, suddenly breaking into a medical conversation between the missionary and her husband.

It showed whither her thoughts were wandering. The twitch of Davidson's face proved that, though he spoke of scientific things, his mind was busy in the same direction. Suddenly, while the doctor was giving some experience of practice on the Flanders front, rather prosily, he sprang to his feet with a cry.

"What's the matter, Alfred?" asked Mrs. Davidson.

"Of course! It never occurred to me. She's out of Iwelei."

"She can't be."

"She came on board at Honolulu. It's obvious. And she's carrying on her trade here. Here."

He uttered the last word with a passion of indignation.

"What's Iwelei?" asked Mrs. Macphail.

He turned his gloomy eyes on her and his voice trembled with horror.

"The plague spot of Honolulu. The Red Light district. It was a blot on our civilisation."

Iwelei was on the edge of the city. You went down side streets by the harbour, in the darkness, across a rickety bridge, till you came to a deserted road, all ruts and holes, and then suddenly you came out into the light. There was parking room for motors on each side of the road, and there were saloons, tawdry and bright, each one noisy with its mechanical piano, and there were barbers' shops and tobacconists. There was a stir in the air and a sense of expectant gaiety. You turned down a narrow alley, either to the right or to the left, for the road divided Iwelei into two parts, and you found yourself in the district. There were rows of little bungalows, trim and neatly painted in green, and the pathway between them was broad and straight. It was laid out like a garden-city. In its respect-able regularity, its order and spruceness, it gave an impression of sardonic horror; for never can the search for love have been so systematised and ordered. The pathways were lit by a rare lamp, but they would have been dark except for the lights that came from the open windows of the bungalows. Men wandered about, looking at the women who sat at their windows, reading or sewing, for the most part taking no notice of the passers-by; and like the women they were of all nationalities. There were Americans, sailors from the ships in port, enlisted men off the gunboats, sombrely drunk, and soldiers from the regiments, white and black, quartered on the island; there were Japanese, walking in twos and threes; Hawaiians, Chinese in long robes, and Filipinos in preposterous hats. They were silent and as it were oppressed. Desire is sad.

"It was the most crying scandal of the Pacific," exclaimed Davidson vehemently. "The missionaries had been agitating against it for years, and at last the local press took it up. The police refused to stir. You know their argument. They say that vice is inevitable and consequently the best thing is to localise and control it. The truth is, they were paid. Paid. They were paid by the saloon-keepers, paid by the bullies, paid by the women themselves. At last they were forced to move."

"I read about it in the papers that came on board in Honolulu," said Dr. Macphail.

"Iwelei, with its sin and shame, ceased to exist on the very day we arrived. The whole population was brought before the justices. I don't know why I didn't understand at once what that woman was."

"Now you come to speak of it," said Mrs. Macphail, "I remember seeing her come on board only a few minutes before the boat sailed. I remember thinking at the time she was cutting it rather fine."

"How dare she come here!" cried Davidson indignantly. "I'm not going to allow it."

He strode towards the door.

"What are you going to do?" asked Macphail.

"What do you expect me to do? I'm going to stop it. I'm not going to have this house turned into—into . . ."

He sought for a word that should not offend the ladies' ears.

His eyes were flashing and his pale face was paler still in his emotion.

"It sounds as though there were three or four men down there," said the doctor. "Don't you think it's rather rash to go in just now?"

The missionary gave him a contemptuous look and without a word flung out of the room.

"You know Mr. Davidson very little if you think the fear of personal danger can stop him in the performance of his duty," said his wife.

She sat with her hands nervously clasped, a spot of colour on her high cheek bones, listening to what was about to happen below. They all listened. They heard him clatter down the wooden stairs and throw open the door. The singing stopped suddenly, but the gramophone continued to bray out its vulgar tune. They heard Davidson's voice and then the noise of something heavy falling. The music stopped. He had hurled the gramophone on the floor. Then again they heard Davidson's voice, they could not make out the words, then Miss Thompson's, loud and shrill, then a confused clamor as though several people were shouting together at the top of their lungs. Mrs. Davidson gave a little gasp, and she clenched her hands more tightly. Dr. Macphail looked uncertainly from her to his wife. He did not want to go down, but he wondered if they expected him to. Then there was something that sounded like a scuffle. The noise now was more distinct. It might be that Davidson was being thrown out of the room. The door was slammed. There was a moment's silence and they heard Davidson come up the stairs again. He went to his room.

"I think I'll go to him," said Mrs. Davidson.

She got up and went out.

"If you want me, just call," said Mrs. Macphail, and then when the other was gone: "I hope he isn't hurt."

"Why couldn't he mind his own business?" said Dr. Macphail.

They sat in silence for a minute or two and then they both started, for the gramophone began to play once more, defiantly, and mocking voices shouted hoarsely the words of an obscene song.

Next day Mrs. Davidson was pale and tired. She complained of headache, and she looked old and wizened. She told Mrs. Macphail that the missionary had not slept at all; he had passed the night in a state of frightful agitation and at five had got up and gone out. A glass of beer had been thrown over him and his clothes were stained and stinking. But a sombre fire glowed in Mrs. Davidson's eyes when she spoke of Miss Thompson.

"She'll bitterly rue the day when she flouted Mr. Davidson," she said. "Mr. Davidson has a wonderful heart and no one who is in trouble has ever gone to him without being comforted, but he has no mercy for sin, and when his righteous wrath is excited he's terrible."

"Why, what will he do?" asked Mrs. Macphail.

"I don't know, but I wouldn't stand in that creature's shoes for anything in the world."

Mrs. Macphail shuddered. There was something positively alarming in the triumphant assurance of the little woman's manner. They were going out together that morning, and they went down the stairs side by side. Miss Thompson's door was open, and they saw her in a bedraggled dressing-gown, cooking something in a chafing-dish.

"Good morning," she called. "Is Mr. Davidson better this morning?"

They passed her in silence, with their noses in the air, as if she did not exist. They flushed, however, when she burst into a shout of derisive laughter. Mrs. Davidson turned on her suddenly.

"Don't you dare to speak to me," she screamed. "If you insult me I shall have you turned out of here."

"Say, did I ask Mr. Davidson to visit with me?"

"Don't answer her," whispered Mrs. Macphail hurriedly. They walked on till they were out of earshot.

"She's brazen, brazen," burst from Mrs. Davidson.

Her anger almost suffocated her.

And on their way home they met her strolling towards the

quay. She had all her finery on. Her great white hat with its vulgar, showy flowers was an affront. She called out cheerily to them as she went by, and a couple of American sailors who were standing there grinned as the ladies set their faces to an icy stare. They got in just before the rain began to fall again.

"I guess she'll get her fine clothes spoilt," said Mrs. Davidson with a bitter sneer.

Davidson did not come in till they were half way through dinner. He was wet through, but he would not change. He sat, morose and silent, refusing to eat more than a mouthful, and he stared at the slanting rain. When Mrs. Davidson told him of their two encounters with Miss Thompson he did not answer. His deepening frown alone showed that he had heard.

"Don't you think we ought to make Mr. Horn turn her out of here?" asked Mrs. Davidson. "We can't allow her to insult us."

"There doesn't seem to be any other place for her to go," said Macphail.

"She can live with one of the natives."

"In weather like this a native hut must be a rather uncomfortable place to live in."

"I lived in one for years," said the missionary.

When the little native girl brought in the fried bananas which formed the sweet they had every day, Davidson turned to her.

"Ask Miss Thompson when it would be convenient for me to see her," he said.

The girl nodded shyly and went out.

"What do you want to see her for, Alfred?" asked his wife.

"It's my duty to see her. I won't act till I've given her every chance."

"You don't know what she is. She'll insult you."

"Let her insult me. Let her spit on me. She has an immortal soul, and I must do all that is in my power to save it."

Mrs. Davidson's ears rang still with the harlot's mocking laughter.

"She's gone too far."

"Too far for the mercy of God?" His eyes lit up suddenly and his voice grew mellow and soft. "Never. The sinner may be deeper in sin than the depth of hell itself, but the love of the Lord Jesus can reach him still."

The girl came back with the message.

"Miss Thompson's compliments and as long as Rev. Davidson didn't come in business hours she'll be glad to see him any time."

The party received it in stony silence, and Dr. Macphail quickly effaced from his lips the smile which had come upon them. He knew his wife would be vexed with him if he found Miss Thompson's effrontery amusing.

They finished the meal in silence. When it was over the two ladies got up and took their work, Mrs. Macphail was making another of the innumerable comforters which she had turned out since the beginning of the war, and the doctor lit his pipe. But Davidson remained in his chair and with abstracted eyes stared at the table. At last he got up and without a word went out of the room. They heard him go down and they heard Miss Thompson's defiant "Come in" when he knocked at the door. He remained with her for an hour. And Dr. Macphail watched the rain. It was beginning to get on his nerves. It was not like our soft English rain that drops gently on the earth; it was unmerciful and somehow terrible; you felt in it the malignancy of the primitive powers of nature. It did not pour, it flowed. It was like a deluge from heaven, and it rattled on the roof of corrugated iron with a steady persistence that was maddening. It seemed to have a fury of its own. And sometimes you felt that you must scream if it did not stop, and then suddenly you felt powerless, as though your bones had suddenly become soft; and you were miserable and hopeless.

Macphail turned his head when the missionary came back. The two women looked up.

"I've given her every chance. I have exhorted her to repent. She is an evil woman." .

He paused, and Dr. Macphail saw his eyes darken and his pale face grow hard and stern.

"Now I shall take the whips with which the Lord Jesus drove the usurers and the money changers out of the Temple of the Most High."

He walked up and down the room. His mouth was close set, and his black brows were frowning.

"If she fled to the uttermost parts of the earth I should pursue her."

With a sudden movement he turned round and strode out of the room. They heard him go downstairs again.

"What is he going to do?" asked Mrs. Macphail.

"I don't know." Mrs. Davidson took off her *pince-nez* and wiped them. "When he is on the Lord's work I never ask him questions."

She sighed a little.

"What is the matter?"

"He'll wear himself out. He doesn't know what it is to spare himself."

Dr. Macphail learnt the first results of the missionary's activity from the half-caste trader in whose house they lodged. He stopped the doctor when he passed the store and came out to speak to him on the stoop. His fat face was worried.

"The Rev. Davidson has been at me for letting Miss Thompson have a room here," he said, "but I didn't know what she was when I rented it to her. When people come and ask if I can rent them a room all I want to know is if they've the money to pay for it. And she paid me for hers a week in advance."

Dr. Macphail did not want to commit himself.

"When all's said and done it's your house. We're very much obliged to you for taking us in at all."

Horn looked at him doubtfully. He was not certain yet how definitely Macphail stood on the missionary's side.

"The missionaries are in with one another," he said, hesitatingly. "If they get it in for a trader he may just as well shut up his store and quit."

"Did he want you to turn her out?"

"No, he said so long as she behaved herself he couldn't ask me to do that. He said he wanted to be just to me. I promised she shouldn't have no more visitors. I've just been and told her."

"How did she take it?"

"She gave me Hell."

The trader squirmed in his old ducks. He had found Miss Thompson a rough customer.

"Oh, well, I daresay she'll get out. I don't suppose she wants to stay here if she can't have anyone in."

"There's nowhere she can go, only a native house, and no native'll take her now, not now that the missionaries have got their knife in her."

Dr. Macphail looked at the falling rain.

"Well, I don't suppose it's any good waiting for it to clear up."

In the evening when they sat in the parlour Davidson talked to them of his early days at college. He had had no means and had worked his way through by doing odd jobs during the vacations. There was silence downstairs. Miss Thompson was sitting in her little room alone. But suddenly the gramophone began to play. She had set it on in defiance, to cheat her loneliness, but there was no one to sing, and it had a melancholy note. It was like a cry for help. Davidson took no notice. He was in the middle of a long anecdote and without change of expression went on. The gramophone continued. Miss Thompson put on one reel after another. It looked as though the silence of the night were getting on her nerves. It was breathless and sultry. When the Macphails went to bed they could not sleep. They lay side by side with their eyes wide open, listening to the cruel singing of the mosquitoes outside their curtain.

"What's that?" whispered Mrs. Macphail at last.

They heard a voice, Davidson's voice, through the wooden partition. It went on with a monotonous, earnest insistence. He was praying aloud. He was praying for the soul of Miss Thompson.

Two or three days went by. Now when they passed Miss Thompson on the road she did not greet them with ironic cordiality or smile; she passed with her nose in the air, a sulky look on her painted face, frowning, as though she did not see them. The trader told Macphail that she had tried to get lodging elsewhere, but had failed. In the evening she played through the various reels of her gramophone, but the pretence of mirth was obvious now. The ragtime had a cracked, heart-broken rhythm as though it were a one-step of despair. When she began to play on Sunday Davidson sent Horn to beg her to stop at once since it was the Lord's day. The reel was taken off and the house was silent except for the steady pattering of the rain on the iron roof.

"I think she's getting a bit worked up," said the trader next day to Macphail. "She don't know what Mr. Davidson's up to and it makes her scared."

Macphail had caught a glimpse of her that morning and it struck him that her arrogant expression had changed. There was in her face a hunted look. The half-caste gave him a sidelong glance.

"I suppose you don't know what Mr. Davidson is doing about it?" he hazarded.

"No, I don't."

It was singular that Horn should ask him that question, for he also had the idea that the missionary was mysteriously at work. He had an impression that he was weaving a net around the woman, carefully, systematically, and suddenly, when everything was ready would pull the strings tight.

"He told me to tell her," said the trader, "that if at any time she wanted him she only had to send and he'd come."

"What did she say when you told her that?"

"She didn't say nothing. I didn't stop. I just said what he said I was to and then I beat it. I thought she might be going to start weepin'."

"I have no doubt the loneliness is getting on her nerves," said the doctor. "And the rain—that's enough to make anyone jumpy," he continued irritably. "Doesn't it ever stop in this confounded place?"

"It goes on pretty steady in the rainy season. We have three hundred inches in the year. You see, it's the shape of the bay. It seems to attract the rain from all over the Pacific."

"Damn the shape of the bay," said the doctor.

He scratched his mosquito bites. He felt very short-tempered. When the rain stopped and the sun shone, it was like a hot-house, seething, humid, sultry, breathless, and you had a strange feeling that everything was growing with a savage violence. The natives, blithe and childlike by reputation, seemed then, with their tattooing and their dyed hair, to have something sinister in their appearance; and when they pattered along at your heels with their naked feet you looked back instinctively. You felt they might at any moment come behind you swiftly and thrust a long knife between your shoulder blades. You could not tell what dark thoughts lurked behind their wide-set eyes. They had a little the look of ancient Egyptians painted on a temple wall, and there was about them the terror of what is immeasurably old.

The missionary came and went. He was busy, but the Macphails did not know what he was doing. Horn told the doctor that he saw the governor every day, and once Davidson mentioned him.

"He looks as if he had plenty of determination," he said, "but when you come down to brass tacks he has no backbone."

"I suppose that means he won't do exactly what you want," suggested the doctor facetiously.

The missionary did not smile.

"I want him to do what's right. It shouldn't be necessary to persuade a man to do that."

"But there may be differences of opinion about what is right."

"If a man had a gangrenous foot would you have patience with anyone who hesitated to amputate it?"

"Gangrene is a matter of fact."

"And Evil?"

What Davidson had done soon appeared. The four of them had just finished their midday meal, and they had not yet separated for the siesta which the heat imposed on the ladies and on the doctor. Davidson had little patience with the slothful habit. The door was suddenly flung open and Miss Thompson came in. She looked round the room and then went up to Davidson.

"You low-down skunk, what have you been saying about me to the governor?"

She was spluttering with rage. There was a moment's pause. Then the missionary drew forward a chair.

"Won't you be seated, Miss Thompson? I've been hoping to have another talk with you."

"You poor low-life bastard."

She burst into a torrent of insult, foul and insolent. Davidson kept his grave eyes on her.

"I'm indifferent to the abuse you think fit to heap on me, Miss Thompson," he said, "but I must beg you to remember that ladies are present."

Tears by now were struggling with her anger. Her face was red and swollen as though she were choking.

"What has happened?" asked Dr. Macphail.

"A feller's just been in here and he says I gotter beat it on the next boat."

Was there a gleam in the missionary's eyes? His face remained impassive.

"You could hardly expect the governor to let you stay here under the circumstances."

"You done it," she shrieked. "You can't kid me. You done it."

"I don't want to deceive you. I urged the governor to take the only possible step consistent with his obligations."

"Why couldn't you leave me be? I wasn't doin' you no harm."

"You may be sure that if you had I should be the last man to resent it."

"Do you think I want to stay on in this poor imitation of a burg? I don't look no busher, do I?"

"In that case I don't see what cause of complaint you have," he answered.

She gave an inarticulate cry of rage and flung out of the room. There was a short silence.

"It's a relief to know that the governor has acted at last," said Davidson finally. "He's a weak man and he shilly-shallied. He said she was only here for a fortnight anyway, and if she went on to Apia that was under British jurisdiction and had nothing to do with him."

The missionary sprang to his feet and strode across the room.

"It's terrible the way the men who are in authority seek to evade their responsibility. They speak as though evil that was out of sight ceased to be evil. The very existence of that woman is a scandal and it does not help matters to shift it to another of the islands. In the end I had to speak straight from the shoulder."

Davidson's brow lowered, and he protruded his firm chin. He looked fierce and determined.

"What do you mean by that?"

"Our mission is not entirely without influence at Washington. I pointed out to the governor that it wouldn't do him any good if there was a complaint about the way he managed things here."

"When has she got to go?" asked the doctor, after a pause.

"The San Francisco boat is due here from Sydney next Tuesday. She's to sail on that."

That was in five day's time. It was next day, when he was coming back from the hospital where for want of something better to do Macphail spent most of his mornings, that the half-caste stopped him as he was going upstairs.

"Excuse me, Dr. Macphail, Miss Thompson's sick. Will you have a look at her?"

"Certainly."

Horn led him to her room. She was sitting in a chair idly, neither reading nor sewing, staring in front of her. She wore her white dress and the large hat with the flowers on it. Macphail noticed that her skin was yellow and muddy under her powder, and her eyes were heavy.

"I'm sorry to hear you're not well," he said.

"Oh, I ain't sick really. I just said that, because I just had to see you. I've got to clear on a boat that's going to 'Frisco."

She looked at him and he saw that her eyes were suddenly startled. She opened and clenched her hands spasmodically. The trader stood at the door, listening.

"So I understand," said the doctor.

She gave a little gulp.

"I guess it ain't very convenient for me to go to 'Frisco just now. I went to see the governor yesterday afternoon, but I couldn't get to him. I saw the secretary, and he told me I'd got to take that boat and that was all there was to it. I just had to see the governor, so I waited outside his house this morning, and when he come out I spoke to him. He didn't want to speak to me, I'll say, but I wouldn't let him shake me off, and at last he said he hadn't no objection to my staying here till the next boat to Sydney if the Rev. Davidson will stand for it."

She stopped and looked at Dr. Macphail anxiously.

"I don't know exactly what I can do," he said.

"Well, I thought maybe you wouldn't mind asking him. I swear to God I won't start anything here if he'll just only let me stay. I won't go out of the house if that'll suit him. It's no more'n a fortnight."

"I'll ask him."

"He won't stand for it," said Horn. "He'll have you out on Tuesday, so you may as well make up your mind to it."

"Tell him I can get work in Sydney, straight stuff, I mean. 'Tain't asking very much."

"I'll do what I can."

"And come and tell me right away, will you? I can't set down to a thing till I get the dope one way or the other."

It was not an errand that much pleased the doctor, and, characteristically perhaps, he went about it indirectly. He told his wife what Miss Thompson had said to him and asked her to speak to Mrs. Davidson. The missionary's attitude seemed rather arbitrary and it could do no harm if the girl were allowed to stay in Pago-Pago another fortnight. But he was not prepared for the result of his diplomacy. The missionary came to him straightway.

"Mrs. Davidson tells me that Thompson has been speaking to you."

Dr. Macphail, thus directly tackled, had the shy man's resentment at being forced out into the open. He felt his temper rising, and he flushed.

"I don't see that it can make any difference if she goes to Sydney rather than to San Francisco, and so long as she promises to behave while she's here it's dashed hard to persecute her."

The missionary fixed him with his stern eyes.

"Why is she unwilling to go back to San Francisco?"

"I didn't enquire," answered the doctor with some asperity.

"And I think one does better to mind one's own business."

Perhaps it was not a very tactful answer.

"The governor has ordered her to be deported by the first boat that leaves the island. He's only done his duty and I will not interfere. Her presence is a peril here."

"I think you're very harsh and tyrannical."

The two ladies looked up at the doctor with some alarm, but they need not have feared a quarrel, for the missionary smiled gently.

"I'm terribly sorry you should think that of me, Dr. Macphail. Believe me, my heart bleeds for that unfortunate woman, but I'm only trying to do my duty."

The doctor made no answer. He looked out of the window sullenly. For once it was not raining and across the bay you saw nestling among the trees the huts of a native village.

"I think I'll take advantage of the rain stopping to go out," he said.

"Please don't bear me malice because I can't accede to your wish," said Davidson, with a melancholy smile. "I respect you very much, doctor, and I should be sorry if you thought ill of me."

"I have no doubt you have a sufficiently good opinion of yourself to bear mine with equanimity," he retorted.

"That's one on me," chuckled Davidson.

When Dr. Macphail, vexed with himself because he had been uncivil to no purpose, went downstairs, Miss Thompson was waiting for him with her door ajar.

"Well," she said, "have you spoken to him?"

"Yes, I'm sorry, he won't do anything," he answered, not looking at her in his embarrassment.

But then he gave her a quick glance, for a sob broke from her. He saw that her face was white with fear. It gave him a shock of dismay. And suddenly he had an idea.

"But don't give up hope yet. I think it's a shame the way they're treating you and I'm going to see the governor myself."

"Now?"

He nodded. Her face brightened.

"Say, that's real good of you. I'm sure he'll let me stay if you speak for me. I just won't do a thing I didn't ought all the time I'm here."

Dr. Macphail hardly knew why he had made up his mind to appeal to the governor. He was perfectly indifferent to Miss Thompson's affairs, but the missionary had irritated him, and with him temper was a smouldering thing. He found the governor at home. He was a large, handsome man, a sailor, with a grey toothbrush moustache; and he wore a spotless uniform of white drill.

"I've come to see you about a woman who's lodging in the same house as we are," he said. "Her name's Thompson."

"I guess I've heard nearly enough about her, Dr. Macphail," said the governor, smiling. "I've given her the order to get out next Tuesday and that's all I can do."

"I wanted to ask you if you couldn't stretch a point and let her stay here till the boat comes in from San Francisco so that she can go to Sydney. I will guarantee her good behavior."

The governor continued to smile, but his eyes grew small and serious.

"I'd be very glad to oblige you, Dr. Macphail, but I've given the order and it must stand."

The doctor put the case as reasonably as he could, but now the governor ceased to smile at all. He listened sullenly, with averted gaze. Macphail saw that he was making no impression.

"I'm sorry to cause any lady inconvenience, but she'll have to sail on Tuesday and that's all there is to it."

"But what difference can it make?"

"Pardon me, doctor, but I don't feel called upon to explain my official actions except to the proper authorities."

Macphail looked at him shrewdly. He remembered Davidson's hint that he had used threats, and in the governor's attitude he read a singular embarrassment.

"Davidson's a damned busybody," he said hotly.

"Between ourselves, Dr. Macphail, I don't say that I have formed a very favorable opinion of Mr. Davidson, but I am bound to confess that he was within his rights in pointing out to me the danger that the presence of a woman of Miss Thomp-

son's character was to a place like this where a number of enlisted men are stationed among a native population."

He got up and Dr. Macphail was obliged to do so too.

"I must ask you to excuse me. I have an engagement. Please
give my respects to Mrs. Macphail."

The doctor left him crest-fallen. He knew that Miss Thompson would be waiting for him, and unwilling to tell her himself
that he had failed, he went into the house by the back door and
sneaked up the stairs as though he had something to hide.

At supper he was silent and ill-at-ease, but the missionary
was jovial and animated. Dr. Macphail thought his eyes rested
on him now and then with triumphant good-humour. It struck
him suddenly that Davidson knew of his visit to the governor
and of its ill success. But how on earth could he have heard
of it? There was something sinister about the power of that
man. After supper he saw Horn on the verandah and, as though
to have a casual word with him, went out.

"She wants to know if you've seen the governor," the trader
whispered.

"Yes. He wouldn't do anything. I'm awfully sorry, I can't
do anything more."

"I knew he wouldn't. They daren't go against the missionaries."

"What are you talking about?" said Davidson affably, coming out to join them.

"I was just saying there was no chance of your getting over
to Apia for at least another week," said the trader glibly.

He left them, and the two men returned into the parlour.
Mr. Davidson devoted one hour after each meal to recreation.
Presently a timid knock was heard at the door.

"Come in," said Mrs. Davidson, in her sharp voice.

The door was not opened. She got up and opened it. They
saw Miss Thompson standing at the threshold. But the change
in her appearance was extraordinary. This was no longer the
flaunting hussy who had jeered at them in the road, but a
broken, frightened woman. Her hair, as a rule so elaborately
arranged, was tumbling untidily over her neck. She wore bedroom slippers and a skirt and blouse. They were unfresh and

bedraggled. She stood at the door with the tears streaming down her face and did not dare to enter.

"What do you want?" said Mrs. Davidson harshly.

"May I speak to Mr. Davidson?" she said in a choking voice.

The missionary rose and went towards her.

"Come right in, Miss Thompson," he said in cordial tones. "What can I do for you?"

She entered the room.

"Say, I'm sorry for what I said to you the other day an' for —for everythin' else. I guess I was a bit lit up. I beg pardon."

"Oh, it was nothing. I guess my back's broad enough to bear a few hard words."

She stepped towards him with a movement that was horribly cringing.

"You've got me beat. I'm all in. You won't make me go back to 'Frisco?"

His genial manner vanished and his voice grew on a sudden hard and stern.

"Why don't you want to go back there?"

She cowered before him.

"I guess my people live there. I don't want them to see me like this. I'll go anywhere else you say."

"Why don't you want to go back to San Francisco?"

"I've told you."

He leaned forward, staring at her, and his great, shining eyes seemed to try to bore into her soul. He gave a sudden gasp.

"The penitentiary."

She screamed, and then she fell at his feet, clasping his legs.

"Don't send me back there. I swear to you before God I'll be a good woman. I'll give all this up."

She burst into a torrent of confused supplication and the tears coursed down her painted cheeks. He leaned over her and, lifting her face, forced her to look at him.

"Is that it, the penitentiary?"

"I beat it before they could get me," she gasped. "If the bulls grab me it's three years for mine."

He let go his hold of her and she fell in a heap on the floor, sobbing bitterly. Dr. Macphail stood up.

"This alters the whole thing," he said. "You can't make her go back when you know this. Give her another chance. She wants to turn over a new leaf."

"I'm going to give her the finest chance she's ever had. If she repents let her accept her punishment."

She misunderstood the words and looked up. There was a gleam of hope in her heavy eyes.

"You'll let me go?"

"No. You shall sail for San Francisco on Tuesday."

She gave a groan of horror and then burst into low, hoarse shrieks which sounded hardly human, and she beat her head passionately on the ground. Dr. Macphail sprang to her and lifted her up.

"Come on, you mustn't do that. You'd better go to your room and lie down. I'll get you something."

He raised her to her feet and partly dragging her, partly carrying her, got her downstairs. He was furious with Mrs. Davidson and with his wife because they made no effort to help. The half-caste was standing on the landing and with his assistance he managed to get her on the bed. She was moaning and crying. She was almost insensible. He gave her a hypodermic injection. He was hot and exhausted when he went upstairs again.

"I've got her to lie down."

The two women and Davidson were in the same position as when he had left them. They could not have moved or spoken since he went.

"I was waiting for you," said Davidson, in a strange, distant voice. "I want you all to pray with me for the soul of our erring sister."

He took the Bible off a shelf, and sat down at the table at which they had supped. It had not been cleared, and he pushed the tea-pot out of the way. In a powerful voice, resonant and deep, he read to them the chapter in which is narrated the meeting of Jesus Christ with the woman taken in adultery.

"Now kneel with me and let us pray for the soul of our dear sister, Sadie Thompson."

He burst into a long, passionate prayer in which he implored

God to have mercy on the sinful woman. Mrs. Macphail and Mrs. Davidson knelt with covered eyes. The doctor, taken by surprise, awkward and sheepish, knelt too. The missionary's prayer had a savage eloquence. He was extraordinarily moved, and as he spoke the tears ran down his cheeks. Outside, the pitiless rain fell, fell steadily, with a fierce malignity that was all too human.

At last he stopped. He paused for a moment and said:

"We will now repeat the Lord's prayer."

They said it and then, following him, they rose from their knees. Mrs. Davidson's face was pale and restful. She was comforted and at peace, but the Macphails felt suddenly bashful. They did not know which way to look.

"I'll just go down and see how she is now," said Dr. Macphail.

When he knocked at her door it was opened for him by Horn. Miss Thompson was in a rocking-chair, sobbing quietly.

"What are you doing there?" exclaimed Macphail. "I told you to lie down."

"I can't lie down. I want to see Mr. Davidson."

"My poor child, what do you think is the good of it? You'll never move him."

"He said he'd come if I sent for him."

Macphail motioned to the trader.

"Go and fetch him."

He waited with her in silence while the trader went upstairs. Davidson came in.

"Excuse me for asking you to come here," she said, looking at him sombrely.

"I was expecting you to send for me. I knew the Lord would answer my prayer."

They stared at one another for a moment and then she looked away. She kept her eyes averted when she spoke.

"I've been a bad woman. I want to repent."

"Thank God! Thank God! He has heard our prayers."

He turned to the two men.

"Leave me alone with her. Tell Mrs. Davidson that our prayers have been answered."

They went out and closed the door behind them.

"Gee whizz," said the trader.

That night Dr. Macphail could not get to sleep till late, and when he heard the missionary come upstairs he looked at his watch. It was two o'clock. But even then he did not go to bed at once, for through the wooden partition that separated their rooms he heard him praying aloud, till he himself, exhausted, fell asleep.

When he saw him next morning he was surprised at his appearance. He was paler than ever, tired, but his eyes shone with an inhuman fire. It looked as though he were filled with an overwhelming joy.

"I want you to go down presently and see Sadie," he said. "I can't hope that her body is better, but her soul—her soul is transformed."

The doctor was feeling wan and nervous.

"You were with her very late last night," he said.

"Yes, she couldn't bear to have me leave her."

"You look as pleased as Punch," the doctor said irritably.

Davidson's eyes shone with ecstasy.

"A great mercy has been vouchsafed me. Last night I was privileged to bring a lost soul to the loving arms of Jesus."

Miss Thompson was again in the rocking-chair. The bed had not been made. The room was in disorder. She had not troubled to dress herself, but wore a dirty dressing-gown, and her hair was tied in a sluttish knot. She had given her face a dab with a wet towel, but it was all swollen and creased with crying. She looked a drab.

She raised her eyes dully when the doctor came in. She was cowed and broken.

"Where's Mr. Davidson?" she asked.

"He'll come presently if you want him," answered Macphail acidly. "I came here to see how you were."

"Oh, I guess I'm O. K. You needn't worry about that."

"Have you had anything to eat?"

"Horn brought me some coffee."

She looked anxiously at the door.

"D'you think he'll come down soon? I feel as if it wasn't so terrible when he's with me."

"Are you still going on Tuesday?"

"Yes, he says I've got to go. Please tell him to come right along. You can't do me any good. He's the only one as can help me now."

"Very well," said Dr. Macphail.

During the next three days the missionary spent almost all his time with Sadie Thompson. He joined the others only to have his meals. Dr. Macphail noticed that he hardly ate.

"He's wearing himself out," said Mrs. Davidson pitifully. "He'll have a breakdown if he doesn't take care, but he won't spare himself."

She herself was white and pale. She told Mrs. Macphail that she had no sleep. When the missionary came upstairs from Miss Thompson he prayed till he was exhausted, but even then he did not sleep for long. After an hour or two he got up and dressed himself, and went for a tramp along the bay. He had strange dreams.

"This morning he told me that he'd been dreaming about the mountains of Nebraska," said Mrs. Davidson.

"That's curious," said Dr. Macphail.

He remembered seeing them from the windows of the train when he crossed America. They were like huge mole-hills, rounded and smooth, and they rose from the plain abruptly. Dr. Macphail remembered how it struck him that they were like a woman's breasts.

Davidson's restlessness was intolerable even to himself. But he was buoyed up by a wonderful exhilaration. He was tearing out by the roots the last vestiges of sin that lurked in the hidden corners of that poor woman's heart. He read with her and prayed with her.

"It's wonderful," he said to them one day at supper. "It's a true rebirth. Her soul, which was black as night, is now pure and white like the new-fallen snow. I am humble and afraid. Her remorse for all her sins is beautiful. I am not worthy to touch the hem of her garment."

"Have you the heart to send her back to San Francisco?" said the doctor. "Three years in an American prison. I should have thought you might have saved her from that?"

"Ah, but don't you see? It's necessary. Do you think my heart doesn't bleed for her? I love her as I love my wife and my sister. All the time that she is in prison I shall suffer all the pain that she suffers."

"Bunkum," cried the doctor impatiently.

"You don't understand because you're blind. She's sinned, and she must suffer. I know what she'll endure. She'll be starved and tortured and humiliated. I want her to accept the punishment of man as a sacrifice to God. I want her to accept it joyfully. She has an opportunity which is offered to very few of us. God is very good and very merciful."

Davidson's voice trembled with excitement. He could hardly articulate the words that tumbled passionately from his lips.

"All day I pray with her and when I leave her I pray again, I pray with all my might and main, so that Jesus may grant her this great mercy. I want to put in her heart the passionate desire to be punished so that at the end, even if I offered to let her go, she would refuse. I want her to feel that the bitter punishment of prison is the thank-offering that she places at the feet of our Blessed Lord, who gave his life for her."

The days passed slowly. The whole household, intent on the wretched, tortured woman downstairs, lived in a state of unnatural excitement. She was like a victim that was being prepared for the savage rites of a bloody idolatry. Her terror numbed her. She could not bear to let Davidson out of her sight; it was only when he was with her that she had courage, and she hung upon him with a slavish dependence. She cried a great deal, and she read the Bible, and prayed. Sometimes she was exhausted and apathetic. Then she did indeed look forward to her ordeal, for it seemed to offer an escape, direct and concrete, from the anguish she was enduring. She could not bear much longer the vague terrors which now assailed her. With her sins she had put aside all personal vanity, and she slopped about her room, unkempt and dishevelled, in her tawdry dressing-gown. She had not taken off her night-dress for four days, nor put on stockings. Her room was littered and untidy. Meanwhile the rain fell with a cruel persistence. You felt that the heavens must at last be empty of water, but still it poured down, straight and heavy, with a maddening iteration, on the iron roof. Everything was damp and clammy. There was mildew on the walls and on the boots that stood on the floor. Through the sleepless nights the mosquitoes droned their angry chant.

"If it would only stop raining for a single day it wouldn't be so sad," said Dr. Macphail.

They all looked forward to the Tuesday when the boat for San Francisco was to arrive from Sydney. The strain was intolerable. So far as Dr. Macphail was concerned, his pity and his resentment were alike extinguished by his desire to be rid of the unfortunate woman. The inevitable must be accepted. He felt he would breathe more freely when the ship had sailed. Sadie Thompson was to be escorted on board by a clerk in the governor's office. This person called on the Monday evening and told Miss Thompson to be prepared at eleven in the morning. Davidson was with her.

"I'll see that everything is ready. I mean to come on board with her myself."

Miss Thompson did not speak.

When Dr. Macphail blew out his candle and crawled cautiously under his mosquito curtains, he gave a sigh of relief.

"Well, thank God that's over. By this time to-morrow she'll be gone."

"Mrs. Davidson will be glad too. She says he's wearing himself to a shadow," said Mrs. Macphail. "She's a different woman."

"Who?"

"Sadie. I should never have thought it possible. It makes one humble."

Dr. Macphail did not answer, and presently he fell asleep. He was tired out, and he slept more soundly than usual.

He was awakened in the morning by a hand placed on his arm, and, starting up, saw Horn by the side of his bed. The trader put his finger on his mouth to prevent any exclamation from Dr. Macphail and beckoned him to come. As a rule he wore shabby ducks, but now he was barefoot and wore only the *lava-lava* of the natives. He looked suddenly savage, and Dr. Macphail, getting out of bed, saw that he was heavily tattooed. Horn made him a sign to come on to the verandah. Dr. Macphail got out of bed and followed the trader out.

"Don't make a noise," he whispered. "You're wanted. Put on a coat and some shoes. Quick."

Dr. Macphail's first thought was that something had happened to Miss Thompson.

"What is it? Shall I bring my instruments?"

"Hurry, please, hurry."

Dr. Macphail crept back into the bedroom, put on a waterproof over his pyjamas, and a pair of rubber-soled shoes. He rejoined the trader, and together they tiptoed down the stairs. The door leading out to the road was open and at it were standing half a dozen natives.

"What is it?" repeated the doctor.

"Come along with me," said Horn.

He walked out and the doctor followed him. The natives came after them in a little bunch. They crossed the road and came on to the beach. The doctor saw a group of natives standing round some object at the water's edge. They hurried along, a couple of dozen yards perhaps, and the natives opened up as the doctor came up. The trader pushed him forwards. Then he saw, lying half in the water and half out, a dreadful object, the body of Davidson. Dr. Macphail bent down—he was not a man to lose his head in an emergency—and turned the body over. The throat was cut from ear to ear, and in the right hand was still the razor with which the deed was done.

"He's quite cold," said the doctor. "He must have been dead some time."

"One of the boys saw him lying there on his way to work just now and came and told me. Do you think he did it himself?"

"Yes. Someone ought to go for the police."

Horn said something in the native tongue, and two youths started off.

"We must leave him here till they come," said the doctor.

"They mustn't take him into my house. I won't have him in my house."

"You'll do what the authorities say," replied the doctor

sharply. "In point of fact I expect they'll take him to the mortuary."

They stood waiting where they were. The trader took a cigarette from a fold in his *lava-lava* and gave one to Dr. Macphail. They smoked while they stared at the corpse. Dr. Macphail could not understand.

"Why do you think he did it?" asked Horn.

The doctor shrugged his shoulders. In a little while native police came along, under the charge of a marine, with a stretcher, and immediately afterwards a couple of naval officers and a naval doctor. They managed everything in a businesslike manner.

"What about the wife?" said one of the officers.

"Now that you've come I'll go back to the house and get some things on. I'll see that it's broken to her. She'd better not see him till he's been fixed up a little."

"I guess that's right," said the naval doctor.

When Dr. Macphail went back he found his wife nearly dressed.

"Mrs. Davidson's in a dreadful state about her husband," she said to him as soon as he appeared. "He hasn't been to bed all night. She heard him leave Miss Thompson's room at two, but he went out. If he's been walking about since then he'll be absolutely dead."

Dr. Macphail told her what had happened and asked her to break the news to Mrs. Davidson.

"But why did he do it?" she asked, horror-stricken.

"I don't know."

"But I can't. I can't."

"You must."

She gave him a frightened look and went out. He heard her go into Mrs. Davidson's room. He waited a minute to gather himself together and then began to shave and wash. When he was dressed he sat down on the bed and waited for his wife. At last she came.

"She wants to see him," she said.

"They've taken him to the mortuary. We'd better go down with her. How did she take it?"

"I think she's stunned. She didn't cry. But she's trembling like a leaf."

"We'd better go at once."

When they knocked at her door Mrs. Davidson came out. She was very pale, but dry-eyed. To the doctor she seemed unnaturally composed. No word was exchanged, and they set out in silence down the road. When they arrived at the mortuary Mrs. Davidson spoke.

"Let me go in and see him alone."

They stood aside. A native opened a door for her and closed it behind her. They sat down and waited. One or two white men came and talked to them in undertones. Dr. Macphail told them again what he knew of the tragedy. At last the door was quietly opened and Mrs. Davidson came out. Silence fell upon them.

"I'm ready to go back now," she said.

Her voice was hard and steady. Dr. Macphail could not understand the look in her eyes. Her pale face was very stern. They walked back slowly, never saying a word, and at last they came round the bend on the other side of which stood their house. Mrs. Davidson gave a gasp, and for a moment they stopped still. An incredible sound assaulted their ears. The gramophone which had been silent for so long was playing, playing ragtime loud and harsh.

"What's that?" cried Mrs. Macphail with horror.

"Let's go on," said Mrs. Davidson.

They walked up the steps and entered the hall. Miss Thompson was standing at her door, chatting with a sailor. A sudden change had taken place in her. She was no longer the cowed drudge of the last days. She was dressed in all her finery, in her white dress, with the shiny boots over which her fat legs bulged in her cotton stockings; her hair was elaborately arranged; and she wore that enormous hat covered with gaudy flowers. Her face was painted, her eyebrows were boldly black, and her lips were scarlet. She held herself erect. She was the flaunting queen that they had known at first. As they came in she broke into a loud, jeering laugh; and then, when Mrs. Davidson involuntarily stopped, she collected the spittle in her mouth and spat. Mrs. Davidson cowered back, and two red spots rose suddenly to her cheeks. Then, covering her face with her hands, she broke away and ran quickly up the stairs. Dr. Macphail was outraged. He pushed past the woman into her room.

"What the devil are you doing?" he cried. "Stop that damned machine."

He went up to it and tore the record off. She turned on him.

"Say, doc, you can that stuff with me. What the hell are you doin' in my room?"

"What do you mean?" he cried. "What d'you mean?"

She gathered herself together. No one could describe the scorn of her expression or the contemptuous hatred she put into her answer.

"You men! You filthy, dirty pigs! You're all the same, all of you. Pigs! Pigs!"

Dr. Macphail gasped. He understood.

W. Somerset Maugham

*

THE VESSEL OF WRATH

THE VESSEL OF WRATH was filmed by the Laughton-Pommer-Mayflower Company of England in 1938. In 1939 the picture was released in the United States as THE BEACH-COMBER by Paramount Pictures. The screenplay adapted by Bartlett Cormack from a version by B. Van Thrall, was directed by Erich Pommer, and starred Charles Laughton and Elsa Lanchester supported by an excellent cast. This film was Laughton's first venture as a producer, and was highly lauded by the critics as one of the foremost pictures of the year.

THERE ARE FEW books in the world that contain more meat than the Sailing Directions published by the Hydrographic Department by order of the Lords Commissioners of the Admiralty. They are handsome volumes, bound (very flimsily) in cloth of different colours, and the most expensive of them is cheap. For four shillings you can buy the Yangtse Kiang Pilot, "containing a description of, and sailing directions for, the Yangtse Kiang from the Wusung River to the highest navigable point, including the Han Kiang, the Kialing Kiang, and the Min Kiang"; and for three shillings you can get Part III of the Eastern Archipelago Pilot, "comprising the N.E. end of Celebes, Molucca and Gilolo passages, Banda and Arafura Seas, and North, West, and South-West coast of New Guinea." But it is not very safe to do so if you are a creature of settled habits that you have no wish to disturb or if you have an occupation that holds you fast to one place. These business-like books take you upon enchanted journeys of the spirit; and their matter-of-fact style, the admirable order, the concision with which the material is set before you, the stern sense of the practical that informs every line, cannot dim the poetry that, like the spice-laden breeze that assails your senses with a more than material languor when you approach some of those magic islands of the Eastern seas, blows with so sweet a fragrance through the printed pages. They tell you the anchorages and the landing places, what supplies you can get at each spot, and where you can get water; they tell you the lights and the buoys, tides, winds and weather that you will find there. They give you brief information about the population and the trade. And it is strange when you think how sedately it is all set down, with no words wasted, that so much else is given you besides. What? Well, mystery and beauty, romance and the glamour of the unknown. It is no common book that offers you casually turning its pages such a paragraph as this: "Supplies. A few jungle fowl are preserved, the island is also the resort of vast numbers of sea birds. Turtle are found in the lagoon, as well as quantities of various fish, including grew mullet, shark, and dog-fish; the seine cannot be used with any effect; but there is a fish which may be taken on a rod. A small store of tinned provisions and spirits is kept in a hut for the relief of shipwrecked persons. Good water may be obtained from a well near the landing place." Can the imagination want more material than this to go on a journey through time and space?

In the volume from which I have copied this passage, the compilers with the same restraint have described the Alas Islands. They are composed of a group or chain of islands, "for the most part low and wooded, extending about 75 miles east and west, and 40 miles north and south." The information about them, you are told, is very slight; there are channels between the different groups, and several vessels have passed through them, but the passages have not been thoroughly explored, and the positions of many of the dangers not yet determined; it is therefore advisable to avoid them. The population of the group is estimated at about 8000, of whom 200 are Chinese and 400 Mohammedans. The rest are heathen. The principal island is called Baru, it is surrounded by a reef, and here lives a Dutch Controleur. His white house with its red roof on the top of a little hill is the most prominent object that the vessels of the Royal Netherlands Steam Packet Company see when every other month on their way up to Macassar and every

four weeks on their way down to Merauke in Dutch New
Guinea they touch at the island.

At a certain moment of the world's history the Controleur
was Mynheer Evert Gruyter and he ruled the people who
inhabited the Alas Islands with firmness tempered by a keen
sense of the ridiculous. He had thought it a very good joke to
be placed at the age of twenty-seven in a position of such con-
sequence and at thirty he was still amused by it. There was
no cable communication between his islands and Batavia, and
the mail arrived after so long a delay that even if he asked
advice, by the time he received it, it was useless, and so he
equably did what he thought best and trusted to his good fortune to keep out of trouble with the authorities. He was very
short, not more than five feet four in height, and extremely
fat; he was of a florid complexion. For coolness' sake he kept
his head shaved and his face was hairless. It was round and
red. His eyebrows were so fair that you hardly saw them; and
he had little twinkling blue eyes. He knew that he had no dignity, but for the sake of his position made up for it by dressing
very dapperly. He never went to his office, nor sat in court,
nor walked abroad but in spotless white. His stengah-shifter,
with its bright brass buttons, fitted him very tightly and dis-
played the shocking fact that, young though he was, he had
a round and protruding belly. His good-humoured face shone
with sweat and he constantly fanned himself with a palm-leaf
fan.

But in his house Mr. Gruyter preferred to wear nothing but a
sarong and then with his white podgy little body he looked like
a fat funny boy of sixteen. He was an early riser and his breakfast was always ready for him at six. It never varied. It consisted of a slice of papaia, three cold fried eggs, Edam cheese,
sliced thin, and a cup of black coffee. When he had eaten it,
he smoked a large Dutch cigar, read the papers if he had not
read them through and through already, and then dressed to
go down to his office.

One morning while he was thus occupied his head boy came
into his bedroom and told him that Tuan Jones wanted to
know if he could see him. Mr. Gruyter was standing in front

of a looking-glass. He had his trousers on and was admiring his smooth chest. He arched his back in order to throw it out and throw in his belly and with a good deal of satisfaction gave his breast three or four resounding slaps. It was a manly chest. When the boy brought the message he looked at his own eyes in the mirror and exchanged a slightly ironic smile with them. He asked himself what the devil his visitor could want. Evert Gruyter spoke English, Dutch and Malay with equal facility, but he thought in Dutch. He liked to do this. It seemed to him a pleasantly ribald language.

"Ask the Tuan to wait and say I shall come directly." He put on his tunic, over his naked body, buttoned it up, and strutted into the sitting-room. The Rev. Owen Jones got up.

"Good-morning, Mr. Jones," said the Controleur. "Have you come into have a peg with me before I start my day's work?"

Mr. Jones did not smile.

"I've come to see you upon a very distressing matter, Mr. Gruyter," he answered.

The Controleur was not disconcerted by his visitor's gravity nor depressed by his words. His little blue eyes beamed amiably.

"Sit down, my dear fellow, and have a cigar."

Mr. Gruyter knew quite well that the Rev. Owen Jones neither drank nor smoked, but it tickled something prankish in his nature to offer him a drink and a smoke whenever they met. Mr. Jones shook his head.

Mr. Jones was in charge of the Baptist Mission on the Alas Islands. His headquarters were at Baru, the largest of them, with the greatest population, but he had meeting-houses under the care of native helpers in several other islands of the group. He was a tall, thin melancholy man, with a long face, sallow and drawn, of about forty. His brown hair was already white on the temples and it receded from the forehead. This gave him a look of somewhat vacuous intellectuality. Mr. Gruyter both disliked and respected him. He disliked him because he was narrow-minded and dogmatic. Himself a cheerful pagan who liked the good things of the flesh and was determined to get as many of them as his circumstances permitted, he had no

patience with a man who disapproved of them all. He thought
the customs of the country suited its inhabitants and had no
patience with the missionary's energetic efforts to destroy a
way of life that for centuries had worked very well. He respected him because he was honest, zealous and good. Mr.
Jones, an Australian of Welsh descent, was the only qualified
doctor in the group and it was a comfort to know that if you
fell ill you need not rely only on a Chinese practitioner, and
none knew better than the Controleur how useful to all Mr.
Jones's skill had been and with what charity he had given it.
On the occasion of an epidemic of influenza the missionary had
done the work of ten men and no storm short of a typhoon could
prevent him from crossing to one island or another if his help
was needed.

He lived with his sister in a little white house about half
a mile from the village and when the Controleur had arrived,
came on board to meet him and begged him to stay till he
could get his own house in order. The Controleur had accepted
and soon saw for himself with what simplicity the couple lived.
It was more than he could stand. Tea at three sparse meals a
day and when he lit his cigar Mr. Jones politely but firmly
asked him to be good enough not to smoke since both his sister
and he strongly disapproved of it. In twenty-four hours Mr.
Gruyter moved into his own house. He fled, with panic in his
heart, as through from a plague-stricken city. The Controleur
was fond of a joke and he liked to laugh; to be with a man who
took your nonsense in deadly earnest and never even smiled
at your best story was more than flesh and blood could stand.
The Rev. Owen Jones was a worthy man, but as a companion
he was impossible. His sister was worse. Neither had a sense
of humour, but whereas the missionary was of a melancholy
turn, doing his duty so conscientiously, with the obvious conviction that everything in the world was hopeless, Miss Jones
was resolutely cheerful. She grimly looked on the bright side
of things. With the ferocity of an avenging angel she sought
out the good in her fellow men. Miss Jones taught in the mission school and helped her brother in his medical work. When
he did operations she gave the anaesthetic and was matron,

dresser and nurse of the tiny hospital which on his own initiative Mr. Jones had added to the mission. But the Controleur was an obstinate little fellow and he never lost his capacity of extracting amusement from the Rev. Owen's dour struggle with the infirmities of human nature, and Miss Jones's ruthless optimism. He had to get his fun where he could. The Dutch boats came in three times in two months for a few hours and then he could have a good old crack with the captain and chief engineer, and once in a blue moon a pearling lugger came in from Thursday Island or Port Darwin and for two or three days he had a grand time. They were rough fellows, the pearlers, for the most part, but they were full of guts, and they had plenty of liquor on board, and good stories to tell, and the Controleur had them up to his house and gave them a fine dinner and the party was only counted a success if they were all too drunk to get back on the lugger again that night. But besides the missionary the only white man who lived on Baru was Ginger Ted, and he, of course, was a disgrace to civilization. There was not a single thing to be said in his favour. He cast discredit on the white race. All the same, but for Ginger Ted the Controleur sometimes thought he would find life on the island of Baru almost more than he could bear.

Oddly enough it was on account of this scamp that Mr. Jones, when he should have been instructing the pagan young in the mysteries of the Baptist faith, was paying Mr. Gruyter this early visit.

"Sit down, Mr. Jones," said the Controleur. "What can I do for you?"

"Well, I've come to see you about the man they call Ginger Ted. What are you going to do now?"

"Why, what's happened?"

"Haven't you heard? I thought the sergeant would have told you."

"I don't encourage the members of my staff to come to my private house unless the matter is urgent," said the Controleur rather grandly. "I am unlike you, Mr. Jones, I only work in order to have leisure and I like to enjoy my leisure without disturbance."

But Mr. Jones did not care much for small talk and he was not interested in general reflections.

"There was a disgraceful row in one of the Chinese shops last night. Ginger Ted wrecked the place and half killed a Chinaman."

"Drunk again, I suppose," said the Controleur placidly.

"Naturally. When is he anything else? They sent for the police and he assaulted the sergeant. They had to have six men to get him to the gaol."

"He's a hefty fellow," said the Controleur.

"I suppose you'll send him to Macassar."

Evert Gruyter returned the missionary's outraged look with a merry twinkle. He was no fool and he knew already what Mr. Jones was up to. It gave him considerable amusement to tease him a little.

"Fortunately my powers are wide enough to enable me to deal with the situation myself," he answered.

"You have power to deport anyone you like, Mr. Gruyter, and I'm sure it would save a lot of trouble if you got rid of the man altogether."

"I have the power, of course, but I am sure you would be the last person to wish me to use it arbitrarily."

"Mr. Gruyter, the man's presence here is a public scandal. He's never sober from morning till night; it's notorious that he has relations with one native woman after another."

"That is an interesting point, Mr. Jones. I had always heard that alcoholic excess, though it stimulated sexual desire, prevented its gratification. What you tell me about Ginger Ted does not seem to bear out this theory."

The missionary flushed a dull red.

"These are physiological matters which at the moment I have no wish to go into," he said, frigidly. "The behaviour of this man does incalculable damage to the prestige of the white race, and his example seriously hampers the efforts that are made in other quarters to induce the people of these islands to lead a less vicious life. He's an out and out bad lot."

"Pardon my asking, but have you made any attempts to reform him?"

"When he first drifted here I did my best to get in touch with him. He repelled all my advances. When there was that first trouble I went to him and talked to him straight from the shoulder. He swore at me."

"No one has a greater appreciation than I of the excellent work that you and other missionaries do on these islands, but are you sure that you always exercise your calling with all the tact possible?"

The Controleur was rather pleased with this phrase. It was extremely courteous and yet contained a reproof that he thought worth administering. The missionary looked at him gravely. His sad brown eyes were full of sincerity.

"Did Jesus exercise tact when he took a whip and drove the money-changers from the Temple? No, Mr. Gruyter. Tact is the subterfuge the lax avail themselves of to avoid doing their duty."

Mr. Jones's remark made the Controleur feel suddenly that he wanted a bottle of beer. The missionary leaned forward earnestly.

"Mr. Gruyter, you know this man's transgressions just as well as I do. It's unnecessary for me to remind you of them. There are no excuses for him. Now he really has overstepped the limit. You'll never have a better chance than this. I beg you to use the power you have and turn him out once for all."

The Controleur's eyes twinkled more brightly than ever. He was having a lot of fun. He reflected that human beings were much more amusing when you did not feel called upon in dealing with them to allot praise or blame.

"But Mr. Jones, do I understand you right? Are you asking me to give you an assurance to deport this man before I've heard the evidence against him and listened to his defence?"

"I don't know what his defence can be."

The Controleur rose from his chair and really he managed to get quite a little dignity into his five feet four inches.

"I am here to administer justice according to the laws of the Dutch Government. Permit me to tell you that I am exceedingly surprised that you should attempt to influence me in my judicial functions."

The missionary was a trifle flustered. It had never occurred to him that this little whipper-snapper of a boy, ten years younger than himself, would dream of adopting such an attitude. He opened his mouth to explain and apologize, but the Controleur raised a podgy little hand.

"It is time for me to go to my office, Mr. Jones. I wish you good-morning."

The missionary, taken aback, bowed and without another word walked out of the room. He would have been surprised to see what the Controleur did when his back was turned. A broad grin broke on his lips and he put his thumb to his nose and cocked a snook at the Rev. Owen.

A few minutes later he went down to his office. His head clerk, who was a Dutch half-caste, gave him his version of the previous night's row. It agreed pretty well with Mr. Jones's. The Court was sitting that day.

"Will you take Ginger Ted first, sir?" asked the clerk.

"I see no reason to do that. There are two or three cases held over from the last sitting. I will take him in his proper order."

"I thought perhaps as he was a white man you would like to see him privately, sir."

"The majesty of the law knows no difference between white and coloured, my friend," said Mr. Gruyter, somewhat pompously.

The Court was a big square room with wooden benches on which, crowded together, sat natives of all kinds, Polynesians, Bugis, Chinese, Malays, and they all rose when a door was opened and a sergeant announced the arrival of the Controleur. He entered with his clerk and took his place on a little dais at a table of varnished pitch pine. Behind him was a large engraving of Queen Wilhelmina. He despatched half a dozen cases and then Ginger Ted was brought in. He stood in the dock, handcuffed, with a warder on either side of him. The Controleur looked at him with a grave face, but he could not keep the amusement out of his eyes.

Ginger Ted was suffering from a hangover. He swayed a little as he stood and his eyes were vacant. He was a man still young, thirty perhaps, of somewhat over the middle height, rather fat, with a bloated red face and a shock of curly red hair. He had not come out of the tussle unscathed. He had a black eye and his mouth was cut and swollen. He wore khaki shorts, very dirty and ragged, and his singlet had been almost torn off his back. A great rent showed the thick mat of red hair with which his chest was covered, but showed also the astonishing whiteness of his skin. The Controleur looked at the charge sheet. He called the evidence. When he had heard it, when he had seen the Chinaman whose head Ginger Ted had broken with a bottle, when he had heard the agitated story of the sergeant who had been knocked flat when he tried to arrest him, when he had listened to the tale of the havoc wrought by Ginger Ted who in his drunken fury had smashed everything he could lay hands on, he turned and addressed the accused in English.

"Well, Ginger, what have you got to say for yourself?"

"I was blind. I don't remember a thing about it. If they say I half killed 'im I suppose I did. I'll pay the damage if they'll give me time."

"You will, Ginger," said the Controleur, "but it's me who'll give you time."

He looked at Ginger Ted for a minute in silence. He was an unappetizing object. A man who had gone completely to pieces. He was horrible. It made you shudder to look at him and if Mr. Jones had not been so officious, at that moment the Controleur would certainly have ordered him to be deported.

"You've been a trouble ever since you came to the islands, Ginger. You're a disgrace. You're incorrigibly idle. You've been picked up in the street dead drunk time and time again. You've kicked up row after row. You're hopeless. I told you the last time you were brought here that if you were arrested again I should deal with you severely. You've gone the limit this time and you're for it. I sentence you to six months' hard labour."

"Me?"

"You."

"By God, I'll kill you when I come out."

He burst into a string of oaths both filthy and blasphemous. Mr. Gruyter listened scornfully. You can swear much better in Dutch than in English and there was nothing that Ginger Ted said that he could not have effectively capped.

"Be quiet," he ordered. "You make me tired."

The Controleur repeated his sentence in Malay and the prisoner was led struggling away.

Mr. Gruyter sat down to tiffin in high good humour. It was astonishing how amusing life could be if you exercised a little ingenuity. There were people in Amsterdam, and even in Batavia and Surabaya, who looked upon his island home as a place of exile. They little knew how agreeable it was and what fun he could extract from unpromising material. They asked him whether he did not miss the club and the races and the cinema, the dances that were held once a week at the Casino and the society of Dutch ladies. Not at all. He liked comfort. The substantial furniture of the room in which he sat had a satisfying solidity. He liked reading French novels of a frivolous nature and he appreciated the sensation of reading one after the other without the uneasiness occasioned by the thought that he was wasting his time. When his young man's fancy turned to thoughts of love his head boy brought to the house a little dark-skinned bright-eyed creature in a sarong. He took care to form no connection of a permanent nature. He thought that change kept the heart young. He enjoyed freedom and was not weighed down by a sense of responsibility. He did not mind the heat. It made a sluice over with cold water half a dozen times a day a pleasure that had almost an aesthetic quality. He played the piano. He wrote letters to his friends in Holland. He felt no need for the conversation of intellectual persons. He liked a good laugh, but he could get that out of a fool just as well as out of a professor of philosophy. He had a notion that he was a very wise little man.

Like all good Dutchmen in the Far East he began his lunch with a small glass of Hollands gin. It has a musty acrid flavour, and the taste for it must be acquired, but Mr. Gruyter preferred it to any cocktail. When he drank it he felt besides that he was upholding the traditions of his race. Then he had *rystafel*. He had it every day. He heaped a soup-plate high with rice, and then, his three boys waiting on him, helped himself to the curry that one handed him, to the fried egg that another brought, and to the condiment presented by the third. Then each one brought another dish, of bacon, or bananas, or pickled fish, and presently his plate was piled high in a huge pyramid. He stirred it all together and began to eat. He ate slowly and with relish. He drank a bottle of beer.

He did not think while he was eating. His attention was applied to the mass in front of him and he consumed it with a happy concentration. It never palled on him. And when he had emptied the great plate it was a compensation to think that next day he would have *rystafel* again. He grew tired of it as little as the rest of us grow tired of bread. He finished his beer and lit his cigar. The boy brought him a cup of coffee. He leaned back in his chair then and allowed himself the luxury of reflection.

It tickled him to have sentenced Ginger Ted to the richly deserved punishment of six months' hard labour, and he smiled when he thought of him working on the roads with the other prisoners. It would have been silly to deport from the island the one man with whom he could occasionally have a heart-to-heart talk, and besides, the satisfaction it would have given the missionary would have been bad for that gentleman's character. Ginger Ted was a scamp and a scallywag, but the Controleur had a kindly feeling for him. They had drunk many a bottle of beer in one another's company and when the pearl fishers from Port Darwin came in and they all made a night of it, they had got gloriously tight together. The Controleur liked the reckless way in which Ginger Ted squandered the priceless treasure of life.

Ginger Ted had wandered in one day on the ship that was going up from Merauke to Macassar. The captain did not know how he had found his way there, but he had travelled steerage with the natives, and he stopped off at the Alas Islands because he liked the look of them. Mr. Gruyter had a suspicion that their attraction consisted perhaps in their being under the Dutch flag and so out of British jurisdiction. But his papers were in order, so there was no reason why he should not stay. He said that he was buying pearl-shell for an Australian firm, but it soon appeared that his commercial undertakings were not serious. Drink, indeed, took up so much of his time that he had little left over for other pursuits. He was in receipt of two pounds a week, paid monthly, which came regularly to him from England. The Controleur guessed that this sum was paid only so long as he kept well away from the persons who sent it. It was anyway too small to permit him any liberty of movement. Ginger Ted was reticent. The Controleur discovered that he was an Englishman, this he learnt from his passport, which described him as Edward Wilson, and that he had been in Australia. But why he had left England and what he had done in Australia he had no notion. Nor could he ever quite tell to what class Ginger Ted belonged. When you saw him in a filthy singlet and a pair of ragged trousers, a battered topi on his head, with the pearl fishers and heard his conversation, coarse, obscene and illiterate, you thought he must be a sailor before the mast who had deserted his ship, or a labourer, but when you saw his handwriting you were surprised to find that it was that of a man not without at least some education, and on occasion when you got him alone, if he had had a few drinks but was not yet drunk, he would talk of matters that neither a sailor nor a labourer would have been likely to know anything about. The Controleur had a certain sensitiveness and he realized that Ginger Ted did not speak to him as an inferior to a superior but as an equal. Most of his remittance was mortgaged before he received it, and the Chinamen to whom he owed money were standing at his elbow when the monthly letter was delivered to him, but with what was left he proceeded to get drunk. It was then that he made trouble, for when drunk he grew violent and was then likely to commit acts that brought him into the hands of the police. Hitherto Mr. Gruyter had contented himself with keeping him in gaol till he was sober and giving him a talking to. When he was out of money he cadged what drink he could from anyone

who would give it him. Rum, brandy, arak, it was all the same
to him. Two or three times Mr. Gruyter had got him work
on plantations run by Chinese in one or other of the islands,
but he could not stick to it, and in a few weeks was back
again at Baru on the beach. It was a miracle how he kept
body and soul together. He had, of course, a way with him. He
picked up the various dialects spoken on the islands, and
knew how to make the natives laugh. They despised him, but
they respected his physical strength, and they liked his company. He was as a result never at a loss for a meal or a mat
to sleep on. The strange thing was, and it was this that chiefly
outraged the Rev. Owen Jones, that he could do anything he
liked with a woman. The Controleur could not imagine what
it was they saw in him. He was casual with them and rather
brutal. He took what they gave him, but seemed incapable
of gratitude. He used them for his pleasure and then flung
them indifferently away. Once or twice this had got him into
trouble, and Mr. Gruyter had had to sentence an angry father
for sticking a knife in Ginger Ted's back one night, and a
Chinese woman had sought to poison herself by swallowing
opium because he had deserted her. Once Mr. Jones came
to the Controleur in a great state because the beachcomber
had seduced one of his converts. The Controleur agreed that
it was very deplorable, but could only advise Mr. Jones to
keep a sharp eye on these young persons. The Controleur
liked it less when he discovered that a girl whom he fancied
a good deal himself and had been seeing for several weeks
had all the time been according her favours also to Ginger
Ted. When he thought of this particular incident he smiled
again at the thought of Ginger Ted doing six months' hard
labour. It is seldom in this life that in the process of doing
your bounden duty you can get back on a fellow who has
played you a dirty trick.

A few days later Mr. Gruyter was taking a walk, partly
for exercise and partly to see that some job he wanted done
was being duly proceeded with, when he passed a gang of
prisoners working under the charge of a warder. Among them
he saw Ginger Ted. He wore the prison sarong, a dingy tunic

called in Malay a baju, and his own battered topi. They were
repairing the road, and Ginger Ted was wielding a heavy pick.
The way was narrow and the Controleur saw that he must
pass within a foot of him. He remembered his threats. He
knew that Ginger Ted was a man of violent passion and the
language he had used in the dock made it plain that he had
not seen what a good joke it was of the Controleur's to sentence him to six months' hard labour. If Ginger Ted suddenly attacked him with the pick, nothing on God's earth
could save him. It was true that the warder would immediately
shoot him down, but meanwhile the Controleur's head would
be bashed in. It was with a funny little feeling in the pit of
his stomach that Mr. Gruyter walked through the gang of
prisoners. They were working in pairs a few feet from one
another. He set his mind on neither hastening his pace nor
slackening it. As he passed Ginger Ted, the man swung his
pick into the ground and looked up at the Controleur and as
he caught his eye he winked. The Controleur checked the
smile that rose to his lips and with official dignity strode on.
But that wink, so lusciously full of sardonic humour, filled
him with satisfaction. If he had been the Caliph of Bagdad
instead of a junior official in the Dutch Civil Service, he would
forthwith have released Ginger Ted, sent slaves to bathe and
perfume him, and having clothed him in a golden robe enter-
tained him to a sumptuous repast.

Ginger Ted was an exemplary prisoner and in a month or
two the Controleur, having occasion to send a gang to do some
work on one of the outlying islands, included him in it. There
was no gaol there, so the ten fellows he sent, under the charge
of a warder, were billeted on the natives and after their day's
work lived like free men. The job was sufficient to take up the
rest of Ginger Ted's sentence. The Controleur saw him before
he left.

"Look here, Ginger," he said to him, "here's ten guilder for
you so that you can buy yourself tobacco when you're gone."

"Couldn't you make it a bit more? There's eight pounds a
month coming in regularly."

"I think that's enough. I'll keep the letters that come for

you, and when you get back you'll have a tidy sum. You'll have enough to take you anywhere you want to go."

"I'm very comfortable here," said Ginger Ted.

"Well, the day you come back, clean yourself up and come over to my house. We'll have a bottle of beer together."

"That'll be fine. I guess I'll be ready for a good crack then."

Now chance steps in. The island to which Ginger Ted had been sent was called Maputiti, and like all the rest of them it was rocky, heavily wooded and surrounded by a reef. There was a village among coconuts on the sea-shore opposite the opening of the reef and another village on a brackish lake in the middle of the island. Of this some of the inhabitants had been converted to Christianity. Communication with Baru was effected by a launch that touched at the various islands at irregular intervals. It carried passengers and produce. But the villagers were seafaring folk, and if they had to communicate urgently with Baru, manned a prahu and sailed the fifty miles or so that separated them from it. It happened that when Ginger Ted's sentence had but another fortnight to run the Christian headman of the village on the lake was taken suddenly ill. The native remedies availed him nothing and he writhed in agony. Messengers were sent to Baru imploring the missionary's help; but as ill luck would have it Mr. Jones was suffering at the moment from an attack of malaria. He was in bed and unable to move. He talked the matter over with his sister.

"It sounds like acute appendicitis," he told her.

"You can't go, Owen," she said.

"I can't let the man die."

Mr. Jones had a temperature of a hundred and four. His head was aching like mad. He had been delirious all night. His eyes were shining strangely and his sister felt that he was holding on to his wits by a sheer effort of will.

"You couldn't operate in the state you're in."

"No, I couldn't. Then Hassan must go."

Hassan was the dispenser.

"You couldn't trust Hassan. He'd never dare to do an operation on his own responsibility. And they'd never let him. I'll go. Hassan can stay here and look after you."

"You can't remove an appendix?"

"Why not? I've seen you do it. I've done lots of minor operations."

Mr. Jones felt he didn't quite understand what she was saying.

"Is the launch in?"

"No, it's gone to one of the islands. But I can go in the prahu the men came in."

"You? I wasn't thinking of you. You can't go."

"I'm going, Owen."

"Going where?" he said.

She saw that his mind was wandering already. She put her hand soothingly on his dry forehead. She gave him a dose of medicine. He muttered something and she realized that he did not know where he was. Of course she was anxious about him, but she knew that his illness was not dangerous, and she could leave him safely to the mission boy who was helping her nurse him and to the native dispenser. She slipped out of the room. She put her toilet things, a night-dress, and a change of clothes into a bag. A little chest with surgical instruments, bandages and antiseptic dressings was kept always ready. She gave them to the two natives who had come over from Maputiti, and telling the dispenser what she was going to do gave him instructions to inform her brother when he was able to listen. Above all he was not to be anxious about her. She put on her topi and sallied forth. The mission was about half a mile from the village. She walked quickly. At the end of the jetty the prahu was waiting. Six men manned it. She took her place in the stern and they set off with a rapid stroke. Within the reef the sea was calm, but when they crossed the bar they came upon a long swell. But this was not the first journey of the sort Miss Jones had taken and she was confident in the seaworthiness of the boat she was in. It was noon and the sun beat down from a sultry sky. The only thing that harassed her was that they could not arrive before dark, and if she found it necessary to operate at once she could count only on the light of hurricane lamps.

Miss Jones was a woman of hard on forty. Nothing in her appearance would have prepared you for such determination as she had just shown. She had an odd drooping gracefulness, which suggested that she might be swayed by every breeze; it was almost an affectation; and it made the strength of character which you soon discovered in her seem positively monstrous. She was flat-chested, tall and extremely thin. She had a long sallow face and she was much afflicted with prickly heat. Her lank brown hair was drawn back straight from her forehead. She had rather small eyes, grey in colour, and because they were somewhat too close they gave her face a shrewish look. Her nose was long and thin and a trifle red. She suffered a good deal from indigestion. But this infirmity availed nothing against her ruthless determination to look upon the bright side of things. Firmly persuaded that the world was evil and men unspeakable, vicious, she extracted any little piece of decency she could find in them with the modest pride with which a conjurer extracts a rabbit from a hat. She was quick, resourceful and competent. When she arrived on the island she saw that there was not a moment to lose if she was to save the headman's life. Under the greatest difficulties, showing a native how to give the anaesthetic, she operated, and for the next three days nursed the patient with anxious assiduity. Everything went very well and she realized that her brother could not have made a better job of it. She waited long enough to take out the stitches and then prepared to go home. She could flatter herself that she had not wasted her time. She had given medical attention to such as needed it, she had strengthened the small Christian community in its faith, admonished such as were lax and cast the good seed in places where it might be hoped under divine providence to take root.

The launch, coming from one of the other islands, put in somewhat late in the afternoon, but it was full moon and they expected to reach Baru before midnight. They brought her things down to the wharf and the people who were seeing her off stood about repeating their thanks. Quite a little crowd collected. The launch was loaded with sacks of copra, but Miss Jones was used to its strong smell and it did not incommode her. She made herself as comfortable a place to sit in as she could, and waiting for the launch to start, chatted with her grateful flock. She was the only passenger. Suddenly a group of natives emerged from the trees that embowered the little village on the lagoon and she saw that among them was a white man. He wore a prison sarong and a baju. He had long red hair. She at once recognized Ginger Ted. A policeman was with him. They shook hands and Ginger Ted shook hands with the villagers who accompanied him. They bore bundles of fruit and a jar which Miss Jones guessed contained native spirit, and these they put in the launch. She discovered to her surprise that Ginger Ted was coming with her. His term was up and instructions had arrived that he was to be returned to Baru in the launch. He gave her a glance, but she did not nod—indeed Miss Jones turned away her head—and stepped in. The mechanic started his engine and in a moment they were jug-jugging through the channel in the lagoon. Ginger Ted clambered on to a pile of sacks and lit a cigarette.

Miss Jones ignored him. Of course she knew him very well. Her heart sank when she thought that he was going to be once more in Baru, creating a scandal and drinking, a peril to the women and a thorn in the flesh of all decent people. She knew the steps her brother had taken to have him deported and she had no patience with the Controleur, who would not see a duty that stared him so plainly in the face. When they had crossed the bar and were in the open sea Ginger Ted took the stopper out of the jar of arak and putting his mouth to it took a long pull. Then he handed the jar to the two mechanics who formed the crew. One was a middle-aged man and the other a youth.

"I do not wish you to drink anything while we are on the journey," said Miss Jones sternly to the elder one.

He smiled at her and drank.

"A little arak can do no one any harm," he answered. He passed the jar to his companion, who drank also.

"If you drink again I shall complain to the Controleur," said Miss Jones.

The elder man said something she could not understand, but which she suspected was very rude, and passed the jar back to Ginger Ted. They went along for an hour or more. The sea was like glass and the sun set radiantly. It set behind one of the islands and for a few minutes changed it into a mystic city of the skies. Miss Jones turned round to watch it and her heart was filled with gratitude for the beauty of the world.

"And only man is vile," she quoted to herself.

They went due east. In the distance was a little island which she knew they passed close by. It was uninhabited. A rocky islet thickly grown with virgin forest. The boatman lit his lamps. The night fell and immediately the sky was thick with stars. The moon had not yet risen. Suddenly there was a slight jar and the launch began to vibrate strangely. The engine rattled. The head mechanic, calling to his mate to take the helm, crept under the housing. They seemed to be going more slowly. The engine stopped. She asked the youth what was the matter, but he did not know. Ginger Ted got down from the top of the copra sacks and slipped under the housing. When he reappeared she would have liked to ask him what had happened, but her dignity prevented her. She sat still and occupied herself with her thoughts. There was a long swell and the launch rolled slightly. The mechanic emerged once more into view and started the engine. Though it rattled like mad they began to move. The launch vibrated from stem to stern. They went very slowly. Evidently something was amiss, but Miss Jones was exasperated rather than alarmed. The launch was supposed to do six knots, but now it was just crawling along; at that rate they would not get into Baru till long, long after midnight. The mechanic, still busy under the housing, shouted out something to the man at the helm. They spoke in Bugi, of which Miss Jones knew very little. But after a while she noticed that they had changed their course and seemed to be heading for the little uninhabited island a good deal to the lee of which they should have passed.

"Where are we going?" she asked the helmsman with sudden misgiving.

He pointed to the islet. She got up and went to the housing and called to the man to come out.

"You're not going there? Why? What's the matter?"

"I can't get to Baru," he said.

"But you must. I insist. I order you to go to Baru."

The man shrugged his shoulders. He turned his back on her and slipped once more under the housing. Then Ginger Ted addresssed her.

"One of the blades of the propeller has broken off. He thinks he can get as far as that island. We shall have to stay the night there and he'll put on a new propeller in the morning when the tide's out."

"I can't spend the night on an uninhabited island with three men," she cried.

"A lot of women would jump at it."

"I insist on going to Baru. Whatever happens we must get there tonight."

"Don't get excited, old girl. We've got to beach the boat to put a new propeller on, and we shall be all right on the island."

"How dare you speak to me like that! I think you're very insolent."

"You'll be O. K. We've got plenty of grub and we'll have a snack when we land. You have a drop of arak and you'll feel like a house on fire."

"You're an impertinent man. If you don't go to Baru I'll have you all put in prison."

"We're not going to Baru. We can't. We're going to that island and if you don't like it you can get out and swim."

"Oh, you'll pay for this."

"Shut up, you old cow," said Ginger Ted.

Miss Jones gave a gasp of anger. But she controlled herself. Even out there, in the middle of the ocean, she had too much dignity to bandy words with that vile wretch. The launch, the engine rattling horribly, crawled on. It was pitch dark now, and she could no longer see the island they were making for. Miss Jones, deeply incensed, sat with lips tight shut and a frown on her brow; she was not used to being crossed. Then the moon rose and she could see the bulk of Ginger Ted sprawling on the top of the piled sacks of copra. The glimmer of his cigarette was strangely sinister. Now the island was vaguely outlined against the sky. They reached it and the boatman ran the launch on to the beach. Suddenly Miss Jones gave a gasp. The truth had dawned on her and her anger changed to fear. Her heart beat violently. She shook in every limb. She felt dreadfully faint. She saw it all. Was the broken propeller a put-up job or was it an accident? She could not be certain; anyhow, she knew that Ginger Ted would seize the opportunity. Ginger Ted would rape her. She knew his character. He was mad about women. That was what he had done, practically, to the girl at the mission, such a good little thing she was and an excellent seamstress; they would have prosecuted him for that and he would have been sentenced to years of imprisonment only very unfortunately the innocent child had gone back to him several times and indeed had only complained of his ill usage when he left her for somebody else. They had gone to the Controleur about it, but he had refused to take any steps, saying in that coarse way of his that even if what the girl said was true, it didn't look very much as though it had been an altogether unpleasant experience. Ginger Ted was a scoundrel. And she was a white woman; what chance was there that he would spare her? None. She knew men. But she must pull herself together. She must keep her wits about her. She must have courage. She was determined to sell her virtue dearly, and if he killed her—well, she would rather die than yield. And if she died she would rest in the arms of Jesus. For a moment a great light blinded her eyes and she saw the mansions of her Heavenly Father. They were a grand and sumptuous mixture of a picture palace and a railway station. The mechanics and Ginger Ted jumped out of the launch and, waist deep in water, gathered round the broken propeller. She took advantage of their preoccupation to get her case of surgical instruments out of the box. She took out the four scalpels it contained and secreted them in

her clothing. If Ginger Ted touched her she would not hesi-
tate to plunge a scalpel in his heart.

"Now then, miss, you'd better get out," said Ginger Ted.
"You'll be better off on the beach than in the boat."

She thought so too. At least there she would have freedom
of action. Without a word she clambered over the copra sacks.
He offered her his hand.

"I don't want your help," she answered coldly.

"You can go to hell," he answered.

It was a little difficult to get out of the boat without showing her legs, but by the exercise of considerable ingenuity
she managed it.

"Damned lucky we've got something to eat. We'll make a
fire and then you'd better have a snack and a nip of arak."

"I want nothing. I only want to be left alone."

"It won't hurt me if you go hungry."

She did not answer. She walked, with head erect, along
the beach. She held the largest scalpel in her closed fist. The
moon allowed her to see where she was going. She looked for
a place to hide. The thick forest came down to the very edge
of the beach; but, afraid of its darkness (after all, she was
but a woman), she dared not plunge into its depth. She did
not know what animals lurked there or what dangerous
snakes. Besides, her instinct told her that it was better to keep
those three bad men in sight; then if they came towards her
she would be prepared. Presently she found a little hollow.
She looked round. They seemed to be occupied with their own
affairs and they could not see her. She slipped in. There was
a rock between them and her so that she was hidden from
them and yet could watch them. She saw them go to and
from the boat carrying things. She saw them build a fire. It
lit them luridly and she saw them sit around it and eat, and
she saw the jar of arak passed from one to the other. They
were all going to get drunk. What would happen to her then?
It might be that she could cope with Ginger Ted, though his
strength terrified her, but against three she would be powerless. A mad idea came to her to go to Ginger Ted and fall on
her knees before him and beg him to spare her. He must have

some spark of decent feeling in him and she had always been
so convinced that there was good even in the worst of men.
He must have had a mother. Perhaps he had a sister. Ah, but
how could you appeal to a man blinded with lust and drunk
with arak? She began to feel terribly weak. She was afraid
she was going to cry. That would never do. She needed all
her self-control. She bit her lip. She watched them, like a
tiger watching his prey; no, not like that, like a lamb watching
three hungry wolves. She saw them put more wood on the fire
and Ginger Ted, in his sarong, silhouetted by the flames. Perhaps after he had had his will of her he would pass her on to
the others. How could she go back to her brother when such
a thing had happened to her? Of course he would be sympathetic, but would he ever feel quite the same to her again?
It would break his heart. And perhaps he would think that
she ought to have resisted more. For his sake perhaps it would
be better if she said nothing about it, naturally the men would
say nothing. It would mean twenty years in prison for them.
But then supposing she had a baby. Miss Jones instinctively
clenched her hands with horror and nearly cut herself with the
scalpel. Of course it would only infuriate them if she resisted.

"What shall I do?" she cried. "What have I done to deserve
this?"

She flung herself down on her knees and prayed to God to
save her. She prayed long and earnestly. She reminded God
that she was a virgin and just mentioned, in case it had slipped
the divine memory, how much St. Paul had valued that excellent state. And then she peeped round the rock again. The
three men appeared to be smoking and the fire was dying
down. Now was the time that Ginger Ted's lewd thoughts
might be expected to turn to the woman who was at his
mercy. She smothered a cry, for suddenly he got up and
walked in her direction. She felt all her muscles grow taut,
and though her heart was beating furiously she clenched the
scalpel firmly in her hand. But it was for another purpose
that Ginger Ted had got up. Miss Jones blushed and looked
away. He strolled slowly back to the others and sitting down
again raised the jar of arak to his lips. Miss Jones, crouching

behind the rock, watched with straining eyes. The conversation round the fire grew less and presently she divined, rather than saw, that the two natives wrapped themselves in blankets and composed themselves to slumber. She understood. This was the moment Ginger Ted had been waiting for. When they were fast asleep he would get up cautiously and without a sound, in order not to wake the others, creep stealthily towards her. Was it that he was unwilling to share her with them or did he know that his deed was so dastardly that he did not wish them to know of it? After all, he was a white man and she was a white woman. He could not have sunk so low as to allow her to suffer the violence of natives. But his plan, which was so obvious to her, had given her an idea; when she saw him coming she would scream, she would scream so loudly that it would wake the two mechanics. She remembered now that the elder, though he had only one eye, had a kind face. But Ginger Ted did not move. She was feeling terribly tired. She began to fear that she would not have the strength now to resist him. She had gone through too much. She closed her eyes for a minute.

When she opened them it was broad daylight. She must have fallen asleep and, so shattered was she by emotion, have slept till long after dawn. It gave her quite a turn. She sought to rise, but something caught in her legs. She looked and found that she was covered with two empty copra sacks. Someone had come in the night and put them over her. Ginger Ted. She gave a little scream. The horrible thought flashed through her mind that he had outraged her in her sleep. No. It was impossible. And yet he had had her at his mercy. Defenceless. And he had spared her. She blushed furiously. She raised herself to her feet, feeling a little stiff, and arranged her disordered dress. The scalpel had fallen from her hand and she picked it up. She took the two copra sacks and emerged from her hiding-place. She walked towards the boat. It was floating in the shallow water of the lagoon.

"Come on, Miss Jones," said Ginger Ted. "We've finished. I was just going to wake you up."

She could not look at him, but she felt herself as red as a turkey cock.

"Have a banana?" he said.

Without a word she took it. She was very hungry, and ate it with relish.

"Step on this rock and you'll be able to get in without wetting your feet."

Miss Jones felt as though she could sink into the ground with shame, but she did as he told her. He took hold of her arm—good heavens, his hand was like an iron vise, never, never could she have struggled with him—and helped her into the launch. The mechanic started the engine and they slid out of the lagoon. In three hours they were at Baru.

That evening, having been officially released, Ginger Ted went to the Controleur's house. He wore no longer the prison uniform, but the ragged singlet and the khaki shorts in which he had been arrested. He had had his hair cut and it fitted his head now like a little curly red cap. He was thinner. He had lost his bloated flabbiness and looked younger and better. Mr. Gruyter, a friendly grin on his round face, shook hands with him and asked him to sit down. The boy brought two bottles of beer.

"I'm glad to see you hadn't forgotten my invitation, Ginger," said the Controleur.

"Not likely. I've been looking forward to this for six months."

"Here's luck, Ginger Ted."

"Same to you, Controleur."

They emptied their glasses and the Controleur clapped his hands. The boy brought two more bottles.

"Well, you don't bear me any malice for the sentence I gave you, I hope."

"No bloody fear. I was mad for a minute, but I got over it. I didn't have half a bad time, you know. Nice lot of girls on that island, Controleur. You ought to give 'em a look over one of these days."

"You're a bad lot, Ginger."

"Terrible."

"Good beer, isn't it?"

"Fine."

"Let's have some more."

Ginger Ted's remittance had been arriving every month and the Controleur now had fifty pounds for him. When the damage he had done to the Chinaman's shop was paid for there would still be over thirty.

"That's quite a lot of money, Ginger. You ought to do something useful with it."

"I mean to," answered Ginger. "Spend it."

The Controleur sighed.

"Well, that's what money's for, I guess."

The Controleur gave his guest the news. Not much had happened during the last six months. Time on the Alas Islands did not matter very much and the rest of the world did not matter at all.

"Any wars anywhere?" asked Ginger Ted.

"No. Not that I've noticed. Harry Jervis found a pretty big pearl. He says he's going to ask a thousand quid for it."

"I hope he gets it."

"And Charlie McCormack's married."

"He always was a bit soft."

Suddenly the boy appeared and said Mr. Jones wished to know if he might come in. Before the Controleur could give an answer Mr. Jones walked in.

"I won't detain you long," he said. "I've been trying to get hold of this good man all day and when I heard he was here I thought you wouldn't mind my coming."

"How is Miss Jones?" asked the Controleur politely. "None the worse for her night in the open, I trust."

"She's naturally a bit shaken. She had a temperature and I've insisted on her going to bed, but I don't think it's serious."

The two men got up on the missionary's entrance, and now the missionary went to Ginger Ted and held out his hand.

"I want to thank you. You did a great and noble thing. My sister is right, one should always look for the good in their fellow men; I am afraid I misjudged you in the past; I beg your pardon."

He spoke very solemnly. Ginger Ted looked at him with

amazement. He had not been able to prevent the missionary taking his hand. He still held it.

"What the hell are you talking about?"

"You had my sister at your mercy and you spared her. I thought you were all evil and I am ashamed. She was defenceless. She was in your power. You had pity on her. I thank you from the bottom of my heart. Neither my sister nor I will ever forget. God bless and guard you always."

Mr. Jones's voice shook a little and he turned his head away. He released Ginger Ted's hand and strode quickly to the door. Ginger Ted watched him with a blank face.

"What the blazes does he mean?" he asked.

The Controleur laughed. He tried to control himself, but the more he did the more he laughed. He shook and you saw the folds of his fat belly ripple under the sarong. He leaned back in his long chair and rolled from side to side. He did not laugh only with his face, he laughed with his whole body, and even the muscles of his podgy legs shook with mirth. He held his aching ribs. Ginger Ted looked at him frowning, and because he did not understand what the joke was he grew angry. He seized one of the empty beer bottles by the neck.

"If you don't stop laughing, I'll break your bloody head open," he said.

The Controleur mopped his face. He swallowd a mouthful of beer. He sighed and groaned because his sides were hurting him.

"He's thanking you for having respected the virtue of Miss Jones," he spluttered at last.

"Me?" cried Ginger Ted.

The thought took quite a long time to travel through his head, but when at last he got it he flew into a violent rage. There flowed from his mouth such a stream of blasphemous obscenities as would have startled a marine.

"That old cow," he finished. "What does he take me for?"

"You have the reputation of being rather hot stuff with the girls, Ginger," giggled the little Controleur.

"I wouldn't touch her with the fag end of a barge-pole. It never entered my head. The nerve. I'll wring his blasted neck. Look here, give me my money, I'm going to get drunk."

"I don't blame you," said the Controleur.

"That old cow," repeated Ginger Ted. "That old cow."

He was shocked and outraged. The suggestion really shattered his sense of decency.

The Controleur had the money at hand and having got Ginger Ted to sign the necessary papers gave it to him.

"Go and get drunk, Ginger Ted," he said, "but I warn you, if you get into mischief it'll be twelve months next time."

"I shan't get into mischief," said Ginger Ted sombrely. He was suffering from a sense of injury. "It's an insult," he shouted at the Controleur. "That's what it is, it's a bloody insult."

He lurched out of the house, and as he went he muttered to himself: "dirty swine, dirty swine." Ginger Ted remained drunk for a week. Mr. Jones went to see the Controleur again.

"I'm very sorry to hear that poor fellow has taken up his evil course again," he said. "My sister and I are dreadfully disappointed. I'm afraid it wasn't very wise to give him so much money at once."

"It was his own money. I had no right to keep it back."

"Not a legal right, perhaps, but surely a moral right."

He told the Controleur the story of that fearful night on the island. With her feminine instinct, Miss Jones had realized that the man, inflamed with lust, was determined to take advantage of her, and, resolved to defend herself to the last, had armed herself with a scalpel. He told the Controleur how she had prayed and wept and how she had hidden herself. Her agony was indescribable, and she knew that she could never have survived the shame. She rocked to and fro and every moment she thought he was coming. And there was no help anywhere and at last she had fallen asleep; she was tired out, poor thing, she had undergone more than any human being could stand, and then when she awoke she found that he had covered her with copra sacks. He had found her asleep, and surely it was her innocence, her very helplessness that had moved him, he hadn't the heart to touch her; he covered her gently with two copra sacks and crept silently away.

"It shows you that deep down in him there is something

sterling. My sister feels it's our duty to save him. We must do something for him."

"Well, in your place I wouldn't try till he's got through all his money," said the Controleur, "and then if he's not in gaol you can do what you like."

But Ginger Ted didn't want to be saved. About a fortnight after his release from prison he was sitting on a stool outside a Chinaman's shop looking vacantly down the street when he saw Miss Jones coming along. He stared at her for a minute and once more amazement seized him. He muttered to himself and there can be little doubt that his mutterings were disrespectful. But then he noticed that Miss Jones had seen him and he quickly turned his head away; he was conscious, notwithstanding, that she was looking at him. She was walking briskly, but she sensibly diminished her pace as she approached him. He thought she was going to stop and speak to him. He got up quickly and went into the shop. He did not venture to come out for at least five minutes. Half an hour later Mr. Jones himself came along and he went straight up to Ginger Ted with outstretched hand.

"How do you do, Mr. Edward? My sister told me I should find you here."

Ginger Ted gave him a surly look and did not take the proffered hand. He made no answer.

"We'd be so very glad if you'd come to dinner with us next Sunday. My sister's a capital cook and she'll make you a real Australian dinner."

"Go to hell," said Ginger Ted.

"That's not very gracious," said the missionary, but with a little laugh to show that he was not affronted. "You go and see the Controleur from time to time, why shouldn't you come and see us? It's pleasant to talk to white people now and then. Won't you let bygones be bygones? I can assure you of a very cordial welcome.

"I haven't got clothes fit to go out in," said Ginger Ted sulkily.

"Oh, never mind about that. Come as you are."

"I won't."

"Why not? You must have a reason."

Ginger Ted was a blunt man. He had no hesitation in saying what we should all like to when we receive unwelcome invitations.

"I don't want to."

"I'm sorry. My sister will be very disappointed."

Mr. Jones, determined to show that he was not in the least offended, gave him a breezy nod and walked on. Forty-eight hours later there mysteriously arrived at the house in which Ginger Ted lodged a parcel containing a suit of ducks, a tennis shirt, a pair of socks and some shoes. He was unaccustomed to receiving presents and next time he saw the Controleur asked him if it was he who had sent the things.

"Not on your life," said the Controleur. "I'm perfectly indifferent to the state of your wardrobe."

"Well, then, who the hell can have?"

"Search me."

It was necessary from time to time for Miss Jones to see Mr. Gruyter on business and shortly after this she came to see him one morning in his office. She was a capable woman and though she generally wanted him to do something he had no mind to, she did not waste his time. He was a little surprised then to discover that she had come on a very trivial errand. When he told her that he could not take cognizance of the matter in question, she did not, as was her habit, try to convince him, but accepted his refusal as definite. She got up to go and then as though it were an afterthought said:

"Oh, Mr. Gruyter, my brother is very anxious that we should have the man they call Ginger Ted to supper with us and I've written him a little note inviting him for the day after tomorrow. I think he's rather shy, and I wonder if you'd come with him."

"That's very kind of you."

"My brother feels that we ought to do something for the poor fellow."

"A woman's influence and all that sort of thing," said the Controleur demurely.

"Will you persuade him to come? I'm sure he will if you

make a point of it, and when he knows the way he'll come again. It seems such a pity to let a young man like that go to pieces altogether."

The Controleur looked up at her. She was several inches taller than he. He thought her very unattractive. She reminded him strangely of wet linen hung on a clothes-line to dry. His eyes twinkled, but he kept a straight face.

"I'll do my best," he said.

"How old is he?" she asked.

"According to his passport he's thirty-one."

"And what is his real name?"

"Wilson."

"Edward Wilson," she said softly.

"It's astonishing that after the life he's led he should be so strong," murmured the Controleur. "He has the strength of an ox."

"Those red-headed men sometimes are very powerful," said Miss Jones, but spoke as though she were choking.

"Quite so," said the Controleur.

Then for no obvious reason Miss Jones blushed. She hurriedly said good-bye to the Controleur and left his office.

"*Godverdomme!*" said the Controleur.

He knew now who had sent Ginger Ted the new clothes.

He met him during the course of the day and asked him whether he had heard from Miss Jones. Ginger Ted took a crumpled ball of paper out of his pocket and gave it to him. It was the invitation. It ran as follows:

Dear Mr. Wilson,—

My brother and I would be so very glad if you would come and have supper with us next Thursday at 7:30. The Controleur has kindly promised to come. We have some new records from Australia which I am sure you will like. I am afraid I was not very nice to you last time we met, but I did not know you so well then, and I am big enough to admit it when I have committed an error. I hope you will forgive me and let me be your friend.

Yours sincerely,
Martha Jones

The Controleur noticed that she addressed him as Mr. Wilson and referred to his own promise to go, so that when she told him she had already invited Ginger Ted she had a little anticipated the truth.

"What are you going to do?"

"I'm not going, if that's what you mean. Damned nerve."

"You must answer the letter."

"Well, I won't."

"Now look here, Ginger, you put on those new clothes and you come as a favour to me. I've got to go, and damn it all, you can't leave me in the lurch. It won't hurt you just once."

Ginger Ted looked at the Controleur suspiciously, but his face was serious and his manner sincere; he could not guess that within him the Dutchman bubbled with laughter.

"What the devil do they want me for?"

"I don't know. The pleasure of your society, I suppose."

"Will there be any booze?"

"No, but come up to my house at seven, and we'll have a tiddly before we go."

"Oh, all right," said Ginger Ted sulkily.

The Controleur rubbed his little fat hands with joy. He was expecting a great deal of amusement from the party. But when Thursday came and seven o'clock Ginger Ted was dead drunk and Mr. Gruyter had to go alone. He told the missionary and his sister the plain truth. Mr. Jones shook his head.

"I'm afraid it's no good, Martha, the man's hopeless."

For a moment Miss Jones was silent and the Controleur saw two tears trickle down her long thin nose. She bit her lip.

"No one is hopeless. Everyone has some good in him. I shall pray for him every night. It would be wicked to doubt the power of God."

Perhaps Miss Jones was right in this, but the divine providence took a very funny way of effecting its ends. Ginger Ted began to drink more heavily than ever. He was so troublesome that even Mr. Gruyter lost patience with him. He made up his mind that he could not have the fellow on the islands any more and resolved to deport him on the next boat that touched at Baru. Then a man died under mysterious circumstances after having been for a trip to one of the islands and the Contorleur learnt that there had been several deaths on the same island. He sent the Chinese who was the official doctor of the group to look into the matter, and very soon received intelligence that the deaths were due to cholera. Two more took place at Baru and the certainty was forced upon him that there was an epidemic.

The Controleur cursed freely. He cursed in Dutch, he cursed in English and he cursed in Malay. Then he drank a bottle of beer and smoked a cigar. After that he took thought. He knew the Chinese doctor would be useless. He was a nervous little man from Java and the natives would refuse to obey his orders. The Controleur was efficient and knew pretty well what must be done, but he could not do everything single-handed. He did not like Mr. Jones, but just then he was thankful that he was at hand, and he sent for him at once. In ten minutes Mr. Jones was in the office. He was accompanied by his sister.

"You know what I want to see you about, Mr. Jones," he said abruptly.

"Yes. I've been expecting a message from you. That is why my sister has come with me. We are ready to put all our resources at your disposal. I need not tell you that my sister is as competent as a man."

"I know. I shall be very glad of her assistance."

They set to without further delay to discuss the steps that must be taken. Hospital huts would have to be erected and quarantine stations. The inhabitants of the various villages on the islands must be forced to take proper precautions. In a good many cases the infected villages drew their water from the same well as the uninfected, and in each case this difficulty would have to be dealt with according to circumstances. It was necessary to send round people to give orders and make sure that they were carried out. Negligence must be ruthlessly punished. The worst of it was that the natives would not obey other natives, and orders given by native policemen, themselves unconvinced of their efficiency, would certainly be disregarded. It was advisable for Mr. Jones to stay at Baru where the population was largest and his medical attention most wanted; and what with the official duties that forced him to keep in touch with his headquarters, it was impossible for Mr. Gruyter to visit all the other islands himself. Miss Jones must go; but the natives of some of the outlying islands were wild and treacherous; the Controleur had had a good deal of trouble with them. He did not like the idea of exposing her to danger.

"I'm not afraid," she said.

"I daresay. But if you have your throat cut I shall get into trouble, and besides, we're so short-handed I don't want to risk losing your help."

"Then let Mr. Wilson come with me. He knows the natives better than anyone and can speak all their dialects."

"Ginger Ted?" The Controleur stared at her. "He's just getting over an attack of D. T.'s."

"I know," she answered.

"You know a great deal, Miss Jones."

Even though the moment was so serious Mr. Gruyter could not but smile. He gave her a sharp look, but she met it coolly.

"There's nothing like responsibility for bringing out what there is in a man, and I think something like this may be the making of him."

"Do you think it would be wise to trust yourself for days at a time to a man of such infamous character?" said the missionary.

"I put my trust in God," she answered gravely.

"Do you think he'd be any use?" asked the Controleur. "You know what he is."

"I'm convinced of it." Then she blushed. "After all, no one knows better than I that he's capable of self-control."

The Controleur bit his lip.

"Let's send for him."

He gave a message to the sergeant and in a few minutes Ginger Ted stood before them. He looked ill. He had evidently been much shaken by his recent attack and his nerves were all to pieces. He was in rags and he had not shaved for a week. No one could have looked more disreputable.

"Look here, Ginger," said the Controleur, "it's about this

cholera business. We've got to force the natives to take precautions and we want you to help us."

"Why the hell should I?"

"No reason at all. Except philanthropy."

"Nothing doing, Controleur. I'm not a philanthropist."

"That settles that. That was all. You can go."

But as Ginger Ted turned to the door Miss Jones stopped him.

"It was my suggestion, Mr. Wilson. You see, they want me to go to Labobo and Sakunchi, and the natives there are so funny I was afraid to go alone. I thought if you came I should be safer."

He gave her a look of extreme distaste.

"What do you suppose I care if they cut your throat?"

Miss Jones looked at him and her eyes filled with tears. She began to cry. He stood and watched her stupidly.

"There's no reason why you should." She pulled herself together and dried her eyes. "I'm being silly. I shall be all right. I'll go alone."

"It's damned foolishness for a woman to go to Labobo."

She gave him a little smile.

"I daresay it is, but you see, it's my job and I can't help myself. I'm sorry if I offended you by asking you. You must forget about it. I daresay it wasn't quite fair to ask you to take such a risk."

For a minute Ginger Ted stood and looked at her. He shifted from one foot to the other. His surly face seemed to grow black.

"Oh, hell, have it your own way," he said at last. "I'll come with you. When d'you want to start?"

They set out next day, with drugs and disinfectants, in the government launch. Mr. Gruyter as soon as he had put the necessary work in order was to start off in a prahu in the other direction. For four months the epidemic raged. Though everything possible was done to localize it one island after another was attacked. The Controleur was busy from morning to night. He had no sooner got back to Baru from one or other of the islands to do what was necessary there than he had to set off again. He distributed food and medicine. He cheered the terrified people. He supervised everything. He worked like a dog. He saw nothing of Ginger Ted, but he heard from Mr. Jones that the experiment was working out beyond all hopes. The scamp was behaving himself. He had a way with the natives; and by cajolery, firmness and on occasion the use of his fist, managed to make them take the steps necessary for their own safety. Miss Jones could congratulate herself on the success of the scheme. But the Controleur was too tired to be amused. When the epidemic had run its course he rejoiced because out of a population of eight thousand only six hundred had died.

Finally he was able to give the district a clean bill of health.

One evening he was sitting in his sarong on the verandah of his house and he read a French novel with the happy consciousness that once more he could take things easy. His head boy came in and told him that Ginger Ted wished to see him. He got up from his chair and shouted to him to come in. Company was just what he wanted. It had crossed the Controleur's mind that it would be pleasant to get drunk that night, but it is dull to get drunk alone, and he had regretfully put the thought aside. And heaven had sent Ginger Ted in the nick of time. By God, they would make a night of it. After four months they deserved a bit of fun. Ginger Ted entered. He was wearing a clean suit of white ducks. He was shaved. He looked another man.

"Why, Ginger, you look as if you'd been spending a month at a health resort instead of nursing a pack of natives dying of cholera. And look at your clothes. Have you just stepped out of a band-box?"

Ginger Ted smiled rather sheepishly. The head boy brought two bottles of beer and poured them out.

"Help yourself, Ginger," said the Controleur as he took his glass.

"I don't think I'll have any, thank you."

The Controleur put down his glass and looked at Ginger Ted with amazement.

"Why, what's the matter? Aren't you thirsty?"

"I don't mind having a cup of tea."

"A cup of what?"

"I'm on the wagon. Martha and I are going to be married."

"Ginger!"

The Controleur's eyes popped out of his head. He scratched his shaven pate.

"You can't marry Miss Jones," he said. "No one could marry Miss Jones."

"Well, I'm going to. That's what I've come to see you about. Owen's going to marry us in chapel, but we want to be married by Dutch law as well."

"A joke's a joke, Ginger. What's the idea?"

"She wanted it. She fell for me that night we spent on the island when the propeller broke. She's not a bad old girl when you get to know her. It's her last chance, if you understand what I mean, and I'd like to do something to oblige her. And she wants someone to take care of her, there's no doubt about that."

"Ginger, Ginger, before you can say knife she'll make you into a damned missionary."

"I don't know that I'd mind that so much if we had a little mission of our own. She says I'm a bloody marvel with the natives. She says I can do more with a native in five minutes than Owen can do in a year. She says she's never known anyone with the magnetism I have. It seems a pity to waste a gift like that."

The Controleur looked at him without speaking and slowly nodded his head three or four times. She'd hobble him all right.

"I've converted seventeen already," said Ginger Ted.

"You? I didn't know you believed in Christianity."

"Well, I don't know that I did exactly, but when I talked to 'em and they just came into the fold like a lot of blasted sheep, well, it gave me quite a turn. Blimey, I said, I daresay there's something in it after all."

"You should have raped her, Ginger. I wouldn't have been hard on you. I wouldn't have given you more than three years and three years is soon over."

"Look here, Controleur, don't you ever let on that the thought never entered my head. Women are touchy, you know, and she'd be as sore as hell if she knew that."

"I guessed she'd got her eye on you, but I never thought it would come to this." The Controleur in an agitated manner walked up and down the verandah. "Listen to me, old boy," he said after an interval of reflection, "we've had some grand times together and a friend's a friend. I'll tell you what I'll do, I'll lend you a launch and you can go and hide on one of the islands till the next ship comes along and then I'll get 'em to slow down and take you on board. You've only got one chance now and that's to cut and run."

Ginger Ted shook his head.

"It's no good, Controleur, I know you mean well, but I'm going to marry the blasted woman, and that's that. You don't know the joy of bringing all them bleeding sinners to repentance, and Christ, that girl can make a treacle pudding. I haven't eaten a better one since I was a kid."

The Controleur was very much disturbed. The drunken scamp was his only companion on the islands and he did not want to lose him. He discovered that he had even a certain affection for him. Next day he went to see the missionary.

"What's this I hear about your sister marrying Ginger Ted?" he asked him. "It's the most extraordinary thing I've ever heard in my life."

"It's true nevertheless."

"You must do something about it. It's madness."

"My sister is of full age and entitled to do as she pleases."

"But you don't mean to tell me you approve of it. You know Ginger Ted. He's a bum and there are no two ways about it. Have you told her the risk she's running? I mean, bringing sinners to repentance and all that sort of thing's all right, but there are limits. And does the leopard ever change his spots?"

Then for the first time in his life the Controleur saw a twinkle in the missionary's eye.

"My sister is a very determined woman, Mr. Gruyter," he replied. "From that night they spent on the island he never had a chance."

The Controleur gasped. He was as surprised as the prophet

when the Lord opened the mouth of the ass, and she said unto Balaam, "What have I done unto thee, that thou hast smitten me these three times?" Perhaps Mr. Jones was human after all.

"*Allejesus!*" muttered the Controleur.

Before anything more could be said Miss Jones swept into the room. She was radiant. She looked ten years younger. Her cheeks were flushed and her nose was hardly red at all.

"Have you come to congratulate me, Mr. Gruyter?" she cried, and her manner was sprightly and girlish. "You see, I was right after all. Everyone has some good in them. You don't know how splendid Edward has been all through this terrible time. He's a hero. He's a saint. Even I was surprised."

"I hope you'll be very happy, Miss Jones."

"I know I shall. Oh, it would be wicked of me to doubt it. For it is the Lord who has brought us together."

"Do you think so?"

"I know it. Don't you see? Except for the cholera Edward would never have found himself. Except for the cholera we should never have learnt to know one another. I have never seen the hand of God more plainly manifest."

The Controleur could not but think that it was rather a clumsy device to bring those two together that necessitated the death of six hundred innocent persons, but not being well versed in the ways of omnipotence he made no remark.

"You'll never guess where we're going for our honeymoon," said Miss Jones, perhaps a trifle archly.

"Java?"

"No, if you'll lend us the launch, we're going to that island where we were marooned. It has very tender recollections for both of us. It was there that I first guessed how fine and good Edward was. It's there I want him to have his reward."

The Controleur caught his breath. He left quickly, for he thought that unless he had a bottle of beer at once he would have a fit. He was never so shocked in his life.

Damon Runyon

*

MADAME LA GIMP

*Hailed as "the first film in the Capra idiom" and a "1938 phe-
nomenon," Runyon's engaging story of a broken down, Broadway flower woman was produced by Columbia Pictures under
the title LADY FOR A DAY. It was directed by Frank Capra
and starred May Robson, Warren William and Glenda Farrell,
supported by Guy Kibbee, Walter Connally, Jean Parker and
Nat Pendleton. It was wisely chosen by motion picture critics
as One of the Ten Best Pictures of 1933.*

ONE NIGHT I am passing the corner of Fiftieth Street and
Broadway, and what do I see but Dave the Dude standing in
a doorway talking to a busted-down old Spanish doll by the
name of Madame La Gimp. Or rather Madame La Gimp is
talking to Dave the Dude, and what is more he is listening to
her, because I can hear him say yes, yes, as he always does
when he is really listening to anybody, which is very seldom.

Now this is a most surprising sight to me, because Madame
La Gimp is not such an old doll as anybody will wish to listen
to, especially Dave the Dude. In fact, she is nothing but an
old haybag, and generally somewhat ginned up. For fifteen
years, or maybe sixteen, I see Madame La Gimp up and down
Broadway, or sliding along through the Forties, sometimes
selling newspapers, and sometimes selling flowers, and in all
these years I seldom see her but what she seems to have about
half a heat on from drinking gin.

Of course nobody ever takes the newspapers she sells, even
after they buy them off of her, because they are generally yesterday's papers, and sometimes last week's, and nobody ever
wants her flowers, even after they pay her for them, because
they are flowers such as she gets off an undertaker over in
Tenth Avenue, and they are very tired flowers, indeed.

Personally I consider Madame La Gimp nothing but an old

pest, but kind-hearted guys like Dave the Dude always stake her to a few pieces of silver when she comes shuffling along putting on the moan about her tough luck. She walks with a gimp in one leg, which is why she is called Madame La Gimp, and years ago I hear somebody say Madame La Gimp is once a Spanish dancer, and a big shot on Broadway, but that she meets up with an accident which puts her out of the dancing dodge, and that a busted romance makes her become a ginhead.

I remember somebody telling me once that Madame La Gimp is quite a beauty in her day, and has her own servants, and all this and that, but I always hear the same thing about every bum on Broadway, male and female, including some I know are bums, in spades, right from taw, so I do not pay any attention to these stories.

Still, I am willing to allow that maybe Madame La Gimp is once a fair looker, at that, and the chances are has a fair shape, because once or twice I see her when she is not ginned up, and has her hair combed, and she is not so bad-looking, although even then if you put her in a claiming race I do not think there is any danger of anybody claiming her out of it.

Mostly she is wearing raggedy clothes, and busted shoes, and her gray hair is generally hanging down her face, and when I say she is maybe fifty years old I am giving her plenty the best of it. Although she is Spanish, Madame La Gimp talks good English, and in fact she can cuss in English as good as anybody I ever hear, barring Dave the Dude.

Well, anyway, when Dave the Dude sees me as he is listening to Madame La Gimp, he motions me to wait, so I wait until she finally gets through gabbing to him and goes gimping away. Then Dave the Dude comes over to me looking much worried.

"This is quite a situation," Dave says. "The old doll is in a tough spot. It seems that she once has a baby which she calls by the name of Eulalie, being it is a girl baby, and she ships this baby off to her sister in a little town in Spain to raise up, because Madame La Gimp figures a baby is not apt to get much raising-up off of her as long as she is on Broadway. Well, this baby is on her way here. In fact," Dave says, "she will land next Saturday and here it is Wednesday already."

"Where is the baby's papa?" I ask Dave the Dude.

"Well," Dave says, "I do not ask Madame La Gimp this, because I do not consider it a fair question. A guy who goes around this town asking where babies' papas are, or even who they are, is apt to get the name of being nosey. Anyway, this has nothing whatever to do with the proposition, which is that Madame La Gimp's baby, Eulalie, is arriving here.

"Now," Dave says, "it seems that Madame La Gimp's baby, being now eighteen years old, is engaged to marry the son of a very proud old Spanish nobleman who lives in this little town in Spain, and it also seems that the very proud old Spanish nobleman, and his ever-loving wife, and the son, and Madame La Gimp's sister, are all with the baby. They are making a tour of the whole world, and will stop over here a couple of days just to see Madame La Gimp."

"It is commencing to sound to me like a movie such as a guy is apt to see at a midnight show," I say.

"Wait a minute," Dave says, getting impatient. "You are too gabby to suit me. Now it seems that the proud old Spanish nobleman does not wish his son to marry any lob, and one reason he is coming here is to look over Madame La Gimp, and see that she is okay. He thinks that Madame La Gimp's baby's own papa is dead, and that Madame La Gimp is now married to one of the richest and most aristocratic guys in America."

"How does the proud old Spanish nobleman get such an idea as this?" I ask. "It is a sure thing he never sees Madame La Gimp, or even a photograph of her as she is at present."

"I will tell you how," Dave the Dude says. "It seems Madame La Gimp gives her baby the idea that such is the case in her letters to her. It seems Madame La Gimp does a little scrubbing business around a swell apartment hotel in Park Avenue that is called the Marberry, and she cops stationery saying this is where she lives, and how rich and aristocratic her husband is. And what is more, Madame La Gimp has letters from her baby sent to her in care of the hotel and gets them out of the employees' mail."

"Why," I say, "Madame La Gimp is nothing but an old fraud to deceive people in this manner, especially a proud old Spanish nobleman. And," I say, "this proud old Spanish nobleman must be something of a chump to believe a mother will keep away from her baby all these years, especially if the mother has plenty of dough, although of course I do not know just how smart a proud old Spanish nobleman can be."

"Well," Dave says, "Madame La Gimp tells me the thing that makes the biggest hit of all with the proud old Spanish nobleman is that she keeps her baby in Spain all these years because she wishes her raised up a true Spanish baby in every respect until she is old enough to know what time it is. But I judge the proud old Spanish nobleman is none too bright, at that," Dave says, "because Madame La Gimp tells me he always lives in this little town which does not even have running water in the bathrooms.

"But what I am getting at is this," Dave says. "We must have Madame La Gimp in a swell apartment in the Marberry with a rich and aristocratic guy for a husband by the time her baby gets here, because if the proud old Spanish nobleman finds out Madame La Gimp is nothing but a bum, it is a hundred to one he will cancel his son's engagement to Madame La Gimp's baby and break a lot of people's hearts, including his son's.

"Madame La Gimp tells me her baby is daffy about the young guy, and he is daffy about her, and there are enough broken hearts in this town as it is. I know how I will get the apartment, so you go and bring Judge Henry G. Blake for a rich and artistocratic husband, or anyway for a husband."

Well, I know Dave the Dude to do many a daffy thing but never a thing as daffy as this. But I know there is no use arguing with him when he gets an idea, because if you argue with Dave the Dude too much he is apt to reach over and lay his Sunday punch on your snoot, and no argument is worth a punch on the snoot, especially from Dave the Dude.

So I go out looking for Judge Henry G. Blake to be Madame La Gimp's husband, although I am not so sure Judge Henry G. Blake will care to be anybody's husband, especially Madame La Gimp's, after he gets a load of her, for Judge Henry G. Blake is kind of a classy old guy.

To look at Judge Henry G. Blake, with his gray hair, and his nose glasses, and his stomach, you will think he is very important people, indeed. Of course Judge Henry G. Blake is not a judge, and never is a judge, but they call him Judge because he looks like a judge, and talks slow, and puts in many long words, which very few people understand.

They tell me Judge Blake once has plenty of dough, and is quite a guy in Wall Street, and a high shot along Broadway, but he misses a few guesses at the market, and winds up without much dough, as guys generally do who misses guesses at the market. What Judge Henry G. Blake does for a living at this time nobody knows, because he does nothing much whatever, and yet he seems to be a producer in a small way at all times.

Now and then he makes a trip across the ocean with such as Little Manuel, and other guys who ride the tubs, and sits in with them on games of bridge, and one thing and another, when they need him. Very often when he is riding the tubs, Little Manuel runs into some guy he cannot cheat, so he has to call in Judge Henry G. Blake to outplay the guy on the level, although of course Little Manuel will much rather get a guy's dough by cheating him than by outplaying him on the level. Why this is, I do not know, but this is the way Little Manuel is.

Anyway, you cannot say Judge Henry G. Blake is a bum, especially as he wears good clothes, with a wing collar, and a derby hat, and most people consider him a very nice old man. Personally I never catch the judge out of line on any proposition whatever, and he always says hello to me, very pleasant.

It takes me several hours to find Judge Henry G. Blake, but finally I locate him in Derle's billiard room playing a game of pool with a guy from Providence for five cents a ball, and the judge is about thirteen balls behind when I step into the joint, because naturally at five cents a ball the judge wishes the guy from Providence to win, so as to encourage him to play for maybe twenty-five cents a ball, the judge being very cute this way.

Well, when I step in I see the judge miss a shot anybody can make blindfolded, but as soon as I give him the office I wish to speak to him, the judge hauls off and belts in every ball on the table, bingity-bing, the last shot being a bank that will make Al de Oro stop and think, because when it comes to pool, the old judge is just naturally a curly wolf.

Afterwards he tells me he is very sorry I make him hurry up this way, because of course after the last shot he is never going to get the guy from Providence to play him pool even for fun, and the judge tells me the guy sizes up as a right good thing at that.

Now Judge Henry G. Blake is not so excited when I tell him what Dave the Dude wishes to see him about, but naturally he is willing to do anything for Dave, because he knows that guys who are not willing to do things for Dave the Dude often have bad luck. The judge tells me that he is afraid he will not make much of a husband because he tries it before several times on his own hook and is always a bust, but as long as this time it is not to be anything serious, he will tackle it. Anyway, Judge Henry G. Blake says, being aristocratic will come natural to him.

Well, when Dave the Dude starts out on any proposition, he is a wonder for fast working. The first thing he does is to turn Madame La Gimp over to Miss Billy Perry, who is now Dave's ever-loving wife which he takes out of tap-dancing in Miss Missouri Martin's Sixteen Hundred Club, and Miss Billy Perry calls in Miss Missouri Martin to help.

This is water on Miss Missouri Martin's wheel, because if there is anything she loves it is to stick her nose in other people's business, no matter what it is, but she is quite a help at that, although at first they have a tough time keeping her from telling Waldo Winchester, the scribe, about the whole cat-hop, so he will put a story in the *Morning Item* about it, with Miss Missouri Martin's name in it. Miss Missouri Martin does not believe in ever overlooking any publicity bets on the layout.

Anyway, it seems that between them Miss Billy Perry and Miss Missouri Martin get Madame La Gimp dolled up in a lot of new clothes, and run her through one of these beauty joints until she comes out very much changed, indeed. Afterwards I hear Miss Billy Perry and Miss Missouri Martin have quite a few words, because Miss Missouri Martin wishes to paint Madame La Gimp's hair the same color as her own, which is a high yellow, and buy her the same kind of dresses which Miss Missouri Martin wears herself, and Miss Missouri Martin gets much insulted when Miss Billy Perry says no, they are trying to dress Madame La Gimp to look like a lady.

They tell me Miss Missouri Martin thinks some of putting the slug on Miss Billy Perry for this crack, but happens to remember just in time that Miss Billy Perry is now Dave the Dude's ever-loving wife, and that nobody in this town can put the slug on Dave's ever-loving wife, except maybe Dave himself.

Now the next thing anybody knows, Madame La Gimp is in a swell eight-or-nine-room apartment in the Marberry, and the way this comes about is as follows: It seems that one of Dave the Dude's most important champagne customers is a guy by the name of Rodney B. Emerson, who owns the apartment, but who is at his summer home in Newport, with his family, or anyway with his ever-loving wife.

This Rodney B. Emerson is quite a guy along Broadway, and a great hand for spending dough and looking for laughs, and he is very popular with the mob. Furthermore he is obligated to Dave the Dude, because Dave sells him good champagne when most guys are trying to hand him the old phonus bolonus, and naturally Rodney B. Emerson appreciates this kind treatment.

He is a short, fat guy, with a round, red face, and a big laugh, and the kind of a guy Dave the Dude can call up at his home in Newport and explain the situation and ask for the loan of the apartment, which Dave does.

Well, it seems Rodney B. Emerson gets a big bang out of the idea, and he says to Dave the Dude like this:

"You not only can have the apartment, Dave, but I will come over and help you out. It will save a lot of explaining around the Marberry if I am there."

So he hops right over from Newport, and joins in with Dave the Dude, and I wish to say Rodney B. Emerson will always be kindly remembered by one and all for his co-operation, and nobody will ever again try to hand him the phonus bolonus when he is buying champagne, even if he is not buying it off of Dave the Dude.

Well, it is coming on Saturday and the boat from Spain is due, so Dave the Dude hires a big town car, and puts his own driver, Wop Sam, on it, as he does not wish any strange driver tipping off anybody that it is a hired car. Miss Missouri Martin is anxious to go to the boat with Madame La Gimp, and take her jazz band, the Hi Hi Boys, from her Sixteen Hundred Club with her to make it a real welcome, but nobody thinks much of this idea. Only Madame La Gimp and her husband, Judge Henry G. Blake, and Miss Billy Perry go, though the judge holds out for some time for Little Manuel, because Judge Blake says he wishes somebody around to tip him off in case there are any bad cracks made about him as a husband in Spanish, and Little Manuel is very Spanish.

The morning they go to meet the boat is the first time Judge Henry G. Blake gets a load of his ever-loving wife, Madame La Gimp, and by this time Miss Billy Perry and Miss Missouri Martin give Madame La Gimp such a going-over that she is by no means the worst looker in the world. In fact, she looks first-rate, especially as she is off gin and says she is off it for good.

Judge Henry G. Blake is really quite surprised by her looks as he figures all along she will turn out to be a crow. In fact, Judge Blake hurls a couple of shots into himself to nerve himself for the ordeal, as he explains it, before he appears to go to the boat. Between these shots, and the nice clothes, and the good cleaning-up Miss Billy Perry and Miss Missouri Martin give Madame La Gimp, she is really a pleasant sight to the judge.

They tell me the meeting at the dock between Madame La Gimp and her baby is very affecting indeed, and when the proud old Spanish nobleman and his wife, and their son, and Madame La Gimp's sister, all go into action, too, there are enough tears around to float all the battleships we once sink for Spain. Even Miss Billy Perry and Judge Henry G. Blake do some first-class crying, although the chances are the judge is worked up to the crying more by the shots he takes for his courage than by the meeting.

Still, I hear the old judge does himself proud, what with kissing Madame La Gimp's baby plenty, and duking the proud old Spanish nobleman, and his wife, and son, and giving Madame La Gimp's sister a good strong hug that squeezes her tongue out.

It turns out that the proud old Spanish nobleman has white sideburns, and is entitled Conde de Something, so his ever-loving wife is the Condesa, and the son is a very nice-looking quiet young guy any way you take him, who blushes every time anybody looks at him. As for Madame La Gimp's baby, she is as pretty as they come, and many guys are sorry they do not get Judge Henry G. Blake's job as stepfather, because he is able to take a kiss at Madame La Gimp's baby on what seems to be very small excuse. I never see a nicer-looking young couple, and anybody can see they are very fond of each other, indeed.

Madame La Gimp's sister is not such a doll as I will wish to have sawed off on me, and is up in the paints as regards to age, but she is also very quiet. None of the bunch talk any English, so Miss Billy Perry and Judge Henry G. Blake are pretty much outsiders on the way uptown. Anyway, the judge takes the wind as soon as they reach the Marberry, because the judge is now getting a little tired of being a husband. He says he has to take a trip out to Pittsburgh to buy four or five coal mines, but will be back the next day.

Well, it seems to me that everything is going perfect so far, and that it is good judgment to let it lay as it is, but nothing will do Dave the Dude but to have a reception the following night. I advise Dave the Dude against the idea because I am afraid something will happen to spoil the whole cat-hop, but he will not listen to me, especially as Rodney B. Emerson is now in town and is a strong booster for the party, as he wishes to drink some of the good champagne he has planted in his apartment.

Furthermore, Miss Billy Perry and Miss Missouri Martin are very indignant at me when they hear about my advice, as it seems they both buy new dresses out of Dave the Dude's bank roll when they are dressing up Madame La Gimp, and they wish to spring these dresses somewhere where they can be seen. So the party is on.

I get to the Marberry around nine o'clock and who opens the door of Madame La Gimp's apartment for me but Moosh, the door man from Miss Missouri Martin's Sixteen Hundred Club. Furthermore, he is in his Sixteen Hundred Club uniform, except he has a clean shave. I wish Moosh a hello, and he never raps to me but only bows, and takes my hat.

The next guy I see is Rodney B. Emerson in evening clothes, and the minute he sees me he yells out, "Mister O. O. McIntyre." Well, of course I am not Mister O. O. McIntyre, and never put myself away as Mister O. O. McIntyre, and furthermore there is no resemblance whatever between Mister O. O. McIntyre and me, because I am a fairly good-looking guy, and I start to give Rodney B. Emerson an argument, when he whispers to me like this:

"Listen," he whispers, "we must have big names at this affair, so as to impress these people. The chances are they read the newspapers back there in Spain, and we must let them meet the folks they read about, so they will see Madame La Gimp is a real big shot to get such names to a party."

Then he takes me by the arm and leads me to a group of people in a corner of the room, which is about the size of the Grand Central waiting room.

"Mister O. O. McIntyre, the big writer!" Rodney B. Emerson says, and the next thing I know I am shaking hands with Mr. and Mrs. Conde and their son, and with Madame La Gimp and her baby, and Madame La Gimp's sister, and finally with Judge Henry G. Blake who has on a swallowtail coat, and does not give me much of a tumble. I figure the chances are Judge Henry G. Blake is getting a swelled head already, not to tumble up a guy who helps him get his job, but even at that

I wish to say the old judge looks immense in his swallowtail coat, bowing and giving one and all the old castor oil smile.

Madame La Gimp is in a low-neck black dress and is wearing a lot of Miss Missouri Martin's diamonds, such as rings and bracelets, which Miss Missouri Martin insists on hanging on her, although I hear afterwards that Miss Missouri Martin has Johnny Brannigan, the plain clothes copper, watching these diamonds. I wonder at the time why Johnny is there but figure it is because he is a friend of Dave the Dude's. Miss Missouri Martin is no sucker, even if she is kind-hearted.

Anybody looking at Madame La Gimp will bet you all the coffee in Java that she never lives in a cellar over in Tenth Avenue, and drinks plenty of gin in her day. She has her gray hair piled up high on her head, with a big Spanish comb in it, and she reminds me of a picture I see somewhere, but I do not remember just where. And her baby, Eulalie, in a white dress is about as pretty a little doll as you will wish to see, and nobody can blame Judge Henry G. Blake for copping a kiss off of her now and then.

Well, pretty soon I hear Rodney B. Emerson bawling, "Mister Willie K. Vanderbilt," and in comes nobody but Big Nig, and Rodney B. Emerson leads him over to the group and introduces him.

Little Manuel is standing alongside Judge Henry G. Blake, and he explains in Spanish to Mr. and Mrs. Conde and the others that "Willie K. Vanderbilt" is a very large millionaire, and Mr. and Mrs. Conde seem much interested, anyway, though naturally Madame La Gimp and Judge Henry G. Blake are jerry to Big Nig, while Madame La Gimp's baby and the young guy are interested in nobody but each other.

Then I hear, "Mister Al Jolson," and in comes nobody but Tony Bertazzola, from the Chicken Club, who looks about as much like Al as I do like O. O. McIntyre, which is not at all. Next comes "the Very Reverend John Roach Straton," who seems to be Skeets Bolivar to me, then "the Honorable Mayor James J. Walker," and who is it but Good-Time Charley Bernstein.

"Mister Otto H. Kahn" turns out to be Rochester Red, and

"Mister Heywood Broun" is Nick the Greek, who asks me privately who Heywood Broun is, and gets very sore at Rodney B. Emerson when I describe Heywood Broun to him.

Finally there is quite a commotion at the door and Rodney B. Emerson announces, "Mister Herbert Bayard Swope" in an extra loud voice which makes everybody look around, but it is nobody but the Pale Face Kid. He gets me to one side, too, and wishes to know who Herbert Bayard Swope is, and when I explain to him, the Pale Face Kid gets so swelled up he will not speak to Death House Donegan, who is only "Mister William Muldoon."

Well, it seems to me they are getting too strong when they announce, "Vice-President of the United States, the Honorable Charles Curtis," and in pops Guinea Mike, and I say as much to Dave the Dude, who is running around every which way looking after things, but he only says, "Well, if you do not know it is Guinea Mike will you know it is not Vice-President Curtis?"

But it seems to me all this is most disrespectful to our leading citizens, especially when Rodney B. Emerson calls "The Honorable Police Commissioner, Mister Grover A. Whalen," and in pops Wild William Wilkins, who is a very hot man at this time, being wanted in several spots for different raps. Dave the Dude takes personal charge of Wild William and removes a rod from his pants pocket, because none of the guests are supposed to come rodded up, this being strictly a social matter.

I watch Mr. and Mrs. Conde, and I do not see that these names are making any impression on them, and I afterwards find out that they never get any newspapers in their town in Spain except a little local bladder which only prints the home news. In fact, Mr. and Mrs. Conde seem somewhat bored, although Mr. Conde cheers up no little and looks interested when a lot of dolls drift in. They are mainly dolls from Miss Missouri Martin's Sixteen Hundred Club, and the Hot Box, but Rodney B. Emerson introduces them as "Sophie Tucker," and "Theda Bara," and "Jeanne Eagels," and "Helen Morgan," and "Aunt Jemima," and one thing and another.

Well, pretty soon in comes Miss Missouri Martin's jazz band, the Hi Hi Boys, and the party commences getting up steam, especially when Dave the Dude gets Rodney B. Emerson to breaking out the old grape. By and by there is dancing going on, and a good time is being had by one and all, including Mr. and Mrs. Conde. In fact, after Mr. Conde gets a couple of jolts of the old grape, he turns out to be a pretty nice old skate, even if nobody can understand what he is talking about.

As for Judge Henry G. Blake, he is full of speed, indeed. By this time anybody can see that the judge is commencing to believe that all this is on the level and that he is really entertaining celebrities in his own home. You put a quart of good grape inside the old judge and he will believe anything. He soon dances himself plumb out of wind, and then I notice he is hanging around Madame La Gimp a lot.

Along about midnight, Dave the Dude has to go out into the kitchen and settle a battle there over a crap game, but otherwise everything is very peaceful. It seems that "Herbert Bayard Swope," "Vice-President Curtis" and "Grover Whalen'" get a little game going, when "the Reverend John Roach Straton" steps up and cleans them in four passes, but it seems they soon discover that "the Reverend John Roach Straton" is using tops on them, which are very dishonest dice, and so they put the slug on "the Reverend John Roach Straton" and Dave the Dude has to split them out.

By and by I figure on taking the wind, and I look for Mr. and Mrs. Conde to tell them good night, but Mr. Conde and Miss Missouri Martin are still dancing, and Miss Missouri Martin is pouring conversation into Mr. Conde's ear by the bucketful, and while Mr. Conde does not savvy a word she says, this makes no difference to Miss Missouri Martin. Let Miss Missouri Martin do all the talking and she does not care a whoop if anybody understands her.

Mrs. Conde is over in a corner with "Herbert Bayard Swope," or the Pale Face Kid, who is trying to find out from her by using hog Latin and signs on her if there is any chance for a good twenty-one dealer in Spain, and of course Mrs. Conde is not able to make heads or tails of what he means, so I hunt up Madame La Gimp.

She is sitting in a darkish corner off by herself and I really do not see Judge Henry G. Blake leaning over her until I am almost on top of them, so I cannot help hearing what the judge is saying.

"I am wondering for two days," he says, "if by any chance you remember me. Do you know who I am?"

"I remember you," Madame La Gimp says. "I remember you—oh, so very well, Henry. How can I forget you? But I have no idea you recognize me after all these years."

"Twenty of them now," Judge Henry G. Blake says. "You were beautiful then. You are still beautiful."

Well, I can see the old grape is working first-class on Judge Henry G. Blake to make such remarks as this, although at that, in the half light, with the smile on her face, Madame La Gimp is not so bad. Still, give me them carrying a little less weight for age.

"Well, it is all your fault," Judge Henry G. Blake says. "You go and marry that chile con carne guy, and look what happens!"

I can see there is no sense in me horning in on Madame La Gimp and Judge Henry G. Blake while they are cutting up old touches in this manner, so I think I will just say good-bye to the young people and let it go at that, but while I am looking for Madame La Gimp's baby and her guy, I run into Dave the Dude.

"You will not find them here," Dave says. "By this time they are being married over at Saint Malachy's with my ever-loving wife and Big Nig standing up with them. We get the license for them yesterday afternoon. Can you imagine a couple of young saps wishing to wait until they go plumb around the world before getting married?"

Well, of course this elopement creates much excitement for a few minutes, but by Monday Mr. and Mrs. Conde and the young folks and Madame La Gimp's sister take a train for California to keep on going around the world, leaving us nothing to talk about but about old Judge Henry G. Blake and

Madame La Gimp getting themselves married too, and going to Detroit where Judge Henry G. Blake claims he has a brother in the plumbing business who will give him a job, although personally I think Judge Henry G. Blake figures to do a little booting on his own hook in and out of Canada. It is not like Judge Henry G. Blake to tie himself up to the plumbing business.

So there is nothing more to the story, except that Dave the Dude is around a few days later with a big sheet of paper in his duke and very, very indignant.

"If every single article listed here is not kicked back to the owners of the different joints in the Marberry that they are taken from by next Tuesday night, I will bust a lot of noses around this town," Dave says. "I am greatly mortified by such happenings at my social affairs, and everything must be returned at once. Especially," Dave says, "the baby grand piano that is removed from Apartment 9-D."

Damon Runyon

*

BUTCH MINDS THE BABY

BUTCH MINDS THE BABY was a delightful light comedy with typical Runyonesque characters and situations. Adapted by Leonard Spiegelglass and directed by Albert S. Rogell, the film was released in 1942 as a Mayfair Universal Production. The cast included Broderick Crawford, Michael Barnitz, Virginia Bruce, Dick Foran and Shamp Howard.

ONE EVENING along about seven o'clock I am sitting in Mindy's restaurant putting on the gefillte fish, which is a dish I am very fond of, when in comes three parties from Brooklyn wearing caps as follows: Harry the Horse, Little Isadore and Spanish John.

Now these parties are not such parties as I will care to have much truck with, because I often hear rumors about them that are very discreditable, even if the rumors are not true. In fact, I hear that many citizens of Brooklyn will be very glad indeed to see Harry the Horse, Little Isadore and Spanish John move away from there, as they are always doing something that is considered a knock to the community, such as robbing people, or maybe shooting or stabbing them, and throwing pineapples, and carrying on generally.

I am really much surprised to see these parties on Broadway, as it is well known that the Broadway coppers just naturally love to shove such parties around, but here they are in Mindy's, and there I am, so of course I give them a very large hello, as I never wish to seem inhospitable, even to Brooklyn parties. Right away they come over to my table and sit down, and Little Isadore reaches out and spears himself a big hunk of my gefillte fish with his fingers, but I overlook this, as I am using the only knife on the table.

Then they all sit there looking at me without saying anything, and the way they look at me makes me very nervous indeed. Finally I figure that maybe they are a little embarrassed being in a high-class spot such as Mindy's, with legitimate people around and about, so I say to them, very polite:

"It is a nice night."

"What is nice about it?" asks Harry the Horse, who is a thin man with a sharp face and sharp eyes.

Well, now that it is put up to me in this way, I can see there is nothing so nice about the night, at that, so I try to think of something else jolly to say, while Little Isadore keeps spearing at my gefillte fish with his fingers, and Spanish John nabs one of my potatoes.

"Where does Big Butch live?" Harry the Horse asks.

"Big Butch?" I say, as if I never hear the name before in my life, because in this man's town it is never a good idea to answer any question without thinking it over, as some time you may give the right answer to the wrong guy, or the wrong answer to the right guy. "Where does Big Butch live?" I ask them again.

"Yes, where does he live?" Harry the Horse says, very impatient. "We wish you to take us to him."

"Now wait a minute, Harry," I say, and I am now more nervous than somewhat. "I am not sure I remember the exact house Big Butch lives in, and furthermore I am not sure Big Butch will care to have me bringing people to see him, especially three at a time, and especially from Brooklyn. You know Big Butch has a very bad disposition, and there is no telling what he may say to me if he does not like the idea of me taking you to him."

"Everything is very kosher," Harry the Horse says. "You need not be afraid of anything whatever. We have a business proposition for Big Butch. It means a nice score for him, so you take us to him at once, or the chances are I will have to put the arm on somebody around here."

Well, as the only one around there for them to put the arm on at this time seems to be me, I can see where it will be good policy for me to take these parties to Big Butch, especially as the last of my gefillte fish is just going down Little Isadore's gullet, and Spanish John is finishing up my potatoes, and is donking a piece of rye bread in my coffee, so there is nothing more for me to eat.

So I lead them over into West Forty-ninth Street, near Tenth Avenue, where Big Butch lives on the ground floor of an old brownstone-front house, and who is sitting out on the stoop but Big Butch himself. In fact, everybody in the neighborhood is sitting out on the front stoops over there, including women and children, because sitting out on the front stoops is quite a custom in this section.

Big Butch is peeled down to his undershirt and pants, and he has no shoes on his feet, as Big Butch is a guy who likes his comfort. Furthermore, he is smoking a cigar, and laid out on the stoop beside him on a blanket is a little baby with not much clothes on. This baby seems to be asleep, and every now and then Big Butch fans it with a folded newspaper to shoo away the mosquitoes that wish to nibble on the baby. These mosquitoes come across the river from the Jersey side on hot nights and they seem to be very fond of babies.

"Hello, Butch," I say, as we stop in front of the stoop.

"Sh-h-h-h!" Butch says, pointing at the baby, and making more noise with his shush than an engine blowing off steam. Then he gets up and tiptoes down to the sidewalk where we are standing, and I am hoping that Butch feels all right, because when Butch does not feel so good he is apt to be very short with one and all. He is a guy of maybe six foot two and a couple of feet wide, and he has big hairy hands and a mean look.

In fact, Big Butch is known all over this man's town as a guy you must not monkey with in any respect, so it takes plenty of weight off of me when I see that he seems to know the parties from Brooklyn, and nods at them very friendly, especially at Harry the Horse. And right away Harry states a most surprising proposition to Big Butch.

It seems that there is a big coal company which has an office in an old building down in West Eighteenth Street, and in this office is a safe, and in this safe is the company pay roll of twenty thousand dollars cash money. Harry the Horse knows the money is there because a personal friend of his who is the paymaster for the company puts it there late this very afternoon.

It seems that the paymaster enters into a dicker with Harry the Horse and Little Isadore and Spanish John for them to slug him while he is carrying the pay roll from the bank to the office in the afternoon, but something happens that they miss connections on the exact spot, so the paymaster has to carry the sugar on to the office without being slugged, and there it is now in two fat bundles.

Personally it seems to me as I listen to Harry's story that the paymaster must be a very dishonest character to be making deals to hold still while he is being slugged and the company's sugar taken away from him, but of course it is none of my business, so I take no part in the conversation.

Well, it seems that Harry the Horse and Little Isadore and Spanish John wish to get the money out of the safe, but none of them knows anything about opening safes, and while they are standing around over in Brooklyn talking over what is to be done in this emergency Harry suddenly remembers that Big Butch is once in the business of opening safes for a living.

In fact, I hear afterwards that Big Butch is considered the best safe opener east of the Mississippi River in his day, but the law finally takes to sending him to Sing Sing for opening these safes, and after he is in and out of Sing Sing three different times for opening safes Butch gets sick and tired of the place, especially as they pass what is called the Baumes Law in New York, which is a law that says if a guy is sent to Sing Sing four times hand running, he must stay there the rest of his life, without any argument about it.

So Big Butch gives up opening safes for a living, and goes into business in a small way, such as running beer, and handling a little Scotch now and then, and becomes an honest citizen. Furthermore, he marries one of the neighbor's children over on the West Side by the name of Mary Murphy, and I judge the baby on this stoop comes of this marriage between Big Butch and Mary because I can see that it is a very homely baby, indeed. Still, I never see many babies that I consider rose geraniums for looks, anyway.

Well, it finally comes out that the idea of Harry the Horse and Little Isadore and Spanish John is to get Big Butch to open the coal company's safe and take the pay-roll money out, and they are willing to give him fifty per cent of the money for his bother, taking fifty per cent for themselves for finding the plant, and paying all the overhead, such as the paymaster, out of their bit, which strikes me as a pretty fair sort of deal for Big Butch. But Butch only shakes his head.

"It is old-fashioned stuff," Butch says. "Nobody opens pete boxes for a living any more. They make the boxes too good, and they are all wired up with alarms and are a lot of trouble generally. I am in a legitimate business now and going along. You boys know I cannot stand another fall, what with being away three times already, and in addition to this I must mind the baby. My old lady goes to Mrs. Clancy's wake tonight up in the Bronx, and the chances are she will be there all night, as she is very fond of wakes, so I must mind little John Ignatius Junior."

"Listen, Butch," Harry the Horse says, "this is a very soft pete. It is old-fashioned, and you can open it with a tooth-pick. There are no wires on it, because they never put more than a dime in it before in years. It just happens they have to put the twenty G's in it tonight because my pal the pay-master makes it a point not to get back from the jug with the scratch in time to pay off today, especially after he sees we miss out on him. It is the softest touch you will ever know, and where can a guy pick up ten G's like this?"

I can see that Big Butch is thinking the ten G's over very seriously, at that, because in these times nobody can afford to pass up ten G's, especially a guy in the beer business, which is very, very tough just now. But finally he shakes his head again and says like this:

"No," he says, "I must let it go, because I must mind the baby. My old lady is very, very particular about this, and I dast not leave little John Ignatius Junior for a minute. If Mary comes home and finds I am not minding the baby she will put the blast on me plenty. I like to turn a few honest bobs now and then as well as anybody, but," Butch says, "John Ignatius Junior comes first with me."

Then he turns away and goes back to the stoop as much as to say he is through arguing, and sits down beside John Ignatius Junior again just in time to keep a mosquito from carrying off one of John's legs. Anybody can see that Big Butch is very fond of this baby, though personally I will not give you a dime a dozen for babies, male and female.

Well, Harry the Horse and Little Isadore and Spanish John are very much disappointed, and stand around talking among themselves, and paying no attention to me, when all of a sudden Spanish John, who never has much to say up to this time, seems to have a bright idea. He talks to Harry and Isadore, and they get all pleasured up over what he has to say, and finally Harry goes to Big Butch.

"Sh-h-h-h!" Big Butch says, pointing to the baby as Harry opens his mouth.

"Listen, Butch," Harry says in a whisper, "we can take the baby with us, and you can mind it and work, too."

"Why," Big Butch whispers back, "this is quite an idea indeed. Let us go into the house and talk things over."

So he picks up the baby and leads us into his joint, and gets out some pretty fair beer, though it is needled a little, at that, and we sit around the kitchen chewing the fat in whispers. There is a crib in the kitchen, and Butch puts the baby in this crib, and it keeps on snoozing away first rate while we are talking. In fact, it is sleeping so sound that I am commencing to figure that Butch must give it some of the needled beer he is feeding us, because I am feeling a little dopey myself.

Finally Butch says that as long as he can take John Ignatius Junior with him he sees no reason why he shall not go and open the safe for them, only he says he must have five per cent more to put in the baby's bank when he gets back, so as to round himself up with his ever-loving wife in case of a beef from her over keeping the baby out in the night air. Harry the Horse says he considers this extra five per cent a little strong, but Spanish John, who seems to be a very square guy, says that after all it is only fair to cut the baby in if it is to be with them when they are making the score, and Little Isadore seems to think it is all right, too. So Harry the Horse gives in, and says five per cent it is.

Well, as they do not wish to start out until after midnight, and as there is plenty of time, Big Butch gets out some more needled beer, and then he goes looking for the tools with which he opens safes, and which he says he does not see since the day John Ignatius Junior is born and he gets them out to build the crib.

Now this is a good time for me to bid one and all farewell, and what keeps me there is something I cannot tell you to this day, because personally I never before have any idea of taking part in a safe opening, especially with a baby, as I consider such action very dishonorable. When I come to think things over afterwards, the only thing I can figure is the needled beer, but I wish to say I am really very much surprised at myself when I find myself in a taxicab along about one o'clock in the morning with these Brooklyn parties and Big Butch and the baby.

Butch has John Ignatius Junior rolled up in a blanket, and John is still pounding his ear. Butch has a satchel of tools, and what looks to me like a big flat book, and just before we leave the house Butch hands me a package and tells me to be very careful with it. He gives Little Isadore a smaller package, which Isadore shoves into his pistol pocket, and when Isadore sits down in the taxi something goes wa-wa, like a sheep, and Big Butch becomes very indignant because it seems Isadore is sitting on John Ignatius Junior's doll, which says "Mamma" when you squeeze it.

It seems Big Butch figures that John Ignatius Junior may wish something to play with in case he wakes up, and it is a good thing for Little Isadore that the mamma doll is not squashed so it cannot say "Mamma" any more, or the chances are Little Isadore will get a good bust in the snoot.

We let the taxicab go a block away from the spot we are headed for in West Eighteenth Street, between Seventh and Eighth Avenues, and walk the rest of the way two by two. I walk with Big Butch, carrying my package, and Butch is lugging the baby and his satchel and the flat thing that looks like a book. It is so quiet down in West Eighteenth Street at such an hour that you can hear yourself think, and in fact I hear myself thinking very plain that I am a big sap to be on a job like this, especially with a baby, but I keep on going just the same, which shows you what a very big sap I am, indeed.

There are very few people in West Eighteenth Street when we get there, and one of them is a fat guy who is leaning against a building almost in the center of the block, and who takes a walk for himself as soon as he sees us. It seems that this fat guy is the watchman at the coal company's office and is also a personal friend of Harry the Horse, which is why he takes the walk when he sees us coming.

It is agreed before we leave Big Butch's house that Harry the Horse and Spanish John are to stay outside the place as lookouts, while Big Butch is inside opening the safe, and that Little Isadore is to go with Butch. Nothing whatever is said by anybody about where I am to be at any time, and I can see that, no matter where I am, I will still be an outsider, but, as Butch gives me the package to carry, I figure he wishes me to remain with him.

It is no bother at all getting into the office of the coal company, which is on the ground floor, because it seems the watchman leaves the front door open, this watchman being a most obliging guy, indeed. In fact he is so obliging that by and by he comes back and lets Harry the Horse and Spanish John tie him up good and tight, and stick a handkerchief in his mouth and chuck him in an areaway next to the office, so nobody will think he has anything to do with opening the safe in case anybody comes around asking.

The office looks out on the street, and the safe that Harry the Horse and Little Isadore and Spanish John wish Big Butch to open is standing up against the rear wall of the office facing the street windows. There is one little electric light burning very dim over the safe so that when anybody walks past the place outside, such as a watchman, they can look in through the window and see the safe at all times, unless they are blind. It is not a tall safe, and it is not a big safe, and I can see Big

Butch grin when he sees it, so I figure this safe is not much of a safe, just as Harry the Horse claims.

Well, as soon as Big Butch and the baby and Little Isadore and me get into the office, Big Butch steps over to the safe and unfolds what I think is the big flat book, and what is it but a sort of screen painted on one side to look exactly like the front of a safe. Big Butch stands this screen up on the floor in front of the real safe, leaving plenty of space in between, the idea being that the screen will keep anyone passing in the street outside from seeing Butch while he is opening the safe, because when a man is opening a safe he needs all the privacy he can get.

Big Butch lays John Ignatius Junior down on the floor on the blanket behind the phony safe front and takes his tools out of the satchel and starts to work opening the safe, while Little Isadore and me get back in a corner where it is dark, because there is not room for all of us back of the screen. However, we can see what Big Butch is doing, and I wish to say while I never before see a professional safe opener at work, and never wish to see another, this Butch handles himself like a real artist.

He starts drilling into the safe around the combination lock, working very fast and very quiet, when all of a sudden what happens but John Ignatius Junior sits up on the blanket and lets out a squall. Naturally this is most disquieting to me, and personally I am in favor of beaning John Ignatius Junior with something to make him keep still, because I am nervous enough as it is. But the squalling does not seem to bother Big Butch. He lays down his tools and picks up John Ignatius Junior and starts whispering, "There, there, there, my itty oddleums. Da-dad is here."

Well, this sounds very nonsensical to me in such a situation, and it makes no impression whatever on John Ignatius Junior. He keeps on squalling, and I judge he is squalling pretty loud because I see Harry the Horse and Spanish John both walk past the window and look in very anxious. Big Butch jiggles John Ignatius Junior up and down and keeps whispering baby talk to him, which sounds very undignified coming from a high-class safe opener, and finally Butch whispers to me to hand him the package I am carrying.

He opens the package, and what is in it but a baby's nursing bottle full of milk. Moreover, there is a little tin stew pan, and Butch hands the pan to me and whispers to me to find a water tap somewhere in the joint and fill the pan with water. So I go stumbling around in the dark in a room behind the office and bark my shins several times before I find a tap and fill the pan. I take it back to Big Butch, and he squats there with the baby on one arm, and gets a tin of what is called canned heat out of the package, and lights this canned heat with his cigar lighter, and starts heating the pan of water with the nursing bottle in it.

Big Butch keeps sticking his finger in the pan of water while it is heating, and by and by he puts the rubber nipple of the nursing bottle in his mouth and takes a pull at it to see if the milk is warm enough, just like I see dolls who have babies do. Apparently the milk is okay, as Butch hands the bottle to John Ignatius Junior, who grabs hold of it with both hands and starts sucking on the business end. Naturally he has to stop squalling, and Big Butch goes to work on the safe again, with John Ignatius Junior sitting on the blanket, pulling on the bottle and looking wiser than a treeful of owls.

It seems the safe is either a tougher job than anybody figures, or Big Butch's tools are not so good, what with being old and rusty and used for building baby cribs, because he breaks a couple of drills and works himself up into quite a sweat without getting anywhere. Butch afterwards explains to me that he is one of the first guys in this country to open safes without explosives, but he says to do this work properly you have to know the safes so as to drill to the tumblers of the lock just right, and it seems that this particular safe is a new type to him, even if it is old, and he is out of practice.

Well, in the meantime John Ignatius Junior finishes his bottle and starts mumbling again, and Big Butch gives him a tool to play with, and finally Butch needs this tool and tries to take it away from John Ignatius Junior, and the baby lets out such a squawk that Butch has to let him keep it until he can sneak it away from him, and this causes more delay.

Finally Big Butch gives up trying to drill the safe open, and he whispers to us that he will have to put a little shot in it to loosen up the lock, which is all right with us, because we are getting tired of hanging around and listening to John Ignatius Junior's glug-glugging. As far as I am personally concerned, I am wishing I am home in bed.

Well, Butch starts pawing through his satchel looking for something and it seems that what he is looking for is a little bottle of some kind of explosive with which to shake the lock on the safe up some, and at first he cannot find this bottle, but finally he discovers that John Ignatius Junior has it and is gnawing at the cork, and Butch has quite a battle making John Ignatius Junior give it up.

Anyway, he fixes the explosive in one of the holes he drills near the combination lock on the safe, and then he puts in a fuse, and just before he touches off the fuse Butch picks up John Ignatius Junior and hands him to Little Isadore, and tells us to go into the room behind the office. John Ignatius Junior does not seem to care for Little Isadore, and I do not blame him, at that, because he starts to squirm around quite some in Isadore's arms and lets out a squall, but all of a sudden he becomes very quiet indeed, and while I am not able to prove it, something tells me that Little Isadore has his hand over John Ignatius Junior's mouth.

Well, Big Butch joins us right away in the back room, and sound comes out of John Ignatius Junior again as Butch takes him from Little Isadore, and I am thinking that it is a good thing for Isadore that the baby cannot tell Big Butch what Isadore does to him.

"I put in just a little bit of a shot," Big Butch says, "and it will not make any more noise than snapping your fingers."

But a second later there is a big whoom from the office, and the whole joint shakes, and John Ignatius Junior laughs right out loud. The chances are he thinks it is the Fourth of July.

"I guess maybe I put in too big a charge," Big Butch says, and then he rushes into the office with Little Isadore and me

after him, and John Ignatius Junior still laughing very heartily
for a small baby. The door of the safe is swinging loose, and
the whole joint looks somewhat wrecked, but Big Butch loses
no time in getting his dukes into the safe and grabbing out two
big bundles of cash money, which he sticks inside his shirt.

As we go into the street Harry the Horse and Spanish John
come running up much excited, and Harry says to Big Butch
like this:

"What are you trying to do," he says, "wake up the whole
town?"

"Well," Butch says, "I guess maybe the charge is too strong,
at that, but nobody seems to be coming, so you and Spanish
John walk over to Eighth Avenue, and the rest of us will walk
to Seventh, and if you go along quiet, like people minding their
own business, it will be all right."

But I judge Little Isadore is tired of John Ignatius Junior's
company by this time, because he says he will go with Harry
the Horse and Spanish John, and this leaves Big Butch and
John Ignatius Junior and me to go the other way. So we start
moving, and all of a sudden two cops come tearing around the
corner toward which Harry and Isadore and Spanish John are
going. The chances are the cops hear the earthquake Big Butch
lets off and are coming to investigate.

But the chances are, too, that if Harry the Horse and the
other two keep walking along very quietly like Butch tells
them to, the coppers will pass them up entirely, because it is
not likely that coppers will figure anybody to be opening safes
with explosives in this neighborhood. But the minute Harry
the Horse sees the coppers he loses his nut, and he outs with
the old equalizer and starts blasting away, and what does
Spanish John do but get his out, too, and open up.

The next thing anybody knows, the two coppers are down
on the ground with slugs in them, but other coppers are coming from every which direction, blowing whistles and doing
a little blasting themselves, and there is plenty of excitement,
especially when the coppers who are not chasing Harry the
Horse and Little Isadore and Spanish John start poking around
the neighborhood and find Harry's pal, the watchman, all tied

up nice and tight where Harry leaves him, and the watchman explains that some scoundrels blow open the safe he is watching.

All this time Big Butch and me are walking in the other direction toward Seventh Avenue, and Big Butch has John Ignatius in his arms, and John Ignatius is now squalling very loud, indeed. The chances are he is still thinking of the big whoom back there which tickles him so and is wishing to hear some more whooms. Anyway, he is beating his own best record for squalling, and as we go walking along Big Butch says to me like this:

"I dast not run," he says, "because if any coppers see me running they will start popping at me and maybe hit John Ignatius Junior, and besides running will joggle the milk up in him and make him sick. My old lady always warns me never to joggle John Ignatius Junior when he is full of milk."

"Well, Butch," I say, "there is no milk in me, and I do not care if I am joggled up, so if you do not mind, I will start doing a piece of running at the next corner."

But just then around the corner of Seventh Avenue toward which we are headed comes two or three coppers with a big fat sergeant with them, and one of the coppers who is half out of breath as if he has been doing plenty of sprinting, is explaining to the sergeant that somebody blows a safe down the street and shoots a couple of coppers in the getaway.

And there is Big Butch, with John Ignatius Junior in his arms and twenty G's in his shirt front and a tough record behind him, walking right up to them.

I am feeling very sorry, indeed, for Big Butch, and very sorry for myself, too, and I am saying to myself that if I get out of this I will never associate with anyone but ministers of the gospel as long as I live. I can remember thinking that I am getting a better break than Butch, at that, because I will not have to go to Sing Sing for the rest of my life, like him, and I also remember wondering what they will give John Ignatius Junior, who is still tearing off these squalls, with Big Butch saying, "There, there, there, Daddy's itty woogleums." Then I hear one of the coppers say to the fat sergeant:

"We better nail these guys. They may be in on this."

"Well, I can see it is good-by to Butch and John Ignatius Junior and me, as the fat sergeant steps up to Big Butch, but instead of putting the arm on Butch, the fat sergeant only points at John Ignatius Junior and asks very sympathetic:

"Teeth?"

"No," Big Butch says. "Not teeth. Colic. I just get the doctor here out of bed to do something for him, and we are going to a drug store to get some medicine."

Well, naturally I am very much surprised at this statement, because of course I am not a doctor, and if John Ignatius Junior has colic it serves him right, but I am only hoping they do not ask for my degree, when the fat sergeant says:

"Too bad. I know what it is. I got three of them at home. But," he says, "it acts more like it is teeth than colic."

Then as Big Butch and John Ignatius Junior and me go on about our business I hear the fat sergeant say to the copper, very sarcastic:

"Yea, of course a guy is out blowing safes with a baby in his arms! You will make a great detective, you will!"

I do not see Big Butch for several days after I learn that Harry the Horse and Little Isadore and Spanish John get back to Brooklyn all right, except that they are a little nicked up here and there from the slugs the coppers toss at them, while the coppers they clip are not damaged so very much. Furthermore, the chances are I will not see Big Butch for several years, if it is left to me, but he comes looking for me one night, and he seems to be all pleasured up about something.

"Say," Big Butch says to me, "you know I never give a copper credit for knowing any too much about anything, but I wish to say that this fat sergeant we run into the other night is a very, very smart duck. He is right about it being teeth that is ailing John Ignatius Junior, for what happens yesterday but John cuts his first tooth."

James Street

*

THE BISCUIT EATER

*Adapted for pictures by Stuart Anthony and Lillie Hayward,
and produced by Jack Moss for Paramount, THE BISCUIT
EATER was chosen as one of the Ten Best Pictures of 1940.
Directed by Stewart Heisler, the film starred Promise, a bird
dog with a pedigree that goes back to 1800, and Billy Lee, nine-
year-old child star.*

*Albany, Georgia, one of the greatest quail hunting centers
in the country, gave THE BISCUIT EATER a world premiere
on April 11, 1940. Paramount had shot most of the picture
near Albany, and a number of the city's 15,000 inhabitants
and their dogs are in the film.*

LONNIE set the greasy bag of table scraps on a hummock of
wire grass and leaned over the branch, burying his face in the
cool water. He wiped his mouth with the back of his hand.
Hundreds of black, frisky water bugs, aroused at his invasion
of their playground, scooted to the middle of the stream,
swerved as though playing follow-the-leader, and scooted
back to the bank.

The boy laughed at their capers. Slowly, he stooped over
the water. His hand darted as a cottonmouth strikes and he
snatched one of the bugs and smelled it. There was a sharp,
sugary odor on the bug.

"A sweet stinker, sure as my name is Lonnie McNeil," the
boy muttered. If you caught a sweet stinker among water bugs,
it meant good luck, maybe. Everybody knew that. Lonnie held
the bug behind him, closed his eyes, tilted his head and whispered, to the pine trees, the branch, the wire grass and anything else in the silence that wanted to hear him and would
never tell his wish: "I hope Moreover is always a good dog."

Then Lonnie put the bug back in the branch. It darted in
circles for a second and skedaddled across the creek, making

a beeline for the other bugs. There were tiny ripples in its wake. The boy grinned. He was in for some good luck. If the sweet stinker had changed its course, it would have broken the charm.

He picked up his bag of scraps, crossed the branch on a log and moseyed to the edge of the woods where the cleared land began. He pursed his lower lip and whistled the call of the catbird, watching the cabin in the field where Text lived with his mother, Aunt Charity, and her brood. Old Charity had a heap of young'uns, but Text was the last. She had listened to her preacher for days during protracted meetings, seeking a fit'n name for her man-child. And because the evangelist took text from this and text from that, she named him Text and reckoned it was a name that God approved. Or else the preacher wouldn't have used it so much.

Lonnie saw Text run to the rickety front gallery of the cabin and listen. He whistled again. Text answered and ran around the house, and a minute later he was racing across the field with a big, brooding dog at his heels. The white boy opened his arms and the dog ran to him and tried to lick his face.

Text said, "Hydee, Lon. Ol' Moreover is glad to see you. Me and him both."

Lonnie said, "Hi, Text. He looks slick as el-lem sap, don't he? Been working him?"

"A heap and whole lot," said Text. "Turned him loose in the wire grass yestiddy and he pointed two coveys 'fore I could say, 'Law 'a' mercy.' He's a prime superfine bird dawg, Lon. He ain't no no-'count biscuit eater."

Lonnie, the son of Harve McNeil, and Text had been friends long before they had got the dog on a mine-and-yours basis, but now they were inseparable. Moreover, the dog was community property between them, and their community was the piney woods of South Alabama, where Lonnie's father trained fine bird dogs for Mr. Ames. The dog had wiped away all class and race barriers between the two.

Moreover's mother had run in the Grand National trials up at Grand Junction, Tennessee—the world series for bird dogs.

Then Mr. Ames had sold her. Moreover's father was a good dog until he killed one of Mr. Eben's sheep, and was shot, according to the code of the piney woods. Harve knew the pup, the outcast of the litter, had a bad streak in him, but had tried to train him only because Lonnie loved the pup. And Lonnie loved him only because nobody else did.

Harve never had been able to get close to the dog's affections. There had been no feeling between them, no understanding. The pup had cowered at Lonnie's feet when Harve had ordered him into the fields to hunt. And when Harve had caught him sucking eggs, he had given him away to a Negro across the ridge.

"He's a suck-egg biscuit eater," Harve had told the Negro. A biscuit eater was an ornery dog. Everybody knew that. A biscuit eater wouldn't hunt anything except his biscuits and wasn't worth the salt in his feed.

The Negro had accepted the dog because he knew he could swap him. That night the dog had stolen eggs from the Negro's henhouse and the Negro had beaten him and called him a low-life biscuit eater. The dog had run under the cabin and sulked.

When Lonnie learned what his father had done with the outcast, he went to Text, and together they went over the ridge to bargain for the dog.

The Negro man was wily. He sensed a good bargain and was trader enough to know that if he low-rated the dog, the boys would want him more than ever. The dog had a cotton rope around his neck and the rope was fastened to a block, and when the dog walked, his head was pulled sideways as he tugged the block. The dog walked to Lonnie and rubbed against his legs. The boy ignored him. He mustn't let the Negro man know he really wanted the dog. The man grabbed the rope and jerked the dog away.

"He's a biscuit eater!" The Negro nudged the dog with his foot. The animal looked sideways at his master and slunk away. "He ain't worth much."

"He's a suck-egg biscuit eater, ain't he?" Lonnie asked. The dog watched him, and when the boy said "biscuit eater" the dog ran under the cabin, pulling the block behind him. "He's scared." Lonnie said. "You been beating him. And ever' time you jump him and you call him 'biscuit eater.' That's how come he's scared. Whatcha take for him?"

The man said, "Whatcha gimme?"

"I'll give you my frog-sticker." Lonnie showed his knife. "And I got a pretty good automobile tire. Ain't but one patch in it. It'd make a prime superfine swing for your young'uns."

The Negro asked Text, "What'll you chip in to boot?"

Text said, "You done cussed out the dawg so far I don't want no share of him. You done low-rated him too much. If he sucks eggs at my house, my maw'll bust me in two halves. Whatcha want to boot?"

"Whatcha got?"

"Nothin'," said Text, "cep'n two big hands what can tote a heap of wood. Tote your shed full of light'r knots for boot."

"What else?"

Text thought for a minute, weighing the deal. "Lon wants that dawg. I know where there's a pas'l of May haws and a honeybee tree."

The Negro man said, "It's a deal, boys, if'n you pick me a lard bucket full of May haws and show me the bee tree."

Lonnie took the block from the dog and led him across the field. Then Text led him awhile. Out of sight of the Negro's shack, the boys stopped and examined their possession.

Text ran his hand over the dog, smoothing the fur. "He's a good dawg, ain't he, Lon? Look at them ol' eyes, and them big ol' feet, and that big ol' long tail. Bet he can point birds from here to yonder. Betcha if he tried, he can point part-ridge on light bread. What we gonna name him, Lon?"

Lonnie said, "Dunno, Text. But listen, don't ever call him—" He looked at the dog, then at Text. "You know." He held his fingers in the shape of a biscuit and pantomimed as though he were eating. The dog didn't understand. Neither did Text. So Lonnie whispered, "You know, 'biscuit eater.' Don't ever call him that. That's what's the matter with him. He expects a beating when he hears it."

"It's a go," Text whispered. "Let's name him Moreover. It's in the Bible."

"Where'bouts?"

"I heard the preacher say so. He said, 'Moreover, the dog,' and he was reading from the Bible."

Lonnie held the dog's chin with one hand and stroked his chest with the other. "He's Moreover then. He's a good dog, Text. And he's ours. You keep him and I'll furnish the rations. I can snitch 'em from papa. Will Aunt Charity raise Cain if you keep him?"

"Naw," said Text. "I 'member the time that big ol' brother of mine, ol' First-and-Second-Thessalonians, fetched a goat home, and maw didn't low-rate him. She just said she had so many young'uns, she didn't mind a goat. I spects she feels the same way 'bout a dawg, if'n he's got a Bible name."

"I reckon so too," said Lonnie, and ran home and told his father about the deal.

Harve told his son, "It's all right for you and Text to keep the dog, but keep him away from over here. I don't want him running around my good dogs."

Lonnie said, "He's a good dog, papa. He just ain't had no chance."

Harve looked at his son. The boy was growing, and the man was proud. "I'm going to work Silver Belle in the south forty," he said. "Want to come along?"

Lonnie shook his head. Harve knew then how much the boy loved his new dog; for, ordinarily, Lonnie would have surrendered any pleasure to accompany his father when he worked Silver Belle. She was the finest pointer in the Ames kennels and Harve had trained her since puppyhood. Already, she had won the Grand National twice. A third win would give his employer permanent possession of the Grand National trophy, and Harve wanted to win the prize for Mr. Ames more than he wanted anything in the world. He pampered Silver Belle. She was a small pointer—so small she had to wear a silver bell when hunting in the tall sage.

After his father and Silver Belle were gone, Lonnie collected the table scraps and went across the branch to Text's.

"Let's work him across the ridge today," Lonnie said. "Papa's got Silver Belle in the south forty and he won't want us and Moreover around."

Text said, "It's a go, Lon. I'll snitch ol' First-and-Second-Thessalonians' shotgun and meet you 'cross the ridge. But that there lan' over there is pow'ful close to Mr. Eben's place. I don't want no truck with that man."

"I ain't afraid of Mr. Eben," said Lonnie.

"Well, I am. And so are you! And so is your paw."

"Papa is not afraid of anything, and I'll bust you in two halves if you say so."

"Then how come he didn't whup Mr. Eben when Mr. Eben kicked his dawg about two years ago?"

Negroes heard everything and forgot nothing. Everybody in the county had wondered why Harve McNeil hadn't thrashed Eben, when the farmer kicked one of the McNeil dogs without cause.

Lonnie was ashamed. He said, "Papa didn't whip Mr. Eben 'cause mother asked him not to, that's why."

"Lady folks sho' are buttinskies," Text said. "All time trying to keep men folks from whupping each other. Lady folks sho' are scutters. All 'cept your maw and my maw, huh, Lon?"

Lonnie said, "Mr. Eben is just a crotchety man. Mother said so. He don't mean no harm."

"That's what you say," Text said. "But he's a scutter from way back. Maw says when he kills beeves he drinks the blood, and Ise popeyed scared of him. His lan' say, 'Posted. Keep off. Law.' And I ain't messin' around over there."

Lonnie often had worked dogs with his father and had seen the best run at field trials. He began training Moreover by inspiring confidence in him. The big dog was clumsy, but Lonnie never upbraided him. When Moreover showed a streak of good traits, Lonnie and Text patted him. When he erred, they simply ignored him. The dog had a marvelous range, and moved through the saw grass at an easy gait, never tiring. He was not spectacular, but constant. He ran with a sort of awkward lope, twisting his head as though he still were tugging a block. But he covered ground. Day after day he trained and worked until the boys panted and stretched on the ground. Then he stood over them.

He had a strange point. He would cock his long head in the air, then turn it slowly toward Lonnie as he came to a point. His tail was like a ramrod. The first time Text shot over him, he cowered. The boys showed their displeasure by ignoring him. He soon was no longer gun-shy and he worked for the sheer joy of working.

"He sho is a good dawg," Text said.

They were working him that day across the ridge near Eben's farm and Moreover, trailing a huge covey, raced through the stubble and disappeared in the sage. When the boys found him he was frozen on a point far inside Farmer Eben's posted land. And watching Moreover from a pine thicket was Eben, a shotgun held loosely in the crook of his arm.

Text was terror-stricken and gaped at Eben as though the stubble-faced man were an ogre. Lonnie took one look at his dog, then at the man, and walked to the thicket. Text was in his shadow. "Please don't shoot him, Mr. Eben," Lonnie said.

The farmer said, "Huh?"

"Naw, suh, please don't shoot him." Text found his courage. "He couldn't read yo' posted sign."

Eben scowled. "I don't aim to shoot him. That is, less'n he gets round my sheep. I was watching his point. Right pretty, ain't it?"

Lonnie said, "Mighty pretty. He's a good dog, Mr. Eben. If you ever want a mess of birds, I'll give you the loan of him."

"Nothing shaking," Eben said. "He's that biscuit eater your paw gave that niggah over the ridge."

Text protested. "Don't go calling him biscuit eater, please, suh. He don't like it."

"He can't read my posted sign, but he can understand English, huh?" Eben laughed. "Well, get him off'n my land or I'll sprinkle him with bird shot."

Lonnie whistled and Moreover broke the point and followed him.

At supper, Lonnie asked his father, "How come you didn't

whip Mr. Eben that time he kicked your dog?"

Harve said, "I've had my share of fighting, son. I don't fight for such foolishness any more. How come you ask?"

"Just 'cause," Lonnie said, and Harve knew his son wasn't satisfied with the reply. He frowned and glanced at his wife. He hadn't punished Eben simply because he didn't think the crime of kicking a dog justified a beating. There had been a time when he thought differently. But he was older now, and respected. He wondered if Lonnie thought he was afraid of Eben, and the thought bothered him.

"I wish we had the papers on Moreover," Lonnie changed the subject. "I want to register him."

Harve said, "I've got the papers, son. You can have 'em. What you gonna do, run your dog against my Belle in the county-seat trials?" He was joshing the boy.

"That's what I aim to do," Lonnie said.

The father laughed loudly, and his laughter trailed off into a chuckle. Lonnie enjoyed hearing his father laugh that way. "It's a great idea, son. So you have trained that biscuit eater for the trials! Where you going to get your entry fee?"

"He ain't no biscuit eater!" Lonnie said defiantly.

His mother was startled at his impudence to his father. But Harve shook his head at his wife and said, " 'Course he ain't, son. I'm sorry. And just to show that me and Belle ain't scared of you and Moreover, I'll give you and Text the job of painting around the kennels. You can earn your entry fee. Is it a go?"

"Yes-sirree, bob," Lonnie stuffed food in his mouth and hurried through his meal. "I'm going to high-tail it over and tell Text and Moreover."

Harve walked down the front path with his son. The boy reached to his shoulders. It was nice to walk down the path with his son. The father said simply and in man's talk, "Maybe I'm batty to stake you and your dog to your entry fee. You might whip me and Belle, and Mr. Ames might give you my job of training his dogs."

Lonnie didn't reply. But at the gate he paused and faced his father. "Papa, you ain't scared of Mr. Eben, are you?"

The trainer leaned against the gate and lit his pipe. "Son," he said, "I ain't scared of nothing but God. But don't tell your mother."

Mr. Ames, the Philadelphia sportsman, sat on the steps of the gun-club lodge and laughed when he saw his truck coming up the driveway. His cronies, who had come to the county seat for the trials—a sort of minor-league series—laughed too. Harve was driving. Silver Belle was beside him. Lonnie and Text were on the truck bed with dogs all around them, and behind the truck, tied with a cotton rope, loped Moreover. Mr. Ames shook hands with his trainer and met the boys.

"We got competition," Harve said, and nodded toward Moreover.

Ames studied the big dog. "By Joe, Harve! That used to be my dog. Is that the old bis—"

"Sh-h-h!" Harve commanded. "Don't say it. It hurts the dog's feelings. Or so the boys say."

Ames understood. He had a son at home. He walked around Moreover and looked at him. "Mighty fine dog, boys . . . If he beats Belle, I might hire you, Lonnie, and fire your father." He winked at Harve, but the boys didn't see him.

They took Moreover to the kennels. They had fetched their own feed. Text ran to the kitchen of the lodge, and soon had a job doing kitchen chores. Moreover's rations were assured, and the best. Lonnie bedded his dog down carefully and combed him and tried to make him look spruce. But Moreover would not be spruce. There was a quizzical look in his eyes. The other dogs took attention as though they expected it, but Moreover rubbed his head along the ground and scratched his ears against the kennel box and mussed himself up as fast as Lonnie cleaned him. But he seemed to know that Lonnie expected something of him. All the other dogs were yelping and were nervous. But Moreover just flopped on his side and licked Lonnie's hands.

Inside the lodge, Ames asked Harve, "How's Belle?"

"Tiptop," said Harve. "She'll win hands down here, and I'm laying that she'll take the Grand National later. I'm gonna keep my boy with me, Mr. Ames. Text can stay with the help."

"What do those kids expect to do with that biscuit eater?" Ames laughed.

"You know how boys are. I'll bet this is the first time in history a colored boy and a white boy ever had a joint entry in a field trial. They get riled if anybody calls him a biscuit eater."

"Can't blame them, Harve," Ames said. "I get mad if anybody makes fun of my dogs. We are all alike, men and boys."

"You said it. Since the first, I reckon, boys have got mad if a fellow said anything against their mothers or dogs."

"Or fathers." Ames suggested.

"Depends on the father," said Harve. "Wish Lonnie could take his dog to the quarter finals, or thereabouts. Do the boy a heap of good."

They were having a drink by the big fireplace. Ames said, "I hope that big brute is not in a brace with Belle. She's a sensitive dog." Then he laughed. "Be funny, Harve, if that dog whipped us. I'd run you bowlegged."

All the men laughed, but when the waiter told the pantry maid the story, he neglected to say that the threat was a jest. The pantry maid told the barkeeper. The barkeeper told the cook, and by the time the story was circulated around the kitchen, the servants were whispering that rich Mr. Ames had threatened to fire poor Mr. Harve because his son had fetched a biscuit eater to the field trials.

The morning of the first run, Text met Lonnie at the kennels, and together they fed Moreover. "Let's put some good ol' gunpowder in his vittles," Text said. "Make him hunt better."

"Aw, that's superstition," said Lonnie.

"I don't care what it is, it helps," said Text.

Lonnie couldn't see any need of tempting luck, so Moreover was fed a sprinkling of gunpowder.

Text said, "I got my lucky buckeye along. We bound to have luck, Lon."

Lonnie was getting too big for such foolishness, but then he remembered. "I caught a sweet stinker not so long ago," he whispered. "And he swum the right way."

"A good ol' sweet-stinking mellow bug?" asked Text eagerly. "Lon, good luck gonna bust us in two halves."

Harve took Silver Belle out with an early brace and the pointer completely outclassed her rival. Her trainer sent her back to her kennel and went into the fields with Ames to watch Moreover in his first brace. He was braced with a rangy setter. Even the judges smiled at the two boys and their dog. Text, in keeping with rules of the sport, gave not an order. Lonnie put Moreover down on the edge of a clover field and the big dog rolled over, then jumped up and loped around the boy, leaping on him and licking his face. Lonnie and Text walked into the field, and Moreover followed. Lonnie whistled shrilly. The big dog jerked up his head, cocked it and began casting. He ranged to the edge of the field and worked in. He loped past a patch of saw grass, wheeled and pointed, his head cocked toward Lonnie, his right leg poised and his tail stiff as a poker.

Lonnie kept his dog on the point until the judges nodded, then whistled him off of it. He called Moreover to the far edge of the field and set him ranging again. He was on a point in a flash.

Ames looked at Harve. "That's a good dog, McNeil. He's trained beautifully. He'll go to the finals with us, sure as shooting."

Harve was beaming with pride. "It proves what I've always preached," Harve said; "that a bird dog will work for a man, if the man understands him. I couldn't do anything with that dog, but he will go to hell and back for my boy and Text."

Silver Belle and Moreover swept through the quarter and semifinals, and news that father and son would be matched in the finals, with the famous Belle and a biscuit eater, brought sportsmen and sports writers swarming to the county seat. Harve and Lonnie slept and ate together, but the man didn't discuss the contest with his son. He didn't want to make him nervous. He treated Lonnie as he would any other trainer. He knew that boys could sense condescension if adults eased up in games and that boys never want their fathers to make things too easy for them.

Harve took Silver Belle to the edge of a field of stubble, and she stood motionless as he snapped a tiny silver bell around her neck. He arose from his knees, patted her fondly and whispered, "Go get 'em girl."

The little pointer dashed into the stubble and soon was out of sight. Moreover rubbed against Lonnie's legs and watched her for a minute, then trotted along her path. There was no order between Lonnie and his dog, only understanding.

The men listened for the tingling of the silver bell that told them the champion was still casting. Through the brush the men sauntered, their senses alert. Suddenly the bell hushed.

Belle was on a point. The delicate little animal was rigid. Her trim body was thrown forward a bit, her nose, perfectly tilted, was aimed toward a clump of sage. She didn't fleck a muscle. She might have been made of marble.

The judges nodded approval. Harve motioned to Belle. She took two steps, stopped, then two more. A roar of wings, a whistle of flight, and the covey of partridge was away like feathered lightning. Guns thundered. Belle didn't bat an eye as the salvo cracked over her. When the echoes died, she began fetching, and when the last bird was laid at Harve's feet, she dashed into the sage again, seeking the singles.

Lonnie had held Moreover while Belle worked. Now he turned the big dog loose. Moreover swung along through the sage at an easy gait. He cast a bit to the right, stuck his nose almost to the ground and found the trail Belle had just made. Then he broke into an easy trot. He never depended on ground scents, but on body scents, and kept his nose high enough to catch any smells the wind blew his way.

About a hundred yards back up Belle's trail, Moreover suddenly broke his trot and eased his nose higher in the air. Then he jerked his head toward Lonnie and froze to a point. His right leg came up slowly, deliberately. He cocked his head in that strange fashion, and the quizzical, comical look came in his eyes. Moreover was a still hunter. He never waited for orders. He held the birds until Lonnie clicked the safety off of his gun. When Moreover heard the click, he began creeping toward the covey. He didn't budge as Lonnie began dropping the birds, and then, without orders, he fetched the dead birds and began casting for singles.

The judges whistled softly. "Most beautiful dog work I ever saw," whispered one. Ames' face took on a worried look. So did Harve's. The big dog had picked up a covey right under Belle's nose.

Belle settled down to hunt. She seemed everywhere. She dashed to a point on the fringe of a cornfield, then held another covey while Harve weeded out the first. She raced over the ridge, her nose picking up scents in almost impossible places. Moreover just loped along, but every time Belle got a covey, he would cast for a few minutes, point, fetch and wait for her to set the pace. She was hunting because she was bred to hunt. He was hunting from habit and because Lonnie expected him to.

It was exasperating. Belle tried every trick of her training, but her skill was no match for his stamina. Her heart was pumping rapidly and she was tired when the men knocked off for lunch. Text ran back to the lodge to fetch food to the field. He strutted into the kitchen and told the servants that Moreover was running Silver Belle ragged.

The servants shook their heads, and one told him that Mr. Ames would fire Harve if Moreover beat Belle. Text couldn't swallow his food. He waited around the fringe of hunters until he caught Lonnie's eye, and motioned to him. "That Mr. Ames sho' is a scutter," said Text, after he told his story. "He's worse'n Mr. Eben. What we goin' do, Lon?"

Lonnie said, "He's half your dog, Text. What you say?"

"We can't let yo' paw get in no trouble on account of us, Lon. He got to have a job."

Lonnie nodded and bit his lip. He noticed that his father's face was drawn as the contest was renewed. Ames was nervous. The two men had worked for years to get Belle to perfection, and win the Grand National for the third time. And here an outcast dog was hunting her heart out at a minor meet. Lonnie thought his father was worried about his job and that Ames was angry.

His mind was made up. He watched Moreover leap across a creek, then race into a field of clover. He and Text were right behind him. Moreover came to his point, jerked his head toward his master and waited.

Lonnie cupped his hands and said hoarsely, "Hep!" It was an order Moreover never had heard. He turned and faced Lonnie. The judges gasped when the big dog left his point. Harve was puzzled.

Ames whispered, "He's breaking. That good-for-nothing streak is cropping out."

"Hep!" Lonnie said it again. The judges didn't hear. Moreover deserted the covey and walked to Lonnie and looked up. Lonnie shouted, "Back to your point, you low-life biscuit eater!"

Moreover tucked his tail between his legs and ran to the lodge and hid under it. Lonnie and Text followed him, without a word to the judges.

Ames looked at Harve for an explanation, and Harve said, "I don't get it. My son called his dog off. He quit."

It took Lonnie and Text a long time to coax Moreover from under the lodge. The dog crawled to Lonnie's feet and rolled over. Lonnie patted him, but Moreover didn't lick his face. The boys were with their dog in the kennel when the prize was awarded to Harve and Silver Belle.

"His feelings are hurt," Lonnie told Text as Moreover lay down and thumped his tail. . . . "I'm sorry I said it, Moreover. I had to."

Text said, "We sorry, puppy dawg. But us had to, didn't we, Lon?"

They loaded the truck, and Harve had his boy sit on the front seat by him. They said good-by and rolled away.

Harve said to Lonnie, "How come you did that, son?"

Lonnie didn't reply and the father didn't press the point. Finally, he said, "Don't ever quit, son, if you are winning or losing. It ain't fair to the dog."

"My dog is mad at me," Lonnie said.

"We'll give him a beef heart when we get home. His feelings are hurt because you threw him down. But he'll be all right.

Dogs are not like folks. They'll forgive a fellow." He knew
Lonnie had a reason for what he had done, and he knew that
if his son wanted him to know the reason, he would tell him.

Back home, Lonnie cooked a beef heart for Moreover and
took the plate to the back gallery where the dog was tied.

Harve said, "Untie him, son. You can let him run free over
here. You don't ever have to keep him over at Text's house,
unless you want to."

He untied his dog and put the food before him. Moreover
sniffed the food and toyed with it. He never had had such
good food before. Lonnie and his father went back into the
house.

After supper, Lonnie went to see about his dog. The meat
hadn't been touched and Moreover was gone.

Harve said, "He's probably gone back to Text's house."

Lonnie said, "I'm going after him."

"I'll go with you," said Harve, and got a lantern.

Text hadn't seen the dog. He joined the search and the three
hunted through the woods for an hour or so, Lonnie whistling
for Moreover, and Text calling him, "Heah, heah, fellow. Heah."

Harve sat on a stump, put the lantern down and called the
boys to him. He had seen only a few dogs that would refuse to
eat beef heart as Moreover had done.

"Text," he said sharply, "did Moreover ever suck eggs at your
place?"

Text rolled his eyes and looked at Lonnie. "Yes, suh." He
was afraid to lie to Harve. "But I didn't tell Lon. I didn't want
to hurt his feelings. Moreover was a suck-egger, good and
proper."

Harve said, "Go on, tell us about it."

"Maw put hot pepper in a raw egg, but it didn't break him.
My ol' brother, ol' First-and-Second-Thessalonians, reckoned
he'd kill Moreover less'n he quit suck-egging. So I got to snitch-
ing two eggs ever' night and feeding him with 'em. He sho did
like eggs, Mr. Harve, and we had plenty of eggs."

Lonnie said sharply, "You hadn't ought to have done that,
Text."

Harve said, "Did you feed him eggs tonight?"

"Naw, suh," said Text. "I reckoned he had vittles at yo' house. We had done gathered all the eggs and maw had counted them by nightfall."

Harve got up. "I'm worried. Let's walk up the branch. . . . Text, you take the left side. . . . Lonnie, you take the right side. I'll walk up the bank."

Lonnie found Moreover's body, still warm, only a few feet from the water. He stooped over his dog, put the lantern by his head, and opened his mouth. The dog had been poisoned. Lonnie straightened. He didn't cry. His emotions welled up within him, and, having no outlet, hurt him.

"I'm sorry I called him a biscuit eater," he said simply.

Text said, "He was trying to get to water. I sho hate to think of him dying, wanting just one swallow of good ol' water."

"Who killed him, papa?" Lonnie turned to his father.

The man picked up the lantern and walked away, the boys at his heels. They walked over the ridge to Eben's house, and Harve pounded on the front gallery until the farmer appeared.

"My boy's dog is dead," Harve said. "Reckoned you might know something about it."

Eben said, "If he was poisoned, I do. He's a suck-egg dog. I put poison in some eggs and left them in the field. Seems he must have committed suicide, McNeil."

"Seems you made it powerful easy for him to get those poisoned eggs," Harve said.

"Ain't no room round here for suck-egg dogs. His daddy was a sheep killer, too. It's good riddance. You ain't got no cause to jump me, Harve McNeil."

Harve said, "He's right, boys. A man's got a right to poison eggs on his own land, and if a dog sucks 'em and dies, the dog's to blame."

Eben said, "Reckon you young'uns want to bury that dog. Buzzards will be thick tomorrow. You can have the loan of my shovel."

Lonnie looked at the man a long time. He bit his lip so he couldn't cry. "Me and Text will dig a hole with a stick," he said, and turned away.

"You boys go bury him," Harve said. "I'll be home in a few minutes."

Lonnie and Text walked silently into the woods. Text said, "He sho was a good dog, huh, Lon? You ain't mad at me 'cause I fed him eggs, are you, Lon?"

"No, Text. Let's wait up here and watch papa. He can't see us."

Back at Eben's gallery, Harve said, "I would have paid you for all the eggs the dog took, Eben. My boy loved that dog a heap."

"Looka heah!" Eben said. "I know my rights."

"I know mine," Harve said. "I always pay my debts, Eben. And I always collect them. I ain't got no cause to get riled because that dog stole poisoned eggs. You were mighty low-life to plant 'em, though. But two years ago you kicked one of my dogs."

"He barked at me and scared my team on the road," Eben said.

"A dog has a right to bark," Harve said, and reached up and grabbed Eben by the collar.

"I'll law you!" Eben shouted.

Harve didn't reply. He slapped the man with his open palm, and when Eben squared off to fight, Harve knocked him down.

In the shadows of the woods, Lonnie whispered to Text, "What did I tell you? My papa ain't scared of nothing cep'n God."

They buried their dog near the branch. Text poured water in the grave. "I can't stand to think of him wanting water when there's a heap of water so close. Reckon if he could have got to the ol' branch he could have washed out that poison? Reckon, Lon?"

"Maybe so."

They were walking to Lonnie's house. "My ol' buckeye and your sweet-stinking mellow bug ain't helped us much, eh, Lon? Luck is plumb mad at us, ain't it Lon?"

Lonnie waited at the gate until his father arrived. "Me and Text saw the fight," he said. "I won't tell mother. Women are scutters, ain't they, papa? Always trying to keep men folks from fighting."

"I'll give you boys another dog, son," Harve said. He peered into the darkness and saw a car parked behind his house, then hurried inside. Mr. Ames was warming himself by the fire and talking with Mrs. McNeil. She went to the kitchen to brew coffee, and left the men alone, after calling for Lonnie and Text to follow her.

Ames said, "I heard why your boy called his dog off. Call him and that little colored boy in here. I can't go back East with those boys thinking what they do of me."

Lonnie and Text stood by the fire and Ames said, "That story you heard about me isn't so. I wouldn't have fired this man if your dog had won. We were joking about it and the servants got the story all wrong. I just wanted you boys to know that."

Harve said, "Yes. But even if Mr. Ames would have fired me, it wouldn't have made any difference. You did what you thought was right, but you were wrong. Don't ever quit a race, once you start it."

Lonnie told Mr. Ames, "My dog is dead. I'm sorry I called him a biscuit eater. He wasn't. I just want you to know that."

Ames lit his pipe and passed his tobacco pouch to Harve. He saw Harve's bloody hand as the trainer accepted the tobacco.

"Ran into some briers," Harve said.

"Lot of them around here." Ames' eyes twinkled. "Just been thinking, Harve. I got some fine pups coming along. You need help down here. Better hire a couple of good men. Know where you can get two good hands? They got to be men who can lose without grumbling and win without crowing."

Harve looked at Lonnie and Text, and smiled. "I know where I can get a couple of good men."

"All right," said Ames, and shook hands all around. "I've got to be going. Good night, men."

Katharine Haviland-Taylor

*

THE FAILURE

THE FAILURE was first filmed in 1933 as ONE MAN'S JOURNEY, starring Lionel Barrymore and May Robson. In 1938 a second film version with the non-committal title A MAN TO REMEMBER, directed by Garson Kanin, was produced by RKO. Budgeted as an inexpensive and minor picture, and finished in fifteen days, this later film was an immediate and unqualified success. Memorable for the excellent performance of Edward Ellis, the cast also included Lee Bowman, William Henry, John Wray and Granville Bates.

A GOOD MANY things had combined, Doctor Eli Watt sometimes thought, to hold him back; but at more drear moments he felt that God had designed him to be a country plug in doctors and now, of course, it was too late to do anything about it. He was pushing sixty, and nights of driving, at first behind old Jenny and then in his car, had made him look eighty, and a tired eighty at that.

Folks generally, Doctor Eli realized, wanted young doctors with well-pressed clothes and polished nails, and at the start of things he'd hoped to be that kind; and here he was in Pleasantville, just where he had started.

He'd been weak, he knew. At twenty-eight he had had a chance to be the assistant to a surgeon who'd reached the top, and he'd been ready to go, when he realized that if he did go no one would care whether little Abner Peters drank milk and that no one would look after Mamie Henise's babies as they came on—sometimes two a year.

He remembered turning down that offer and remembered the surgeon's prophecies.

"Do you mean to tell me, Watt," the surgeon had said, "that

you're going to bury yourself in that one-horse town for the sake of a charity practice?"

The then-young Watt flushed. "It's hard to explain," he answered thickly.

"I'd think so, Watt," said the surgeon, and he smiled a little but without mirth; then suddenly he was irritable. "Look here," he went on sharply, "I'm going to tell you what you'll come to if you stick there. I've noticed your capabilities; a good many of us have. You can be a great doctor if you turn your back on a fringe of human weaklings who are better dead, anyway. If you don't turn your back on them you'll be an over-worked, underpaid hack."

Young Watt had nothing to say, and he went back to Plea-santville in a thoughtful and hardening mood.

He guessed rather certainly that he ought to leave. He guessed less surely, that someone would turn up to look after Mamie Henise and little Abner Peters and the rest of them. He even began, that night, to look around his office to see what was worth the trouble of packing, and his dreams of the future began to form as he opened the drawers of his desk to turn over the clutter. The top drawer held English wal-nuts which had been delivered as part payment on opening a boil. The second drawer held a more varied assortment; there were rolls of bandage. He picked one up, to find it stained with oil, and then he remembered how old Andrew Arnold had driven in to say, "My girl, she burned herself with spillin' an oil lamp. *How much fer comin' out?*" Old Andrew was tight as the bark on a tree.

"How much'll you pay?" asked young Watt.

"Fifty cents and not one cent more," Andrew stated and, words out, his jaw clamped like a trap.

"All right," said young Watt, "I'll be with you in a minute," and he had gone to save a life, for fifty cents.

Also in that second drawer was a moire silk bookmark, cross-stitched, rather unevenly, with the statement that the Lord would provide. Little Aggie O'Brien had made that for Doctor Watt after he had gone out to the O'Brien farm one night, to find diphtheria, and small Aggie fighting a fast-closing throat.

Mrs. O'Brien held the lamp steadily while he used his knife. Once he had seen tears coursing down her brown lined cheeks, yet she had smiled. "I'm cryin' because I was that scared afore you come," she said.

It was nights of such pattern that, even then, were making him look old, and that gave him a series of pictures in which black surrounded the yellow square of a farmhouse door that silhouetted the someone waiting for "Doc."

He'd never get on, he knew, if he stayed.

In the bottom drawer he found amidst more clutter some lamb's wool that made him think of Mrs. Armhime, who had needed rest and had no chance for it, and had needed an operation that she wouldn't have.

"Not even you, Doc, could get me through that; I ain't right for it," she stated; "and there's my kids, you know—five of 'em. If you can keep me above ground till next year, when Molly's fourteen, why, then she can do for 'em."

They thought he was God, to measure their time, to grant requests to live till the kids could manage. And somehow he had kept Mrs. Armhime and a lot of women of Mrs. Armhime's group alive until something in extremely pliant young fabric was able to churn and bake.

Young Doctor Watt closed the lowest drawer of his desk. And as he closed it he knew he could not leave. He mopped his brow. "God," he said, "I've got to miss it. I know I'm weak, but I just can't go, and I hope You'll see Your way to forgive me!"

And he knew, slumping in the chair by his desk, that he must plug along to be a failure.

Two years after that his sister's husband died, and she and her boy came to live with him; and, as Lucy's boy grew, Doctor Eli transferred his own dreams to the youngster.

He took young Jimmy with him often when he made country calls. The boy wanted to be a doctor.

"We'll manage Vienna for you," Doctor Eli would say.

"Yes."

"A year, anyway."

"Yes."

"It's not that their technique is better, but the hospitals offer you every chance to study cases. Now I knew a fellow —he was in my class and he wasn't very smart, but now he's at the top. You see, he went to Vienna."

The tales were long and they were interrupted only by the opening of humble doors through which the doctor disappeared with his bag.

A long bag, young Jimmy learned soon, meant a delivery. He didn't think he'd fool with obstetrics; they took too much time. But his uncle, who then seemed very old to Jimmy, seemed to like them. He'd reappear, after absences that sometimes stretched for hours, gray with fatigue, but smiling. He would almost always say, "She's doing fine; a nice boy" —or "girl"—but when things went wrong, it knocked him.

As Jimmy grew he didn't see the point. "The thing to do," he decided at sixteen, "is to manage a practice, but not let it manage you."

At seventeen he knew his uncle for a country doctor who would never "expand," and at twenty-two he was telling his uncle how the big fellows did it.

Thus the years, and now Doctor Eli Watt sat in his office, which had grown as shabby as he from years of overwork and little in money to do with. He was tired, and the whole day had been patterned to bring facts home. That morning he had taken Rebecca Kyle to the hospital of the big town, some twenty miles away, where his nephew was practicing.

Big modern hospitals nowadays made Doctor Watt feel apologetic; everyone in them knew so well what they were doing. The modern appliances that he didn't half understand made him feel humble. He always tiptoed down the corridors, and when the floor head called him by name, before he'd known it he'd said, "Thank you." That was the way of it.

Jimmy was to operate on Rebecca, three days later. She was to have intravenous glucose preparatory to operation; a new dodge. Old Doc Watt had wandered to the ward after Rebecca was settled and for a little time he sat by her bed. She seemed to want him to stay around a while.

"Doc," she began hesitantly.

"Yes, Becky?" he said gently. She was one of his babies.

"Doc, if I shouldn't get well of this, you look after Tilly, won't you? She takes the cold that easy."

"Why, you know I would," he answered. Then something in the look she gave him made his throat feel tight.

"I knowed you would," she stated, "but I just had to ask like that. It makes me feel better to have you say what I know."

"I'm going home now to give her a little bottle of sugar pills," said Doctor Watt.

Becky smiled. "That'll tickle her," she said happily. She lay thinking of her child, but it seemed right to have old Doctor Watt near as she did this.

"You haven't a thing to worry about," said Doctor Watt. "You know my nephew is operating."

"I know."

"None better, Becky."

"I know," she answered dutifully.

"He's a wonderful surgeon."

"Sure; I know, Doc."

He had to leave then, but before he quitted the hospital he searched out his nephew. Jimmy had been operating, and he appeared in his white, the sterile mouth gauze dropped under his chin.

"What have you been doing?" asked Doctor Watt hungrily.

"Simple appendectomy."

"I see. I brought in Becky Kyle."

"Did you?" A nurse stood waiting with Jimmy's overall. Another stood by with hand lotion. In a corner someone was cleaning instruments.

"She feels a little nervous," said Doctor Watt.

"Scheduled for Thursday, isn't she?" asked Jimmy.

"Yes, Thursday at ten; and, Jim, she'd feel easier if she could talk to you first."

"Oh, good heavens!"

"Well, maybe you can't make the time for it," said Doctor Watt apologetically.

"'Fraid I couldn't. I have a full week. Coming to the Medical Association meeting?"

"Well, if I can get it in," Doctor Watt answered. "Hilda Archer's baby has pneumonia and I have to be around considerably. I guess you remember Hilda? She was Hilda Jones and she lived in that big house on Elm Street."

Jim did not remember Hilda.

He was cleaned up now, and Doctor Watt inspected his suit with interest. You could see it was a real expensive suit.

"Finished for the day?" he asked.

"No. I have a duodenal ulcer at two; nice case."

"Wish I could stay and see it," said Doctor Watt, "but I got to be getting on."

He turned then to the door, but another thought came to him. Rather uncertainly he retraced his steps.

"How's Miss Cynthia?" asked Doctor Watt. She was, to Doctor Watt, "Jim's girl."

"Quite as usual. She always asks about you, by the bye, Uncle Eli."

"A nice girl," said Doctor Eli heartily; "fine folks she has back of her, but she's not uppish about it."

Jim didn't seem to like this for some reason. "Socially quite suave," he murmured.

"What?" asked Doctor Watt.

Jim led his uncle from the operating room, a white, beautifully manicured hand upon his uncle's shabby coat sleeve. "I meant," he explained patiently, "that she has those gifts I'd expect in a wife."

"Is it fixed?" asked Doctor Watt. He had paused in the corridor.

"Seems so," Jim answered, smiling. The old chap was amusing and—rather pathetic. Suggesting that he, Jim, go in to see this Becky—was it Kyle? No wonder his uncle was worn out and done.

"Well, I'm real glad," said Doctor Watt; he stood nodding, smiling. "That never came my way," he added, "but now I'm kind of getting it through you, the way I do other things."

He thought of a packet of letters in his desk that were post-marked Vienna.

"I guess," he murmured, "that you never will know what you've done for me. Your life holds everything I used to dream, a long while back, might be in mine. And now, to cap it all, you're going to be spliced to Miss Cynthia Morgan; a genteel, lovely young lady if ever there was one!"

"Utterly," Jim agreed. He looked at his watch. "I'm no end sorry," he said, "but I'll have to get along. I'm lunching with Babcock."

"Babcock?" asked Doctor Watt incredulously. "Not *the* Babcock?"

"Who else? He's here for a clinic."

Babcock himself, Doctor Watt reflected, and Jim lunching with him and saying it like that; as if it didn't matter. He'd look around pretty carefully leaving the hospital, Doctor Watt decided, and maybe he'd get just a little peek at him. It would be something to remember.

He asked, voice hushed, what Babcock looked like, and Jim answered, bored, "Oh, like a lot of other people—"

Doctor Watt hesitated, then he spoke. "Jim," he said, "if you don't think Doctor Babcock would think it was kinda pushing of me, you tell him his writings have meant a lot to an old country doctor. It's a little thing, but it might please him."

Without hearing, Jim nodded.

That done, Doctor Watt tuned up his car to turn toward home. On the way he stopped at a flower shop, where he selected a cineraria of violently purple bloom that stood in a pot wrapped in pink plaited paper.

This he had sent to Miss Cynthia Morgan, and on his card he wrote, "A little engagement present for a very lovely young lady." And he went home warmed by the thought of her pleasure.

But at home his elation dwindled. He kept thinking of the hospital, the hurry there, the way Jim had looked, his lunching there with—the great Babcock. It wasn't that he didn't want Jim to have all he had, but it made his own life seem lean.

He had only yawning doors to remember, with simple country people waiting in them for him.

Nothing glorious.

And going to town now seemed to do him up pretty badly. He was getting old.

His telephone tinkled; wearily he answered. He heard, "Doc, you're to come to Greiner's place. Baby has the fits."

He rose slowly to pack a bag. Maybe on the way home he could look in to see Hiram Askins. He guessed one more call wouldn't kill him and Hiram was eased up considerably by describing his pains.

There was a little package on his desk he saw for the first time. He unwrapped it; it held a somewhat worn billfold in which was a note that read: "Dear Doc, This belonged to Henry, and I thought maybe, since I can't pay you no money, it would be something." And it was signed "Mrs. Henry Burger."

"Well, that was nice!" he thought. Suddenly he had to sit down in his desk chair again. He sat holding the purse, looking at it, but seeing the hospital, the bustle there. What was making him feel so old and useless and done?

It was mighty nice of Mrs. Burger. Jim would laugh, Doctor Watt knew, if he saw the billfold. But maybe God knew there were some ways of failing that weren't so bad as others. Of course he was a failure.

Babcock; Jim lunching with him.

His eyes were smarting; what the deuce was the matter with him? "I guess," he thought, "Babcock was the man I wanted to meet more than any other."

He rose then, with the recollection that Baby had the fits. He hurried, leaving, troubled by having kept anyone waiting.

Jim certainly had worn a fine suit, he thought, riding. Jim had lunched with Babcock. He'd try to get in to see Becky again on the chance that Jim wouldn't have time for a visit with her. Jim wouldn't exactly understand, but there were real reasons that she should be heartened and pulled through. She came of a weak stock.

There ahead was the house he was to visit. The door was opened and someone framed by door jambs was awaiting him.

The someone turned to call a triumphant, "Doc's comin', Mom!"

He parked his car and picked up his bag, to move up the path to the door.

"Well now," he said, stepping into the house, "we won t worry! Everything's going to be all right." And a woman began to cry, the way they would when he came and things seemed a little better to them.

Hot water and plenty of it—he guessed the city fellows would try some kind of rays he'd never heard of—and in a few moments the baby was quiet.

He sat, waiting to be sure everything was all right.

The man shambled in. "I can't pay you anything now, Doc," he said.

"That'll be all right, Lem," the doctor answered.

The woman raised her eyes from her baby's face. "When you come," she said, "it was like God stepped into our house."

"I'm only an old hack," he stated, a little bitterly; then he smiled and his voice softened. "But God and the country doctor," he added, "they're both there when they're needed."

When he left, a little girl followed him to his car, clinging to a fold of his coat. The woman stood in the doorway, holding the baby; she waved. The man said a gruff "Thanks, Doc," without looking away from his child.

Doctor Watt drove off and toward Hiram Askins' mortgaged farm.

That night was bad; there was a first baby and a man who grew afraid of death as the shadows absorbed all the world he knew. He had a few hours' sleep, to rise to another stretch of work. Doctor Watt reflected, as he ate his breakfast, that if Jim had time maybe he would tell him someday about what Babcock said while they ate together. He'd get out Jim's Vienna letters some night. He hadn't read them for a long time.

Then activities began; house filled with the usual calls and some that were unusual. At noon he gave sugar pills to the younger set and he looked at a pet cat with a sore paw. He took pins for payment, thinking of Jim, and of how Jim would laugh—a trifle scornfully.

After his midday dinner he had a little time and he decided he'd get out Jim's letters from Vienna, and for quite a stretch of minutes he had quite a chance to look hungrily at words that were the bloom of his dreams. He became so absorbed that it was difficult to adjust quickly to the present, as he had to do when a long, smart car drew up at the curb.

Miss Cynthia Morgan was in it. He scanned his vest, to brush it ineffectually. His shirt was dirty, too, he realized.

Mrs. Gaunt, his houskeeper, admitted Cynthia, and it was Mrs. Gaunt who flung open the office door, with a harsh "Someone fer to see you, Doc."

Then Cynthia came across the room to him, both white hands outstretched.

"Maybe," said Doctor Watt, after their greeting, "you'd rather sit in the parlor; maybe that would be more suitable for you? Your dress is so fine."

She shook her head, and to his dismay he saw that she was trying not to cry; she said, in a stifled voice, "I love it—here!"

"Well, then we'll sit here," he said, and she took the chair at the side of his desk that faced the light. It was old-fashioned, he felt, but he could learn a lot about how he could help a patient, from the shifting play of expressions. Of course the big men used blood tests and all that, and of course he was behind the times. Miss Cynthia Morgan drew a deep breath as he settled. "I never can tell you," she said, "what the lovely flowers meant to me!"

She was a beautiful young lady, he decided; all the look of race was there, and more—kindness.

"Well, I just thought they'd please you," he admitted. He laughed. "You know," he added, "I drove home thinking of your surprise at getting them, and it made me very happy."

She said unsteadily, "You're a darling person!" and then she was crying.

He leaned forward to take her hand. "Why, my dear child," he said, "what's troubling you?"

Then he waited. It seemed she couldn't stop crying; but at

length she managed to say, "I can't—I can't marry Jim—"

Doctor Watt's face changed. It was a considerable blow. He liked her so much; he'd never liked any other young lady half so well; and, too, he wanted the best for Jim.

"Well, if you can't, you can't, you know," he murmured.

She rubbed her eyes briskly, but tears still darkened her long lashes, to mat them to points.

"I want to explain," she said.

"You take your time," said Doctor Watt.

And yet again he waited. At length she began.

"He doesn't understand what is important," she stated.

Doctor Watt's heavy eyebrows drew close; he wanted to understand, but he couldn't.

"I mean," she went on, "everything *you* have he's missed!"

"I?" asked the old doctor. He looked around. "Why, I don't know," he confided slowly, "just what I do have!"

"You wouldn't know," she agreed. "You don't think of yourself. Don't you see? He's thick and cruel."

"Jim?"

"Yes."

"No, I don't," he answered a little stiffly. Then he realized he must do all he could to fix it because of Jim.

"Miss Cynthia," he said, "you know what Jim needs is someone like you. His mother died when he was eighteen, and while I did the best I could, I guess I wasn't much hand at raising even a one-child family. Of course, I had a lot to do always —with calls and so on—"

"He had every chance, being near you, to have what he lacks," she asserted, and her voice was a trifle strident.

"He's a great success, Miss Cynthia."

"You think so?"

"Why, my dear child, I know so."

"I don't see it."

Again his brows drew close; he couldn't get it, her point of view. Why, Jim was going to reach the top of the ladder. He tried to explain this, and still she was not convinced.

Then she saw the letters and she knew the writing on the envelopes. Without apology she picked one up. "You were rereading them?" she asked, words again a little blurred.

"Well, yes, I was," he said.

"How often does he come to see you?"

"Oh, ever and again."

"Exactly what does that mean, Doctor Watt?"

"Well, I mean once in two or three months. He's a busy man, Miss Cynthia."

She said nothing; her small, sweet chin was hard; her eyes, too, were hard.

Doctor Watt realized that he wasn't reaching her. He leaned forward again, hands on his knees, elbows out. "He's a big man," he stated. "Why, he lunched with Babcock the other day."

"You're a big man," she said. "You could stay here all your days without anyone ever hearing of you, and you'd be a big man."

He laughed. It seemed really funny to him; to hear anyone calling him a big man.

There was no convincing her, or changing her, Doctor Watt found as the call drew out. She felt that Jim had failed, somehow, and he couldn't make her see that Jim was a coming man and even now a big man.

She rose when a clock-stroke made her know she'd been an hour in the old office. Doctor Watt rose, too. She neared him; he felt her hands on his shoulders and he looked down into her deep blue eyes.

"I wish," she said, "that there were some measure for people like you! Some measure that would tell you what you have done and of your success. But it is the people who are never heard of who do the most in the world, and the hard ones travel up—up—up!"

Then, to his great surprise, she kissed him. No one had kissed him for years.

She went off then, and he sat looking at the chair in which she'd sat. Poor Jim. And what a lovely lady she was, despite very strange ideas. He must go to town to see Jim soon. Maybe he could manage that on the morrow. He must do all he could for Jim. The bell of his telephone tinkled.

But it was not until Friday that he went to town, and he went then because Jim sent for him. Becky Kyle's case, seeming very simple, had taken a wrong turning, from no more, it seemed, than her waning interest in life.

Jim met his uncle in the corridor outside the ward. Jim looked older and tired. He was taking it hard, Doctor Watt saw.

"I don't know what's the matter with her," said Jim, "but she'll die, if something can't be done. I don't want to lose a case that's so simple. It's absurd."

"I'll talk to her," said Doctor Watt.

"Do you mind if I come with you?" asked Jim; he seemed changed, different.

"Certainly not," said Doctor Watt.

He entered the ward; Jim followed him. He sat down by Becky's side and Jim stood at the foot of her bed. The screen was near; the one that meant the ward must be isolated from death and the troubles of the dying.

"Well, Becky," said Doctor Watt.

She opened her eyes a second, but they closed again.

"It's looking mighty nice out our way," said the doctor next. "The lilacs by your house are coming out."

Again she opened her eyes; this time she kept them open a little longer.

Doctor Watt talked on; of home and all she knew; of those dear and familiar things that had been dimmed by pain.

When his voice dropped away she whispered a question; it was, "How's my baby?"

The doctor spoke out loudly; he said, "Crying for you, Becky," then he rose.

"I think," he said, when with his distinguished nephew in the corridor, "that your patient has turned the corner. I can tell you she's going to get well."

It was the next week that Jim asked his uncle to go with him to the County Medical Association dinner. Doctor Eli Watt was surprised and deeply pleased.

"That is nice! And mighty kind of you," he said, "and of

course I'll come; that is, if Mary Smith's baby appears when it should."

Jim smiled affectionately, and not with seared enjoyment as at those who will follow wrong roads. "You'll have to come," he said; "there's a reason."

But Doctor Eli Watt was late that night, the baby having delayed its arrival. He reached town tired; it had been a long, hard confinement and his arms still ached and his knees felt shaky.

He made his way to the rooms slowly, thinking that perhaps he could still eat a course or two of the dinner that he knew would be mighty fine. He hadn't had a chance to eat anything since morning.

To his surprise he found that the dinner had not yet begun and that the group seemed to be waiting. And when he appeared the big fellows kept coming up, greeting him, it seemed, especially, and more than one of them said, "Very honored to be here, Doctor Watt."

Then he found his place; it was at the head of the table. He settled timidly after he had asked the man at his right whether there had not been some mistake. The man, a stranger, said, smiling, that he thought not, and the dinner began.

Doctor Watt ate heartily. "I'm pitching in pretty hard," he explained to this man on his right, "but I haven't eaten since morning. Some of my people have been real sick and they certainly keep you going—"

The man was studying him closely, he realized, and this made Doctor Watt speak. "My name's Watt," he said, "I'm a country doctor. I know you're a stranger, and what might your name be?"

"Babcock," said the stranger.

Doctor Watt blinked. And suddenly his nephew rose to speak; Doctor Eli Watt began to shake, and cold sweat trickled from his brow. His nephew was telling about how he, an old country plug in doctors, had saved Becky Kyle's life, and it sounded very well. Too well; of course, it was true, but it wasn't psychiatry; it was sense.

And someone else rose to tell of what he—Eli Watt—had done in a country town.

The dinner was for him; he had to lay down his fork, his hand was shaking too disastrously.

And then all around the table men were pounding with feet and clapping and calling, "Watt! Watt!"

He rose; he saw them through a blur, he began to speak, a tear slipped down his cheek.

"Gentlemen," he said, "I'm sorry about this, acting this way, but nothing like this has ever happened to me before, and you see, I know what I am, a failure, and when you get to knowing that—a thing like this can hurt, because—I can't explain. And as for Becky Kyle, gentlemen, I don't know anything about the mind, so you mustn't give me any credit. I couldn't keep up, there was too much to do. I can only use sense. But to be here, and know you have room for me, a very humble man beside you all—" he had to pause. "That's something," he ended, "that I'll never forget, and it'll help me to go on till the end at taking care of my folks—"

Then he sat down; and he had to wipe his eyes.

Doctor Babcock turned to him. "I wish," he said, "you'd come down to look at a patient of mine that I haven't the wisdom to get inside. You have—"

Doctor Babcock talked on; asking his opinion. Other men turned to him. He sat, forgetting hunger and the need to eat; smiling, for the most part silent; very tremulous.

Once and again he thought, "Why, this can't be true!" and once he whispered it.

At eleven he started back to his village and his folks. He was still dizzy.

Passing the Morgan house, he saw from a light that someone was still up, and temptation won him and he stopped his car. If the person who was up was Miss Cynthia, he wanted to tell her of this; this great thing that had happened to him.

It was she who was up and she opened the door to him.

"Miss Cynthia," he said, "I guess stopping so late must seem queer to you, but I want to tell you about my evening. You'll never believe it, but Jim gave a dinner for me and he had the cream of the profession there. And they made speeches."

She said, warmly, "Darling!" She put her hands on his shoulders; she raised her face, she kissed him.

"Nothing they said was true, I must admit," he said, "but it's a thing I'll never forget. I'll keep it around in my heart, the way I keep Jim's letters from Vienna in my desk. I just can't tell you the nice things they said, and I sat at the head of the table with Babcock, *the* Babcock, on my right. . . . Yes, sir, and they had ten courses."

"Jim did it?" she asked.

He drew a deep breath and nodded. "And, funny thing," he said, "at the start and before I knew that dinner was for me, I was awful tired, and now I feel as if I could lick a hyena single-handed. And another funny thing, I have a case out there—back in the hills—and I was discouraged about her, but now I know I can pull her through. But I mustn't be keeping you up."

She patted his hand, held between hers. "I told you you were wonderful," she said.

"I?" he asked.

She was smiling.

"Wonderful," she repeated. She went on, "And you can tell Jim I've changed my mind; tell him I've decided I have to be related to you. And tell him, too, that tonight made me feel he is going to reach the top some day and be a worthy successor of his uncle."

He sat in his office an hour later, smiling mistily. They had all greeted him as an equal, a man of importance. Well, maybe he had done some things. He wondered whether God remembered the day when he had turned his back to getting on, because his sick folks needed him.

"I couldn't do anything else," he murmured, "and I guess maybe God understands better'n I do. And now I have that dinner."

The telephone tinkled. He answered it. "Doc," he heard, "you're to come up to Seefey's place; the missus is bad."

He realized the ten miles ahead of him as he started his car, but the thought of them and a night call didn't tire him as usual. He was feeling young again, he realized, and he could go, with any luck, for a good many years longer. And suddenly he wanted those years as he had in his young days; years for work; years in which he could give to those who had need of all he could give. . . . He looked up; the stars were bright and they seemed close.

"A little more time," he said, as his patients, who must live, seemed to speak to him, "and then whatever You want." And he added, seeing a long table, faces turning his way, his distinguished nephew speaking of his work, which seemed, after all, to count, "And *thank You!*"

The house lay ahead; the door was open—he knew by the square of yellow printed against the night.

And someone, seeing the headlights of his car, turned to call, "It's all right! Doc he' a comin'!"